BOROUGH OF POOLE
551074125 U
550842861 5

Dance until Dawn

Berni Stevens

First published in digital and print on demand format
as *Fledgling* in 2011

Published 2014 by Choc Lit Limited
Penrose House, Crawley Drive, Camberley, Surrey GU15 2AB, UK
www.choc-lit.com

A CIP catalogue record for this book is available
from the British Library

ISBN 978-1-78189-132-2

Printed and bound by CPI Group (UK) Ltd, Croydon, CR0 4YY

For Bob and Sam.

Acknowledgements

Dance until Dawn has emerged like a phoenix from the embers of one short story and a novel. The main characters, Will and Ellie, are now a part of my family, and hopefully, are here to stay. We've grown stronger together, been on the Authonomy website together, and made it through the editing process – in various guises.

My love of vampire folklore must be mainly attributed to Bram Stoker's *Dracula*, Sheridan Le Fanu's *Carmilla* and Polidori's *The Vampyre*. Since reading them, I've read everything I could find, featuring our fanged friends. In fact, I thought myself an 'expert' until I joined the Dracula Society. The Society is for fans of Gothic literature, film and theatre, and some of its members put me to shame with their knowledge of genre folklore and fiction. I'm grateful to the Society for its friendship and support.

Mostly I feel so privileged to be a Choc Liteer! Thanks to everyone in the wonderful Choc Lit team, especially the lovely Choc Lit authors who welcomed a lowly cover designer to the fold.

Huge thanks also go to my husband, Bob, and son, Sam, for believing I could write. You're the best!

Prologue

Portland Hospital, London W1.

31 January

The only sound I could hear in the dark, quiet room was the gentle beep of the life support monitor. Elinor lay immobile and pale as death in the hospital bed, yet her exquisite face still looked perfect, framed with vibrant contrast by her glorious copper-coloured hair. Only the slight rise and fall of her chest showed that any life remained. How much of that life could be attributed to the machines in the room, I have no idea. Medical technology has moved ahead with incredible speed.

I remained in the shadows by the window, mesmerised by the sight of her – so fragile, so very still. How many times have I waited and watched for her outside the stage door? Hoping for a glimpse of her at least. I find it difficult to believe in this tragic turn of events.

For almost twelve months, I had watched Elinor dance on stage, admiring her energy and grace. I am almost ashamed to admit that I have become utterly infatuated with this girl. For me, the seduction of women is easy; it is rare my advances are rejected. This is not arrogance, merely a statement of fact. But for some reason this little dancer is different – I felt almost nervous to approach her, like a young inexperienced boy in the throes of a first crush.

After months of watching her from the shadows, I attended Glastonbury Festival because I knew she would be there. I watched her from afar, whilst enjoying the eclectic selection of music. Music appears to give her such joy. Against my better judgement, I even sat with her for a few wonderful, stolen moments. How long ago that feels now.

A few short weeks later, I happened to overhear a conversation at a party between some of Elinor's friends, and I became determined to attend the event at all costs. She fills my thoughts. I could not have stayed away.

How could I have foreseen the dreadful accident, which has caused her to lie in this hospital bed, attached to tubes – tubes that apparently hold her precious life in the balance?

The sound of voices outside in the corridor forced my thoughts to return to the present. The door opened, and a large wedge of yellow light filtered into the room. Two men – presumably doctors – discussed Elinor without any emotion, almost as though she were some kind of scientific experiment. I had to force myself to stay still when all I wanted to do was kill them for their callousness. The main topic of their consultation seemed to be when to terminate her existence, when to actually unhook her from the machines that kept her alive. I knew it was time to intervene. A world without Elinor would be intolerable.

The door closed behind them, and I became enveloped in darkness once more. The monitor's lights blinked back at me as I walked towards her.

Chapter One

Awakening

I hate the dark. People always come and hurt me in the dark.

The old childhood fear flooded my body and, with fingers that trembled, I groped through the darkness for the bedside lamp. My hand met only empty air until it brushed against a clammy wall. Where had the lamp gone? The table? I blinked my eyes several times and waited as they gradually became more accustomed to the darkness. I could make out brick walls now, but no windows. Weird. The absence of windows meant no street lights could shine in through the curtains ... *OK Ellie, wake yourself up, this has to be another one of your random, stupid dreams.*

I screwed my eyes shut again, counted to ten and then opened them wide. Nope. Still the same unfamiliar four walls. *What the—?*

I strained my ears as I listened for the normal sounds of Crouch End life on a—whatever day or night this was. Nothing. No cars. No sounds of people on their way home from clubs, with their laughter and conversation drifting up to my first floor window. Nothing at all.

What I could hear was a faint rhythmic sound; it sounded like the constant drip of water. A tap? Perhaps I hadn't turned the bathroom tap off properly – or perhaps it's the kitchen tap? Actually, almost every washer in the place must be past its sell-by date now. Not being the most handy person in the world is always a problem, and there's no way I could pay a plumber his exorbitant hourly rate just to change a washer. Being between DIY-savvy boyfriends means there's no one to call on for help either.

I looked around again. I could see the bleak room more or less in its entirety for the first time now. Still no window. Why? Also, how could I see almost perfectly in what appeared to be pitch darkness?

A cold stab of fear stirred in my stomach. I could see in the dark, this wasn't my flat – or even my bed for that matter – and I had no recollection of my arrival here. Wherever the hell 'here' was.

I looked at the bed. It looked narrow and felt hard to the touch, even with the excuse for a mattress that covered it. There were no bedclothes, just a solitary pillow, which still bore the indent of my head. I didn't feel convinced about being awake, so I pinched my arm – hard. It hurt – a lot. So … definitely awake then. I looked down at my grubby jeans and mud-covered trainers. Wait … I'd slept in my *clothes*?

The night just got worse. I looked up at the bare brick walls again. *Oh God, I must be in prison. I must have been really drunk, caused a scene somewhere and got myself arrested.* That seemed the only explanation. Totally out of character, but an explanation nevertheless. Except I'd never been arrested in my life – I'd never broken the law. Not even had a speeding ticket. I felt guilty if I picked an apple from someone's tree, so a life of crime would not have been for me. *What the hell?*

Did prison cells have windows? I wasn't sure they did, but I'd never been in a cell – until maybe now. There were no windows for sure.

My mouth felt dry and parched, and I looked around again for any kind of table that might hold a glass of water. Surely even prisoners were allowed a drink? I ran my tongue over dry, cracked lips, as my eyes darted around the dark room. I hoped to find something that would give me some kind of reassurance. I wanted to know that I hadn't been imprisoned – or worse – *kidnapped*. I felt so thirsty, really very thirsty. This thirst, like I'd never had before, suddenly became all-consuming in its ferocity.

I couldn't even remember where I'd been for the last few days. It must have been one hell of a party, if it had been a party. I just hoped it had been worth it, although at that moment it appeared debatable.

A slight sound from a corner of the room made me jump violently, and in sudden panic I leapt from the bed. Somehow I found myself crouched in the opposite corner to the sound, with no recollection of ever getting there. A tall figure stood across the room, and I stared up into a pair of vaguely familiar green eyes. Although *why* they seemed familiar didn't make any sense.

'Good evening.' His deep voice was almost gentle.

Speak nicely to the potential lunatic. 'Who the hell are you?' *Or not.* My own voice sounded hoarse as though it either hadn't been used for a while, or I'd been screaming ... a lot.

He didn't answer.

This might not be good. If I had been put in some kind of a cell – and he was here too –really, this wasn't good at all.

'Don't men and women have separate cells anymore?' I pressed myself against the wall as I stood up very slowly on legs that trembled.

'Is that where you think you are?' The cultured tones held a tinge of sarcasm.

'Feel free to enlighten me.'

'You are here because I brought you here.'

Oh crap. The nauseous fear in my stomach churned. Trust me to get myself trapped in some weirdo's fantasy world.

'You don't have any right to keep me here.' I tried to sound braver than I felt. He moved farther into the room and the nearer he came to me, the more terrified I felt that he would attack. But he merely stared down at me from his superior height, with no expression at all on his handsome face.

Now, I'm used to people who stare down at me. I'm a little over five-foot-three in height, so believe me, I'm not easily intimidated by tall people. But there appeared something *unsettling* about this man, for want of a better word. His very presence drew me to look at him, and his hypnotic gaze held my own, until I found it difficult to look away.

That he had been generously endowed in the looks department wasn't in dispute, but there are some historians who claim the Marquis de Sade had been good-looking too. Didn't stop him from hurting his victims though, did it? *Sadist* seemed a word that could easily be associated with this man, although I couldn't say why exactly. I watched him from my corner, taking in his appearance properly.

He stood with hands on slim hips, which caused the black leather jacket to gape open and reveal a close-fitting white T-shirt over a lithe, muscular torso. I dropped my eyes, which didn't help, because they were now on a level with snug blue jeans.

When I looked back up at his face, his lips curved slightly, as if he knew exactly why I had averted my gaze.

'I have every right to keep you here,' he said at last. 'You belong to me now.'

'I don't know where you're from, or who the hell you think you are,' my voice shook with fear and anger, 'but around here women pretty much choose where they want to be – and with whom. I choose not to be here and certainly not to be with you. So open the door and let me out. *Now*.'

He gave a short bark of laughter at that and sauntered closer.

'Stay the hell away from me.'

'Or what?'

'*Or* I'll execute one of the best moves in women's self-defence known to man.'

'And arguably one of the most painful.' He didn't look that bothered.

'The police will be looking for me,' I tried a different tactic.

'Somehow I seriously doubt that.'

'What do you mean?'

'Correct me if I am wrong, but the police do not generally continue searching for a person who has been pronounced dead and buried.'

Warning bells jangled loudly in my head now. I've met some pretty weird people in my twenty-five years, many of them in the theatre, but he appeared to be the weirdest to date, and possibly the most dangerous.

I stared at him, trying to think of a reply. He stared back, his face expressionless. He could have been a waxwork for all the emotion he didn't show. His pale skin stretched tautly over well-defined cheekbones and a straight, aristocratic nose. Glossy thick black hair, almost long enough to reach his broad shoulders, framed his face and dark eyebrows frowned above incredible green eyes that appeared to glow in the dark. His thick eyelashes would have made him look feminine were it not for the sheer masculinity of his features – eyelashes, incidentally, that most women would kill for.

But it was his eyes that drew me back to staring at him every time. They weren't just green; they were like a cat's eyes. Unblinking. Intrusive. Like a predator. I shivered. His full lips twitched into a slight smile as I stared at him. I decided to carry on pretending that I felt brave. *Buried? Dead and buried.*

'Buried? Yeah, because I just look so damn buried, don't I?' I waggled my fingers in front of my face, suddenly noticing the lack of rings. My fingers hadn't been ringless for at least ten years, apart from performances of course. 'Did you steal my jewellery?'

He gave me a mocking look. 'Do I appear to be a jewel thief to you?'

'What you *appear* to be, is some kind of perverted creep who's drugged me, shut me up in a dungeon *and* stolen all my rings.'

He raised a dark brow. 'Interesting.'

Well he might have found it all fascinating but I was just plain terrified.

'So?' Trying to brazen this out seemed a good idea. After all, if I kept him talking, maybe he would go off the idea of hurting and/or raping me. That's what people did in films after all. Keep the lunatic talking for as long as possible, to give the police time to find them. Hysterical thoughts flitted at a frantic pace through my muddled brain.

'I am not a lunatic,' he said and my eyes widened with shock.

'Did I say that aloud?' More confused and incoherent thoughts hurtled around, and I shook my head hoping to clear it. I felt as though my brain had been removed altogether, and the space left behind had been stuffed with wet cotton wool, or bubble wrap, or something.

'Unfortunately for you, I am able to pick up on your thoughts whether I wish to or not,' he replied with nonchalance.

'Well, stay the hell out of my head, you invasive bastard.'

His lips twitched again, and he sauntered to the far end of the bed. I twisted to keep him in my view and watched him warily. He ignored me, lowered his lean frame easily onto the bed and patted his jacket pockets before producing a rather battered pack of cigarettes. He lit one and with a creak of leather, leaned back on his elbows.

'Now I know this is a nightmare,' I said almost in relief. 'Smoking? Who the hell smokes in a public place these days?'

'As far as I am aware, this is not a public place.'

'Well, I hate the smell of smoke, and I hate the idea of dying from passive smoking because of some selfish bastard who smoked all over me.'

He turned to look at me then. 'Where were you when I said you were already dead and buried?'

I froze at his words. I had heard them but I didn't understand them. I felt more and more as though I were somehow trapped in a horror movie, and destined to be turned into some kind of body suit. Although if memory served, most of the women in that particular movie were large and, being a professional dancer, I didn't think there would be too much of my body to make up a suit. Certainly not one that would fit him anyway. I mentally cursed whoever had made me watch that DVD.

I watched him sitting on the bed, smoking. He hadn't threatened me exactly, but he exuded an aura of deadly strength, which dissuaded me from any attempt to make a run for it. Assuming I could find a door of course. I looked around in the vain hope that I'd spot an escape route.

'You must be a very sick person.' He ignored me. Again.

He stood up in one swift, graceful movement, dropped his half-finished cigarette to the floor and ground it out with his heel. I ran to the opposite side of the room, and pressed myself against the wall again, my eyes wide and really afraid now. He walked towards me, very slowly, holding his hands up at waist level, palms out. 'Do not be afraid, little fledgling.'

A searing pain tore through my stomach at that moment, and I wrapped my arms around myself as nauseous cramps took hold. My body trembled with a violence I couldn't control and I sank to the damp floor.

'What's happening to me?'

'Your body needs to adjust to the change.'

Casually he reached out as though to touch my face.

I jerked back from his hand. 'Don't touch me! Don't

ever touch me. I want to go home. Let me go home. You have no right to keep me here.'

He slowly raised both hands again, as though in surrender, but let his arms fall back to his sides as he stepped back away from me. He regarded me with a calm expression. 'As your maker, I am afraid I have every right.' His tone froze me again. 'The last thing this city needs is a young renegade vampire running around, so you have to be contained.'

I closed my eyes as further spasms attacked my body. Then his words sank into my confused brain.

'*Vampire?*'

'That is what I said, yes.'

'You really are insane.'

'You could be forgiven for thinking so.'

I found myself thinking of the body suit again – I really shouldn't watch horror films, I'm just not brave enough.

'What are you going to do to me?' I asked against my better judgement.

'Now that really is the question is it not?' he countered. 'Several interesting ideas immediately spring to mind, but none I feel like sharing at present.'

I watched his face. There wasn't even a flicker of emotion as he answered me, and I felt a chill of fear run through my body again. If this *was* a dream, now would be a really good time to wake up.

'What is this place?'

'It belongs to me.'

'So you own a chain of dungeons?'

Amusement flickered briefly across his face as he moved slowly to the opposite end of the room, turning back when he reached the wall. He leaned back against the wall, almost mirroring my own position and sighed as he ran an elegant hand through his hair. For some reason, I suddenly wanted to run my own fingers through that silken mass of hair, and I pushed my hands behind my back, in case the urge took precedence over my more rational feelings.

'Do you know any good plumbers?' I asked, feeling better with him further away from me.

He raised a dark brow in question.

'To stop whatever is causing that sound of water.'

'This is an old building,' he replied. 'Around two hundred and sixty years old, to be precise, and the cellars are damp. There was no such thing as damp proofing in the Georgian era, therefore, dampness in a house of this age is unavoidable. I apologise if it causes you distress.'

The stomach cramps chose that moment to return – with a vengeance, and I doubled over in agony. 'What have you done to me?'

His voice came now from the darkest shadows. I strained my eyes to see where he'd gone. 'Only feeding will make the pain cease.'

I heard myself moan as the pain intensified and became aware that he'd left the room. I don't know how I knew, because he'd made no sound. But I just did.

I wondered what drugs he'd injected me with to get me here. I could already be dying. Actually, dying would be better, at least the pain would be gone. That had to be proof I wasn't dead. Dead people didn't feel pain, did they?

Pervert. How many women did he have in his other dungeons?

He was probably on his way even now to his own home, leaving me trapped somewhere underground where no one would ever find me.

I went back over to the bed and pulled myself up onto it. Another wave of pain assaulted me, and I closed my eyes as cold tears trickled down my cheeks.

I didn't want to die in this damp, dark place.

I didn't want to die away from my friends.

I didn't want to die ...

10 February

It has been a few weeks since I have written in this journal. Somehow I feel it is important to record Elinor's rebirth and progress.

Unfortunately, I already fear her conversion is going to tread a somewhat rocky path.

I had watched the fledgling when she struggled her way out of the grave. She looked so small and fragile, and yet she fought like a warrior to free herself from the earth. I felt full of admiration for her tenacity. I have seen many rebirthed vampires in my long existence, but she was among the quickest to emerge from the grave that I have ever witnessed.

Initially, she asked for my help, but then terror set in, and she ran away like the wind. Alas for her, she could never be swifter than me, and I was already at the cemetery gates when she arrived.

She ran instinctively to her old home, and I followed. I saw her staring down at me from the upstairs window. Her feeling of terror reached me from where I stood, and I knew she had not yet grasped the fact that she was dead.

I crossed the road to the house and climbed the stairs to her apartment. Standing in the open doorway, I watched her for a few minutes before she sensed I was there. I knew I would have to be strong, assertive – perhaps even cruel – in order to get her to go with me that night. I did not relish that particular part of my role, but if I once softened, it would all be for nothing.

She argued and wept, whilst trying to keep a distance between us at all times. She even threw a chair at me – brave for one so young – especially as she was consumed with terror and disbelief. Yet still the relentless time advanced. For her own safety she had to be safely tucked below ground level long before dawn, or I would lose her, not just to the daylight hours, but because her mind would be lost to me. She needed to be asleep soon in order to cope with the first night of the change. If necessary, I would render her unconscious, but I wanted to avoid that, if at all possible.

Eventually, I resorted to jumping from the second-floor window with her in my arms, in an effort to demonstrate immortality. Unfortunately, that only caused her terror to intensify, but at least we were out of the apartment.

Luckily for me, the Thirst gripped her when we were outside and she collapsed. I managed to find a cab, using the excuse of inebriation to explain my comatose 'girlfriend'. She did not awaken even when I carried her downstairs to the cellar. Thus passed the first night of her rebirth, and the first night she has seen me as the monster I truly am.

11 February

The sun had almost set when I went back to the cellar. I unlocked the heavy door and slipped inside the room, making sure to lock the door behind me. Security must be paramount, especially for these first uncertain nights.

After the fledgling's disorientation with her rebirth last night, I find myself wondering what she will be like tonight. It is not unusual for a new vampire to forget the last few days of its human life. There is, after all, an unprecedented amount of information to take in. First and foremost, the fledgling needs to recognise the terrifying reality of its own death, followed by the *undead* realisation. It is a lot for a human brain to take in – or rather, a former human brain.

I know I will have to assert my dominance over her quickly, much as one would in order to train a young animal. I also know she will be terrified and the dismal surroundings of the cellar will not have helped, but I have no choice. She has to be contained for at least four nights, maybe more, and she must be watched over, perhaps even counselled. I have no way of knowing, as yet, how she will react to anything.

Above all else, I have to keep her safe.

Once again, I wondered whether I had made the right decision to turn her. The fact that I first saw her more than twelve months ago is somewhat irrelevant now. She was unaware of my existence for much of that time. But I had not been prepared for the horrific accident that very nearly terminated her existence.

Fate forced my hand, made the decision for me and now there is no way back. I can only hope she will not despise me for it. The world without her presence would have been a dreary place indeed.

I know I have to be patient, I need to win her trust before I can hope for anything more. Somehow I do not think it is going to be easy.

I watched as life began to return to her body, and I knew she dreamt in the way only a vampire can. Just before the awakening, when the daylight hours are chased away by night shadows, this is when we dream, and the dreams are rarely pleasant. Sometimes, in the case of fledglings, the dreams take the form of flashbacks from the previous human life. Add to the dreams, the first ravening thirst of the newly fledged, and the reasons for incarceration become apparent.

I could tell the child's dream consumed her with terror, and I began to talk to her to bring her out of it. I talked softly, speaking her name, and asked her to return to me – her maker. Our bond should be strong even in these early stages. I knew she would hear me.

I should have known things would not run smoothly. It has been many decades since I have instructed a fledgling, and I have never before been emotionally attracted to one. In fact, I have not actually made a fledgling for over a century.

Time really is of the essence, and I have to get her to feed as a matter of some urgency.

I was somewhat surprised by her behaviour towards me. I had not exactly expected her to fall into my arms with words of undying love, but I was disappointed, to say the least, by her complete lack of any positive feelings. Again, I suppose I feel I already know her well ... but she does not remember me.

At the moment, all she feels is the pain of the Thirst, and anxiety at finding herself imprisoned. I am the person she will trust least, yet, ironically, I am the one she needs the most. She does not know the real reason I made her into one of us, and I cannot tell her – at least, not yet. She will not understand fully until her brain begins to function normally. I can only hope that she responds to feeding.

Chapter Two

Despair

It was completely dark when my eyes snapped open. I lay still for a moment waiting for pain, nausea or anything else to kick in. It didn't. So far, so good.

I sat up carefully and slid my legs over the edge of the bed. I looked around my prison, and as my eyes became used to the darkness, I could just make out a door in the far corner. Unfortunately, it looked pretty solid.

My mouth felt as if it had been scoured with sandpaper, and again I felt very thirsty. It felt like the kind of thirst caused by serious dehydration. A thirst that grows more unbearable with every passing minute.

Thirsty ... So very thirsty. I licked my dry lips.

I suddenly wondered whether there were rats in here, and immediately swung my legs back up on the bed so I could sit cross-legged. I didn't want rats running over my feet – the very thought made my stomach churn.

There were no creepy green eyes glowing in any of the corners, which meant I was alone – at least for the moment. But a new conviction gnawed inside me, one that said *he'd* be back soon, and I'd never see the outside world again.

I wondered if anyone had missed me? Were they looking for me? I had a big circle of friends, surely *someone* would have contacted the police when I didn't show up for work? Oh ... *work* ...

More than anything I longed to be back in the familiarity of the garish hustle and bustle of the theatre. I even longed for the gruelling, strenuous rehearsals, and the usual biting comments from the choreographer, as he strived to get the best from us – his dancers. I missed music too, and I wanted to be with people. Most of all, I wanted to be *outside*.

The only sound in this eerie place was the faint *drip*, *drip*, *drip* of water. It must be the damp running down from the walls just as *he* had said. I shuddered. No wonder the sound of water had constantly been used as an implement of torture. It also explained how plumbers could charge so much ... and why people in cheap apartments went crazy ... the dodgy washers in all the taps made them drip constantly and the sound drove them all mad. I remembered how yesterday I'd nearly fooled myself into thinking I was still at home and the only problem I had to worry about was a faulty washer.

Being incarcerated made my brain lurch into manic overdrive, and my imagination is rife at the best of times. I couldn't imagine why he'd brought me to this place, but whatever his plans were, they couldn't be good. The one comfort I had was that if he wanted to kill me, surely I'd already be dead? But didn't he say I *was* dead already? Sick, sick man. I wished he'd get on and do whatever he intended to do and just get it over with.

Time had no meaning at that moment. I had no idea whether it was day or night. I never wore a watch, that's what mobile phones were for – as well as making calls, obviously. Calls ... mobile ... of course ...

I jumped up from the bed to look around, but there was no sign of my bag as far as I could see. So no phone either, then. Damn.

If this was evening, shouldn't I be at the theatre? I must have missed rehearsals. I'd lose my job. Surely *someone* had missed me?

The door opened and *he* strode in, his tall frame silhouetted in the light from the old-fashioned oil lamp that he carried. The yellow flame flickered in the damp air as he moved further into the room.

He stood the lamp carefully on the floor and then came towards me.

Terror gripped me, and convinced that he'd pull out a knife at any moment, I ran to the end of the bed and squatted down, in an effort to make myself as small as possible. I pressed back against the hard damp wall, feeling thankful that most of the narrow bed now stood between us.

'Don't come any closer,' my voice sounded thin and hoarse.

'My apologies, I forgot about the lack of light in here,' he said. His voice sounded calm, almost matter of fact – he could have been talking about the weather.

I pushed shaky hands through my long tangled hair, and rocked back and forth. I didn't want him any closer to me, I really didn't.

He continued to move closer. How I wished I could push myself through the wall in order to get away. I bit my lip to prevent a frightened sob from escaping.

The now familiar pain suddenly clawed at me from inside my body, and I screamed in agony. I began to babble, sounding incoherent even to my own ears. 'Do something! Help me! Let me go … please, give-me-my-*life*-back.'

'I cannot give you that,' he said. 'I can give you almost anything else.' He paused. 'But not that.'

'The pain …'

'The pain you feel is the Thirst. It is caused by your need to feed. With each night you abstain, the pain will grow, and you will become weaker.'

'So feed me.' I gasped as another onslaught of pain caused me to double over again.

He brought a silver phial from his pocket and stood in front of me.

'You should try to sup from this,' he suggested, as he held it out to me.

Warily I took the phial from him, even though my hand shook with the effort. The smooth surface felt strangely warm, and I risked a glance at him. His face was devoid of any expression, as usual, except for his eyes, which glowed eerily with their hypnotic green light. I pulled the stopper out from the bottle and sniffed gingerly at the opening. It smelt odd, yet strangely familiar, a musky, almost metallic aroma.

'What's in here?' I asked.

'What you need to survive,' he replied.

'Is it poison?'

Yeah right, like he'd tell me if it was. *Yes, of course it's poison, so I can peel your skin off and get someone to stitch it back together once you've died a revolting and painful death.*

'It is not poison.'

I had no way to know whether he was speaking the truth or not. His impassive face belied the gleam in his expressive eyes. I raised the bottle to my lips, even as I fought against the voice inside my head, warning me, screaming at me not to drink from it. My legs trembled, and I sat down on the bed before I fell over.

'It will lessen the pain.'

Anything that could lessen the gut-wrenching pain in my stomach had to be worth a try. Against my better judgement, I took a large swig from the bottle and realised, far too late, what it was as I swallowed.

Blood.

The warm, viscous liquid made me gag almost the moment it went down my throat. Retching, I toppled off the bed onto my knees, and vomited violently. A dark red stain covered the flagstones, reminding me of what I'd attempted to drink. What *he* had made me drink.

I stood and hurled the phial at my tormentor as I screamed obscenities at him. Words I didn't even realise

I knew. My fear of him had been replaced by horror and disgust at what he'd made me do.

He caught the phial easily in one hand, his face composed and devoid of expression. 'For such an innocent-looking beauty you have a man's colourful use of the English language.'

'Sexist bastard,' I added for good measure.

My insides still felt queasy, and I screwed my eyes shut. My mouth filled with bile and I could still taste the strong metallic taste of blood. In fact, I didn't think I would ever be rid of that foul taste.

'*Why*?' I demanded. 'Why are you making me drink blood?'

'Blood is the staple diet of the vampire,' came the calm reply.

'You're obsessed with vampires. You perverted creep.'

'Why do you suppose I am keeping you here?'

I raised tear-filled eyes to his.

'Because you like torturing women.'

'No.'

'You just want to torture *me*.'

'No.'

'Rape me.'

'I do not condone rape.'

'Kill me.'

'You are already dead.'

I felt the cold realisation of utter despair. This man would never release me. Whatever his plans were, getting me a cab home wasn't among them. I had never felt so alone in my life. I might live alone, but I was rarely there on my own. I was rarely there period. Rehearsals, matinee shows, and evening performances all took up most of my waking hours.

Shit.

Rehearsals.

'I have to go to work,' I said. 'I'm late for rehearsal.'

'I think your colleagues would be rather alarmed to see you.'

'What?' I looked at him again and he returned my look calmly.

'You have not been at work for five weeks, maybe more.'

'Five *weeks*? Why?' Horror filled me afresh at this new information.

'It is rather unusual for dead people to continue with their former careers in my experience.'

'There you go again with the dead people crap,' I muttered. 'Can I have a mirror?'

'I fear a mirror will not be of any use to you.'

'Why?' *I wish someone would give me my brain back ...*

'Vampires cast neither reflections nor shadows.'

'Yeah right,' I said bitterly. 'If I *believed* in vampires, which for your information, I *don't*.'

'How terribly unfortunate for us both.' An amused tone had crept into his deep voice.

So it seemed I'd lost my job, as well as being imprisoned by a blood-drinking, vampire-obsessed psychopath, plus I could never put makeup on again because I didn't have a reflection, apparently. Nothing left for me then. He had obviously been removing my identity ... or something ... for ages. Wasn't there a film about that too? I held my head in my hands, trying to keep track of the frantic thoughts as they whirled around.

'Who or *what* are you?'

'You may call me Will.'

'I can think of things I'd rather call you,' I replied. 'So *what* are you? You say you aren't a lunatic, so what are you? Serial killer? Rapist? Or just a pervert?'

He walked towards me again, and I scuttled up the bed away from him.

'I am your sire. Your maker, if you like,' he began. 'Like you, I too am a vampire, although I have been a vampire for over three hundred years.'

'You need to get out more,' I shook my head again. 'Take my advice and ditch the horror DVDs, they're melting your psycho brain.'

'I understand that this is rather a lot to take in,' he said. 'But I would appreciate it if you would stop referring to me as either psychotic or perverted.'

'Well *I'd* appreciate not being kidnapped and shut in this filthy hole.'

'*Touché.*'

Will moved away from me, then turned suddenly to pin me with his emerald gaze.

'It is imperative that you feed soon,' he said, his voice still calm but with a thread of something else in it now. It sounded like fear ... but no ... surely it couldn't be.

'And if I won't?' I looked down at the red stain on the floor again.

'You will not survive.'

'Is that a threat?' I asked.

'Fact.'

'I will not drink blood.'

'I am very much afraid you will have to.'

I did look up at him then. He still held the phial in his left hand.

'I have no idea who or what the hell you are, but I am not drinking blood, you—you disgusting pervert!' My voice rose to a near hysterical scream at the end of the sentence. I could feel tears fill my eyes again, which threatened to fall, and I struggled to prevent them.

He sighed and bent to retrieve the stopper from the phial. After he had replaced it, he slipped the phial into his coat pocket and got out a pack of cigarettes. He put one between his lips, struck a match, and lit it, regarding me over the glow from the flame. I watched him from my safe distance.

'Very well,' he began, 'allow me to tell you a few home truths.'

I went to speak, but he raised his hand with an authoritative gesture, and I fell silent.

'Against my better judgement I have allowed you to give vent freely to your anger and frustration. You have, I believe, used most of the obscene language in the English-speaking world. Now you will listen to me, if you value your survival.'

I felt another thrill of fear slice through me at his cold words, but said nothing.

'In order to survive in our world, you have to feed. The food of the vampire is blood. If you do not feed, your flesh will wither and fall from your bones, yet you will not die. Your beauty will be lost, and your mind—*you* will be lost, and that I cannot allow.'

I made no comment. The man was mad, clearly deranged, and I was his prisoner. If I said anything he didn't like, he might turn into a raging maniac. He looked strong. I felt sure he could pull me apart with his bare hands.

'Yet you still do not believe me.'

I looked at him. He looked so calm and *reasonable*, standing there smoking his cigarette. The feeble light from the sputtering lamp chased some of the shadows from his handsome face and illuminated those incredible eyes. I shook my head slowly. He leaned away from the wall to extinguish his cigarette.

'I have no idea why your first attempt at feeding made you sick, I have never before witnessed such a phenomenon. I can only surmise it is because you have retained more humanity than most during the change. But then, I always knew you were unique.'

I thought he might have been making a joke, but if he was, his face showed no sign of humour.

'You don't know anything about me,' I retorted.

He raised his eyebrows at that and walked slowly back towards me.

'Your name is Elinor Jane Wakefield but most people call you Ellie. You are twenty-five years old and a dancer by profession. You live alone, or at least you used to live alone, in a first floor apartment in a Victorian house in Crouch End, North London. You are an only child, your parents are dead, and you were brought up by foster parents, whom you left at the tender age of eighteen to attend dance college. You enjoy going to popular music concerts and festivals and you dance like an angel.'

I stared at him, completely dumbfounded. How the hell did he know all that? Will continued, his face still impassive.

'I also know that you have never been truly in love, which is something I intend to rectify.'

The sheer arrogance of the man astounded me almost more than his in-depth knowledge of my life.

'Now I know you're insane,' I spat.

'A trifle optimistic I grant you. But insane? No.'

'What are you going to do to me?'

I felt a rush of cool air, and found myself pinned to the wall so suddenly, and with such force, that my head smacked into it. I saw stars for a split second. His strong hands held my arms above my head and, once again, I hadn't seen him move.

I stifled a panicky scream of terror. He regarded me almost lazily as he traced one elegant finger softly down my cheek, and brought it to rest against my lips, his other hand easily keeping both of mine captive. My face tingled where he had touched it – ice and fire at the same time. He prised my mouth open with his finger and ran it lightly over my canine teeth. His breath was cool on my face as he spoke in quiet even tones. 'Have you not felt the change in your teeth child? Have you not ran your tongue over those oh-so-delicate points?'

I swallowed the hysteria rising in my throat. I would not let him see how afraid I was.

I would not. I chose not to answer his question, either. I merely stared defiantly into his eyes.

He leaned in even nearer, and spoke softly, his lips very close to mine. Almost touching, but not quite.

His words sounded strangely loud. 'If my main objective was merely to have sex with you, would I not have taken my pleasure many times already?'

Still I didn't answer. His close proximity was having a strange effect on me. His lips were close enough to kiss and ... I ... wanted to. My eyes widened at the thought and he swiftly drew back, just far enough away so he could see my eyes. His look was mocking now.

'What do you think you could ever do to stop me taking whatever I want?' He released me abruptly, and I let out a shaky breath as he moved away across the room.

The silence between us became almost tangible but he didn't seem inclined to break it. Reaching into his coat pocket, he brought out the silver phial, and turned it slowly in his hands, almost reverently.

'I won't drink blood again, and you can't make me,' I said quickly.

I couldn't bear the thought of attempting to swallow the repellent stuff again.

Will shot me a serious look. 'I should not have to make you. You should yearn to drink blood, in fact, your very essence should be filled with desire for the taste.'

'Well it isn't.' I yelled at him in agony and sheer frustration, clutching my stomach as the pain seared through it again. 'You just want me dead.'

Will came closer again and stared down at me. 'If I wanted you truly dead, little fledgling, trust me on this, you would be very dead. Although you are indeed dead to the human world, you still exist, as do I. But in order to *remain* in existence you have to feed.'

'I won't drink blood!' I almost screamed the words in despair. 'I just *can't*.'

Will continued to stare down at me, his arms folded. 'If you are really adamant that you will not feed tonight, then I should warn you that you will feel even worse tomorrow,' he said.

'So what?' I asked.

'So you must at least try to take some blood. I am afraid it is the only way.'

I gripped the edge of the bed, and stared at my trainers. They looked so normal. How could anything look that normal when nothing would ever be the same again? Will was still and quiet, as he observed me intently. I could feel his eyes on me even though I wasn't looking at him. I pressed my hands to my stomach as the pain started up again.

'If you would permit me to simply hold you, the pain will lessen,' said Will.

I looked up at him in surprise. 'I'd rather have the pain,' I ground out through gritted teeth.

He didn't try to force the issue, and I felt glad he didn't. If he was in any way put out by my refusal, it certainly didn't show. He merely shrugged and walked to the other side of the room. Lighting another cigarette, he watched me with his eyes slightly narrowed, as though his thoughts were too scary to share.

'How long do you intend to defy me?' he asked after a few minutes.

I looked at my trainers again. 'Who died and made you King?'

'Ah, the sulky child act.'

I did look up at him then, and a flood of hot anger suddenly suffused my whole body. 'I have every right to be sulky and angry!' I shouted. 'I didn't choose to be here. You brought me here for some revolting purpose that I don't even want to think about. I want to go home.'

'This is your home now.'

'Wonderful.' I almost spat back. 'Very cosy. Locked up in a disgusting, damp cell with no lights, no bathroom and not even a change of clothes.'

Will merely raised his eyebrows.

'Why am I here?'

'You are here in order to remain safe and undetected by the human world.'

'But I *am* human,' I began, but faltered when I saw his expression.

'I am afraid you are no longer human. As I constantly have to explain, you are now a vampire, and a very young vampire at that. I am your maker, and it is my dubious pleasure to instruct and care for you.'

'So I really am dead then?' I was finding our conversations becoming ever more bizarre. 'If that's true … you must have murdered me already.'

'I sired you. Brought you over. It is not the same as murder,' he replied.

'Bloody well is from where I'm sitting,' I said.

'Dead is just dead,' he shrugged elegantly. 'We are undead, we do not age, we cannot contract any disease, and we are extremely difficult to kill.'

'Sunlight would do it.' I couldn't believe I was even having this conversation. I must have surely been deep within some weird nightmare.

'Indeed it would,' he agreed conversationally. 'Why else would you be in my cellar where there are no windows?'

'I hate the dark.' I shook my head slowly as I realised he

had actually told me I was in his cellar. His *cellar*? 'I really hate the dark.'

'That could be yet another potential problem for a creature of the night.'

I looked up swiftly. I thought he might have made another joke at my expense, but no expression showed on his face. His eyes held a wicked glint, however, and I held his gaze briefly before I looked down again.

'So you have brought me to this existence on some kind of whim?'

'I never have whims.'

'You must just be a selfish bastard then. You came along and took me from my life and forced me into yours without so much as a by your leave. You gave me no choice ... I wanted children one day ... ' my voice cracked in anguish at that thought.

A strange look passed across his face at my outburst, and he was silent for a while as though mulling over my angry words.

'You are right,' he said at last, surprising me. 'I am a selfish bastard. I tend to take what I want when I want it, but regrets will not solve anything now.'

Another uneasy silence grew between us. Eventually I looked up at him. He just stared at me, his expression guarded.

I clutched at my stomach as the Thirst attacked me again.

'Help me,' I gasped.

Suddenly it was as if Will had changed his own personal channel, flicked a switch that said 'normal Will' and the previous conversation had never taken place.

'It would be so much easier, for us both, if you would accept that which you cannot change, and allow me to help you move on,' he replied, his voice still quiet.

'Why should I make things easy for *you*?' I said, and

gasped at another surge of pain. 'I don't even know who the hell you are. You're nothing to me.'

'The fact that I am your maker means we have an unbreakable bond whether you like it or not.' He arched an eyebrow. 'Although it rather appears to be "not" at the moment.'

'So, I'm stuck with you,' I retorted. 'I don't have to *like* you.'

He burst out laughing at that, which startled me. I watched him warily. This mercurial Will was disconcerting, to say the least.

'No, you do not have to like me, little fledgling,' he said, with laughter still in his deep voice, 'but you will, given time.'

'In your dreams, sunshine,' I muttered as the pain in my stomach grew stronger. 'Leave me the hell alone.' I curled up on the bed again like a wounded animal and closed my eyes. I didn't hear Will walk away. All I heard was the slight creak of the door as it opened.

'You have yet to meet the others too,' he said from the door. 'That should be most entertaining.'

I heard the key in the lock. It clicked with a sound of finality.

I opened my eyes, so I could watch the door in case he came back, then listened for a few minutes, but there was nothing to be heard except the occasional drip of water. He didn't come back, so I curled up on the bed, with my arms around my stomach. At least when he was in the room, I had something else to concentrate on, even if it was only the arguments. Alone, I just felt weak and ill.

I wondered why he hadn't insisted that I try to feed again. Perhaps he was bored of me already and wouldn't come back any more. The pains in my stomach intensified, and I raked my nails down my arms in an effort to counteract the all-consuming pain of the Thirst – if that really was the cause.

'Someone help me,' I whispered into the darkness.

I closed my eyes and longed for a release of any kind. To escape from this interminable pain. Death would be preferable to this.

12 February

I confess to some considerable anxiety about the fledgling's lack of desire to feed.

She must have sustenance soon or the pain from the Thirst will become all-consuming and it will erode her mind until her brain no longer functions. Once this happens I cannot help her, and she will have to be destroyed. I cannot even contemplate the horror of such an outcome.

But I will not give up on her. If I have to force-feed her, I will do so. I refuse to lose her now.

Perhaps this is the outcome of my turning an intelligent woman from the twenty-first century. Women today are so different from the women of my own era. Modern women are confident in their ability to live their lives as they wish. They often live alone without man or family and I have found this strange beyond belief. My little fledgling has lived alone for years, and quite happily, it seems. She forged a career from her own talent, and worked hard to maintain that career.

I will not lose her to the Thirst.

I will not.

Chapter Three

Desperation

I opened my eyes to yet another dark and lonely night. I sat up and groaned at the now familiar pain that ravaged my body. Will had warned me that I might feel worse unless I fed, and feel worse I certainly did. Fully awakening from the blessed unconsciousness to this painful awareness certainly held no joy for me. The tortuous agony raged around inside me like a trapped voracious beast over which I had no control.

In a pathetic effort to fight the pain, I rampaged around the small cellar and screamed out loud, as I smashed my fists against the walls until I bled.

I shouted for someone to come. No one did.

I sobbed as the Thirst tried to tear me apart from the inside. Sinking to the floor, I raked my fingernails down my arms. Tiny rivulets of cold blood trickled down from the wounds as I cried for someone to come. Even *him*. Anyone.

After a while, I sank to the floor, exhausted, and hugged my knees as I rocked back and forth like a lunatic. Where was my tormentor? Didn't he want to come and laugh at me? Hatred for him flooded me like cold fire, mingling with the red-hot pain of the Thirst.

'Where are you, you bastard?' I muttered to myself. 'Hiding away somewhere like the coward you are?'

Suddenly the door opened and he came in, the man responsible for all this. *Will*.

He looked cool and as handsome as ever, while he regarded me with that unusual cat-like stare of his. His eyes flicked to the damage I had done to my arms, and he gave me an exasperated look. He put his lamp on the floor and I glowered at him but said nothing.

'You have to stop this,' he said tersely.

'*You* make it stop,' I almost snarled back. 'You made it happen. You make it stop.'

With just two swift strides he towered above me, and I stared up at him defiantly. The air around him felt electric, dangerous. He looked like a predator about to strike.

'I'm not afraid of you,' I lied. 'You're just a bully.'

He suddenly grabbed me by my wounded upper arms and lifted me easily to my feet. I struggled more from a sense of pride than from any belief that I could get away.

'Oh, but you *are* afraid of me,' he corrected, 'and so you should be. I can be a very frightening person.'

'That just proves you're a bully,' I retorted. 'So. Put. Me. *Down*.'

With a harsh laugh, he let go of me so abruptly that I lost my balance and fell to the floor. I looked around for some kind of weapon. Something – well anything I could use against him. Delusional, really, as Will might be many things but stupid didn't appear to be one of them.

He licked my blood from his fingers lazily as he sat down on the bed, and his mesmerising eyes continued to hold my gaze. He raised dark brows as I swore at him in frustration.

'Please behave yourself, fledgling.' His mild tone held a hint of amusement.

I stood with as much dignity as I could muster, clutching my stomach as the pain erupted again. I fought to swallow the animalistic noises rising in my throat.

'I really hate you.'

He didn't bother to reply, merely lit a cigarette and leaned back on his elbows. I carried right on glaring at him, as the unfamiliar temper flared up inside me again, almost keeping pace with the Thirst. I ran my fingers through my tangled hair, and felt despair that it would ever look nice again. Still, what did it matter? I was dead wasn't I? Only other dead people were going to see it apparently.

'I don't. Want. To. Be. Here.' I emphasised each word. I watched him for some kind of a response. His face remained impassive and calm. He continued to smoke his cigarette, occasionally pursing his lips to make perfect smoke rings.

'Don't you understand? I don't want to be here and I *hate* you!'

He frowned, but still made no comment.

'Why don't you say something?' The incessant pain forced tears to my eyes.

'I rather thought you were talking enough for both of us,' he replied at last. His voice sounded as calm as ever, but with just a touch of something else. It still sounded like amusement to me, and that angered me even more.

'Bastard,' I muttered, more to myself than to him.

I began to pace the room, uncomfortably aware that his eyes never left me. Suddenly, he stood and crushed out his cigarette on the floor. I scuttled to the other side of the small room, keeping as far away from him as I could. He raised a sardonic eyebrow in my direction.

'But you are not afraid of me, of course,' his lips twitching into a slight smile.

'Why are you still here?' I demanded. 'Take me home.'

'You are in no position to order me around, little fledgling.'

'Stop calling me that. My name is Ellie.'

'I am well aware of that, and when you start behaving like Ellie, I shall call you Ellie.'

'What the hell do you mean?'

He favoured me with a steady look. 'Exactly what I say. Think about it.'

Thinking wasn't something I could do at this particular moment. I was in too much pain and the art of thought and articulate conversation eluded me.

I sank to the floor and rested my head on my knees, which gave me a sudden feeling of *déjà vu*. I had done this before ... felt like this before.

When? Why?

I cried quietly, not wanting to give him the satisfaction of seeing me fall apart.

'Elinor,' he said softly, and I looked up in surprise.

I recoiled in shock to find him squatting down in front of me, and once again, I hadn't even heard him move. How did he do that? I swallowed the hard lump of fear in my throat, nearly choking with the effort.

I brushed the tears away with the backs of my hands and his eyes softened. I hugged my arms around my cold body, as I rocked back and forth again on the floor. He put his hands on my shoulders to stop me, and the strength of his touch made me shiver.

His face was very close to mine now and against my better judgement I found I was looking straight into those vivid eyes.

'Elinor,' he said my name again, so softly, yet it sounded loud at the same time. I wanted to cover my ears. 'You have to help yourself a little here, you know.'

I shook my head slightly, still mesmerised by his eyes.

'I'm cold.' Even to my own ears, I sounded pathetic.

He stood then and lifted me to my feet at the same time. 'That feeling will soon pass once you have fed,' he assured me. 'But I will get you something else to wear for now.'

Then he was gone again, and I was left alone in the middle of the dank, dark room.

He seemed to be gone only for a heartbeat, and then he was back with a dark-blue sweatshirt, which he handed to me. 'Put this on.'

'How can I be cold if I'm dead? Am I really dead?'

He sighed. 'Just humour me and put the sweater on.'

I obeyed almost without thinking, and he looked pleased.

'This is your last night off. Tomorrow night you will have to feed in order to survive.'

I wasn't sure whether that was a threat or another statement of fact. 'I don't understand,' I said bleakly.

'As I have already told you, the Thirst will become more ferocious with each night you refuse to feed.'

I shuddered at the thought of the pain becoming any worse. 'Why can't you make the pain stop?'

'I have told you before that I can remove your pain.'

'I don't believe you. It's probably just a pathetic excuse to touch me.'

'If you truly believe that, then you could not be more wrong. I am not suggesting anything untoward. I have no need to make excuses for anything, pathetic or otherwise. There are plenty of women who would be more than happy for me to touch them, if I so desired.'

Arrogant, sexist and *a bully.*

'So go get one of them and leave *me* the hell alone.' My petulant remark caused him to laugh aloud.

'It is not that simple, child.'

He eyed me sardonically, almost as though he could read my thoughts. *Didn't he say he could?* I pulled the sleeves of the sweatshirt down over my hands and revelled in the warmth of it. He watched my every move with those expressive eyes, causing me to send him a reproachful glare.

'Why?'

'Why, what?'

'Why isn't it more simple for you to just go and find some woman who actually wants to be with you?'

He sat back down on the bed. 'My duty, first and foremost, is to you, my little fledgling. I made you. You are mine. Deny it all you wish, but you cannot alter the fact.'

One of his hands was already up to stop my protest. 'It is imperative that I get you feeding,' he continued, 'although, I have to confess, I have never come across a more difficult fledgling.'

I felt a small flare of satisfaction at that. 'So I'm unusual?'

'Difficult,' he corrected.

'Please let me go home.'

'I am afraid that is not an option.' His voice was firm, and with that parting shot, he stood and left the room, taking the only source of light with him.

And just like that I was alone again, alone with the terrifying darkness and the intolerable pain of the Thirst.

13 February

At least the fledgling and I are now conversing, albeit not exactly in a friendly manner. I am certain our rapport will improve eventually, but it is going to be a slow process. I admire her spirit, and I hope that once she accepts the inevitable, she will accept me too. I suppose I could have saved myself much angst by explaining how I came to bring her over to vampirism, but something has prevented me. Pride? Fool-hardy arrogance perhaps? I know I do not want merely her gratitude for preserving her existence. Ultimately, I want her to love me for myself.

I cast my thoughts back to an evening last summer when I had gone to watch her dance in *Chicago*, a fairly modern musical by my standards. Her vivacity had shone then, too. I had been amazed that the producer had cast her in the chorus rather than in the role of Roxie Hart, although I suppose she was not well known enough to take a main role.

I still love the theatre, I always have. I love the atmosphere, the tangible air of expectation just before the curtain rises, and, of course, the performance itself. I am rarely disappointed. Elinor danced beautifully that night, and I was entranced. So much vivacity emanating from one so fragile.

I went back night after night to see her perform. She always gave everything to her performance, and I suspected she would give her all to anything she was passionate about.

Someday, I hope she will be passionate about me.

Chapter Four

The Thirst

When I found myself still in Will's cellar the following night, I had to finally admit that this was no nightmare. At least not one I could wake from. I still couldn't remember how I came to be here, and for the life of me couldn't begin to understand what Will was hoping to achieve. With his looks, I didn't think he'd ever have a problem getting any woman he wanted, so what was the big deal with me? I had no illusions about myself, being in any kind of show business will do that for you. Constantly surrounded by taller, slimmer and more beautiful people doesn't do a whole lot for one's self-esteem, believe me. I'd failed many an audition because of my height – or lack of it, and sometimes because of my red hair too.

My stomach felt as though something was stabbing me from the inside, and the searing intensity of the pain made me gasp and double over each time it flared. But I refused to sit and feel sorry for myself.

Forcing myself to stand, I went towards the door, or where I imagined the door should be.

I hated the dark. I'd told him that, the bastard. Did he get some kind of kick out of keeping me locked up here in the dark? Despite his protests to the contrary, he had to be some kind of pervert.

I felt my way along the damp, slimy wall until I found the door. Metal. Perfect for a prison, I thought bitterly. I kicked it in frustration and was gratified when it made a loud noise that reverberated around the walls.

I pictured Will upstairs somewhere entertaining and having to explain the noises coming from his cellar. I kicked the door again and again, amazed at my own strength. At this rate I'd be able to break the door down and get out of this damn place.

The room was suddenly flooded with harsh electric light, and I closed my over-sensitive eyes against its intrusive glare. The door opened outwards, and because I was leaning against it, I cannoned into a large immovable object, which turned out to be the man himself. His eyebrows rose in surprise, and he put his hands on my shoulders to steady me.

'Are you having fun?'

'You left me alone in the dark again.'

He continued to keep me at arm's length, and his strong hands curled like steel bands around my arms. He walked us both back into the room and kicked the door shut, as he regarded me with interest.

'As you can see, I have now arranged electricity in this part of the house for you,' he said as if he'd just paid for dinner at the Ivy. 'That should alleviate some of your discomfort.'

'Shutting me in this ... *cell* is what's causing my discomfort.'

'It is a necessary precaution for the moment, I am afraid,' he replied. 'I apologise. Again.'

He dropped his hands from my arms and I turned away from him, walking further into the room.

'I am afraid we need to address the problem of your feeding tonight.' His voice was quiet.

'I can hardly wait to see what you come up with this time.'

To my surprise, he turned back to the door and opened it again. Glancing back over his shoulder he inclined his head at me. 'Would you accompany me?'

'Is there a choice?' I countered.

'Not really.'

'Great,' I muttered. 'OK, lead the way to another dark and miserable place, I'm all yours.'

'Would that, that were true.' An amused tone had crept into his voice again.

Against my better judgement, I followed him. It got me out of this cellar after all, even if it did only lead to another. My 'dungeon' turned out to be connected by a small passageway to another door, which, in turn, opened onto what appeared to be an old wine cellar. I had no idea where this place was, but any house that had cellars, plural, had to be pretty old, very big, and worth a considerable amount of money. *Hadn't he said the house was Georgian*? If we were still in London, we were talking millions.

I clutched my stomach as the Thirst made its presence known again. I stumbled and missed a step. Will's arm immediately encircled my waist to prevent me from falling, and I flinched at his touch. He let me go at once. Perhaps he wasn't a pervert then, just a sadist.

As we walked further into the wine cellar, I became aware that I could actually hear a heartbeat. A strong smell of unwashed flesh pervaded my nostrils at that point, and I gagged. Someone else was in this cellar and they were definitely alive.

Looking around, I noticed the crumpled form of a skinny young man as he lay comatose on the floor.

'What the hell have you done?' I whispered in horror.

'Sent out for a take-away,' came the flippant answer.

'Most take-aways are pizza or Chinese.'

'I discovered this one attempting to break into my house,' came the cold reply.

'So ... what? You thought you'd smash his brains in and then drink him dry?' My voice trembled.

Will gave a harsh laugh. 'I will neither drain him nor kill him. Although I admit to being sorely tempted to do both.' He pushed the man's body over with a contemptuous flick of his boot. 'You will snack on him, and then I shall call our worthy police to have him arrested.'

'Well I don't know much about vampires,' I said. 'But even I know that there will be visible puncture wounds, and I am *not* biting into him or any other human. That's the grossest thing you've come up with yet.'

Will turned to face me. 'There really is no choice child,' he said quietly. 'It is the survival of the fittest, which, I can assure you, will be you, rather than this piece of pond life.'

I pushed my tangled hair out of my eyes as I looked down at the man again. I became aware of the smell of warm blood and my body suddenly craved the taste.

I knew then that Will had told the truth all along and my body wanted blood. Wanted it badly.

God help me, I wanted to taste him. I could feel the surge of the Thirst and my whole body trembled with the ferocity of it. I turned wild, frightened eyes to Will who merely began to lead me towards the man.

My body shuddered at the conflict and I struggled involuntarily against Will's iron grip. He held me fast, apparently without any effort at all on his part, talking softly to me all the time even though I paid no attention to the words.

My body wanted blood, but my brain didn't agree.

'I *can't*.' I was frantically struggling to free myself from his grasp. 'Not from a person.'

'Yes. You can,' reassured Will. 'It is your nature. I would have allowed you to feed from a bottle, but you refused that. This is now the only way forward for you. Your instincts will take over and help you to feed.'

'Blood made me sick,' hysteria made my voice rise. 'Sucking blood from a person is revolting—I can't—I won't—'

'Yes, you will,' he corrected. 'You cannot go another night without sustenance, you have to believe me.'

I shook my head, trying to clear my jumbled thoughts.

I can't drink blood. Why is he making me do this? What kind of monster is he?

I was vaguely aware that Will was speaking again, but I didn't want to listen to him. A sob caught in my throat, and my body shuddered.

The ravening Thirst now consumed me, any rational thoughts I had became clouded, and I trembled from head to foot. I could feel the insistence of the Thirst, which seemed to dictate I should drink blood from the unconscious man on the floor. I looked up at Will, and fancied that the cold look in his eyes softened for just a moment.

'I will help you. Trust me.'

'I must have trusted you once, and all that got me is dead.'

He rolled his eyes in exasperation. 'I *will* help you.'

I looked down at the unfortunate man, who sported a large bruise on his cheek. I had no doubt that bruise had been courtesy of my green-eyed jailer. Will hauled him up with one hand, keeping a firm grip on my arm with the other. He held the man upright, as though he weighed nothing at all, and turned back to me. 'Feed little one.' He released my arm.

The Thirst surged through my whole body again, and I shuddered violently. My hand shook when I tentatively touched the man's arm. It felt so *warm*. I could hear the hypnotic beat of his pulse, and even smell the blood that pumped through his veins and around his body; blood that flowed so very close to the surface of his skin. I could hear the pounding of his heart, controlling the blood ... warm lifeblood circulating his unconscious body ... *blood* ...

My nostrils flared again.

'Feed,' Will repeated.

'I don't know how,' I whispered, closing my eyes against the pain that racked my body. 'I don't know what to do.'

'Your body will dictate what to do. Move closer.'

With faltering steps, I moved close to the unconscious man. All at once, my body urged me to feed, to sink the fangs I was now aware of into the unfortunate man's neck. But my brain clung to the last vestiges of humanity it had left, and urged me to stop. *What was I thinking?* I moved in a little nearer, but it didn't help. I felt confused, disorientated and very frightened.

I drew in a shaky breath, and sank to my knees, with cold tears trickling down my face. '*I can't.*'

I expected Will to be angry, but he didn't seem to be. He let the man fall back to the floor callously and moved as if to take me in his arms. I stood up in sudden panic and shook my head as I moved swiftly away from him. My stomach churned with nausea and my eyes filled with tears of self-pity as I looked up at Will. 'Let me die. Please ... just kill me.'

He came close and watched me for a few moments. 'If you would come here to me,' he held his arms wide, 'I could help remove the pain.'

I shook my head. 'You're supposed to be helping me, not seducing me.'

'I *am* trying to help.' He sounded exasperated.

I closed my eyes as the Thirst raged inside me. 'Then, for God's sake, help me.'

'Let us just take one step at a time.' He started to draw me back towards my cellar, but I shook my head again, trying to pull away from his grasp. 'No. I don't want to go back there. Please don't lock me in there again.'

He scooped me up easily in his arms, carried me back to the other room, and over to the bed, onto which he unceremoniously dumped me. I rested my head on my drawn-up knees and shook uncontrollably as the pain continued to slice through my stomach like so many sharp knives. Will put his hands gently on my shoulders, holding my gaze with his own, when I looked up at him.

'I will not leave you alone for very long,' he said. 'Just sit here for a moment. I will even leave the door open for you, and I shall return swiftly, that I promise.'

I continued to stare at him while I decided whether or not I could trust him. His eyes gleamed brightly in the artificial light, their depths as deep as any ocean, but his expression looked sincere enough. I wrapped my arms around myself once more, as tremors again took hold of my body. He traced the backs of his fingers so very gently down my tear-stained cheek, and even that brief, soft touch made my body shiver in anticipation of another touch. I closed my eyes, not trusting myself to look into those feral eyes anymore.

'I shall be right back.'

Then he was gone. I felt his absence immediately, it was as though a part of myself had been torn away, and that scared me almost more than anything else in this never-ending nightmare. I'd never been dependent on another person and I didn't want to start now. I closed my eyes tightly, willing the awful vibrations in my body to stop. If this was eternal life, I'd take death – death for all eternity sounded blissful at this moment in time.

I kept my eyes closed as I told myself to try and ignore the Thirst and my unwarranted anxiety at Will's absence. After a while I became suddenly aware of his return, and the smell of fresh blood.

Warm, fresh blood that was very close.

My eyes snapped open to see Will in front of me holding a china mug. My fuddled brain managed to register the fact it had *Buffy the Vampire Slayer* printed on in blood-red lettering, but I felt far too ill to appreciate the irony.

Will knelt down close to me and held the mug out. But I still trembled and couldn't have taken it from him, even if I had wanted to, and I wasn't sure I did want to. He stood back up and sat beside me, putting his free arm firmly around my shoulders. I went to move away, but the moment he touched me, the shuddering inside my body quieted, and I turned to look at him in surprise.

'Sip this very slowly.' He watched me intently.

I looked at the thick, red liquid and felt my stomach heave. 'It will make me sick again.'

'No. I do not believe it will.'

He held the mug to my lips and I sipped, very, very slowly at first, but then as the taste overwhelmed me, I drank faster and faster, gulping down the warm, metallic thickness of it as fast as I physically could.

'Slowly. I can provide more.'

I finished the contents of the mug at a more sedate pace and turned to look at him, both amazed and revolted at what I'd done.

'I will get more.' With that, he left the room again.

Oh, I knew where the blood was coming from, my own human drinking fountain, but I had no idea how that much blood was finding its way into a mug so quickly. I didn't want to ask either. Will returned with a full mug and held it out to me. 'Are you able to hold this?'

I nodded and took it from him. When I had finished, the excruciating pain at long last subsided. I felt revitalised, almost alive again, and certainly well enough to hold his gaze steadily with my own.

'Thank you – I think,' I said and was rewarded by a devilish grin.

'The pleasure is mine. Although I confess my intentions are partially dishonourable. I intend to return to my romantic seduction programme when you are feeling up to it.'

'So that's your evil plan.'

The grin widened with a flash of gleaming fangs. He stood there in front of me, all satanic seduction personified. I bet he didn't get turned down too often. In fact, I felt convinced he didn't get turned down *ever*.

'Do you need more sustenance?'

I nodded, not trusting myself to speak, and he took the mug from me once more. He reappeared a few minutes later, and handed me the refilled mug.

'Finish this while I tidy things up,' he said. 'I shall be back soon.'

'But you will come back?' I felt suddenly and inexplicably afraid of being left alone.

'Of course.'

I was continuing to sip at the warm contents of the mug, when memories began to flood my head noisily and colourfully, each jostling for prior position. I almost fainted at the onslaught. Fragmented pictures swam luridly around, as conversations from previous days resounded, jangling and harsh. I saw a bizarre image of myself, fighting desperately to get out of a closed coffin deep beneath the earth. Images that caused my eyes to fly open in an attempt to break free of them. *What world of madness was this?* 'Let us go little vampire.' Will's voice, deep and commanding. When? *Where?*

Other memories continued to assault my brain, most of them jumbled and confused. I couldn't separate what was grim reality from what appeared to be horrifying dreams. Perhaps this revolting cellar was, in fact, the dream? Although sadly, that seemed much more likely to be wishful thinking on my part.

Strangely, I found I could now remember more of my previous human life, although events were somewhat haphazard and in no particular order.

Where *had* I first met Will? How had I ended up here in this predicament? *Drinking blood?*

I stared down at the nearly empty mug. There was a little of the warm liquid left at the bottom and my stomach suddenly churned violently.

In a fit of violent remorse, I stood and hurled the mug

across the room, just as Will reappeared. He caught it deftly with a movement that was preternaturally swift and almost too fast to see.

'Trying to save on the washing up?'

'Did you kill him?' I had to know.

'No need. I merely called the police, and had him arrested for attempted breaking and entering. His various bruises were obviously my pathetic attempts at self-defence.'

'What about his lack of blood or holes in his neck?' I persisted.

'By the time he appears in the Magistrates' Court his blood will have replenished itself and there are no marks on his neck.'

I wanted to ask how the blood had been taken but felt afraid to.

'I extracted the blood straight from a vein, by means of tubes and machinery, in much the same way as a nurse would, from a blood donor. Which, in fact, he was.' Will smiled at his own joke.

'Where the hell did you get that kind of equipment? And stop taking questions out of my head.'

'Money buys most things,' was the reply. 'Your questions are bombarding me somewhat at the moment and it is a little difficult to differentiate the ones spoken aloud to the ones you are thinking.'

That could be a problem if I was thinking about escaping at any time.

'I would not advise that,' Will said, proving my point. 'You would never survive without my guidance.'

'Who guided you?'

His face became impassive again, his eyes unfathomable, although they glittered like angry emeralds. 'It is a long and extremely unpleasant story.'

I decided to change the subject fast.

'Will I get better?'

'Better?' He threw me a quizzical look. 'What *do* you mean, child?'

'Better at being a vampire,' I replied, frowning at him. 'I seem to be pretty useless at it so far.'

He moved closer and I stared up at him.

'Now that you are beginning to feed, you will be fine. I am the best teacher you could have, after all.'

I searched his face for sarcasm and found none. He seemed so confident, who was I to burst his bubble?

I decided, however, not to tell him about my returning memories, I wasn't ready to confide in him. He was too arrogant ... too controlling ... too ... too bloody everything actually. If he could pick up on my thoughts, he was welcome to the memories as well. If I couldn't make any sense out of them yet, then he sure as hell wouldn't be able to.

'Would you care to take a walk?'

I looked at him in amazement. Anywhere away from this dank cellar would be sublime. 'Walk? Where?'

'Outside, of course.'

Outside? In the open air? That had to be his best idea yet.

I wondered whether it was day or night. 'Is it sunny?'

He favoured me with a mocking glance. 'I sincerely hope not.'

I just stared at him again.

'Vampires are unable to go out in the sun, little fledgling,' he said. 'We are creatures of the night. Surely you knew that?'

Yes, of course I had known that, I'd watched loads of *Buffy* reruns with everyone else, and I've often ogled Eric Northman from *True Blood* too, but somehow I hadn't likened any of it to my own state. Fiction was fiction. But now the realisation hit me like a sledgehammer: it would mean living in darkness for eternity.

'You mean I'll never see the sun again?'

He already knew how much I hated the dark.

He looked pensive for a moment. 'You can look at it through darkened glass, but you will never again be able to go out in direct sunlight. As a fledgling, you will not even awaken until after the sun has set. For that, I am truly sorry.'

I let this latest bombshell sink in and looked disconsolately at the floor.

'Would you like to take a bath?' He changed the subject swiftly.

I looked up in surprise and he gave me a wry smile. 'I am trying to make this easier for you, but you will have to meet me halfway, as I am considerably out of practice.'

I decided to humour him. 'A bath would be good. Different clothes would be even better.'

He nodded and motioned me to follow him back through the doorway.

Will led me back through the other cellar – the man had gone, of course, and there was no trace of him, just a lingering smell of blood, which probably only a vampire would notice.

We passed through another doorway and Will led the way up some stairs. A door at the top opened onto a small landing and he opened another door to reveal an enormous bathroom. It appeared to be almost the size of my whole flat in Crouch End, so he had to be one very wealthy vampire.

The sunken bath was huge, it looked as though it could easily accommodate four people with room to spare. I wondered idly what kind of parties vampires went in for, then decided I really didn't want to know. An ornate hand basin against the far wall had an antique oak cupboard above it, and in the corner of the room was a large glass cubicle, housing a modern, state-of-the-art shower, which I made a mental note not to use whenever Will was around. It was just a little too see-through for my taste.

The toilet looked to be an early Victorian design, with a high cistern, an elaborate chain with enamel pull, and an oak seat. *Do vampires have normal bodily functions?* Somehow I didn't think so. The floor was made up of large flagstones, which looked centuries old to my untrained eye. Just how old was this place again? The walls were partly tiled with plain, gleaming white tiles, and the rest of the walls were painted an ivory colour. The brass taps glinted in the soft lighting and I noticed there were no windows. This bathroom seemed to be completely vampire-friendly, and it also felt as though we were still underground.

Will turned on the gleaming taps and spun around to face me. 'Bubbles?' he held up two different, expensive-looking bottles. I nodded, and he unscrewed the ornate cap from one of the bottles to add some fragrant liquid to the water. Immediately, the room filled with the aromatic scent of cedar wood.

It was round about then I realised I was going to have to undress in order to have a bath, and I had a feeling he wasn't the type to leave while I did so.

I stood uncertainly near the door, and watched him warily.

I argued silently with myself. I'd only known him a few days, and he'd already turned me into a vampire, so how much worse could it get?

The bath filled up quickly, a little too quickly for my liking, and then he was coming toward me. His mocking look was back as he stood in front of me, hands resting on his slim hips.

'Shy Elinor?' He asked, surprising me by using my name.

'Where I come from, ladies have their baths alone,' I replied.

'Then I shall go and find you some other clothes while you get in the bath,' he said, with a courteous gesture of hands, and I nodded again, feeling relieved.

He went out through a second door, opposite the one we had entered, and I hastily stripped off my filthy jeans, both sweatshirts, and underwear. I stepped tentatively into the warm, frothy water and sat down, making sure the bubbles covered absolutely everything from my chin down. The feel of the warm, foamy water against my cold, sensitive skin was overwhelming, and I closed my eyes as I gave myself up to the somewhat erotic sensation.

Will came back in, carrying faded blue jeans and a dark-blue jumper. I didn't want to ask about underwear. Best not to mention underwear at this point.

'How is the water?'

'Wonderful,' I wondered if he was just going to stand there and watch me. His presence seemed to fill the room and I sank lower under the water.

'I take it you would not be too keen on company in the bath.'

'Don't even think about it.'

He smiled. This was all going to go to hell in a minute. I could feel it.

He squatted down beside the bath, trailing his hand lazily in the bubbles. I moved backwards carefully, away from his hand, trying not to disturb the bubbles too much, and felt suddenly grateful that the bath was so huge.

He watched me, his green eyes glinting.

'I could, however, wash your hair for you,' he offered.

I looked at him suspiciously then, and he laughed.

'I would like to say I do not bite,' he said, 'however, you definitely know it is not the case.'

I desperately wanted my hair to feel clean and tangle-free again, but I didn't trust him an inch. He leaned his arms on the side of the bath and looked at me, as he raised his eyebrows.

'So ... little Elinor ... do you trust me with your lovely red hair?'

'I would love clean hair,' I said. 'Just don't try anything.'

His lips quirked upwards.

It was all going to go horribly wrong if he attempted any kind of seduction routine on me. I wasn't even sure I would be able to tolerate his hands in my hair, let alone anywhere else. He moved behind me and my whole body tensed as his fingers touched my hair. I felt his palms gently cupping water over the tangled mass, and then those strong, sure fingers began to massage shampoo into my hair and scalp. My body gradually began to unwind as the tension left it, and I closed my eyes, allowing myself to relax properly for the first time in what felt like months. He rinsed off the shampoo thoroughly, and ran his fingers through my hair, gently straightening out the tangles.

Lightly, teasingly, his hands suddenly slid down my bare shoulders. His touch made me gasp, and my skin tingled like ice and fire together where his fingers had been. He softly kissed the back of my neck – a gentle, fluttering kiss like a velvet butterfly winging its way down my body.

I moved away from him, with one violent shove that sent the water sloshing around to reveal more of my upper body than I was happy with.

'How did I know you would take advantage?' I said scathingly. 'Dead or alive, men are all the same.'

'So call me predictable.' He held up his hands in mock surrender as he stood. His t-shirt was soaked, and clung rather distractingly to his muscular body. I averted my gaze quickly and for once felt safer with him standing.

'You enjoyed my company once,' he sighed.

As I couldn't even remember where I'd even met him, I found his remark somewhat confusing.

'Even if we'd met under different circumstances, I very much doubt I'd have found you even passably attractive,' I lied.

He arched an eyebrow at that. 'We did, and I can assure you, I was not found wanting.'

So why can't I remember?

I had sunk right down in the water again to ensure the bubbles came right up to my neck. There was no way on this earth I would get out of the bath with him still in the room.

'Let me show you my world,' he said, once again changing the subject. '*Our* world.'

'I want to get dry and dressed first. In private.'

'So shy,' he mocked me again. 'How very refreshing.'

He inclined his head at me before he left through the opposite door again, closing it firmly behind him. I waited for a few minutes, half-expecting him to return at any moment. When he didn't, I got out of the bath, and hurriedly wrapped myself in a towel. I dried and dressed quickly with shaking hands. The clothes he'd chosen were my own, and I was glad of the familiarity, although how he'd come by them I couldn't remember. I was glad he had supplied underwear too, although I wasn't sure how I felt about him actually handling it. A strange feeling clenched at my lower body at the thought, and I tried to ignore it in a wave of foreboding.

'Do you want to bring the rest of your clothes?'

I was sitting on the floor in my flat, leaning against my wardrobe door. Will had pulled a holdall from the top of the wardrobe and was stuffing clothes into it. I watched him put my life into a bag and still I did nothing. Why wasn't I running away?

'Let us go, little vampire'

A brief baring of his white teeth in a semblance of a

smile and I began to shake my head again and again, no … no … I would not go anywhere with this man.

I blinked several times and the elegant bathroom swam back into focus. Where had that memory come from? When had Will been in my flat packing my clothes? That he had, in fact, packed my clothes was evident because I was wearing them. God I wanted my brain back. I was beginning to accept I couldn't ever have my old life back, but surely recovering more of my memories would help me get through this bizarre time. Although now that I had bathed, my hair was clean and I wore clean clothes, I actually felt better for the first time in … How long had it been?

My body felt strong, athletic. Coiled and ready for … For what? I usually felt like this when I'd had a good rehearsal and the adrenaline was pumping around my body in anticipation of the next performance. I towelled my hair as dry as possible and looked around for a comb or a brush.

Will came back in at exactly that moment, looking devastatingly handsome in black jeans and a dark-red shirt. I pushed that thought out of my head immediately. No man had the right to look that sexy. He handed me a silver-backed hairbrush and I looked at him in amazement. How had he known?

'I have been around a very long time,' he said, answering my thoughts. 'I think I know when a lady needs a hairbrush.'

I took the brush and began to ease it through my tangled hair, when, without warning, he took the brush back from me, my nerveless fingers giving no resistance.

'Permit me.'

He brushed my hair back from my face, watching me all the time. Gradually he brushed out all of the tangles, easing the brush through the full length of my hair. Finally, putting the brush down, he ran his hands through the silky thickness of it, his gaze lingering on my face. Oh this man was good. Centuries of practice, I supposed.

'So beautiful,' he murmured, almost to himself. 'I hope you never tie it up.'

'Only for work.' I realised I'd replied almost without thinking.

His long black eyelashes lowered over his eyes seductively, just for a moment, but it was enough to make my body clench again. Just what the hell was happening to me? I bent down and pulled on my trainers, using the action to cover my confusion. I was more at ease when we were arguing, and it seemed suddenly odd to be having a near normal conversation with the man who'd murdered me. Brought me over. *Sired* me. Whatever.

'What's through there?' I asked, motioning toward the opposite door.

'Maybe some night you will find out.'

14 February

Elinor is in my bath as I write, and the urge to just go in and claim her is overwhelming. To think of her just two rooms away, naked, is tantamount to torture. But I have vowed not to rush her in any way. She is not like any of the other women I have met in the last fifty years or so, and she is certainly not like other vampire women. For this, I am grateful, and my intention is to keep her thus. She has retained a certain innocence and vulnerability, and must therefore be protected. The thought of any man taking advantage of her fills me with feelings I had thought long dead, buried along with my human existence.

One of the advantages of being immortal is that there is no need for haste, and I am prepared to bide my time. Elinor needs to be made aware that physical entertainment is not my main criteria, although one day it will be most welcome and, I have no doubt, enjoyable. There are other factors to consider and resolve first.

We are about to take a walk and I rejoice at the progress that has been made.

Chapter Five

Hampstead

Will led the way downstairs to a far door in the first wine cellar, which he unlocked and waved me through. I found myself in a walled garden, and stood entranced for a moment, to revel in the sounds and smells of the dark winter night.

Old flagstones covered the entire garden floor area, and a huge ornate stone urn stood majestically in the centre. A profusion of dark ivy tumbled over the sides of the urn, which gave the appearance of a living fountain created by foliage. The high brick walls that surrounded the secluded garden were also cloaked in a similar glossy ivy. The effect was tranquil and beautiful.

A heady fragrance wafted across to me on the night air, and I looked around to find the source. I spotted a bushy, trailing plant that clung tenaciously to the far wall. An abundance of white, star-shaped flowers gleamed against the glossy leaves.

'Night-flowering winter jasmine.' Will's voice came from my left, and I jumped, having forgotten for a moment he was there.

I continued to look around, noticing a lovely stone bench, on which I could easily imagine Will whiling away the night hours, doing whatever it is old vampires do in their spare time.

The night sky drew my gaze upwards, and I stared at the twinkling stars. I breathed in the cold air and my body tingled. I felt revitalised. My head seemed unusually clear, too, and a surge of something akin to happiness flooded through me. I felt almost free – that is, except for my handsome prison officer, of course. I didn't think I'd be getting rid of *him* any time soon.

Will watched me quietly, smoking a cigarette. 'How do you feel now?'

'Better.' My tone still sounded resentful.

His gaze travelled over me and lingered on my hair. 'Your hair looks like spun gold in this light.'

I turned away from him to look back at the house, without acknowledging his rather poetic compliment. I've never been very good at accepting compliments graciously and I didn't feel exactly gracious towards him anyway.

'Is this your house?' I looked back at the large, square building silhouetted behind us. It certainly looked big.

He didn't reply at first.

'Does it matter?' he said at last.

'It might matter if someone else came in during the day.'

'It has been my house for many years.'

I wondered how many exactly. Just how old was he? As old as the house? *Older?*

He strode over to the wall, and pressed a combination of numbers on a very modern key pad, which, I presumed, unlocked the heavy oak door. He held the door open for me, with a strange old-fashioned flourish, and I wondered for the umpteenth time which century he was from. Strange how I'd gone from disbelieving every word he uttered to some kind of acceptance. Must have something to do with drinking blood. My stomach roiled again at the memory. Dear God, I hoped I didn't have to do that every night.

We went through the opening and out onto the pavement outside. The door swung shut behind us with a heavy *thud* and *click*. I wondered how Will's 'burglar' had ever thought he could break in here. It was like Fort Knox.

'He had the audacity to attempt a break-in through my front door,' Will's deep voice interrupted my thoughts. Again.

'I don't remember coming here.'

'You were unconscious.'

'What? Why?'

'Your strength went long before the dawn. You collapsed in the cab.'

'When you kidnapped me I suppose.'

He didn't comment.

'Shall we go to Hampstead?' *Ah, changing the subject again.* Hampstead? So we were still in North London. I'd had a feeling that we were miles out of town, but I was so pleased to discover we weren't. For some reason, I felt less vulnerable in my own city. Perhaps a part of me still thought I could make a run for it back to Crouch End. At least I knew the way. Maybe I could turn into a bat and fly there.

We walked in silence for about fifteen minutes, and as we neared Highgate Tube Station I was momentarily surprised when Will turned in. I was even more surprised when he bought two tickets from the machine. He raised an eyebrow at my expression.

'Problem?'

'Couldn't we just walk to Hampstead? It's not far and it would be much quicker than messing around on tubes.'

'It is and it would,' he agreed, 'but I thought you might like to do something more normal.'

'So we buy Travelcards?' Must tell him about Oyster Cards at some point.

'Yes.'

We swiped our tickets, and passed through the barriers. For one fleeting moment, I felt as though I was on my way to the theatre. Then I remembered I could never go back there, and a wave of desolation and sadness washed over me.

Sadness – because I would never again dance on a stage. I had always known that a professional dancer's working life was criminally short, but I was only twenty-five. Well,

I had been only twenty-five. Guess I'd never be twenty-six or even thirty now, which was a kind of bonus.

My eyes flicked around the small tube station, taking in the familiar red and blue London Underground logo, the film posters peeling from the walls, and a few people walking toward the platforms. An ordinary, everyday scene. Suddenly the disorientation and grief for what had been my life hit me with devastating finality. I looked down in an effort to control the tears I felt brimming in my eyes, and tried to swallow the ache in my throat. I felt Will's hands on my shoulders, which forced me to stop walking. He put his forefinger under my chin, and raised my face up to his. His expression was impassive as usual, but his eyes were full of concern.

'I realise this must be painful and difficult for you. I just want to prove there are many wonderful things you can still see and do, but if you want to return to the house … if it is too soon for you … ?' He stopped, his eyes searching my face for a response. A traitorous tear escaped, and trailed its dismal way down my cheek. Will trapped the tear with his finger, and put it in his mouth. 'What do you think?'

'I do want to go out. It's just … '

'It is just that the first time is the most difficult,' finished Will. 'Is it not the case with a lot of things?' His eyes took on a wicked glint and my heart felt a little lighter in spite of everything.

He put a proprietary hand underneath my elbow and guided me down to the platform. My first instinct was to shake him off, but the weird feeling made me feel really afraid, and to be honest, his touch felt kind of reassuring. We took the first available tube to Camden Town, where we changed to get a Hampstead train. I hadn't been on the Underground for a while – I usually preferred to take a bus wherever possible, or walk. I'm not too good at being underground, although I felt that wasn't a fact worth sharing. So ... I'm scared of the dark, claustrophobic when underground and in small spaces, and not too keen on drinking blood. Way to go for a vampire.

I couldn't ever recall the trains being quite so loud, and jumped violently as a tube roared into the station. Will covered my ears with his hands, as if he had known the noise would cause me pain.

Mercifully, our journey was short and I felt relieved when we got out at Hampstead. We were the only two people in the lift going up to street level. Will leaned back against the lift wall, while his vivid eyes travelled languidly down my body and then back up to my face.

'We have very acute hearing,' he said. 'That is why your ears hurt on the tube. You will get used to it.'

'The hurting or the hearing?'

He made no reply, just continued to watch me with a slight smile on his face.

How weird was everything tonight? I wished more memories of my life would emerge. The flashbacks I'd experienced so far had only added to the turmoil inside my head.

The lift doors opened and we stepped out. Several people looked our way, most of them female, who stared unashamedly at Will, although he didn't appear to notice.

'Very stealthy, with the undercover bit.'

He turned to look at me then, and his eyes gleamed with fiery green sparks. 'Is there a point you wish to make?'

'Well we can hardly mingle, and pass for human, with half of North London lusting after you.'

'Sarcasm does not become you.' He led the way out of the station.

'Oh I think it suits me pretty well.'

Will turned right, and began to stride up Heath Street at such a speed that I had to run to catch up with him. For some reason I felt I'd scored a point – petty, I know.

Hampstead had always been a favourite haunt of mine, and now it seemed that I would be haunting *it. Fancy that.* Its houses and apartments were astronomically expensive, and it did tend to veer towards the pretentious sometimes, yet still managed to retain a wealth of old-world charm. Hampstead had really captured my imagination from my very first visit. I loved it here. Somewhat misguidedly, I'd even thought I might actually live in Hampstead one day. Unfortunately, when I checked out a few estate agents in the vicinity, it didn't take too long to discover that the paltry salary of a dancer wouldn't come anywhere near to buying a litter-bin in the area, let alone an apartment.

A lot of Hampstead's inhabitants were actors, writers, and well-known artists, including an infamous talk show host and his glamorous script writer wife, with a few millionaires thrown in for good measure. Famous authors seem to have migrated to Hampstead in their droves over the years, as many a blue plaque gracing an old house proclaimed. The most famous by far was the nineteenth-century poet John Keats. Although he only lived in Hampstead for a relatively short time, he managed to gain both a blue plaque and the dubious honour of having his house turned into a museum.

But it was such a wonderful place to visit – both in good weather and bad. The good weather always drew people out for long walks on the vast expanse of the Heath, and to Kenwood House for open-air concerts and firework displays. There's always something going on in Hampstead.

During the winter and bad weather, the plethora of good restaurants and lively bars still attracted plenty of people, not forgetting the ever-popular Everyman Theatre.

I'd always felt that Hampstead looked like a beautiful rural town that had been dropped into North London by mistake. Although a hundred years ago it would have been a country town – maybe even a village. I remembered from somewhere that it had been a spa town in the seventeenth century, a fact proven by the existence of an old pub called *The Flask*, where people had travelled many miles to get their flasks filled with Hampstead's healthy spa water. Where I had actually *obtained* that particular piece of information still eluded me. My capacity for hoarding trivial information had clearly returned to full strength. But I still longed for the more important memories to return ... like where the hell I'd met Mr Spooky Will Whatever-His-Other-Name-Is.

A lot of my favourite shops graced Hampstead's elegant High Street, and also some of my favourite cafes. I had no idea whether or not vampires ate proper food, but I somehow doubted they could. I felt convinced that eating in restaurants and cafes would now become another part of my past.

I looked in at a shop window as we passed on our way uphill, and came to an abrupt halt in front of its gleaming surface.

No reflections.

No me, and no Will. Just as he'd said the other night. *Nothing*.

I remembered my dream of a few nights ago, if it *had* been a dream. Just what the hell was going on with my head? I rubbed at the shop window with the sleeve of my sweatshirt and in my mind's eye I saw the bathroom mirror back in my flat.

I rubbed at the bathroom mirror. All I could see reflected in it was the bathroom.

Not myself.

What the–?

I rubbed at the mirror again, making the sleeve of my

top sodden from the steam, and I pressed my fingertips against the now shiny surface.

Nothing.

No me.

Tentatively, I ran my hands over my face. Everything was where it should be. I could feel my nose, cheeks, mouth ... I looked down at my body and it looked perfectly normal to me. It was definitely there. Okay ... whatever I'd eaten after the show last night – if I could remember what the hell I had eaten last night – was never going to be on my menu again.

What was it with my dreams at the moment? Perhaps I should just never eat again, and then I'd have pleasant dreams. I'd be really skinny too.

I went back into my bedroom, and looked around at yet more confusion. The duvet and the pillows had gone from my bed. Only the bare mattress remained to mock me. When had I done that? Why?

A strange compulsion made me go to the window and look down to the street below. As I looked, a tall dark-haired man looked back up at me. His eyes reflected the light from the nearby street lamp, and his eerie gaze went through my body like a lightning bolt. Gasping, I clutched at the windowsill. I shut my eyes tightly, and when I opened them again, he was gone.

I returned to the present, and discovered I was very close to the shop window, with my fingertips still pressed to its cold surface. I shivered and turned to find Will watching me.

'You were outside my flat ... '

'So your memory is beginning to return?' Will looked pleased.

'I couldn't see myself in the bathroom mirror ... '

'No shadows, no reflections.'

'I'm not sure I can cope ... '

'You will get used to it in time, I assure you.'

'Well, at least I won't have any more fat days.'

He raised a dark brow.

I was making an effort to regain some sense of proportion. Inside I was screaming – screaming so loud, and so hard, that I knew I'd never stop. I'd never be able to put makeup on again, or dry my hair in front of a mirror – even supposing I could get hold of something as trivial as a hair dryer. How would I ever know if I looked presentable enough to go out? What the hell did I look like now?

Will regarded me seriously for a moment, then said gallantly, 'I very much doubt you ever had any "fat days", whatever they are.'

'I had at least five a week. Dancers have to rehearse in front of full-length mirrors. There's nothing quite like a studio full of skinny dancers to make you feel like Jabba the Hutt.'

He favoured me with a slight smile but didn't make any further comment, and we continued on up the hill. He probably had no idea who Jabba the Hutt was anyway, so my feeble attempt at a joke would have fallen flat.

I slowed as we neared the place where Maxwell's restaurant used to be. It was still a restaurant, noisy and busy as always, virtually seething with life. I could *feel* it.

Will stood quietly watching me, his calm presence strangely soothing.

'I used to come here a lot when it was called Maxwell's, meeting friends for birthdays.'

'Although you were always searching for that elusive something I believe, which I intend to provide.'

I was amazed at his words. His utter confidence bordered on arrogance, considering the circumstances.

'You are altogether too full of yourself.'

He didn't reply. After a few minutes' silence, I tried again.

'What makes you think I will ever want anything from you?' My sarcastic tone would have wilted a lesser man, but Will merely turned to me and said calmly, 'Vampire intuition.'

Whatever the hell *that* was. We started to walk towards Jack Straw's Castle. So many things had changed. I could remember when it had still been a famous pub, but unfortunately it had recently been redeveloped into luxury flats, and swiftly sold for exorbitant prices. Although, to be fair, who wouldn't want the chance to live in a historic listed building, overlooking the Heath, yet still within walking distance of Hampstead Village and its shops? I'd have given a kidney to live there. Of course I realised undead kidneys might not be too useful, when all is said and done, so there was another money-making option out of the window.

'A walk on the Heath would be good,' Will suggested, mercifully interrupting my bizarre train of thought.

I looked at him, horrified. 'At this time of night? Are you mad? It's not safe.'

He laughed derisively at that. '*Bogeymen* going to get us?'

'Well, muggers or even rapists might.'

Still laughing, he shook his head. 'Very unlikely, plus I am far more likely to be propositioned on the Heath than you are.'

It would have to be one suicidal son of a bitch to try that.

We went walking on the Heath, of course. There weren't many people around, it was February after all. Most normal folk were indoors, snug in their centrally heated homes. Since I'd fed, some of the bone-deep coldness in my body seemed to have lessened, although my skin still felt cold to the touch.

I looked at everything through new eyes, and heard

so many different sounds with my heightened sense of hearing. It seemed as though all my senses had become enhanced, not just my hearing. I could smell the damp, cold earth. I could smell ... people ... and blood. A tremor shivered through me, and Will put a reassuring hand on my arm.

I turned to look at him. 'Is it the Thirst again so soon?'

Suddenly, I felt more than a little worried that I might suddenly lose control, leap on an unsuspecting tourist and sink my shiny new fangs into him.

He shook his head. 'No, it is just your body reacting to the smell of blood. It is because you are newly fledged.'

'You make me sound like a chicken.'

He led the way towards Parliament Hill. We climbed to the top of the hill, and stood looking down at the lights of London, twinkling in the dark night. This had always been one of my favourite views, although I'd never been brave enough to venture here at night. What other secrets could possibly be lurking down there, in that teeming metropolis?

'I wonder if there are any more vampires down there?' I said aloud.

'Twenty-five.'

I looked at him in utter amazement. 'How can you possibly know that?'

He raised a dark brow at me as though I had no right to question him. 'There are no vampires in London that I do not know about,' he replied with a trace of arrogance. 'London is my city, my *territory*, if you like.'

'What *are* you then, some kind of king?' I sounded flippant and wondered, too late, whether he'd be angry.

'I am the Elder of this city.' His reply was matter-of-fact. I had no idea what an Elder was, but it sounded important.

'Why? Because you're the oldest?'

'The strongest.'

I couldn't think of anything to say to that, so I said nothing. Unusual for me. I wondered how come London wasn't infested with vampires. Why wasn't everyone a vampire?

'Turning humans is against the law of this city,' he answered my unspoken question. Again.

'So how come you didn't keep your fangs to yourself?'

'There were ... extenuating circumstances.'

'One rule for you and another rule for the masses.'

'If you like.'

I looked unseeingly back down at the city. Of all the arrogant ... *extenuating circumstances*? I fought against a rise of temper. The man was insufferable.

To calm myself, I concentrated on the view below me, and inhaled the scents of the night.

I could almost feel some of the pulses of the inhabitants below. I sensed their living bodies. I knew they were there. It was a most peculiar sensation. I had never realised, until now, that night smelt so very different from day. My nostrils flared, and the cold night air filled them again with its exotic, alluring scents. I dug my nails into the palms of my hands and breathed in the heady elixir of earth, people, animals and the fragrant, winter night air.

I watched the headlights of the traffic moving far below, tiny specks of light that buzzed around the city like manic fireflies. A city literally pulsing with human life. Everyone with a purpose – except for me. I no longer had any purpose.

I was conscious of Will's cool presence at my back. I could see him in my mind even though I faced the other way. Weirder and weirder.

Why had he turned me? My head buzzed with unanswered questions. I wondered if there was a more sinister reason behind Will's actions. Although I seriously doubted there could be anything much more sinister than murder or making vampires.

I didn't want to go back to that dank, dark cellar and I really, really didn't want to be locked up again. But I had begun to realise that I actually didn't have a choice. I was too new to survive the change alone. I really did need Will's help. Not that I was ever going to admit that to him, he'd probably take it as an invitation for other things. He stood quietly at my side now, not attempting anything either verbally or physically, which could well be a first for him.

Somehow, I knew we'd have to leave soon. I heard him strike a match, and turned to look at him. He smoked a cigarette while he watched me with an almost indulgent look.

'We have to go soon.'

'Must we?' I turned back to look at the city again.

'We will come again, I promise.'

'*You* promise. What are *your* promises worth?'

'I will always keep my promises to you. Whatever else you think of me, you need to know that I always keep my word.'

I didn't answer and he turned slowly to begin the walk down the hill, obviously confident that I would follow.

I followed.

There didn't seem any other choice. After all, I didn't have anywhere else to go. My friends thought I was dead, my flat almost certainly had new tenants in it by now, and more importantly I had absolutely no idea how to be a proper vampire. I couldn't even feed properly. I certainly couldn't see myself doing a 'Countess Dracula' on anyone in order to get blood.

I suspected Will would have prevented my escape before I'd gone very far anyway, and that would have simply meant more arguing. I felt tired, more than a little strange, and certainly not strong enough to take on Will. Staying with him seemed the best option for the moment. I could wait.

As we left the Heath, he again took hold of my arm and I was too tired, for once, to protest or even comment. I noticed he watched me intently, and felt surprised when he hailed a cab. He helped me in and swung in after me, giving the cab driver his address.

'No tubes?' I had to ask.

He gave a slight shake of his head, and turned in the seat to look at me.

'Are you feeling all right?'

'Yeah, peachy.' I leaned back in the seat and closed my eyes.

Soon we were back in Highgate, and the cab drew to a halt outside the back of the house. Will helped me out and paid the driver. He waited until the cab had disappeared around the corner, and then drew me towards the door in the garden wall.

I stumbled.

My legs felt sluggish and too heavy for me to move properly. I found it difficult to even put one foot in front of the other. Will caught me against him, and manoeuvred us both skilfully through the doorway, closing the door behind us.

'What's happening?'

'Dawn,' came the terse reply.

Had we really been out that long? I couldn't remember.

'Help me.' I clawed desperately at the front of his jacket.

He didn't reply, merely scooped me up effortlessly and carried me inside to the cellar, where he placed me on the bed. All my limbs felt heavy and useless, as though my body had been pumped full of a strong anaesthetic, which slowly and relentlessly rendered me immobile. I realised I'd never been conscious at the approach of dawn before, and felt terrified now at the prospect.

I looked for Will and found him close, looking down at me.

'I'm afraid.'

'I know.'

He sat down next to me on the narrow bed, and took one of my hands in both of his. 'There is nothing to fear, I promise you. Just close your eyes, give yourself to the dawn and rest. I shall see you at the next sunset.'

'Don't leave me ... ' *How pathetic I sounded.*

'I shall be right here.'

I could feel the dawn's approach. A suffocating, strangled sensation gradually crept through my body. It felt leaden and immovable. My acute awareness of the different sensations terrified me, and my eyes opened wide again. Will immediately placed cool fingers on either side of my head and whispered words in Italian that I didn't understand, although I felt strangely comforted by them. He continued to talk softly, lulling me as though I were a child, and eventually my eyes fluttered shut again. The dawn strengthened its hold.

14 February

St Valentine's Day, a ridiculous Victorian obsession, yet a rather fitting date for our first walk together. I could hear so many different thoughts flitting through her head, poor child; she is still so afraid, so disoriented and still understandably angry.

Later

I stood watching her for a while. I knew that, I too, would soon have to retire. The dawn pressed against my brain, and my limbs felt weary. Even after three hundred years I must still succumb at some point.

Elinor lay like a sleeping angel, and her newly washed hair fanned out across the pillow, like glorious living flames. Her thick eyelashes, several shades darker than her hair, cast little shadows on her flawless cheeks. God, she is beautiful. Part of me felt shame and sorrow for having wrought this existence on her, but the selfish, ruthless part of me felt only joy that she was here. With me. Had I not turned her, she would be but dust beneath the earth now, and that would have been a travesty. My own existence has been lonely for too long. I needed a companion and I chose her. That I gave her no choice, as she so accurately pointed out, does not—*must* not matter. I could not let her simply cease to exist, but she does not know that yet.

I reached out tentatively to touch her cheek, and suddenly felt more of a predator than when I hunt. I withdrew my hand. For some reason she is making me feel everything more acutely than I have for decades. Can it be that she will make me a better man? *A nicer monster?*

I could not ignore the insistence of the dawn any longer, and with a last look at my lovely captive I left the room, locking the door behind me. I did not think she would wake before me, but for my kind security has always been essential. How else would we have survived for so many centuries?

I went upstairs to my own room and surveyed the elegant furnishings with ironic detachment. The large four-poster bed mocked me with its emptiness, and I grimaced as I took off my clothes and lay down to rest. Hopefully, someday soon, I will have my chosen companion here with me, but somehow I know it is not going to be an easy path.

I am content with the progress this night though. I am pleased – nay, relieved – that she has at last taken some blood. Certainly, now she has the taste, the actual feeding should become easier for her.

I find her more desirable each time I set eyes on her, and her constant rejection of me is eroding my soul. Contrary to mythical belief, vampires do have souls. Modern literature and films have changed us almost beyond our own recognition. Some of us are governed more by the presence of the soul than others. I suspect my little one will retain much of her soul. It is easy to spot the truly evil among us within a few hours of their rebirth and she is definitely not one of them. It is the main reason our laws demand that the maker should always take responsibility for its own fledgling and look after its schooling. I have not allowed any vampire to turn a human in London for many decades. It is too dangerous in a city such as ours.

It would take but one young vampire to turn renegade and the city would be over-run in a relatively short time.

As the Elder of the city of London, it is my responsibility to ensure that the other vampires adhere to our laws. Most of us feed only on the willing, or those who live on the streets. We rarely kill when we feed, to do so would be tantamount to greed and sheer blood lust. There is also the risk of exposure should the body count rise. Fledglings tend to get carried away with the overwhelming taste of warm blood during the first few nights of their rebirth, and thus can easily kill. It would not take too many bodies being discovered drained of blood to regenerate the vampire myth and proclaim it as truth.

It is actually forbidden to bring a human across without permission from the Elder of the city, but thankfully I do not have to explain my own actions.

Unfair, perhaps, but lucky for me.

I think the nights ahead will be difficult, but I remain optimistic. Elinor has begun to feed. I will not lose her.

Who knows what the next sunset will bring.

14 February, the previous year
Highgate, London

Valentine's Day. The Victorians loved this day, they celebrated with handwritten poetry and gifts of flowers. I wonder how many of them realised the tradition stemmed from celebrations for an early Christian saint named Valentinus. Although, apparently, the first association with actual romance should be accredited to Geoffrey Chaucer in the Middle Ages.

So, on Valentine's night, I sit alone, writing this journal, just as I have done for more than three hundred years. Many things have changed over the centuries, not least the actual journal – and the writing implement. Perhaps one day I shall even use a computer, although the thought makes me smile.

I do not indulge in self-pity, for I choose to live alone. I am dangerous. Too dangerous, perhaps, to live with others. As a vampire – or, more precisely, the Vampire Elder of London – my responsibilities are many and varied, such is the penance for eternal life.

I have taken many lovers over the decades – a man is a man no matter how old he may be. But none have stayed. The human lovers perished, the vampires either left, or I tired of them. Never have I found the one true love for whom my non-beating heart yearns. Until ... perhaps now – and I feel the urge to record my thoughts.

The awakening passion I feel for the beautiful red-haired dancer I first noticed some weeks ago at the Adelphi Theatre has hit me hard and fast. For some reason I cannot erase her from my memory. She moves like a dream, her grace and beauty so bright – like a captive star. She holds me in her thrall, and I have since returned several times to watch her performance. She never disappoints.

I cannot concentrate at the moment and feel the need to be outside in the cool beauty of the moonlight.

Later

Once again, I found myself standing just over the road from the stage door of the Adelphi, and stood watching for my quarry from the darkness of a convenient doorway. Eventually she emerged, surrounded by her friends. I heard them call her 'Ellie'.

To my surprise she looked across the road – directly at me – and smiled. I felt as if my heart would burst. Could it be she had actually noticed me? Spotted me in the gloom?

An old woman stood nearby, selling long-stemmed red roses, and on impulse I purchased them all – at an exorbitant price – and took them across the road to 'Ellie'.

She stopped when I stepped in front of her, and blushed most becomingly. She looked up at me with startling eyes like twin sapphires. I had never been so close to her before.

I wished her a happy Valentine's Day and told her she danced like an angel, at which she laughed a little self-consciously. As she accepted the flowers, she said perhaps I could tell her choreographer that. Her friends had stopped a little way up the road in order to wait for her, and were looking back at us with more than a little curiosity.

She said she had to go and I stepped back to allow her to pass.

With her arms full of red roses, she walked away from me, glancing back to smile again before disappearing into the night.

Chapter Six

Reluctance

The Thirst began to rage the moment my eyes were open. Clutching at my stomach, I toppled off the narrow bed onto the floor, the reverberation of my agonised screams loud in the darkness. 'Will!'

I attempted to stand, but didn't have enough strength, so I curled into a ball on the floor and wrapped my arms around my body. The lights came on then, and I sensed Will's presence before I felt him beside me.

'It's worse. Why is it worse?'

Strong hands lifted me up and set me back onto the bed.

'Calm down.'

'You're never here at sunset,' I accused him through gritted teeth, as another wave of cramps and nausea clenched my stomach into a tight knot. He made no reply. I closed my eyes as the Thirst attacked me relentlessly. Tears welled beneath my eyelids, and I screamed again with pain.

'Do something – anything.'

'*Anything*? Are you sure?'

I nodded.

Without a moment's hesitation, he pulled me into his arms and enfolded me within them, like a kind of strait-jacket. Instantly the searing pains began to subside. I wriggled feebly against his strong hold but managed only to get my hands flat against his chest in order to put some space between us.

He looked amused. 'You did say *anything*.'

I glared. 'Even when I'm feeling like crap, you take advantage.'

He stood up slowly, his eyes still glowing with amusement. 'You need to feed.'

Even I could have worked that one out. Little old newbie vamp me. I gave him a somewhat jaded look. I felt sure he'd try to push his advantage while I was still feeling weak, but he merely helped me to stand. My legs weren't feeling strong enough to support my weight and Will supported me with ease.

'Shall we try again?'

Keeping one arm firmly around my waist, he guided me through the doorway and into the next cellar. Once again, I could smell warm blood and the Thirst was pleased. A man lay on the floor, his torso propped up against the damp wall, and his legs splayed out in front of him. His head drooped onto his chest and his eyes were closed. If it hadn't been for the slight rise and fall of his chest, I would have thought him newly dead.

'Another burglar?'

Will laughed a soft, sexy laugh that sent a sudden thrill through me from head to toe. Some distant part of my brain wondered how often he'd used that laugh as a tool of seduction.

'Please tell me you're not expecting me to bite him.'

'That was my original plan I admit. Do you think you can?'

I stared at him a little desperately. The man on the floor still looked like a man, not food. I really didn't want to feed straight from a person. Will pushed me gently towards the unfortunate man, stopping me once I was very close to him.

Fascinated, I watched the man's pulse beating in his throat. I could even hear it beating in my head. I sniffed the air and smelt the warm blood coursing through his veins.

I wanted blood. *Needed blood*. I knew that now. But he was still a *man* – not food, not really.

I looked at Will, who watched me silently, waiting for

me to make a move. I stayed still, unsure and unhappy. Will crouched down and turned the unconscious man's face to one side, stroking the neck invitingly with his other hand.

'This is the bit you bite.' He sounded like a sarcastic teacher. 'There is a very nice vein here called the jugular, and it contains nourishing, warm blood. Very good for little vampires.'

I crouched down too, and put a tentative hand out to touch the man's neck. I felt the warmth of his blood just below the skin's surface. I slid my fingers over the pulse. Its measured throb seemed hypnotic. I looked at Will again, and he smiled encouragingly – well, encouragingly for him, anyway. I moved in closer to the man, and stroked his warm throat.

I had a sudden flashback to myself at the age of ten, cuddled into my father's neck, and I moved back onto my heels so suddenly that I lost my balance and sprawled on the floor.

I drew my legs up, and put my head on my knees. I felt weak and very hungry, but I still could not feed on a person. Will squatted down in front of me, and put his hand under my chin, raising my face until he could see my eyes. I looked into those spectacular green eyes as he arched dark eyebrows at me. 'What is the real problem here?'

'He's a *person* – someone's lover, husband or father.' I closed my eyes as another bout of pain attacked me.

'I did not ask you to kill him.' Will's voice was oh-so-reasonable. 'Just feed, and I will then take him back to where I found him. He can afford to lose a pint or so, people often donate that much and recover in an hour.'

'He'll have bite marks. People will come looking for us.'

'People do not actually believe in vampires, Elinor. You did not. In fact, I am not so sure you do even now.' He stood up, and helped me to my feet again, holding my arm firmly. 'So, I ask again, what exactly are you having the problem with?'

'Seeing him just as food and not as a person. I know, I'm an evil monster now, and I should be able to feed from him, but I really can't. My head won't let me.'

'Well, I am having some considerable trouble seeing you as an evil monster.' Will smiled, but the smile was gone instantly, as he saw the look on my face. 'Child, you need to feed to survive. It is the rule of nature. Every creature on earth needs to feed to survive. Humans kill animals for food, animals kill other animals for food. We need blood in order to survive. A vampire deprived of blood is a frightening sight, believe me, I have seen it.'

'What happens?' I vaguely remembered the answer.

'Vampires cannot die. We are undead. It is the blood that animates us, allows us eternal life.'

'What happens?'

He gripped both of my arms with his strong hands and stared down at me, his eyes glinting eerily. 'A vampire that cannot, or will not, feed becomes a walking skeleton. It does not die, but its flesh withers and falls from its bones. Trust me on this, it is not a pretty sight.'

Will spoke, I realised then, from painful experience. His eyes stared into space, looking at a place I never wanted to see. 'I will *not* allow that to happen to you.'

I bowed my head, as a fresh bout of pain and nausea tried to tear me apart from the inside. Will held my arms, and cursed quietly under his breath. I looked up at him, startled, and he ran a hand through my hair, winding a thick bunch of it around his fist tightly, so I couldn't look down again.

'Do you understand me? I will not allow you to waste away in front of my eyes.'

'I can't do this,' I said, my voice sounding strained. 'Why couldn't you have just left me alone?'

Will stared at me, still holding my hair firmly. 'I will do whatever it takes to get you feeding properly.' He began leading me back towards the man, who was still mercifully unconscious.

Releasing his hold on my hair, he knelt and took hold of the man's arm. He got a small penknife from his jeans pocket, and swiftly sliced open the man's flesh. Blood welled from the cut immediately and the now all too familiar buzzing started in my head.

Will dipped his fingers in the blood and, leaning forward, put his fingers to my mouth.

Before I knew it, I had licked them clean without even thinking about it.

Warm, nourishing blood. I licked my lips, all the while staring at Will.

He smiled a self-satisfied smile.

'Come here to me kitty,' he coaxed softly. 'Come and drink.'

I found myself on the floor next to the man without even realising I'd moved nearer. Will lifted the man's arm towards me, and the smell of warm, living blood pervaded my nostrils and my senses.

'Drink.'

I leaned towards the arm, but a wave of gut-clenching nausea swept through me, and I shook my head.

'I can't. Not from a person. Please don't make me.'

Will stood in one smooth, elegant movement and held his hand down to me. After a moment's hesitation, I took it and allowed him to help me up. His strong fingers clasped mine, and his eyes glittered like emeralds as he looked down at me. Releasing my hand, he gently moved a strand of hair from out of my eyes, his touch lingering on my face slightly longer than it needed to.

'Back to the china mug, I think. Come back and sit down and I will sort it out for you.'

He guided me back through the cellar to the narrow bed in my 'cell' and made me sit down. He stood and looked at me for a while without speaking a word.

'I suppose I'm more trouble than I'm worth.'

He raised an eyebrow. 'If I thought that, you would not even be here.'

I was suddenly very sure of that. I didn't think Will would ever allow himself to be compromised in any way, or take on anything that wouldn't directly benefit him. I wasn't quite sure yet where I came in, but I felt convinced I'd find out before too long. I had a feeling he had some kind of game plan, and somehow I would have an integral part to play.

I looked at him as he stood in front of me, this tall, dark charismatic stranger who appeared to know me so well already. Who somehow seemed able to awaken a primal desire in me with just the slightest touch of his hands, or a deep laugh. How the hell I had managed to become entangled in all this weirdness seemed to be a question I had no hope of answering.

I was still having trouble remembering many details of my last few days as a human, yet I could now remember much of my earlier life. I wanted to remember how I had become a night creature, and, more importantly, I really wanted to know *why*.

'I will be back as soon as I can,' Will said, interrupting my thoughts, and I nodded. He returned after about fifteen minutes carrying the *Buffy* mug.

'You couldn't find something less ironic?' I commented, and a smile quirked his lips briefly.

'It is functional, and she is fictional.'

Good point. I took the mug and sipped at the contents. This was marginally better than staring at a comatose person whilst drinking. If I had to drink the stuff at least I could pretend it was something else when it was in a mug.

'Perhaps I could have some vodka in it next time?' I suggested, with an attempt at a feeble joke.

He simply took the now empty mug from me and went to refill it. All the time I couldn't see where it came from, I seemed to be all right. Perhaps I could be a blindfolded vampire.

Will returned within minutes and handed me the newly filled mug.

'I need to return our friend,' he said. 'I may be a little while. Would you like to go out when I return?'

I sipped at the mug's contents with my eyes closed, and I remembered the trauma of my return the previous night. What little confidence I did have instantly evaporated.

'Could I just sit in the garden and look at the moon?'

'Of course, if that is your preference.'

He strode toward the door, but turned back when he reached the doorway. 'That sounds almost romantic. Perhaps we should have done that on Valentine's Day.'

'You are so full of crap.'

His deep laugh floated back to me. He never missed a chance. One minute, he was the scary creature of the night who'd brought me forcibly to this existence, and the next he was like any other man who fancied his chances with a woman. He leaned against the door frame, a vision in denim and leather. I'd met many gorgeous men in the last few years, but most had turned out to be either complete bastards, or nice – but gay. *Cynical? Me? Oh yeah.*

'I have been called a bastard many times,' he said. 'But I am definitely not "gay" in the modern meaning of the word.'

'Stay the hell out of my head.'

'My apologies. I shall be gone about half an hour. Would you like to take a shower or bath?'

'Are you going to trust me in your bathroom alone?' I put the empty mug down on the floor.

'Not entirely,' he replied. 'If you would like to shower

or bathe, I shall provide everything you need and then lock you in.'

'You really know how to make a girl feel special don't you?'

'Yes or no?'

Anywhere was preferable to that miserable cellar, and I really fancied standing under that state-of-the-art shower for about twenty minutes.

'It's a yes, of course.'

He waved me through the doorway and I followed him upstairs to the bathroom. It was still gleaming and spotless, and I wondered vaguely who cleaned it. Somehow, I couldn't picture Will doing it.

'Can I have some other clothes?'

'Of course. Do you have any preferences?'

'These jeans are fine, but I'd like clean ... underwear ... and a black top. Any top will do, and my leather coat if you have it.' I stumbled over the underwear request, feeling embarrassed, but for once, he behaved like a gentleman, and ignored my awkwardness. He merely nodded and went through the opposite door. He came back a few minutes later with a bundle of my clothes that, to my delight, included my much-loved leather coat. I smiled to see it, remembering how hard I had saved in order to buy it two years ago. I'd worn it so much, the leather now felt meltingly soft, and the coat fit me like a glove. It was worth every penny I had paid for it.

'Nice coat.'

'I know.'

Will put the clothes down on a nearby wooden chair, and taking a bunch of keys from his pocket, locked the door he'd just come in by. He walked over to the other door, and I couldn't resist another cheap jibe.

'You really trust me alone in your house, don't you?'

He turned back to regard me with a kind of detached amusement. 'It is as much for your own safety as mine.'

Oh yes, that made a lot of sense – not. I watched him go out, and heard him lock the door behind him. From the exact moment he left, I missed him. *Strange*. I really hoped he wasn't wearing down my resistance. This existence was going to be hard enough to bear without me developing a crush on the head honcho. I really did not want to become part of the harem I felt certain he had stashed away somewhere.

I stripped off my clothes and walked over to the shower. Sliding back the door, I turned the shower on and closed the door behind me. Powerful warm jets of water doused me immediately, and I revelled in it. I lifted my face up to the shower head, and let the hot water cascade through my hair and down my body.

It felt glorious. I closed my eyes, and just stood under the jets, feeling the massaging effect of water against my skin. Grabbing a bottle of shower gel from the shelf, I poured some into my hand and began to soap my body. I glanced at the label. Armani – I might have guessed it would be nothing but the best, although it was a little too spicy and masculine for my taste. Perhaps I could persuade Will to buy something more feminine for me. I snorted with amusement at the thought of him walking around Boots the Chemist with a wire basket.

Then I started wondering how he did, in fact, buy things: clothes, toiletries – even furniture for his house. Of course that started me wondering if he even *had* any furniture in his house. I hadn't seen any of the rooms above basement level after all. Perhaps they were all empty, cobweb-ridden and damp, just like a vampire's lair in the movies, or Miss Haversham's dining room in *Great Expectations*. But somehow I couldn't picture Will tolerating discomfort.

Good to see my fertile imagination had survived the transition even if my more recent memories hadn't.

I turned off the shower, stepped out and pulled a huge towel off the rail to wrap around my wet body. Just in time too, as a key turned in the lock, and Will came back in. His interested gaze took in my towel-clad form with one sweep as he closed the door behind him.

'Very fetching.'

'Well you can fetch yourself into another room while I get dressed.'

'Whatever my lady wishes,' he replied.

'I am not your lady.' I told his retreating back as he disappeared through the other door. Aggravating bastard.

I went over to the oak cupboard and sifted through various bottles, but found only expensive masculine colognes and nothing whatsoever to interest me. I was definitely going to write a shopping list.

I dressed quickly and picked up the hairbrush Will had used on my hair before. I found myself wishing I had something to tie it up with just to be annoying. Childish? Maybe. But as he seemed fond of calling me 'child', it seemed fitting.

A soft knock on the far door startled me.

'What?' I said somewhat ungraciously.

'May I come in?' Will's voice still sounded tinged with amusement.

'It's your house, apparently. Plus you have the key.'

Said key turned in the lock, and Will entered the bathroom.

'I was merely being polite.'

He picked up my coat and held it up for me to put on. I eyed him warily, but his look was innocent enough. I turned my back to him and slipped my arms into the sleeves of my beloved coat. To my surprise, he let go of the coat – and me – immediately, without any lingering touch whatsoever. I wasn't sure whether to be relieved or insulted, and that worried me.

Will went and opened the far door, then gestured me through. 'Let us go and see this moon of yours.'

15 February

Elinor requested to sit in the garden. I was surprised at first, because I thought she would prefer to be anywhere rather than my house. Then I realised her confidence would undoubtedly be somewhat dented after her collapse last night. Remiss of me not to think of it.

There is so much to be done to ensure her happiness and well-being. I truly never thought it would be such a task. However, I am confident it will be very worthwhile.

Chapter Seven

Moonlight

Will led the way through the other cellar, to the door that I knew opened onto the walled garden at the back of the house. We went out into the cold night. The dark sky was clear, with just a sliver of winter moon, shining bright and alluring. I stared up at it, feeling an affinity with her cold beauty. 'It's so beautiful.'

'As are you,' said Will.

'Okay, who are you, and what have you done with Mr Spooky?' I responded to a compliment in my normal flippant manner, much to my own surprise.

'Is that who I am?' he murmured, and I twisted around to look at him.

The moonlight shone on his dark hair, and illuminated his pale chiselled features, accentuating the cheekbones. His eyes glowed with an ethereal light. I looked at him as he gazed down at me with those incredible eyes. Oh yeah, there was definitely something really spooky about him. His expression appeared softer than usual, which I found confusing, and I stepped away from him in sudden panic. His expression instantly became amused again.

Suddenly I wondered what it would it be like to be held throughout the night in those strong arms. The thought leapt unbidden into my head, followed by even more treacherous thoughts ... Like how it might feel to be held close, really close, to his naked, muscular body as his strong, elegant hands caressed me, and to actually kiss those incredibly tempting lips.

I swiftly dispelled the all too vivid images from my mind, just in case he picked up on my thoughts. I glanced at him, flustered, and he raised an eyebrow as though he had actually read my mind.

'I'm not used to compliments,' I said.

'Then you must truly have known only blind idiots,' he commented, walking towards the stone bench near the urn. He sat down, and I followed, but remained standing. In a paranoid fashion, I took great care not to stand within grabbing distance. I wondered whether it had been a good idea to come out here, if potentially it would give him the wrong idea, or, actually, *any* ideas. I felt uneasy being so close to him in the romantic moonlight, yet his amusement felt almost tangible when he angled his head to look up at me.

'Are you so afraid of me that you will not sit down?'

'I was afraid the first time I met you. I should have run away while I still had the chance.'

I had a sudden flashback to Caroline's party. Joe had been there with his latest squeeze and I had gone alone, at least I *think* I had. But I could now recall leaving the party with a tall, handsome stranger. Guess who? I stared out into the night as I remembered making coffee in my flat for Will, chatting as though I had known him for years. Not one of my more sensible decisions clearly.

'It was you at Caroline's party, wasn't it?' I asked, still not looking at him.

'I thought you were always aware of that.' His answer was soft.

'Maybe I was.'

'Please sit down,' he invited. 'I will not harm you.'

'No, you already did that.'

He shook his head slightly. 'Sit down,' he said again. 'I promise to be a perfect gentleman.'

A sudden laugh escaped before I could stop it. I did actually feel a little ridiculous standing up. He hadn't made any advances after all. I felt as though the 'lady doth protest too much'.

So I sat down, but not too close, there was no point in tempting fate, and certainly no point in tempting Will. He continued, however, to look completely at ease.

The night wrapped itself around us like a living, breathing thing. I could hear the faint noise of traffic from the main road, but otherwise we could have been anywhere at all, or even in the middle of nowhere. It didn't feel as though we were in a city. The occasional high-pitched squeak of a bat punctuated the distant traffic sounds, adding to the feel of being in the middle of the countryside.

Will slid a pack of cigarettes from his jacket pocket, pulled one out, and put it between his lips. He took a box of matches from the same pocket and struck one. As the flame illuminated his face, he looked at me above its brightness as he lit the cigarette.

'How long did you say you have been in this house?' I asked, breaking the silence.

'I did not say,' he replied. 'So what shall we play now?' He raised his eyebrows, his expression mischievous.

'How about we play "give Ellie a break?"'

Will's laugh was soft and sexy, and the sound curled around like gentle fingers of velvet inside my stomach, making me very aware of his close proximity. 'As you wish. I shall endeavour to curb my clumsy, amorous overtures.'

'Not good enough, you need to promise to behave.'

'Are you always going to be so unadventurous?' He sighed.

'Absolutely. It's time you realised that not all women are yours for the taking.'

'That is rather harsh,' he said. 'I do not remember ever stating I wanted *all* women.'

I didn't respond to that. He somehow managed to make me feel ill at ease whenever the conversation got personal. I was sure the more I rejected him, the more he would come on to me. Just like human guys – perhaps death didn't change people much after all.

'How did you become a vampire?' I asked, keen to change the subject again.

'I was bitten,' came the dry response.

'You know what I meant,' I said, and he nodded.

'Yes, of course I do,' he said. 'One day I will tell you the whole terrible story, but I do not think you are ready to hear it yet.'

'What does *that* mean?'

He sighed again. 'It is something that is very personal to me, and is simply not relevant at the moment.'

Well, that certainly told me. I felt convinced he would have been made by a woman anyway. Probably some incredibly sexy female vamp he hadn't been able to resist. I wondered where she was now. I wondered what she looked like and whether she was likely to come back and claim him, and then I pushed those thoughts out of my head. Like I cared anything about his initiation anyway. *Stupid Ellie.*

'Elinor,' he said quietly, and I looked at him in surprise.

'Most people call me Ellie.'

'I am not most people,' he said. 'I want you to know that I will endeavour to keep my distance romantically, unless, or until, you choose otherwise. I want you to feel safe with me, and I want you to trust me.'

Well that was a surprise, and a pleasant one too. Things would be a lot easier if I only had to concentrate on the problem of feeding, and not worry that he might pounce on me at any time.

'I rarely pounce,' he reassured me.

'You're in my head again,' I said.

'The first move must be yours,' he said, and ground out his cigarette on the ground, before he leaned back and crossed one long leg over the other.

'Well, don't hold your breath.' I looked back up at the sky.

We sat in silence for a while, looking at the moon and the dusting of stars that had become visible. He began to talk about Italy, and other places he'd lived, and then went on to talk about North America, surprising me with his knowledge of the desert. He described the many stars that could be seen in the clear night skies, and as he described the velvety heat of the night there, I felt as though I could actually feel it around me, like a blanket. I'd never been to America, but he made it sound wonderful. I wondered when he had lived there and why.

I found myself wondering why he'd come back to England, but didn't feel inclined to ask. I just listened to him talk. His voice sounded beautiful, so soothing and hypnotic, and I became captivated.

Strangely, he told me nothing of a personal nature, no information about any relationships, past or present, and I was still too intimidated by his powerful presence to ask. I listened as he described life in Victorian London, and wondered whether he'd been in London all the time since then, or whether he had still travelled. How did vampires travel? Surely time zones could be dangerous ... flying would be paramount to suicide, wouldn't it?

'In the early days I travelled by ship,' he answered my unspoken question. 'But in latter years I purchased my own aeroplane.'

'You own a *plane*?' I asked incredulously. 'Just how rich are you? Who flies it?'

He gave a slight smile. 'I can fly it myself, but I usually hire a pilot,' he said. 'It is not difficult.'

I tried to imagine 'parking' a plane in Highgate and failed.

'It is kept at Elstree Aerodrome,' he said. 'Many people keep their private aircraft there.'

This man was a constant surprise. But I supposed there

were many things that could be done if the whole of eternity stretched out in front of you. He probably needed something to alleviate the boredom.

'You're a revelation,' I said.

'You are mocking me.'

I began to feel a heaviness invading my body again, and looked upward.

The night sky was beginning to lighten ever so gradually in the east, and I could feel the dawn's approach as it began to affect my body.

Will stopped talking, and glanced up at the sky.

'Time for little fledglings to be asleep,' he said. He held my arm as we both stood up.

We started back towards the house.

'How are you doing?' he asked.

'I—I'm having trouble with my legs again,' I said as cold fear shivered through me.

He swung me up into his arms immediately, and carried me easily towards the cellar. As he set me down on the bed the approach of dawn had already begun to infiltrate my body, rendering my limbs almost useless. The lack of coherent thoughts made further conversation impossible. My eyelids felt heavy, and I looked at Will through narrowed eyes. He seemed a long way away.

He stroked my hair away from my forehead gently. 'Do not try to fight it, little one. Relax and it will not be so painful. Close your eyes.'

I closed my eyes obediently and allowed the dawn to take me until the next sunset.

15 February

I am filled with uncustomary happiness. I have spent a whole night with Elinor, almost without any arguments or recriminations. I think she is beginning to trust me a little at last. I so want to see her laugh as often as she did whilst alive, and I feel that time is coming ever closer. I wonder whether perhaps I talked too much, but I wanted to ease the tension that seems to be ever present between us. I know it was the right thing to do, in stating that I would keep my distance. I saw the relief in her eyes and I felt some of the tension leave her body. Not flattering I admit, but I want her to feel safe with me, not to fear my every move. At least she doesn't flee every time I stand up now, for which I am grateful.

I vow to be waiting for her when she awakes at the next sunset. My timekeeping tends to be a little tardy at times, especially when I have to hunt for both of us.

I watched her for a while ... my beautiful fledgling ... with her lustrous hair, so like Emily's in length and colour, yet her looks and personality are so very different to Emily's. This tiny vampire child will be a force to be reckoned with someday, I am already sure of that. I need to tread softly and carefully, but I am an expert at treading softly.

I shall always remember the dismal winter day we buried Emily. It was 1705. Rain poured down incessantly from heavy brooding skies over Highgate Village, and the darkness mirrored my emotions as I stood numbly by the open mausoleum. The biting wind cut through my clothes, like a malevolent sword, but it did not matter. Nothing mattered anymore. Emily, my beautiful young wife, had been taken from me, together with our stillborn son. My whole family had been wrenched from me in one single night of pain and agony. How I wished I could have died alongside them. Without Emily and my son, my life had no meaning, no future. My guilt knew no bounds. She had loved me unconditionally, and I had strived to care for her in return. That I cherished her was without question. But *love* . . .? What is love? Nevertheless, I missed her.

Long, lonely weeks passed interminably, as night after night I returned to the mausoleum, still numb with grief. I always sat inside the mausoleum next to Emily's tomb, and I spoke to her often as though she could hear me. I liked to think she could. On one such night, my solace was interrupted by a female voice with a slight foreign inflection. I felt anger beyond belief at the intrusion and told the woman in no uncertain terms to leave. When I looked up, she still stood nearby, her eyes glinting almost silver in the light of the moon.

'Why are you still here?' I demanded.

'Because I can help. One so handsome should not be grieving.'

'My wife and son are barely cold in their tomb. Have you no pity?' I grated the words out.

'I want only to help you, *cara*,' she said again.

'Unless you can raise the dead, there is no help you can give me.'

'I am the dead,' she said.

When I looked up again, she had gone.

A few minutes later, I too, left the tomb, and locked its heavy doors behind me. My tranquil time with Emily had been ruined by the strange woman's intrusion. I turned to walk toward the cemetery gates, only to be confronted again by the woman who suddenly appeared in front of me. I stopped, frustrated, and looked down at her. Her deep-blue eyes mesmerised me, as their different hues sparkled and glinted.

'What are you?' I whispered.

'Your salvation, William,' she replied, as she closed the distance that remained between us.

Her eyes suddenly blazed with an intense blue fire that removed my free will and sucked my very soul into their depths. I felt as if I had tumbled headlong into a bottomless black hole that nothing on God's earth could ever stop.

I became dizzy and nauseous, until an intense, sharp pain made me cry out. I heard her voice as it spoke softly to me in a foreign tongue. I even heard her laugh once, a cold, mirthless sound that chilled me to the very bone.

'Now you are mine,' she said as darkness overwhelmed me.

They found my body the next day, and buried me in the family mausoleum next to Emily, never knowing that earthly confines would never hold me. Three nights later, I rose and she was waiting for me.

'What have you done?' I asked, my voice hoarse, and my brain not altogether functioning in a normal way.

'I have removed all of your earthly pain,' she replied.

She turned and walked away, and I found myself following her. It was almost as though she knew without question I would follow, for she never once turned back to look at me. A carriage waited at the cemetery gate, with two gleaming black horses harnessed between the shafts. The driver sprang from his seat the moment he saw her approaching and opened the carriage door. She got in without a backward glance and I followed. The driver closed the door behind us, and a few moments later, we drove away from everything I had ever known, and everyone I had held dear.

After about twenty minutes, the woman rapped on the ceiling of the coach and it slid smoothly to a halt. I glanced out of the window and noticed we had stopped somewhere in a poorer part of the city. Rotting rubbish festered in the rain-sodden gutter, and its stench hung on the damp night air. The street was deserted except for a lone lady of the night, who perked up considerably at the sight of the coach. She began to walk towards us, obviously hoping for some lucrative work.

My companion turned to me with a cold, tight-lipped smile. 'Time for your first feed, William,' she said softly.

She opened the carriage door and sprang lightly down to the street. 'Come.'

Obediently, I joined her on the pavement, and watched as she went to meet the other woman. I followed her slowly, at a loss to guess what her intention could be. The horses snorted as I passed them, their harnesses jingling as they tossed their heads. Steam rose from their sweat-covered flanks, and one horse stamped a hoof impatiently, making a hollow clang on the cobbles with its iron shoe.

The prostitute walked toward us, hands on plump swaying hips. She smiled with uneven, tobacco-stained teeth. 'Well looky 'ere,' she said. 'Wot a pretty pair. I'll do the pair of yer fer a guinea. Nah – I'll do *'im* for free.' She cackled as she wiggled her hips and walked an uneven circle around me.

My companion grabbed the woman by her frizzy hair in a movement almost too fast to follow. She suddenly bared gleaming fangs, and sank them into the hussy's dirty neck, drawing a bubbling fountain of warm blood from the jugular vein. I made a startled noise of disgust, but the moment I saw the blood, a thirst stirred within my body – an all-consuming thirst such as I had never felt before. She pushed the nearly unconscious woman towards me. Almost as one hypnotised, I drank from the wound. God help me. I fed on a helpless woman.

'Very good, William,' my maker, Khiara, purred. She leaned forward to take the prostitute's limp body back from me. To my horror and eternal shame, I did nothing as she broke her neck with one callous snap, and threw the broken body into the gutter.

'We do not make many new vampires,' she remarked casually, wiping her dainty, blood-covered hands on a silk handkerchief. 'We prefer to keep our numbers to a select few.'

I still stared at Khiara, rendered speechless by the night's events.

'We are the undead. *Vampyre. Nosferatu*,' she said. 'There are many names for us.' She trailed cold fingertips down either side of my face, and stared at me with her incredible fathomless eyes, the like of which would never be seen in any human countenance.

'I made you, William, and you now belong to me. Together we shall travel the world, and cause mere mortals to weep in despair and fall at our feet.'

Chapter Eight

Truth

The first breath shuddered through my body and forced me to sit up. My eyes snapped open and I gasped aloud from the ferocity of regaining consciousness. I closed my eyes again immediately when the light came on and almost blinded me.

'I am here.' Will's voice sounded calm. 'It is all right.'

My body continued to shudder uncontrollably as I felt him come nearer to the bed. I hugged my arms around my body, and, after a while, looked up at him. He had dressed in his customary black t-shirt and faded denim jeans, with a black leather belt pretending to hold the jeans up, although they didn't appear to need any help. His dark hair gleamed in the artificial light, and he stood with his hands on his hips as he regarded me seriously.

'Have you been here all the time?' I asked, finding words difficult to form and my voice hoarse.

'I wanted to be here when you awoke,' he replied.

He was like a politician, never answering the damn question. He bent down to pick up a mug from the floor, which he handed to me with a glimmer of a smile. 'Breakfast in bed.'

I took the mug with trembling hands, and began to sip the contents slowly. Strangely, the Thirst hadn't made its presence felt yet. I dreaded the pain of that more than anything else.

'Hopefully the early feeding will prevent the pain,' he said, answering my thoughts again.

I continued to drink from the mug until it was empty. Will took it back from me without a word and left the room. I knew he was filling it from some poor 'donor' he'd found. He reappeared and handed me the refilled mug.

When I'd finished, my head cleared and I felt good, apart from a slight burning sensation in my stomach that I chose not to mention. It didn't seem to be as bad as usual, so I decided to ignore it.

'Bath or shower?' Will asked, raising dark eyebrows.

'Bath,' I replied.

He nodded and gestured for me to follow him upstairs, which, like a good little fledgling, I did. The bathroom looked inviting, but then anything would be inviting after the dank and miserable cellar room. Apart from another dank and miserable cellar of course.

Will put the brass plug in place, and turned on the taps. He took the cap off one of the bottles, and poured it liberally into the running water.

'Plenty of bubbles,' he said. 'Embarrassment free.' His eyes sparkled with wicked glints, and I narrowed my own at him suspiciously. He put the cap back on and replaced the bottle.

'I shall be back in about thirty minutes or so,' he said. 'Will you be all right?'

'I've been having baths on my own for about twenty years,' I said sarcastically. 'I think I can manage.'

'Your clothes are in the dressing room,' he said and I stared at him in surprise. 'I am trusting you to not leave, or set fire to my house in my absence.'

'Are you insured?'

'For around ten million,' he replied. 'But please curb any arsonist tendencies all the same.'

'Your house will be safe with me,' I said, and he nodded, leaving the bathroom by the other door.

Well, that was a turn up for the books. Will hadn't locked me in. A vast improvement. But I didn't say I wouldn't look around did I? I listened for any sounds but heard nothing, so, unable to contain my curiosity, I opened the door opposite. It opened onto a bedroom, although merely calling it a 'bedroom' didn't do it justice.

The room was dominated by a huge oak four-poster bed. It looked pretty ancient to me, with beautiful carvings decorating the posts and the headboard. Dark-blue velvet drapes hung down from the top and surrounded the bed, almost reaching the floor. Two matching velvet upholstered chairs stood one on either side of the bed, and a carved oak chest stood against the far wall. The floor consisted of aged oak floorboards, no doubt polished many times over the decades, and which gleamed softly in the dim light. Expensive-looking rugs were scattered about the floor and the overall effect was one of luxurious, but masculine, elegance. I wouldn't have expected anything less for Will. There were no windows, so I assumed the room was in the basement.

I wondered how many floors there were to this house. Although if it was indeed Georgian, as Will had once said, the chances are there would be four. I knew there were quite a few Georgian houses in Highgate and Hampstead, I'd often walked around, admiring them, and wishing I could have a look round inside. Little did I know I'd end up a prisoner in a cellar of one of them. Perhaps I'd even walked by this very house, never dreaming a vampire owned it. Not the kind of thing one dreams about after all – well not in the sane world anyway.

I hadn't taken much notice of my surroundings the night we'd walked to Highgate tube station, but I remembered it took about fifteen minutes or so to get there. By my reckoning I thought we were probably somewhere near Swains Lane. Highgate West Hill perhaps, Holly Terrace or maybe Oakeshott Avenue. All those streets had beautiful Georgian houses. But that would put Will's house strangely close to the famous cemetery. You'd have thought he'd want to keep well away from the tourists and Goths who frequented the cemetery. Maybe it appealed to his sense of humour. I didn't know him well enough to comment.

I walked across the bedroom to the large double doors in the far wall. I opened them to discover what Will had called the 'dressing room'. It was nearly as large as the master bedroom with a double bed against one wall and cupboards along another. I pulled open one of the cupboard doors, and my clothes were indeed hanging neatly together on one side. I rifled through until I found a short denim skirt, a black sweater and my long, black boots. I discovered underwear and a pair of black tights in a drawer beneath the wardrobe. A mite presumptuous, I thought, putting my clothes in here. Although in fairness there was no sign of his own clothes.

'Do you like it?' Will's deep voice came from behind me, and I started guiltily, turning around with an armful of clothes.

'I'm sorry, I didn't mean to be nosey—' I began, flustered.

'Yes you did,' he said. 'So, do you like it?'

'Yes of course, it's beautiful.'

'Good. I was not looking forward to re-decorating.' He turned and went through to the master bedroom and back into the bathroom. I followed with a last look at the lovely bedroom, closing the door behind me.

'When you promised not to set fire to my house, I did not expect you to try and flood it instead,' he said dryly as we entered the bathroom to see the huge sunken bath very nearly full.

'I forgot about the taps,' I said. 'Is that your bedroom?'

Will was busy turning off the taps, and when he looked at me his expression was carefully blank. 'Well, let me see,' he said, sitting on the edge of the bath, and folding his arms. 'This is my house and no one lives here but me, and now you, so I suppose it must be my bedroom.'

'Well, I don't think much of your hosting skills,' I said. 'Locking me in a cellar while you sleep there.'

He ran his fingers through his thick dark hair and his eyes shone mischievously as he looked at me. 'Any time you wish to share, you only have to say.'

'You wish,' I said, trying for cool, but sounding embarrassed instead.

He stood up then, and grabbed hold of my arms to pull me nearer. I struggled to free myself but he just laughed. The look he gave me was a hundred percent male, mixed with predatory vampire sex appeal. An unexpected flicker of desire fluttered through my stomach. Although it might have been fear. It was hard to tell the difference.

'Let. Me. Go,' I hissed. The feel of his lean, muscular body against mine suddenly had a disturbing effect on my self-control. 'You promised no pouncing.'

He looked down at me with his amazing eyes, which were now so disconcertingly close, and a slight smile played over his sensual lips. Another surge of unwarranted desire swept through my body and I shivered. He released me as suddenly as he'd grabbed me, and touching my cheek softly with cool fingertips said, 'I apologise most profusely Elinor, I forgot myself.'

'What makes you think I'll ever want to sleep with you anyway?' I said, more angry with myself than him at that moment.

He smiled with more than a hint of arrogance. 'You will not be able to resist me forever. I do know that.'

'You arrogant bastard.' I just felt angry now. *Of all the ...*

Raising an eyebrow at my angry words, he grabbed me around the waist and swept my legs from under me with a swift, and clearly practised movement, which sent both of us crashing toward the floor. He put out his free hand just before I would have landed on the tiles and lowered us both, very slowly, the last couple of inches. This put him dangerously close and – *er* – dangerously on top. His body pressed against mine again, and I was now close to panicking. My hands moved automatically to his chest, to put some space between us, and his amused gaze followed the movement.

'Defensive,' he commented. 'I really shall have to cure you of that.'

'Are you going to add rape to your list of crimes against me?' I tried to push him off me.

'Absolutely not,' he said. 'Rape is not something I would ever condone, but I have already told you that.' He stood up swiftly, his legs straddling my body, and looked down at me with a serious expression. 'So who hurt you?' he asked.

I looked at him in amazement. The man was unbelievable and very intuitive. Infuriatingly intuitive.

'I don't do casual sex,' I said stalling for time, and this time he did laugh.

'Well, that is blatantly obvious,' he said. 'It did not take too long for me to work that out. Although, frankly, I have no intention of being casual about sex with you.'

He reached down, and offered me his hand to pull me to my feet. As I stood, I noticed his unusually serious expression, and he took hold of my chin between thumb and forefinger, 'But if he is still around, whoever he is, I will kill him,' he murmured very softly.

I stared up at his face again, expecting to see his usual teasing expression, but for once it was absent.

'I have to go back out for a while. Will you be all right alone?' he asked.

'I'm getting in that bath,' I replied, and my voice trembled, because I still felt pretty shaken.

'So you are.' The Will who was always in complete control had returned, almost as though the previous conversation had never taken place. He brushed my lips softly with the pad of his thumb. 'You really have no idea of your allure do you?'

'Perhaps you've lived like a monk too long,' I said. 'I think anyone would look good after a while.'

He frowned and shook his head slightly. 'Never put yourself down, Elinor, certainly not to me. I shall be about fifteen minutes.' With that parting comment, he was gone, leaving me to have a solitary bath in peace. I stripped off and got into the bath, luxuriating in the scented bubbles. The bath was indeed so full, I could probably have swum in it. I tried to time fifteen minutes, but I felt so nervous about Will's return I washed myself in record time, and hurriedly got out of the bath to wrap myself in one of the huge towels.

I listened for sounds of Will's return, but the house stayed silent. I pulled out the plug to let the water run away and dried myself. I dressed myself in seconds, which is something I've always been good at, as most dancers are. I felt calmer with clothes on, and even happier with my heavy boots on. A swift well-aimed kick in a certain place should deter him from any more of his silly games.

I couldn't believe him. One minute he apologised, and the next, he pounced again. Infuriating, arrogant ...

I wondered how long he would be, and looked at the bedroom door. *Would he be angry if he caught me snooping upstairs? Did I care? What the hell, he's already killed me, turned me into a vampire, shut me in a cellar – oh, and he even expects me to like him into the bargain – and eventually sleep with him too.* I decided I was definitely allowed to snoop.

I opened the door to the bedroom and went in there again. I spotted another door opposite the double doors, so I made for that and opened it. It revealed stairs going upwards, which were carpeted in the same dark blue as the drapes that hung around Will's bed. I went straight up those stairs of course.

I remembered the parts in horror movies where the

heroine goes either up or down a dimly lit staircase, the music rises to a crescendo and the whole audience is thinking, 'Is she mad? Why is she going up (or down) those stairs?'

Well, here it was for real, except I was supposed to be one of the scary monsters now. Not that I could ever beat Mr Spooky when it came to being scary.

At the top of the stairs, I found myself in a large reception hall, with a Georgian front door. Several other doors led off the hall, and an elegant staircase wound its way up to the other floors. Behind one of the doors, a telephone started to ring, and I jumped. Oh yeah, I was really good at being scary. After a few rings, an answerphone clicked in and I recognised Will's voice, inviting the caller to leave a message. A deep voice with an American accent spoke then, 'This is Honyauti. I shall be with you in two weeks' time.' I heard the click of the call being terminated.

I stood in the hall and debated whether to go on upstairs, or look in the room with the telephone. At least in the movies you could tell by the music which room to go in, or when things were about to get truly scary.

I heard a door shut downstairs. Feeling like a guilty child, I went quickly downstairs to the bedroom, arriving just as Will came through the other door.

He eyed my short skirt appreciatively. 'Been looking around again, Elinor?' He gave a slight smile. 'Shall I give you the official tour, then?' adding, 'Trust a woman to want to look everywhere.'

'If I wasn't always shut in the cellar, maybe I wouldn't be so nosey.'

'I have already said that my bed is your bed. Whenever you wish to share it, you have only to say,' he gave a nonchalant shrug.

He never gave up.

I followed him up the stairs I'd just come down. As we

reached the reception hall, I turned to him. 'You've got a phone message.'

'And did you just happen to hear who was calling?' Will's voice dripped with sarcasm.

'Yes, someone called Hon-y-owtee or something.'

He smiled and headed for the door to his right. I followed, not wanting to miss the chance of seeing another room.

We went into a large drawing room, where a magnificent fireplace dominated part of one wall. It looked like an original Georgian fireplace to me, but I'm no expert. All the walls were plain ivory in colour, and unadorned by any pictures. The large windows were concealed behind heavy wooden shutters, and deep red velvet curtains were draped in front of them. A double safety measure, I supposed, in case Will strolled in during the afternoon. I'd already discovered that he 'slept' less than I did.

A large dark-red leather chesterfield stretched along one wall, with an old pine chest in front of it, which was clearly being used as a table, seeing as it had cigarettes, matches, and a pile of newspapers on it. Both recesses on either side of the fireplace contained bookshelves stuffed to overflowing with books of all shapes, sizes, and ages; so it appeared even centuries-old vampires read books.

There was a huge state-of-the-art, flat-screen television on the opposite wall, with a small table underneath on which a DVD player sat. I felt surprised at seeing them; somehow I'd imagined Will would be a complete technophobe. But I suppose time weighs heavily when one has an eternity to find amusement.

Several red leather armchairs, which matched the colour of the sofa, were scattered around the room, and beautiful oriental rugs graced the polished wooden floorboards.

The telephone rested on top of a carved antique cabinet and the answer machine was indeed flashing. Will pressed a button and played the message.

'Good,' was all he said. He reached for the cigarettes and, putting one between his teeth, picked up the box of matches. As he struck a match, the light from the flame illuminated his face briefly, accentuating his chiselled features, and I had a flashback again to the fight I'd had to get free from the grave, and how I came face to face with him. He flicked the match into the fireplace and regarded me with his steady gaze. 'What is it?'

'Just remembering.'

'What are you remembering?' Interest suddenly sparked in his eyes.

'Fighting my way out of a coffin and coming face to face with you.'

'What about before that?' he persisted. 'Do you remember anything about before?'

I tried to remember my last few days as a human, but the memories were still missing, and all I could recall was feeling sick and afraid. 'You killed me.'

Will flung his cigarette into the fireplace with an angry gesture and spun around to face me. His eyes flashed and he looked more dangerous than I'd ever seen him. I stepped back.

'And you seem determined to make me pay for that for all eternity,' he said scathingly, 'unless we talk about it, right here, right now.'

'I—'

'Sit down.' His voice was harsh and uncompromising, a tone he'd never used with me before. I backed away from him, suddenly afraid, and he swore savagely and colourfully under his breath.

'Did you hear me? I said, sit the fuck *down*, Elinor!'

His anger was palpable and it turned my spine to ice.

I sat.

I was shocked to hear him resort to profanities. That alone was enough to scare the hell out of me.

He stared at me, his eyes glinting dangerously, and I resisted the urge to gulp. I watched him warily, and wondered why he'd suddenly become so angry.

He began to pace the room like a caged panther, every bit as graceful, but infinitely more dangerous.

I opened my mouth to speak, but he turned back to me, and the look in his eyes shut me up. I really wished he would stop pacing, it made me nervous.

He stopped suddenly and looked at me. I met those livid eyes without a flinch, although it wasn't easy. He bent to pick up his cigarettes and matches again, and I watched him light one, then toss the packs back onto the pine chest. He looked at me without a trace of his usual humour, and that bothered me more than I felt prepared to admit.

'I am one of the most patient men you will ever meet,' he said at last, 'and probably *the* most patient vampire.'

I said nothing. I do occasionally know when to keep quiet.

'But even my patience is not endless. I am doing everything I can to help you come to terms with what you are. Not just because it is my duty, but because I want to. It is about time you realised that resenting me for your death and rebirth is not helping either one of us. It certainly prevents you from moving on.' He paused to drag on his cigarette. 'I have not sired a fledgling for centuries, yet I chose to give you eternal life, Elinor. Do you not yet realise what a compliment it is? What it tells you about my feelings for you?'

I fiddled with my fingers, an old childhood habit I'd developed after my parents' deaths – usually when confronted by angry foster parents, who were unable to cope with my grief. I'd never been good at discussing anything personal, having had to hide my feelings for so many years. So I didn't speak, I just watched him, and hoped his anger would subside soon.

'I was hoping you would remember your last day as a human on your own, but for some reason the events have evaded your memory. I can only assume the reason for that is because it was so traumatic.'

'Whose fault was that?' I muttered, and jumped violently, as Will smashed his fist on the pine chest in front of me causing the lid to crack.

'It was not mine!' He almost snarled.

I sat back farther in the sofa, my eyes wide with shock. This was a Will I didn't know at all. The change in him was terrifying. Gone was the charming, elegant man I had become accustomed to, and in his place stood a demonic entity. I watched as he struggled to regain his self-control. He turned away from me to face the fireplace, and leaned his hands against the mantelpiece, with his head lowered.

'Will—'

'Elinor, please do not speak to me for the moment,' his voice was deep with emotion. I stayed silent, wanting only to run from the room, anywhere away from him would have been good at that moment.

'And stay where you are,' he added.

The silence grew between us, stretching uncomfortably, and I knew I wouldn't break it. I continued to watch him, wondering again why he'd lost his temper so quickly. At last, he faced me, his face stern and uncompromising. I went to speak, but he held up his hand with the authoritative gesture I'd begun to know and hate.

'Listen to me,' he said in quiet, even tones. 'Four days before your death, you were knocked down outside the theatre by a drunken driver.'

I gasped in shock.

'I was there watching the stage door, and I saw it happen. I called for an ambulance, but had to leave before it arrived. I could not risk having to give evidence in a human court in daylight.'

Chapter Nine

Honesty

I remained motionless, staring at Will in horror. I really had no memory of an accident, and although I felt sure he spoke the truth, part of me didn't want to believe it.

Run down by a car?

Will lit yet another cigarette, and smoked for a few minutes without a word. Then he continued, holding me captive with his bright gaze. 'The driver did not stop.'

'They never got him?'

Will shook his head slightly. '*They* did not. No.'

'What are you saying?'

'He is of no consequence to this conversation,' he replied firmly, and I knew without question that the driver was dead.

Will walked towards me, and I sprang up ready to run. He raised his hands in surrender.

'Please sit back down,' he said, returning to his place in front of the fireplace.

I sat down slowly, trying to make sense of it all.

'Elinor, you were attached to a machine enabling you to live, and I happened to be in the room when the doctors decided to switch it off.'

I refrained from asking what the hell he was doing in the room in the first place.

'I could not let you die,' he said. 'I was already in love with you, and I appreciate that is difficult for you to comprehend, because your memory has not completely returned, but it is a fact. I did the only thing I could, in order to keep you on this earth, which was to turn you. I know it was an evil act, and I am well aware that it was wrong – especially in your eyes – but I find it difficult to feel any remorse whatsoever over my actions.'

I sat in silence. All this time I had been blaming Will for my death, and he'd allowed me to continue with that train of thought. He had in some strange way saved me. I couldn't think of a thing to say. Tears filled my eyes and trickled slowly down my cheeks. Will immediately came and knelt in front of me. His anger seemed to have abated now, and his eyes were full of nothing but concern. He took hold of both my hands and stroked one hand gently with his thumb. Just that one small gesture made me catch my breath. With his other hand he gently brushed the tears from my face.

'Elinor, forgive me. I am so sorry you had to hear this from my lips,' he said. 'I should have spared you the sight of my wrath. I fear my temper over ran good sense. The last thing I wanted to do was frighten you.'

'I was already dead?'

Will shook his head. 'No but you were very close to death. You would not have survived the night. I hope one day you will find it within your heart to forgive me, for bringing you into this existence that you find so abhorrent.'

I looked at him kneeling there, glossy dark hair flopping over his dark eyebrows, the glorious eyes and sculpted perfection of his face.

'I would be completely dead if it wasn't for you?'

He nodded, his face grave. He stood up slowly, running his hand through his hair again. He walked back again to the fireplace, away from me, giving me some space. I felt grateful for that, having him too near confused the hell out of me … amongst other things.

Will leaned back against the mantelpiece. He continued to search my face with his bright gaze.

I looked at his tall lean body, and for a moment I nearly forgot what we were talking about. No matter what I did or didn't feel for him, I could still appreciate the beauty of his face and body. Indifference was, unfortunately, impossible.

'Do you still not remember anything at all yet about the night you died?' he asked at length.

'I remember that I thought I was drowning. Then I could see only complete darkness,' I said slowly. 'So much darkness.' I shuddered.

'Ah yes, the darkness,' he gave a rueful grin that instantly made his face look boyish. 'Only I could turn someone with a phobia about darkness and the sight of blood.'

'I'm having trouble just getting my head around all of this,' I said. 'You let me think that you turned me merely because you wanted me for some reason. You let me go on thinking that.'

'Do not have any illusions about me,' he interrupted me. 'I am neither a hero nor some kind of reformed black knight.' He gave me a small smile. 'I would definitely have found a way to turn you at some point.'

'Against my will?' I had to know.

He shook his head. 'Preferably not, no. I had hoped to persuade you to fall in love with me, and then I would have given you the choice.'

I looked down. It seemed as though all of this had been planned for a while, but the hit-and-run driver had inadvertently moved things on.

'The worst thing for me about this ... *existence*, is that everything I've ever known ... everyone I've ever known ... well, it's all been taken away from me. Gone. My whole life has just *gone*. You *say* you care about me, yet you shut me in a dark cellar when you know I hate the dark. I'm forced to drink blood to survive, and I've never been able to stand the sight of the stuff. I just feel so alone, and I don't think I will ever be any good at this – especially as I really, *really* don't want to bite people.'

I stopped my self-pity rant to look up and find his gaze now sympathetic.

'You are not alone,' he said. 'You will never be alone, that I promise. I will never leave you, and, of course, I do care for you. I certainly do not want you to be so afraid of me. That is painful to me. Every time you cry, your tears erode a part of my soul.'

'You do have a way with words,' I said with a small smile, 'You weren't friends with Shakespeare by any chance?'

'Even I am not that old,' he said. 'Although I did hang out with Byron a few times.'

Will started to pace the room again, eventually coming to a halt and sitting on the pine chest in front of me. His knees nearly touched mine. I tensed. He immediately moved back.

'Do you wonder, Elinor, why you were on my radar, so to speak?'

I nodded. 'There are plenty of better looking girls in London. You could probably have anyone you fancied.'

'It had to be you, and only you, from the first moment I saw you.'

'Which was?'

'About a year ago,' he watched me closely.

A year? I couldn't hide my astonishment. 'You stalked me for a whole *year?*'

He gave a small smile then, and the humour crept back into his eyes at last. I felt as though I could now breathe out after a long time of holding my breath, although any withholding of breath by a member of the undead fraternity would cause little discomfort if the truth be known.

'I prefer the term *observed*,' he said dryly.

'That's still a bit pervy,' I was feeling braver, 'and some pretty serious ... *observing*.'

'I can see why you would think that.'

I'd often suspected Will was somewhat tenacious and single-minded, but even so, a *year*?

'I think I searched for you even before I knew of your existence,' he continued. 'I have been searching for my soul mate for many years. Decades actually. But when I met you, I knew I had found her.'

I was stricken into silence. How could any of this be possible? How could a several-hundred-year-old man suddenly decide I was his soul mate? Where did that come from? It was the stuff of fantasy, B-movies and cheap novels. Things like this just didn't happen in the real world. I shook my head again, and Will reached across to take one of my hands.

'I know you are finding this all very difficult to come to terms with. It is one of the reasons I did not want to tell you about the accident yet.' He gave a small rueful smile. 'But you inadvertently forced the issue and I lost my temper.'

'That is one very scary temper you have.'

'Elinor,' he raised my hand to his soft lips and kissed it. 'I apologise yet again. I do seem to be making a complete mess of everything in more ways than one. I promised no pouncing and yet I pounced, not just once, but twice. I had also promised myself that I would not tell you about the accident for a while and yet I have.'

'Good to know you're not perfect,' I said. 'Because that would just be dull.'

Will laughed, his face immediately lighting up and his eyes gleaming. What a difference.

A knock at the front door made us both stand up. A key sounded in the lock and I looked at Will in consternation.

'Get behind me.'

I hesitated for a split second.

'Do it now.'

If Will was worried then I was worried. I stood behind his tall frame and he put one arm behind himself to wrap around me.

There was a sharp knock on the drawing room door and I felt the tension leave Will's body.

'Come on in Luke,' he said, his deep voice sounding relaxed.

The door opened and a tall blond man walked in.

'Good evening Will,' he said.

Will nodded, and gestured to one of the armchairs. 'Have a seat.'

Luke loped across the room, and folded his long frame into the nearest armchair. Will still protected me with his body, and I began to feel a little foolish. I tried to remove his arm, but it was like trying to move a tree.

'Is this the new fledgling?' asked Luke, nodding at what little he could see of me.

Will brought me around to the side of his body so that Luke and I could see each other. He kept a hold of my arm in a possessive grip as I stared at the newcomer. Luke's fair hair hung in waves, almost to his broad shoulders, and his eyes were the colour of cornflowers. He was definitely a vampire, I could feel it. Casually dressed in black sweater, jeans and a brown leather jacket, he seemed completely at ease, although his eyes looked me over with frank curiosity. I didn't know whether vampires bothered with body building exercises, but he certainly looked as though he did.

'Elinor this is Luke,' said Will.

'Hallo Luke,' I said. *Very original Ellie, and very eloquent.*

'Hallo Elinor,' said Luke. 'It is good to meet you at last.'

What did he mean by *at last*?

'Luke has always been aware of your arrival,' said Will.

'She looks well,' commented Luke, his eyes travelling up and down my body with interest.

'She looks infinitely better than she did a few nights ago,' said Will.

'*She* is standing right here,' I said.

'A fact I am very well aware of,' Will glanced at me.

Luke hid a smile, and I wondered whether he was in any way subservient to Will. Why did he have a key to Will's house and why did he knock at both doors and come in anyway?

'Luke is my second,' said Will. 'He has a key to all my properties, it is a safety precaution. He knocks out of courtesy.'

'Stay out of my head,' I said. 'Believe me, there's enough going on in there at the moment without you joining in.'

Will crossed to the sofa and sat down, gesturing for me to do the same. I sat in one of the armchairs in a deliberate act of defiance, which he chose to ignore. He turned back to Luke. 'Is something wrong?'

Luke shrugged. 'I believe so, yes,' he replied. 'There has been an odd occurrence that I thought I should make you aware of.'

Odd occurrence? Now why didn't I like the sound of that?

Will lit the inevitable cigarette. It was probably a good job he was dead because those things would have killed him for sure. He turned an amused glance my way.

'But you are not going to scold me are you?' It was a statement rather than a question.

'I wouldn't presume,' I said.

'May I say, Will,' ventured Luke, 'that you appear to have met your match?'

'No, you may not,' said Will. 'So what appears to be the problem?'

'A body was discovered in Waterlow Park this morning,' said Luke. 'Drained.'

Will swore under his breath. Even I could understand the significance of that. 'Sounds as though someone has found out about Elinor.'

'What the hell does that mean?' I asked.

'I have already explained the rules of the city to you,' said Will. 'Therefore the only likely candidate to drain a human would be a fledgling who lacked self-control. As it is forbidden to turn a human without my express permission, it appears the only fledgling vampire in London is you.'

I stared at him, horrified. 'But you know it wasn't me, I've been here with you since—'

'I know that, you know that and Luke knows that,' he replied. 'Unfortunately no-one else knows that.'

'Someone apparently does know of your existence and is deliberately implicating you,' said Luke.

'So if it *was* me—and you both know it wasn't—what would happen?' I wasn't sure I actually wanted to hear the answer.

'Under normal circumstances, the fledgling would be tracked down and staked.' Will said. 'However, these are not normal circumstances and, luckily for you, what I say goes.'

I had a sudden vision of enraged villagers descending on the house with flaming torches and pitchforks and stared at Will wide-eyed.

'It must be Khiara,' he said to Luke.

'After all this time?' asked Luke. 'Why?'

'Because she is Khiara,' said Will. 'It is what she does best.'

Luke shook his head slowly. 'Surely we would know if she was in London.'

'Not if she wished to remain undetected. As long as she kept her distance, I would not detect her presence.'

'Waterlow Park is hardly a distance.'

'Khiara would not do any dirty work herself.'

'Good point.'

I followed their conversation with ever increasing horror. When I couldn't stand it any longer I stood up in agitation.

'Hold on just a damn minute,' I said loudly.

Both men turned to look at me. Luke with the detached interest one would show an irritating child who wanted attention, and Will with his usual amusement. But at least I had their attention.

'Can someone please explain what the hell is going on here? And who the hell is this Khiara person?'

Will and Luke exchanged glances.

'You really do have your work cut out,' said Luke.

'Oh, you have no idea,' agreed Will with a resigned shrug.

'Who's going to tell me?' I persisted.

'Khiara is my maker,' said Will to me. 'I have not seen her for nearly two hundred years.'

'She's born a grudge for two hundred years?' I asked. 'She must be a Scorpio.'

Will's lips twitched. 'I could not say,' he said. 'All I know is that my life has been uncomplicated in the extreme for very many years, but the moment I bring another woman to my house, someone begins to sully my territory. She is the only creature on this earth who is vindictive enough to instigate revenge two centuries on.'

'She needs to get a life.' I muttered. 'Or another death.'

Luke laughed. 'I like her.'

'I knew you would,' said Will.

'So what do we do?' I asked, as I sat back down.

'*You* will do nothing,' he said. 'I, too, shall do nothing at this stage either.'

'Oh, good plan,' I said sarcastically. 'So when the angry villagers torch your house, will you do something then?'

'You have seen far too many cheap horror films,' he replied.

'Does this woman know where you live?' I asked. 'I mean if you can sense her, surely she would be able to sense you too, and find you here eventually?'

Will looked impressed. 'Beauty *and* brains,' he said.

'Don't patronise me,' I said, annoyed.

'It was a compliment.'

'Trust me, it wasn't.'

Will turned to Luke. 'You are younger than I, do you understand her?'

Luke looked thoughtful. 'I think she is inferring that you think it unusual for a woman to be beautiful, yet intelligent, and that generally it is not possible to be both.'

Will looked back at me and raised his eyebrows.

'What he said,' I agreed.

'Elinor, I am well aware that you have considerable intelligence; as far as I am concerned that has never been in question. Plus your appearance speaks for itself.'

'You definitely spent too long with Byron,' I said.

At that moment the phone rang and Will rose to answer it.

'Yes?' Not one for bothering with a good telephone manner obviously. He listened for a while, and nodded his head every now and again. 'I appreciate that Jake, thank you.'

He came back and sat down. 'Jake has come across some unknown vampires in the Camden area. One very large male, who could be Grigori, plus a blonde woman who could very well be Josephine. When he challenged them, they got into a car and drove off. He says they went towards Chalk Farm.'

'So if it is Grigori and Josephine, Khiara is almost certainly in London too,' said Luke. 'What would you like me to do?'

'Contact all of our people and tell them everything, and also tell them about Elinor. You need to assure them the renegade is not ours. Everyone should be very alert and security conscious. Especially when going out to feed, I do not want to lose anyone.'

'Consider it done.'

Luke stood up and Will stood too. They clasped

hands like two ancient warriors, and Will gripped Luke's shoulder. 'Take care my friend.'

Luke nodded and turned to me. 'It was good to meet you Elinor.'

'You too.' I said.

The door closed behind him, and after a few seconds I heard the front door close too. I stared into space thinking about this latest development. 'Will your people think it was me anyway?'

'Absolutely not,' Will said firmly. 'I trust Luke implicitly to say the right things where you are concerned.'

'What can we do?' I asked. 'There must be something.'

'We keep a very low profile and let Luke handle things for the moment.'

'If my profile was any lower, I'd be back in the grave.'

'Feeding could be a potential problem too ...' He was obviously thinking aloud. 'I cannot risk bringing anyone here for a while.'

Great, just when I was getting accustomed to room service and drinking the revolting stuff from a mug, it all goes to pot again.

Will crossed back to the phone and, picking it up, keyed in a few numbers.

'I need a favour,' he said. 'Yes. That would be plenty, many thanks. If you deliver to the usual place, I shall leave payment for you there.'

He replaced the phone.

I looked questioningly at him.

'I have made arrangements for some blood to be delivered from the hospital.'

'Someone could die if we take the hospital's blood.'

Will shook his head. 'I very much doubt that,' he said. 'We only take the more common blood groups. You would do well to worry more about your own well-being at this moment in time.'

That made me feel so much better. Not.

Will sat back down on the sofa and watched me for a while. I knew he was about to ask me something personal, so I mentally braced myself.

'I would still like to know who destroyed your faith in men.'

I said nothing at first, just looked at him. Eventually I shook my head.

'Tell me.'

'Why does it matter to you? It all happened a long time ago, and you don't have any right to ask me about it.'

'You are quite correct of course, I do not have the right to ask you such a personal question,' said Will. 'But I think your past is still playing a part now. It stands between us like an ugly spectre and I would very much like to exorcise it.'

I thought about whether to trust Will with the information. I didn't know him well enough to know how he would take the knowledge of my hideous abuse at the hands of the one person I should have been able to trust. Deciding there was nothing to lose, I closed my eyes against the painful memories.

'Foster father.' I whispered, reluctantly remembering events I'd buried deep in my memory for years – revolting things I had never wanted to surface again. I watched his face anxiously, expecting to see it show disgust with me, the dirty child, problem child, lying child. But his gaze was sympathetic, almost kind.

'How old were you?'

'Twelve,' I replied. 'My parents died in a car accident when I was eleven.'

Will stood up, cursing under his breath. He started to pace, and I felt anxious in case his temper erupted again. 'How does a maggot like that ever become a foster father?'

'No one believed me. He was plausible and very

charming to the people who mattered. His wife didn't believe me either, and I became branded a problem child. But he was always seen as the nice guy who had kindly taken in an orphan with problems, and given her a nice home.'

'No wonder you "don't do casual sex", it makes perfect sense.' He said. 'How long did it go on?'

'Until I was fifteen. Then they took in another, younger, girl. He transferred his attentions to her—I tried to help her—' I broke off as more images flashed before my eyes. Scenes that had long been relegated to the dark recesses of my memory. Strange how they were all still there, and yet I still couldn't recall the accident.

Will stood still and crouched down in front of me. 'Once again I find myself wishing I could take the pain away from you,' he rested his hands either side of me on the arms of the chair. Strangely, I didn't feel penned in by him for once. The only emotion I could feel from him was concern. 'I meant what I said before, Ellie, if I ever find him, he is a dead man.' He stood slowly, and touched my hair briefly, before crossing back to the sofa and sitting down again.

'You called me Ellie,' was all I could find to say.

A slight smile touched his lips. 'I believe I did. The night is yet young, would you care to take a walk?'

'Is it safe to leave the house?'

'We shall no doubt find out.'

I felt as though I needed some air after all the events of the night, so I stood up and nodded. 'Let's go then.' I sounded braver than I felt.

Will stood too and, crossing to the door, opened it for me. He strode across the reception hall to a Victorian coat-stand, and took down my coat and his jacket, handing me mine. I slipped it on, hugging it around myself as he pulled on his jacket. His t-shirt strained across his chest as he did so, and I would have had to be made of stone not to enjoy the view. A fact that I am sure Will was well aware of. He opened the front door with a flourish, and I went out in front of him.

So this was the front of the house. The door itself was a typical Georgian door, painted in traditional black, with a glass fanlight at the top. Will flicked the hall light on as we left and locked the door behind us. Stairs led down from the door to the paved parking area in front of the house, which was surrounded by high brick walls in much the same way as the garden at the back of the house. Huge wrought iron double gates stood majestically in the centre of the walls and were firmly closed.

Will went to a key panel in the wall, and when he tapped in some numbers the gates swung quietly open. After we'd gone through, they swung closed again with a clang.

'Not exactly a caller-friendly house is it?' I said.

Will pointed to a mailbox set in the wall. 'Post or deliveries go here. Luke and Stevie both know the combination for the gates at the front and back of the house but anyone else has to ring the entry phone.'

Well, he certainly took no chances with security, and at that moment in time I was pleased he didn't. If there were unfriendly vampires in London trying to implicate me in murder for whatever reason, all precautions were good.

'Who's Stevie?' I asked, suddenly realising he'd unwittingly given me another name.

'He is the manager of my club and a good friend, you will meet him soon.'

'You have a Georgian mansion in Highgate, a plane in Elstree and now I find you own a club.' I was beginning to wonder how much money this man had.

'When one has been around as long as I have, one accumulates,' he said.

We walked to the end of the road where Will turned

into Oakeshott Avenue, and from there he headed toward Swains Lane.

We were making for the cemetery.

'Are you deliberately trying to scare me?' I asked him.

He turned his head to look down at me. 'Perhaps. You may need to hang on to me if you become frightened.'

'So that's your evil plan,' I said.

His soft laughter ran through me as though he'd touched me.

Oh, he had plans all right.

16 February

I curse my foul temper and I curse the fact that Elinor had to hear the full story of her tragic accident from my own lips. I wanted her to remember under her own volition. I do not know why I felt it would make a difference, but somehow I believed it would.

I know she believes that I sought out and killed the driver who caused her to almost die, and she is correct in her assumption. She knows me better than I thought she did. But I could not allow that creature to live.

How could anyone drive into another person and then not stop to give assistance? Why do the human courts not have fitting punishment for a crime such as this? I would not think twice about retribution for such an appalling act. In fact, I did not.

I feel our somewhat fragile relationship, if indeed it can be called such, is more fragile than ever at the moment. I have succeeded in scaring her twice in the bathroom, even instilling the belief I would rape her. Then I terrified her further with my revolting show of temper.

In a way I am relieved that Luke came when he did, as I think his presence calmed things down a little. Although his news was nothing I really wanted to hear. I am convinced Khiara is now in London, and it is the very last thing I need to contend with, at the moment. The woman is bad news, and her entourage the main source of intrinsic evil. They will only cause problems within the City.

Protocol among us decrees that a visiting 'kiss of vampires' should seek the permission of the city's Elder before arriving. The fact Khiara did not is an arrogant declaration of animosity, and a direct insult to me. To allow one of her entourage to so blatantly drain a human, and then leave the body for all and sundry to see, is tantamount to throwing down the gauntlet. I am not sure how to play this just yet, but my main objective is to keep Elinor safe, and preferably far away from Khiara.

Chapter Ten

Changes

As we walked along Swain's Lane towards the cemetery, I began to wonder about getting in.

'It'll be locked.'

Will gave me a wicked grin as he dangled a large key in front of my nose. 'Courtesy of the Friends of Highgate Cemetery.'

'So you joined a society of ageing middle-class snobs just to get a key?'

'No, I merely relieved one of them of the key. I felt it was too much responsibility for her.'

Best not to delve any deeper into that little scenario, I decided. He really was a law unto himself.

When we reached the imposing gates, he did indeed unlock them and wave me through. I gave him a long-suffering look as I walked past him.

He locked the gates behind us, pocketing the key, and led the way into the depths of the cemetery. Good that I wasn't at all scared then. I followed him down narrow, moss-covered paths that twisted and turned like a maze between huge Victorian tombs and their neighbouring ivy-clad gravestones.

We passed the tomb of Queen Victoria's dog trainer and startled a badger foraging for food. It bared its ferocious yellow teeth at us, and Will bared his own white teeth back. The badger backed off.

I looked around at the tombstones jostling against each other, like so many uneven teeth, all vying for the best position. Masses of dark prolific ivy cloaked neighbouring headstones, shielding them from human eyes.

The atmosphere was brooding and intense, almost as

though the cemetery itself was waiting for something – or someone. Somehow, I didn't feel convinced we were the only supernatural visitors tonight.

Will stopped at a convenient tomb and lowered his lean frame to the ground. He leaned back against the tomb and stretched his long legs out in front of him. As usual, he looked comfortable and completely at ease. 'Have a seat.' He patted the grass beside him.

I reluctantly sat down, being careful not to get too close. I didn't think I could trust him, especially after his earlier display of temper. I doubted whether there would ever come a time when I didn't feel a bit afraid of him. He, perversely, still seemed to believe I'd hop into bed with him sometime soon, even after everything that had happened and everything that had been said. Incorrigible. Hundreds of years of never being turned down, I suspected. It would do him good to be rejected for a change.

I leaned back against the tomb, and listened to the mingled sounds of the night, the bark of a fox, the faint squeak of a bat, and the small nocturnal animals that scurried through the undergrowth to hide from the night's predators. I could even hear the distant sound of traffic. Yet, strangely, I actually felt better than I had for a long time.

It was me who broke the silence. 'Do you have any Irish blood in you?'

His short bark of laughter was spontaneous and, as usual, at my expense.

'Well let me see, Irish, Asian, Caucasian, whoever happens to be around really … would you like a list?' He gave me an amused look.

'Funny man,' I said, exasperated, as I realised too late the absurdity of what I'd just said. I took a sneaky peek at his perfect profile, admiring the way the moonlight picked out the lines of his face, and made his amazing eyes into something otherworldly. He twisted around to look at me, as if on cue.

'We could start our affair here.' He sounded deceptively innocent. 'Are you up for that?'

'No—and you stay exactly where you are,' I said. 'Any more pouncing of any kind and you'll see how good I can be at self-defence.'

He grinned and put his hands up in mock surrender. 'As you wish. But you look so delectable sitting there, I am finding it extremely difficult to keep my distance.'

'Try bloody harder.'

'Surely I can just kiss you?'

He had moved suddenly closer with the graceful quiet stealth of a predator, and my eyes widened in shock.

I moved away at once – I suddenly realised I didn't exactly trust myself either when he was so near.

'Where is the harm in one simple kiss?' His breath whispered a sudden chill across my cheek. He'd moved in close to me again, and I hadn't even noticed. Could this be the acclaimed 'vampire magnetism' I'd seen TV vampires use on humans in *True Blood*? I really did watch far too many DVDs.

'Am I so repulsive that you would deny me something so innocent?' He put his fingertips gently to my jaw, and made me face him.

He was really, disturbingly close.

His eyes reflected the moonlight, yet glowed with intelligence and humour.

'You are so very beautiful.' He murmured almost to himself, his hand now cradling my face.

I felt as if I could drown in his eyes, and involuntarily tensed in anticipation of his kiss. He kept his hand on my face, and leaned in closer, until his lips found mine in a gentle, almost chaste kiss. His lips were like velvet, yet I felt the burn of his touch run through my whole body like an electric shock. Disturbingly, his kiss felt really familiar, almost as though we had been together for years. Fear of the unknown flooded me, and when he drew back to look at me I scooted away from him at once.

'Was that so bad?' he asked dryly.

I looked at him without speaking, and he laughed aloud as he settled back against the tomb again. He lit a cigarette and blew smoke upwards, still smiling to himself. 'What *am* I going to do with you?'

'Is that a rhetorical question?'

'Perhaps.'

We sat in silence for a while. Will looked completely relaxed as he happily smoked his cigarette, while I sat nervously at his side, not knowing what to say or do. I felt like a virgin on her first grown-up date. I didn't trust him. I wasn't even sure I liked him. But he certainly possessed a magnetism that drew me to him like the proverbial moth to a flame. How very aggravating.

He finished his cigarette, stood up abruptly, and looked down at me with an unfathomable expression.

'Shall we go?' He offered me a hand.

After a moment's hesitation, I took it, and he pulled me to my feet.

'As you are clearly not going succumb to my advances, we may as well go home.' He raised his eyebrows hopefully. 'Unless you *are* going to succumb?'

'Home.' I said firmly.

'So heartless, Elinor. Cruel and utterly heartless.'

After leaving the cemetery safely locked behind us, we walked in silence towards Will's road. Several times during the walk the burning sensation in my stomach made itself known and I rubbed it surreptitiously, or so I thought. Will put his hand on my arm. 'Are you in pain?'

'A little.' I always put all pain down to the Thirst, and so I hadn't mentioned anything to Will.

When we reached the front gates, Will swiftly keyed in the combination and they swung open. Once they were secure behind us, he gripped my arms and turned me to face him.

'Describe the pain.'

'Burning. Sharp, it's only the Thirst again.'

'No. It is not.'

Without another word, he lifted me in his arms, and somehow managed to unlock the front door whilst carrying me. He strode across the hall, down the stairs to his bedroom, and dumped me on his bed.

'Point to where the pain is,' he said tersely.

Obediently I pointed in the general direction of my belly button and he frowned.

Without any further conversation, he took my coat off and threw it to the floor, then went to remove my skirt.

'Hey,' I said. 'What the hell are you doing?'

'Elinor, just this once, please be quiet.'

Then my skirt, boots and tights were off too, leaving me in my jumper and underwear and lying flat on my back on Will's bed. *Marvellous*. I went to sit up but he prodded me in the chest and forced me back down.

'Keep still.' His gaze travelled up my legs to my belly. 'Oh *merda*!' He spat out the words.

'What?'

'Your belly has been pierced with silver.'

'I know that. I was there.'

'We cannot wear silver,' he said. 'This thing will have to come out. Have you been suffering like this all the time? Why the hell have you not told me before?'

'Well we weren't exactly having friendly conversations before, and I've had a couple of other things on my mind since.' I ground out through gritted teeth. 'It's *burning*.'

Will looked grim. 'Yes, it would. Stay still.'

He went into the bathroom, returning with a dry face flannel.

'This is going to hurt. Do you want me to knock you out?'

'Don't you bloody dare,' I said, still through clenched teeth.

He peered down at me and smiled briefly. 'Then at the risk of sounding like an old Hammer horror film, look into my eyes.'

I gave a rather hysterical snort in spite of the pain, and he put the flannel in my mouth.

'Bite that,' he said. 'It will be preferable to your tongue.'

I wondered whether it was just his way of keeping me quiet, but obediently bit into it anyway, and then stared into his eyes. I watched the different shades of green glint and sparkle, like deep pools of emerald fire, so perfect to submerge in. He was fiddling with the clasp to the bolt, and the pain seared through my stomach again. My teeth sank further into the flannel, and I felt relieved it wasn't my tongue. I clenched my fists and tried to just concentrate on his eyes. His handsome face looked stern as he freed the bolt part of the rod.

The burning sensation grew stronger, making me arch my back.

'I am going to pull it out now.'

As he pulled, the pain caused me to scream in agony, but luckily my screams were muffled by the flannel. Then, at last it was over, and Will removed the flannel from my mouth. My hair stuck to my head in damp tendrils, and he moved it out of my eyes with gentle fingers – fingers that were burnt from gripping silver. Tears streaked down my face and he brushed them away.

He sat on the edge of the bed. 'It is gone Elinor. Everything is all right now.'

Everything was so bloody far from being all right, I couldn't think of a suitable comment other than: 'Thanks.'

'Pleasure.' The word was said with some irony. 'So, who the hell got you ready for burial?'

'How should I know? I was dead.'

I hugged my arms around my semi-naked lower body, feeling suddenly vulnerable. Strangely, Will didn't press his advantage, he merely pulled the duvet up to cover me. 'Dawn is close, you had better rest here.'

'I don't think so,' I struggled to sit up.

He stood up, putting his hands on his hips. 'Relax, Elinor, please. Your honour will remain intact,' he flashed me a wicked grin. 'Until you no longer wish it to remain intact, that is. I shall be resting in the dressing room should you need me.'

I could feel the dawn pressing inside my head. My body was already feeling so leaden and heavy, and I knew I should protest more ... I did try to protest more ... but I felt too strange and tired. That bed felt like sheer luxury after the narrow bed in the damp cellar.

I closed my eyes, trying to relax as Will had taught me, and tried not to fight the oncoming dawn.

I think I felt his lips brush my forehead gently, and then my body became useless as the sleeping death took me again for the daylight hours.

17 February

I enjoyed our walk together as we took in the solitude of the cemetery. I have taken many walks there, but always alone. What a difference a companion makes. I wanted to hold her, and kiss her until she begged for mercy, but I have frightened Elinor enough tonight to last a decade.

How I love to watch the moon's silver rays touch her delicate features, seeing how they play in her wonderful hair and light up her beautiful eyes. I could watch her forever. No doubt she would think me truly insane if I said as much to her.

I think the romance is sorely missing in this century, people are cynical, marriages do not last, and monogamy seems a thing of the past. What chance will there be for a relationship that I want to last for eternity?

Although I felt sympathy for her pain with the strange silver decoration in her stomach, I cannot help but be joyful that she is now asleep in my bed.

At last.

I have no doubt she will be angry when she wakes at sunset. I wonder whether she will even believe that I slept in the dressing room.

Still, I always knew she would be a challenge, and I am man enough to look forward to that.

Chapter Eleven

Thoughts

When the first breath of night woke me, I soon realised where I was, but that didn't reassure me in any way. As usual, my thoughts were a little jumbled at first, but I knew beyond any doubt I was in Will's bed. The fact I'd woken there at all disturbed me; the fact that I couldn't remember *why* or even *how* I came to be there filled me with horror. I looked up at the dark blue canopy of the four poster, and then, in a moment of abject panic, looked to my right in case Will still slept there, but thankfully there was no sign of him. The other half of the bed still looked pristine, and the pillow hadn't been marred by an indent of a dark head. I turned to look around the other side of me. The man in question sat in a chair by the bed, mercifully fully dressed in black jeans and a dark blue long-sleeved sweatshirt. He looked cool, calm, and good enough to eat – and I didn't even like him. Much. He was reading a copy of the *Ham & High*, which, to the uninitiated, is the *Hampstead and Highgate Express*, the local paper for people privileged enough to live in this exclusive area. He glanced up the moment I looked at him.

'Good evening Elinor,' he said. 'How are you feeling?'

'What the hell am I doing here?' I asked without preamble.

He made a wry face. 'Somehow I knew that would be your first question.'

'So what's the answer?'

He folded his arms behind his head and leaned back in the chair. 'You do not remember?'

'If I remembered I wouldn't be asking.'

'Good point,' he agreed. 'You had a problem with a

silver bolt through your belly and I had to remove it. You were in agony.'

Ah. I immediately wanted to look under the duvet to see whether I was naked, but my pride wouldn't let me.

'I had to remove your skirt, and, yes, you were awake at the time,' he said helpfully, 'and, yes, all your other clothes are still in place. Untouched by vampire hand.' He held up both hands, palms out, and wriggled long fingers at me.

I narrowed my eyes at him, not altogether sure whether he was teasing.

He gave me a patient, almost condescending look. 'You tend to keel over just before dawn, wherever you are. You had been in considerable pain, and I decided to leave you where you were – with, I hasten to add, no ulterior motive.' He smiled.

I favoured him with a contemptuous snort.

'Nothing happened,' he continued. 'Nothing intimate will ever happen without your consent. When will you learn to trust me?'

'After yesterday? Probably never.'

'How unfortunate.'

'So there was no more pouncing of any kind?'

'Call me old-fashioned, but I always think it more fun to have a reciprocating partner.'

'So all your previous pouncing was—?'

He sighed. 'A grave mistake on my part, for which, I have apologised. At least twice.'

I gave him a withering look and his lips twitched. 'I meant what I said the other night, Elinor.'

'To which particular bit of poetic nonsense are you referring?'

'I truly want you to feel safe with me.'

Safe? What a joke. The only time I felt safe was when I was unconscious and that was only because I couldn't feel anything at all. I surreptitiously checked under the duvet to make sure I still wore my jumper before I sat up.

Will gave a knowing smile. 'Now that you are awake, I shall go and get you some nourishment.'

'Room service now, huh?'

He gave a slight nod and left the room. I waited until the door closed behind him and then slid out of bed to retrieve his newspaper. It seemed an age since I'd looked at any news, and although this would be mainly local news, at least it would give me some insight to the outside world. I scrambled back into bed and glanced at the headline. Oh. It wasn't going to help. The large newsprint virtually screamed out at me.

BODY FOUND IN
WATERLOW PARK IDENTIFIED.

I read on. Apparently, the murdered girl had been a barmaid called Angie Wilson, and she had been on her way home from work. What she'd been thinking of walking alone in the park at night, I had no idea. Still, no one deserves to be drained of blood and left in the park like a piece of discarded rubbish. Will came back in at that point, carrying the inevitable mug of 'nourishment'. He frowned when he saw me reading the paper.

'You do not need to read that.'

'What am I? Twelve?' I retorted. 'It sort of concerns me, so I think I should be allowed to read it.'

He handed me the mug. 'Always the feisty one,' he murmured. 'Be my guest.'

I sipped at the mug's revolting contents, trying to forget what I was actually drinking. I wondered why the blood was warm, when I knew for a fact that Will had said he wouldn't be bringing any more 'donors' back for a while. I gave him a look of surprise.

'Microwave,' he said.

'What?'

'You were wondering how I managed to get the blood to body temperature,' he said. 'I may not have reason to cook but I am adept at using a microwave.'

I spluttered into the mug. Against all the odds I had found something amusing. Who'd have thought?

Will grinned. A real, natural, knock 'em-dead grin. When he wasn't being scary Mr Spooky or trying to be the big seducer, he really was quite something.

'It is a great relief to me that you are rediscovering your sense of humour,' he said.

'Don't push it,' I said.

'I think we should go out tonight,' he changed the subject with his usual swiftness. 'But clearly you need to get dressed first.'

'Clearly,' I agreed, 'and I'd like a shower.'

Will made an expansive gesture with his hands, '*La mia casa e la tua casa*,' he said.

Sounded Italian to me, and very sexy when he said it.

'Well, I got *house*.'

'My house is your house.'

'Somehow it sounded better in Italian.'

'The language of lovers,' Will smiled.

'Give it a rest, Mr Spooky.' I pulled a face at him. 'Can you just be somewhere else for half an hour so I can get that shower?'

'Of course,' he said. 'I shall be in the drawing room and honoured if you would join me when you are ready.'

'Definitely far too much time with Byron,' I muttered as he left the room.

18 February

I write this entry whilst I wait for Elinor. I know she will not be too long, so I must be swift.

The arrival of the Italian vampires has not come at a good time, if indeed there ever could be a good time for such a thing. I cannot – dare not – leave Elinor alone for a second, however, I do need to show myself at the club soon. I need to be visible around town, in order to convince the enemy that I am a force to be reckoned with. I may have to take her with me, which is a worrying prospect. Perhaps I should instead leave her in the house guarded by Luke, but I am reluctant to let her out of my sight. I need to make a decision soon.

I had planned to take Elinor to Camden tonight, but perhaps we should stay closer to home.

I need to think.

Chapter Twelve

Camden

Several nights after the belly bar incident, I was still spending my days in Will's bed, and still without him too, which had been my choice. He seemed preoccupied and more than a little distant. Part of me felt relief at the distance, but a niggling part of me missed our verbal wrangles.

Nothing had been seen or heard of the intruders and there had been no more murders. I hoped they'd gone back to Italy, but that was almost certainly wishful thinking.

On this particular night I sat up, clutched the duvet to me, and waited for my senses to catch up with my body. Will lounged at the end of the bed, wearing only a pair of snug-fitting black jeans, his long legs stretched out in front of him, crossed at the ankles, his bare feet relaxed. His dark hair looked damp and smelt newly washed. His torso gleamed like living marble in the soft lighting and he looked like an erotic dream – or would that be *nightmare*? He rested his back against one of the carved bed posts as he wrote busily in a leather bound book.

He stopped writing as I sat up, and smiled at me, his eyes shining. 'Are you hungry?'

I shrugged. 'I suppose so.' I never seemed able to muster up any enthusiasm for obligatory vampire food. God, if only I'd been a vampire when I was a dancer, I'd never have had any weight issues at all.

Will swung his legs off the bed and stood up, treating me to the full glory of his muscled upper body, so pale in stark contrast to his black jeans.

'Then I shall go and perform my nightly magic with the microwave,' he said, picking up his book and pen, and moving toward the door. I didn't answer. He knew my revulsion for blood hadn't gone away and he also knew how difficult it was for me to force some down each night. Thankfully the pain of the Thirst seemed to have abated with the regular feeding, and Will had said that there might be a possibility I would only need to feed three or four times a week. Apparently not all vampires need to feed every night, and those who do so are either motivated by greed, or are just new and filled with blood-lust. *I am still one of life's mysteries it seems. Or death's mysteries ... whatever.*

Will came back in the room carrying a china mug and handed it to me. 'Drink without looking,' he advised. I sighed and drank the foul contents whilst watching him take a long-sleeved black sweatshirt from a drawer. He pulled it on, covering his tempting body. Turning to look at me, he said, 'I thought we might go to Camden tonight.'

'Goth Central?' I asked. 'Why?'

'To make a change from the cemetery, and to see how you react when surrounded by people.'

I didn't like the sound of that. 'React?'

'Do not panic,' he reassured me. 'If I thought for one moment you could not cope, I would never risk taking you.'

'Well, that makes me feel a lot better.'

'It is time for you to get up.'

I was well aware of what I was wearing under the duvet, and it wasn't an awful lot, and somehow I didn't feel ready to give Will another peep show. I had never been particularly comfortable parading around half-naked in front of a boyfriend; although Will wasn't in the boyfriend category, and let's face it, he wasn't exactly a boy either.

'Can you pass me my jeans?'

He raised an eyebrow. 'Why the demure school girl act? I believe I have seen you in your underwear before.'

'When I was in agony and nearly unconscious,' I retorted. 'I thought you men from yesteryear were supposed to be gallant.'

'And I thought dancers ran around half-naked a lot of the time.'

'You've been mixing with the wrong kind of dancers. We tend not to run around half-dressed in front of strangers. Especially male strangers.'

'So, suddenly I am a stranger again,' he sighed as he turned away. Going over to the farthest chair, he picked up my jeans where I'd left them just before dawn, and threw them across to me. 'I shall be upstairs.' With that parting shot, he left the room.

It was unlike Will to take offence quite so quickly – if at all. Perhaps he had grown tired of me, and I wondered what would happen if he had. Supposing he threw me out onto the streets to fend for myself? I shuddered – that was not a good thought.

I got out of bed and grabbed some clothes from the dressing room before collecting my jeans where he'd thrown them. Then I went downstairs to take a quick shower.

When I went upstairs I found Will talking on the phone. He glanced at me as I entered the room, waving me to the sofa. He was clearly not a happy vampire. I hoped it wasn't my fault. *Paranoid? Me?*

'I shall be there. Goodnight Luke.' Will replaced the phone on its dock and faced me.

'What's wrong?' I asked.

'Nothing that need concern you.'

'Great. So why don't you just open the front door and boot me out, it'll probably solve all your problems.' My tone was acerbic.

He raised his eyebrows in surprise. 'From where did that little diatribe emerge?'

'Your off-hand behaviour, your patronising refusal

to include me in recent events and all this bloody secret squirrel rubbish.'

'Secret squirrel?' He looked genuinely puzzled.

'If you don't want me to either treat you like a stranger or to feel like one myself, then try including me,' I said. 'If you are genuine in wanting a relationship with me, then I can tell you now, you're going about it all the wrong way.'

'I have formed that opinion myself,' he said with a wry grimace. 'I apologise if you have felt somewhat superfluous to various discussions. I suppose I am just a three-hundred-year-old man trying to relate to a twenty-five-year-old woman. Men from my century did not discuss battle strategies with their women, in fact they did not discuss much at all with their women.' He shrugged and leaned back against the carved cabinet. 'I am trying—'

'You got that right,' I agreed. 'Very bloody trying.'

I was rewarded with a wicked grin.

'You always have an answer,' he said. He moved to sit in the armchair opposite me. Leaning back, he crossed one leg over the other whilst resting his arms on the arms of the chair. He appeared as relaxed as usual, although there was an air of apprehension about him that I'd never felt before.

'Elinor, I am going to have to become more visible for a while.'

'You look pretty visible to me.'

He ignored my pathetic attempt at humour, merely lit a cigarette and looked at me through the plume of smoke that curled upward. 'How well known are you in North London?'

I was surprised at the question. 'You know I was never famous.'

'No, you misunderstand,' he corrected me. 'I simply want to know if you have many friends and acquaintances in this part of London.'

'Well there's Greg and Fliss, the couple who lived

downstairs in my old place,' I replied. 'Then there's Caroline, Joe and the rest of the gang in Crouch End. Some of the chorus live in the Wood Green and Turnpike Lane areas. I don't know anyone in this part of Highgate though, I never mixed in those kind of circles.'

He nodded, frowning again. 'What I need to know is, if we go to Camden, are you likely to bump into any of your old friends?'

Ah, the penny finally dropped. Of course, anyone from my old life would probably have a heart attack to see me wondering around Camden supposedly alive and well.

'It's possible I suppose,' I said.

'Perhaps we should change your appearance?'

'You can forget either cutting or dying my hair.'

'Changing your hair is the very last thing I would ever suggest,' Will looked horrified. 'I thought perhaps different clothes to the kind you normally wear, just for a while at least.'

I narrowed my eyes at him. 'Do not even presume to make me wear some Laura Ashley floral creation or a taffeta ball gown.'

Will laughed, and I realised I had actually missed his laugh over the last few days. He did seem to be growing on me lately, which was potentially not good. He stood up, and threw his cigarette butt into the fireplace.

'Well, that would be rather extreme,' he agreed. 'The thing is, I need to make an appearance at my club fairly soon, and I do not want to leave you here alone.'

I didn't want to be left alone either.

'So who's coming after you, or us, exactly?'

'I am pretty certain now that it is Khiara. Which is why I need to visit my club. She or her people will certainly go to my club at some point, and if someone informs her that I have been absent for some months, she will come here.'

'Who would tell her?'

'Anyone with whom she comes in contact. A vampire of Khiara's age is highly skilled at extracting information.'

I really didn't like the sound of that. 'I thought you would be able to sense her if she came near here.'

'That is so, yes. But if she arrives mob-handed as it were—'

'Which is why you don't want to leave me here on my own,' I understood now.

'Exactly so.'

'Shit.'

'As you so colourfully say.'

The reason for Will's distraction was now very apparent. I stood up.

'I could go and find my incredibly attractive woolly hat if you like?'

'If you would be so kind,' he nodded. 'At least by covering your glorious hair, you will not stand out quite so much.'

I went back downstairs and rummaged around in the dressing room cupboard until I found my black hat. Unfortunately, I wasn't going to be able to see what it looked like in a mirror, so I'd just have to hope that I didn't end up looking like a complete prat. I pulled my hair back, twisted it in a knot and then pulled the hat over it. It felt OK. Mentally shrugging, I ran back upstairs.

'If people laugh—' I began as I went into the room.

'You look adorable,' Will interrupted. 'Shall we go?'

Fifteen minutes later we were on the platform at Highgate tube station, just as a train arrived. We squeezed ourselves into a carriage crowded with people going home from work, and I felt decidedly nervous. So many people.

Since I'd been feeding regularly, some of the pain and horrific tension had eased, and I felt calmer, more rational. But I wondered what would happen in the summer hours, would I stay asleep for longer? Sunset would be hours later after all.

My attention suddenly returned to the feel of warm bodies and their throbbing pulses all around me, which presented a very real problem. I hadn't been this close to so many people since my rebirth. The last time we had travelled on a tube it had been after the commuters' rush, and there were far less people. This felt ... uncomfortable. I was beginning to feel a bit panicky, hemmed in on all sides by warm, living bodies.

I could hear their pulses.

I could definitely smell their warm blood.

I looked up in wide-eyed panic at Will. Never one to miss an opportunity, he slipped his arms around my waist and pulled me up against his body, almost as though he knew exactly how I was feeling – which he probably did. His touch, miraculously, calmed me down and I breathed a sigh of relief. The headlines that raged in my head thankfully evaporated, erasing, '*Female lunatic attacks commuters on the Northern Line.*'

We got off at Camden Town and made our way to the exit.

Camden was always busy at almost any time of the day or night, and we walked up the High Street toward the market. The stalls stood empty now, closed up for the night, but the streets were still crowded. The pavements bustled with people of all ages, colours and creeds, all busy going somewhere; home from work, out for the evening, or just for a walk.

I had always been fascinated by the huge number of Goths and vampire wannabees who congregated in the Camden area. It seemed to attract them like a magnet. Possibly because of the amount of Goth clothes and jewellery shops in Camden. I had always loved to browse in them, although I would never have been brave enough to wear any of the more outrageous outfits. The streets were full of the flamboyant and Gothic that evening – some girls carried handbags or backpacks in the shape of coffins or skulls. They stood in little clusters, preening their multi-coloured hair that had been gelled to stand up in gravity-defying spikes. Their eye makeup, lips and fingernails were all painted black, and a few of the girls wore magenta-coloured net underskirts beneath their tight-fitting black dresses. They looked oddly attractive, like an exotic tribe peculiar to North London. Will and I passed by them, and were completely ignored in our comparatively boring attire of jeans and leather coats.

How amusing to think two real vampires had just walked quietly by them and they hadn't even spared us a glance. Although having said that, it wasn't strictly true, as several girls had spared Will more than a glance, but I was beginning to get used to it. Strangely, he never seemed to notice the attention he attracted.

He looked down at me and, with a mischievous smile, offered his arm.

I gave him a strange look, but slipped my arm though his anyway without comment.

'We cannot have you getting lost in the crowds can we?'

'Apparently not.'

We went down the steps to the Regents Canal towpath and stood for a while, watching and listening. The canal itself glittered like a black ribbon, moving at a sluggish pace, its many secrets hidden in the murky depths. There were a few people walking along the canal path, mostly couples.

We passed by the Pirate's Castle, which I thought should probably be renamed Dracula's Castle, although the younger kids might not like it as much. We walked slowly past the moored barges in the visitors' basin. Music blared out from a few of them, but nothing recognisable.

The night's scents were an almost overwhelming concoction of exotic food and people. I felt full of anticipation, yet had no idea why. It was good to be out and walking about. Almost as though nothing untoward had ever happened.

As we reached Cumberland Basin, Will stopped and raised his head. His nostrils flared. I watched him, seeing him then for what he was – a very dangerous predator. He looked back at the *Feng Shang* Chinese floating restaurant and I followed his gaze, looking at the diners silhouetted against the brightly lit windows.

'I need to feed, but there are rather too many witnesses.'

'Could put them off their noodles.'

I had never seen Will feed, and to be honest, I didn't relish the thought of it at all. If he only ever picked on beautiful women, I didn't think I could stand by and watch him. I truly didn't know how it would affect me. I had a sneaking suspicion I might feel jealous, even though I had no right to. I didn't much like the idea of him observing my quandary either.

I looked across the canal at the beautiful Regency houses with gardens leading down to their private moorings. Many of the houses had their own boats and I wondered just how much money it would take to live here. The majority of the houses had at least four floors, with roof gardens and terraces as well as regular back gardens. The nearer we walked to Regents Park and St Johns Wood, the more opulent the houses became.

'Are those your dream houses, Elinor?' Will had obviously been watching me.

'If I were still human perhaps. But there are rather too many neighbours for our kind of lifestyle.'

'True.'

Secretly I thought Will's Georgian mansion in Highgate was better by far.

We walked in the direction of the zoo and I sniffed

the air, now thick with the pungent aroma of different animals. Not always a plus, these enhanced senses. Will turned to me, 'Hunting is common sense, always try to find someone on their own, for obvious reasons, or lure them away from other people. Be discreet, be quick and then get the hell away from the spot as soon as possible. That is all there is to it, other than knowing when to stop feeding so you do not kill them.'

'Why are you telling me this?'

'Should anything happen to me, you will need to find your own food.'

'Is anything likely to happen to you?'

Will stopped walking and clasped his hands to his heart with an overly dramatic gesture. 'I do believe she is beginning to care. Be still my beating heart.'

'Our hearts don't beat.'

He smiled then, taking my arm and threading it back through his again. 'So true again, my very clever Elinor.'

'I thought you said you only fed on the willing.' I changed the subject quickly.

'Most are willing for me,' he said with a touch of arrogance. 'Would you like to hunt with me?'

I shook my head violently. 'No, of course not.'

'Then I shall leave you here for just a few minutes, and return as soon as I can.'

'Leave me?' I felt horrified. 'You're going to leave me here *alone*?'

Will stopped walking again and put his hands on my shoulders. Gently, he tucked an escaping tendril of hair back under my hat.

'Elinor, should anything untoward happen, I will know immediately, and I shall return to your side with all speed, do not worry.'

'Worry is my middle name.'

'My mistake, I thought it was Jane,' he bent down and kissed my forehead.

We were level with the Snowdon Aviary before he turned to me again. 'Stay right here, I shall only be a few minutes.'

Yeah, yeah only a few minutes. I found it odd that Will felt confident enough to leave me alone. I wasn't sure whether to be pleased or annoyed. He clearly didn't expect me to run off, although I had no doubt he could track me down before I'd got very far.

I had no idea what would happen if I needed to choose and feed from my own victims. Choose or starve, I supposed. For the moment I preferred drinking from a china mug and not knowing where the contents had come from.

I hoped Will wouldn't be long, I hated being here on my own. Standing alone on a canal path in the dark wasn't exactly my idea of fun. Or exactly safe either.

I heard footsteps behind me and turned around, hoping to see Will. Unfortunately it was two male city types who'd clearly had more to drink than was good for them. Perfect.

'All alone? I don't think it's safe to be all alone here. Do you Clive?' said the taller of the two. 'P'raps you'd like to come along with us?' His upper crust accent sounded slightly slurred and just as though he had a plum stuck in his larynx.

'I'm waiting for my boyfriend,' I said, and wished Will would miraculously appear.

'He seems to be a tad late doesn't he?' said the other, and they both laughed. They sounded like a couple of snotty hyenas.

The first man waved an open whisky bottle under my nose. 'Fancy a little drinky girly girl?'

'No.' I wished Will would hurry the hell up.

'Not too friendly is she?' said Clive, draping his arm across his mate's shoulders.

'Oh, I think she could be persuaded to be a lot more friendly.' They both leered drunkenly at me.

Shit.

'Go. Away.' I said. *Come on Will, how the hell long does it take you to feed?* Unless of course he was doing something else as well ... but I really didn't want to think about that.

'Only if you say pretty please.' The two of them laughed uproariously. *Hilarious.*

'The lady said go away I believe,' Will's voice came from behind me, and I turned to him with relief. *At bloody last.*

He sauntered up to my side and put an arm possessively across my shoulders.

'Shall we go?' he said to me, and I nodded. *Yes, somewhere far away from these two jackals.* As we passed the two men, I screamed at a sudden flash of steel, as one of them drew a knife, and the next thing I knew, both of them were lying on the ground not moving.

'What have you done?' I gasped in horror. 'Please tell me you haven't killed them.'

'They needed their heads banging together,' Will shrugged. 'No harm done, they were just drunk.'

'Just *drunk*? They had a *knife*.'

'They were merely intoxicated children, Elinor,' he said gently. 'Trust me when I say I can tell the difference between the truly evil, and the feeble posturing of drunken little boys.'

I looked around to see if anyone had noticed, but luckily there was no one in close proximity.

'Shall we leave them to sleep it off?' Will took hold of my arm again, and guided me back the way we'd come. We soon arrived back at the steps, which led to the street above, and for once I felt relieved to be back amongst the throng of other people. We mingled with the crowds that headed for the various pubs and clubs.

Wonderful, bustling Camden. It felt almost possible to touch the energy humming through it. So many interesting people. So much *life*.

Will strode through the crowds with his confident, graceful stalk – coupled with his looks, it made him pretty tricky to ignore. Even I couldn't ignore him all the time.

Will glanced down at me. 'Do you fancy a walk, or do you want to go home?'

'I'd like to walk on the Heath,' I suddenly wanted to feel the relative freedom of open space that only the Heath could provide.

'Then that is exactly what we shall do.'

25 February

I did not feel confident in my decision to take Elinor to Camden, almost from the very moment we arrived. But I needed to see how she would react amongst a crowd of humans before taking her to the club. I have to make an appearance there soon. Luke confirmed this tonight. He had information about two of Khiara's people who have already visited the club, although as yet there have been no sightings of the lady herself.

I fear for Elinor's safety but I have absolutely no intention of leaving her alone in Highgate, so she will have to accompany me when I visit the club tomorrow. It is to be hoped her former friends do not frequent the place. I know Elinor has never been there, but she seems to have had so many friends.

She appears happier of late, and I hope she is warming towards me a little. I confess I never thought it would be so difficult to win her round. The arrogance of age undoubtedly.

Chapter Thirteen

Feelings

Will and I walked in companionable silence for a while. We wandered past the Old Stables, a part of Victorian London history, which apparently looked much the same from the outside as it did when the stables were first built. The original loose boxes were still almost intact inside, with iron bars on top of each wooden partition to separate the stalls. Many of the floors even boasted the original flagstones. During the day the stalls housed antiques, bric-a-brac, old toys and faded lithographic prints, although one section was now an art gallery, one so trendy it made your teeth hurt.

I remembered the huge redevelopment of the Old Stables that started in 2007, when about twenty-five of the original railway arches were exposed and utilised. Huge fibreglass statues of horses now stood on the original cobbles, with Victorian figures, carriages and blacksmiths, all adding to the authenticity and incredible feel of the place.

Bands often played in the trendy gallery in the evenings, and part of me longed to go in and listen to some music, although I felt it probably wouldn't be a very good idea.

'I remember when this was a bloody horse hospital,' said Will, with a shake of his head.

I glanced at the sign above the iron gates. *1854*. 'You should, you're much older than the stables. Didn't you say something about being three hundred years old?'

'I see I walked right into that little compliment. Yes, I have been around for over three hundred years. Are you going to tell me I wear well?'

I laughed. He didn't look a day over thirty. 'I could

probably say whatever I like, seeing as you can't look at your own reflection.'

He raised a dark brow in my direction. 'Be careful young lady, you have to rely on my judgement now as to your own appearance. After all, *you* are the one wearing a woollen hat.'

I went to thump his arm, but he caught my fist and held it firmly, smiling at my futile attempts to free it. He laced his fingers through mine and gestured towards the entrance to Chalk Farm tube station with our linked hands.

'Would you prefer to get a train to Hampstead?'

I shook my head. 'I'd rather walk, it doesn't hurt my ears as much.'

If the truth were to be told, I was actually enjoying the walk with Will. He held my hand in a strong grip, and I found I didn't want to pull mine away. Strange but true.

I looked at his strong profile, and covertly admired it, or so I thought. He angled his head to look at me. 'Now what?'

I just smiled but didn't answer. It seemed a little naïve to say I liked to look at him, when only a few nights ago I'd hated him for supposedly causing my death.

We walked onto Hampstead, and by the time we reached the Heath I felt the first spots of rain.

'We're going to get wet,' I said.

'Does it matter?'

'Well, I've got a woolly hat,' I smiled. I felt happy to be away from the claustrophobic confines of the house for a while. It made me feel almost normal.

At that moment, the heavens opened and rain poured down, soaking us in seconds. Will turned his face up to the sky, letting the rain run down it in rivulets. He suddenly released my hand and ran up the hill towards Kenwood House in an incredible blur of movement. When he got near to the top, he yelled down at me.

'Come on, slowcoach, get up here!'

I ran up the hill towards him, but when I got close, he ran off again. I slowed to a walk and eventually reached the top of the hill, where I found him in a tree, dangling from a thick branch by one hand.

I looked up at him. 'You are way too old to be climbing trees.'

His teeth flashed white in the darkness. 'You need to lighten up.' He put his other hand on the branch and swung himself lithely to the ground. Grabbing hold of my hands, he swung me round in a circle. 'Tell me you love this feeling Elinor,' he said, and stopped us so that he could look down at me. I stared back without a word. He'd completely flipped now, obviously.

'Come on, admit it, you never felt this alive before you were dead.'

Dreadful jokes seemed to be a speciality of his. I watched him as he stood in front of me, hands on his hips, laughing at me, *again*, and even with his rain-soaked hair flopping into his eyes, he looked gorgeous. I couldn't help but smile back at him. Even after my constant rejections of him, he retained his sense of humour and, for the most part, his patience.

'I thought we vampires were supposed to be all glowery and scowling,' I said.

'Well, I can be, if that is your preference. Would you like me to be more traditional?'

'God, no.'

'I do not think it has much to do with Him.'

The rain still poured down, but Will seemed to enjoy getting wet. He gripped my shoulders. 'Can you feel the power?'

Power? Was that a trick question? I shook my head, letting him see the confusion in my eyes.

'*Your* power. Can you feel it?' he said again, giving me a little shake.

I thought about it for a moment. 'I feel strong, is that the same thing?'

He dropped his hands from my shoulders and stepped back from me, raising his arms to the heavy night sky. He stood still for a moment, and then grinned with pure evil joy, if such a thing is possible.

'The power of the vampire.' He said with sudden passion. 'Tell me you can feel it Elinor. *Embrace* it. Feel it as it runs through your veins like liquid fire. You are strong – you are immortal. You will never grow old and, like me, you are beautiful.'

I laughed at that, and found I'd inadvertently moved in closer to him. I hadn't even realised what I was doing. He looked surprised.

'Now that *is* new.' He said. 'I like it.' He put his arms around me, and pulled me closer.

I rested my hands on his chest lightly and looked up at him. I wondered what would happen next. His eyes were like green glass as he watched me, his expression suddenly serious. 'It is your call.'

I moved my hands up to his broad shoulders, which removed my last bastion of defence, and he moved nearer until our bodies were pressed together. It felt right, somehow. For the first time, it actually felt right. Something inside me seemed to open up, and I raised my face to his as he bent to kiss me. The first kiss was soft, sensuous, almost tentative, and his lips felt gentle on mine. I relaxed into his embrace, and the heat between us suddenly ignited. His kisses became possessive and demanding. He ran his tongue along my lips and then slid it inside my mouth, exploring me urgently – expertly. My arms unwittingly wound around his neck, and I was vaguely aware that my feet no longer touched the ground.

When he eventually set me back down, and we drew

slowly apart, I couldn't for once think of a thing to say. He kept his arms around me, as if afraid I would push him away again.

'Well, that was certainly worth waiting for,' he said.

'I'm not sure I know what just happened.' I said, half-joking.

'It is the old maker, fledgling bond kicking in. At bloody last.'

My head still reeled from his kiss as we made our way slowly back down the hill. The man certainly knew how to kiss for sure. But what had I started – and did I really want to start anything at all?

The rain had eased off now, but we were both completely soaked through to the skin. Will took hold of my hand again, and even that felt unbearably sensual. My whole arm tingled from just the touch of his hand, and I couldn't help wondering if it felt the same to him. He looked at me, and his look was confident now, the look of a man who believes he has almost won the woman at last. His lips curved into a satisfied smile.

'We need to find ourselves a cab home.'

Back at the house, I followed Will into the drawing room and noticed the answer machine flashing. He pressed the replay button, and Luke's deep voice spoke. 'This is Luke. Please call me back.'

Will dialled some numbers and tucked the receiver under his chin as he lit a cigarette.

'Luke,' he said after a few seconds. He listened for a while, but although I listened intently, I couldn't hear Luke's words, much to my annoyance.

I wandered over to the bookshelves and looked at the titles on the spines. A battered copy of Bram Stoker's *Dracula* grabbed my attention. Fancy that, I thought, and pulled it out. I sank down in the nearest armchair and was halfway through the first chapter when Will put the receiver down.

'Good book?' he asked.

'Possibly,' I said. 'I've never read it before.'

Will turned the book up to see the cover. 'Ah, Vlad, poor bastard, supposedly the inspiration for one of the most famous vampire stories ever written. Good job he never knew about it.' He sat down in the chair opposite, and regarded me with his usual amused expression. I felt a little nervous now we were back in the house, alone, and I think Will had picked up on it. I have never been exactly wonderful at relationships, probably due to the abuse I'd suffered at such a young age. I always found it difficult to put my trust in any man.

My first real relationship had been at dance college, a rather sweet affair that lasted several years, but ended as we grew apart. Then there was the disastrous time with Joe the Love-Rat, a not-so-wonderful experience I wasn't too keen on repeating.

Will clearly had centuries on me, and I found the knowledge somewhat daunting. I wondered how many women he'd slept with over the decades, and how many times he'd actually been in love. I gave myself a mental shake.

'Vlad?' I asked, in an effort to keep a conversation going.

'A fifteenth-century prince from Southern Romania. Fought the Turks and delivered exceedingly dire punishment to his enemies,' said Will. 'Vlad Tepes the Third. He impaled some of his enemies alive on spikes, and as they slipped down the spikes they were disembowelled. If they were lucky, he just chopped their heads off and stuck them on the spikes. Hence his nickname, Vlad the Impaler.'

'Well, aren't you a mine of grisly information?'

He shrugged. 'I have had plenty of time to read over the years.'

'What did Luke want?' I thought a change of subject would be good.

'He wanted to make sure we were still going to be at the club tomorrow.'

'And are we?'

'Yes. The club is in Hoxton. Did you or your friends ever go clubbing there?'

'You must know I was at work most nights,' I said. 'According to you, you were watching the show most nights too.'

'What of your friends?'

'I'm pretty sure they don't go out in Hoxton.' I replied. 'I don't have to wear a woolly hat to a trendy club do I?'

Will's lips twitched, and I had a sudden vivid flashback to his passionate kisses. His gaze dropped to my own lips at the same time. 'Little Elinor, always with something to say,' he said, his voice suddenly deeper. 'Would you care to see whether your peculiar brand of humour stands up to me in bed?'

I did a mental gulp, and shot him a wary look. 'One kiss isn't a passport to sex,' I said firmly.

He did laugh at that. 'Somehow I did not think it would be. May I at least escort you to the bedroom?' He stood up, walked over to me, and held his hand out. I put my hand in his, and he helped me up. He kept hold of my hand as he pulled the wet hat from my head with his other hand. My damp hair fell freely to my shoulders, and he ran his hand through it as he stared down at me with an unfathomable expression.

'Is this not the moment where I say, "Why Ms Wakefield, you are quite beautiful?"'

'Only if you want to become a cliché,' I replied. *Safety in humour*.

'We would not want that now, would we?' he murmured.

He traced his fingertips down my cheek so very lightly, and my body reacted instantly to his touch. 'The *when* is entirely up to you. I shall try my hardest not to influence you in any way. You need to be sure.'

I looked up at him again and nodded. 'I'm sure you have enough notches on the bedpost for the moment anyway.' The words were out of my mouth before I could stop them. *Perfect. Well done Ellie. What a cool thing to say.* He held me away from him, so he could see my face. 'I fear I did lose count some time ago.'

Somehow he'd missed the point. I frowned and looked down, knowing his words hadn't helped my feeling of inadequacy. In fact, he hadn't helped the situation at all. He put his forefinger under my chin and tilted my face up to his. 'Have I upset you somehow?'

'I'm just worried I'll be a huge disappointment. That once you've slept with me, you'll dump me.'

He raised his eyebrows at that. 'You have a pretty low opinion of me, it seems.'

'Of men in general.'

'At least it's not personal, then?'

I shook my head. 'I need time,' I said. 'I'm only just coming to terms with the whole vampire thing, and the thought of trying to make a relationship work as well is terrifying.'

He put his hands inside the sleeves of my sweater, running his fingertips gently up and down my skin. His touch made me shiver, and I wasn't sure whether it was from fear or anticipation.

'We have eternity before us,' he said softly. 'I certainly have no intention of jeopardising any potential relationship for one night of sexual gratification.' He slipped his arms around my waist, pulled me closer and spoke with his lips against my hair. 'I watched you for more than a year. I followed you around whenever I could. If I had once thought I would tire of you after bedding you, I would never even have entertained the idea of bringing you here.'

I raised my face and looked up at him, 'Well that's you nicely sorted, what about how I feel? Supposing *I* can't make it work, what happens then?'

'It will work.'

I opened my mouth to speak, but he kissed me gently on the lips to prevent any further conversation.

'You and I are meant to be,' he said eventually.

'Meant to be what?' Sometimes he said the weirdest things. He just gave me a roguish grin and the serious moment passed.

'It is late, Elinor, if you do not retire soon, I fear you may keel over on me again.'

'Thanks for that wonderful picture,' I said with a grimace.

He merely offered his arm again with his old-fashioned courtly gesture. I took it and he did indeed escort me downstairs. Being contrary, I wasn't sure whether to be sorry or relieved when he left me to get ready for bed, promising to come back and sit with me as the dawn permeated my body.

7 March

This evening was wonderful. I love to be in Elinor's company. She has begun to relax at last, and the sound of her laughter is music to my ears. Some things have not changed over the centuries, and the act of a man doing ridiculous things to make his woman laugh has remained with us. If I have to swing from trees to bring the light back into Elinor's eyes, then I shall do so. To kiss her once again after what feels an eternity felt sublime, and I think we are indeed forging our bond as it should be, at last.

I found myself thinking back to last summer when I had gone to the Glastonbury Festival with Stevie and the others. Initially the plan had been to find new bands to play at the club, but I had discovered Elinor would be there too, and the festival suddenly became even more interesting.

June, the previous year

Jake and Roxanne were more than happy to drive me on the Thursday afternoon. They usually went anyway. Unfortunately, Luke had to remain behind in London. It is never a good idea to leave one's territory undefended, and as Luke is my second, he has to be there whenever I am not.

A three-day music festival is not exactly my idea of fun, but Jake and Roxy were regular attendees of concerts and festivals and I had to be there because I knew Elinor would be there.

Jake drove a camper van with blacked out windows. He assured me the sun's rays would never be able to infiltrate the cabin beyond. He had also fitted heavy wooden shutters, and they would be closed and locked from the inside during the day, for added security. I admired his ingenuity.

I remembered the necessity of being able to mingle unnoticed among the crowds, so I had dressed in old Doc Marten boots, faded and torn denim jeans, secured by an old black leather belt with a heavy brass buckle and a black vest t-shirt. I added an ancient gold Celtic symbol on a leather thong around my neck, and took my oldest black leather jacket, in case the English summer decided to erupt with thunderstorms and torrential rain, as is its wont. Not that adverse weather affects me particularly, but I needed somewhere to keep my cigarettes dry. I also took a pair of dark glasses to protect my over-sensitive eyes from the stage lighting rigs, which I knew would be a major part of the various shows.

Stevie decided to come with us at the last minute, leaving Errol to manage the club. I was relieved in many ways to have his company. As a werewolf the sun holds no problems for him, and having a day-walker with us would certainly alleviate my feelings of insecurity. Stevie and I also wanted to check out some of the lesser known bands, with a view to booking them for the club.

Of course the main reason I wanted to be present was Elinor. I was, and am, drawn to be near her whenever it is possible. Strange for me – since my rebirth as a vampire I have had no allegiances with any one woman. Plenty of dalliances of course, for being a vampire does not change one's urges, and I like women – rather too much sometimes. But the moment I laid eyes on Elinor, some six months before then, I knew nothing would ever be the same. I wanted a partner for eternity, and that, as they say, is a whole different ball game. I want her, but I refuse to turn her against her will, she must have the choice. I do not know as yet how this will play out, but I am convinced she is the one. It is something I feel deep within me. The Prophecy of Porphyry foretells what is meant to be, and I am sure I am right. Only Stevie and Luke know of the Prophecy. I have kept the details from the others for the moment, and it has to be this way.

Once we had parked the van Jake and Roxy went off for a look around, and I wandered toward the nearest stage with Stevie. Massive trucks and generators were scattered everywhere, the huge stages were already assembled, and hoards of large sweating men were setting up various PA systems and complicated lighting rigs. To a seventeenth-century man it looked like witchcraft, although I actually consider myself more of a twenty-first-century man now, in many ways. I've been to so many bloody rock concerts in the past year – mainly to catch sight of Elinor – that I have become an expert on a lot of current music. It is helpful for the club at least.

Stevie and I stood together, and watched the activity for a while. He knew I would disappear to feed quite soon, just as I knew he would go somewhere quiet to 'change' and hunt. We had agreed to meet at the top of the Tor later, leaving the two young vampires to do their own thing, whatever that might be.

I wandered over the fields, watching crowds of people converging from all sides – it is always interesting, being among so many people with pulses. I needed to feed and feed soon, so I watched for an opportunity to arise, whilst keeping my eyes hidden behind my dark glasses.

A pretty little blonde emerged from one of the toilets, and began to pick her way over the hard, sun-baked grass. I swiftly moved in front of her to grasp her arm. Thinking she had in fact stumbled, she looked up at me with a smile on her lush lips.

'Thanks,' she said.

I pushed the sunglasses on top of my head, giving her the full effect of my vampiric gaze. She stared back at me with her lips parted and I knew her mind was already mine. She was ready to be taken. I smiled at her with closed lips, there seemed no sense in scaring her. Without speaking a word, I drew her arm through mine, and began to walk away from the main crowds. She just stared at me the whole time with instant infatuation, which is one of the many useful attributes of a master vampire. I led her to an oak tree at the edge of the first field, and pulled her behind it. Pushing her gently against the bark of the tree, I kissed her on the lips, gradually moving my own lips across her cheek and down her soft, white throat. She smelt of sunshine and fragrant freesias, but underneath

I could smell her warm blood. The pulse beating in her neck tempted me to run my tongue over it. She moaned softly and I ran my hands up her back, pulling her in closer to my body. I kissed and nuzzled her soft neck, then swiftly sank my fangs into the vein. Sweet, warm blood filled my mouth. She was young, and the blood was like an aphrodisiac. I drank from her, as she moaned in ecstasy beneath me.

Most humans experience orgasm at the moment of feeding, and luckily for us, that's usually all they remember afterwards. I took enough to sustain me, but not enough to either render her unconscious or harm her. The saliva of a vampire makes blood coagulate, and I made sure that she no longer bled from the jugular vein. Her eyes were still closed in utter bliss, and she trembled a little as I propped her limp body against the tree. She would rest awhile now and never remember what had actually happened.

'Thank you,' I whispered.

I made my way swiftly towards the Tor and spotted Stevie near the top of the grassy hill, leaning back on his elbows, and watching a group of musicians playing tribal drum music. There was always some kind of weird shit going on at Glastonbury Tor.

The Holy Grail is reputed to be buried beneath Chalice Spring on this steep hill – buried supposedly by Joseph of Arimathea. I could almost believe it, the land itself seemed to pulsate with ancient life, and I do not just mean myself and Stevie. I dropped down to sit next to him, and he nodded towards the drummers. 'They're not bad.'

I nodded in agreement, and we sat for a while, smoking and watching the crowd.

'Is she here?' asked Stevie and I shook my head.

'Not yet.'

I would know when she arrived. I would sense her – feel her presence. Already I am connected to her, and we haven't spoken a word to each other yet. Strange things, prophecies.

On Friday afternoon I opened my eyes and wondered where I was for a moment. Then I looked around the dark interior and spotted Jake and Roxy entwined in each other's arms on a narrow bed. In the distance I could hear conflicting music from several directions and the noise of the crowds in various different audiences. There was a soft knock at the door. I rose and crossed the floor to the door to unlock it.

'Come in Stevie,' I said, stepping back from the daylight I knew would pervade the van. Stevie came in, and hurriedly closed the door behind him.

'I've booked a couple of new bands for the club,' he said, 'I think they'll be big.'

I nodded my approval. I trusted Stevie's opinion in all things to do with modern music, he'd never been wrong yet.

'What's the time?'

'Half an hour to sunset,' he replied, 'and hotter than hell out there.'

We sat and chatted until the sun set. I knew she was here now, I could feel her presence and I felt anxious to see her.

Jake suddenly sat up as if an alarm had gone off, and Roxy followed suit a few minutes later. Stevie started to tell us about a man who had ridden to the festival on a Sinclair C5 from the other side of Oxford, which is more than a hundred miles away when travelling the back roads. It was the fourth year running he had travelled to Glastonbury in that way, in spite of getting heatstroke one year and a flat battery another year, resulting in the necessity to sleep in a supermarket car park. He was now clearly one of the festival's 'celebrities'. Mortals were getting madder with every decade and, thankfully, a lot more interesting too.

I stood up, anxious to seek out my quarry and the others stood too. Jake and Roxy were hoping to catch Primal Scream on the 'Other Stage', assuming a well-known band with a name like that would not have played earlier in scorching sunlight. We left the van and Jake secured it behind us. I made my way to the Pyramid stage. I knew instinctively that Elinor would be there. Stevie followed me, whilst Roxy and Jake went off on their own. The air was thick with the smell of hamburgers, hot dogs, onions and beer. I had no doubt the smells would be of vomit and worse things later, but tried not to think of it.

I spotted her immediately, even though she was tiny – almost bird-like. Her lithe body was dressed in a black halter neck top, and tiny denim shorts, which showed her dancer's legs to full advantage. Her glorious titian hair hung almost to her tiny waist, and I do not think I have ever seen anything more beautiful. Stevie followed my gaze and growled his approval. I raised an eyebrow in his direction and he smiled with a flash of incredibly white teeth.

Stevie is nearly as tall as me, and with his shoulder length dark hair and piercing blue eyes, he looks the epitome of an ancient Celtic warrior – apart from his pierced eyebrow and modern tattoos, which place him securely in the present day. He always gets more than his fair share of women, and, being a werewolf, he ages considerably slower than normal humans, although he is not immortal.

I felt more than happy to stay and watch Elinor, so Stevie took himself off to find something to eat. I wasn't sure whether he would hunt rabbits and deer, or whether he would simply eat several hamburgers – the choice was his to make. Elinor stayed near the front of the Pyramid stage, and as time went by, I realised she had been making sure of a good spot to see U2. I watched her supple body sway to the music of Biffy Clyro and Morrissey, I could not take my eyes off her, she was completely mesmerising. I have yet to ever see another human or vampire who could entrance me even half as much.

In the early hours of the morning, when the music had all but finished for the night, I followed Elinor back to the tent that she shared with two other girls. I wanted to ensure her safety, and the last thing I wanted was another man anywhere near her. I stayed outside listening to their laughter for a while and then went in search of a snack.

The next night, Stevie and I had seen the Chemical Brothers and Alice Gold before we made our way to the Pyramid Stage again to see Elbow and Coldplay. The atmosphere was electric, the crowd deafening in their approval. Stevie and I managed to keep the immediate area around us completely clear of people. Even though no one would realise there was a werewolf and a vampire in their midst, we gave off enough of a dangerous aura to keep people from getting too up close and personal.

Elinor was in the crowd just as I knew she would be, and I watched her covertly from behind my dark glasses. Stevie was surprised I had not yet invited her out, but I want to watch her for a few months longer. I had to be sure.

By Sunday I was beginning to tire of the smells of Glastonbury: fried food, sweaty bodies, the stench of overflowing toilets and the underlying cloying, sweet smell of marijuana. Sometimes the enhanced senses of a vampire are more of a hindrance than a help. The music had been good, however. Stevie and I spent some time watching acts on the BBC Introducing Stage. He assured me he would be able to sign some of the newer acts for the club. The names of bands become stranger every year; Crow Black Chicken, for example, make names like U2 and the Rolling Stones sound almost boring. However, I found myself admiring the energy of Jake Bugg's performance. Stevie was convinced he would be the 'next big thing'. I watched the Vaccines and actually quite enjoyed the Kaiser Chiefs, although Elinor wasn't visible in the crowd, and I needed to be wherever she was. So Stevie and I returned to the Pyramid Stage, where I could once again see my lovely quarry, and keep her in my sights at all times. The more I saw of her, the more I wanted her. I had become obsessed with her, and I knew I had to have her.

The Festival ended, unusually, with a performance from Beyoncé, hardly an expected finale for the Festival – although no doubt Elinor was interested in the dancing. There was, however, ecstatic approval from the sweating crowds, especially when hundreds of cascading fireworks filled the summer night's sky.

After the last notes of music had died away, some of the festival fans bedded down for their last night, although many had already left, and the fields looked decidedly emptier than on previous nights. The different noises gradually lessened, and I walked amongst the debris of empty beer cans and bottles, greasy hot dog and hamburger trays, even a certain amount of used condoms. Some people had been sensible at least. I found myself walking towards Elinor's tent and, to my surprise, I saw her sitting outside, drinking from a bottle of beer. She looked up at my approach and smiled. I felt a thrill of recognition run through my body as I smiled back.

'I saw you watching Beyoncé,' she said.

At least she had not realised I had been watching her and not Beyoncé, that would have been embarrassing. But I felt surprised she had actually noticed me. So much for my 'under cover' tactics. Admittedly I hardly look like one of Beyoncé's fans.

Against my better judgement, I sat down on the grass opposite her. Pulling my cigarettes from the pocket of my jeans, I offered her one, which she refused politely. I lit one for myself, and sat watching her as she sipped from her bottle.

'Do you always wear sunglasses at night?' she asked.

Obligingly I pushed the glasses on top of my head. She drew in a breath as she looked into my eyes.

'Green eyes,' she murmured, 'like a cat's.'

I reached forward and ran a gentle finger down her smooth cheek. 'You are so beautiful.'

She smiled, and, feeling encouraged, I leaned in closer to brush her lips with mine. I ran my hand through her lustrous hair, and when I deepened the kiss, she wound her arms around my neck, dropping her bottle onto the hard grass. Regretfully, after a few moments, I pulled gently away. I knew I should leave while it was still possible.

As I drew back from her, I held her gaze. Her eyes were beautiful. So blue and intense, fringed by thick lashes.

'Until we meet again.' I touched her hair gently, and stood up abruptly. She still stared after me as I walked swiftly away. Any lingering doubts I felt had been dispelled. From that moment on, her destiny was assured.

Chapter Fourteen

Nightmares

Vampires surrounded me. Beautiful female vampires. They appraised and held me captive with their eyes – dead, cold eyes. I tried to back away, but they simply moved closer. Even the air around me felt full of threat and menace. The vampire women were so near to me that I could feel their cold breath on my face.

I tried to tell them I was a vampire too, but they laughed. One of them was so close, I heard her jaws snap together when she ground her small white teeth. One of the other women put a cold hand on my arm, and I jumped. They all laughed again, and the sound was like shards of broken glass falling on ice.

I could feel sharp fingernails as they dug into my arms. I knew they had drawn blood because I could feel it trickling down my bare arms. I knew what they intended – they were going to rip me apart with their bare hands.

There would be no coming back from this. I knew that too, beyond any doubt. There were too many of them, and they were incredibly strong.

It was all too late. I was too late. Too late to be a real vampire, and too late to make things work with Will. *Will.*

'Elinor.' A deep, familiar voice. '*Ellie*, it is all right. Open your eyes. Come back to me.'

I tried to fight my way out of a black tunnel, but my arms hurt, and someone gripped me by the shoulders. Someone called my name over and over again. I struggled to free myself, but couldn't move. Whimpering in fear, I continued to struggle.

'*Elinor.*'

My eyes opened wide, and I took in the first frantic

breath of the night. I trembled and shivered and tried in vain to sit up. Will knelt over me on the bed, his strong hands gripping my shoulders. The moment I looked at him, he pulled me into his arms.

'What the hell was that? Some kind of vision?' My voice shook.

'Ssssh. It was not real.'

'There were so many—they wanted to destroy me.'

'It was not real,' he said again.

'How do you know what I saw?'

'I saw the same events,' he said, 'and I know who they are.'

'*How* could you see?'

'We have a connection, Elinor. I have explained this.'

'Was it Khiara? Will she come here?'

'Possibly,' he replied. 'But you will be safe with me.'

He cradled me in his arms, and I clung to him like a frightened child. He murmured endearments and gently kissed the top of my head.

'They were almost certainly sent by Khiara.' He said almost to himself. 'She used to be able to invade my dreams wherever I was, but I am too strong now. It appears she can invade your dreams because you are connected to me, plus you are young, and not very strong as yet.'

He sat down next to me on top of the covers, and kept one arm around my shoulders as he pulled the duvet up and tucked it around me.

'She can never hurt you physically through dreams, and the other members of her motley crew most certainly cannot.'

'But they can scare the hell out of me.'

His lips twisted into a small smile, 'They can indeed scare the hell out of you.'

'What did it mean?'

Will was silent for a moment, his dark brows pulled

together in a frown, while his hand played absent-mindedly with strands of my hair,

'There is no denying that Khiara knows of your existence,' he said at last, 'and it is fairly obvious she is not too happy about it.' His lips curved in a smile again.

I realised to my embarrassment that I was still clinging to Will, and made a movement to draw away, but he tightened his hold.

'There will be no more running away,' he remonstrated. 'I think we have both endured enough of that.'

'I'm not exactly used to depending on anyone,' I said.

'That is evident,' he said. 'Would you like nourishment, or would a bath better soothe your nerves?'

'What about the Thirst?'

'I think there is time. You are stronger each night.'

I nodded. The thought of wallowing in a hot bath was too tempting to turn down.

Will swung his legs off the bed, but when he went to move away from me panic descended again, and I clutched at his arm. 'I don't want to be left alone yet.'

'Then come with me.'

When I hesitated, he went into the other room, and returned seconds later with a man's dark blue silk shirt. Throwing it across to me, he said, 'Put that on, it should be long enough to cover all you want to.'

He was an intuitive man. An aggravating, domineering and often arrogant man, but oh-so intuitive.

'Thanks,' I muttered. I pulled the shirt on and buttoned it under cover of the duvet.

I slid out from the bed and when I stood up the shirt almost reached my knees.

'It looks better on you than it ever did on me,' said Will. 'I think you should wear it often.'

He walked over to the door that led to the bathroom, where he stopped to wait for me. When I reached him, he put his hands on either side of my face and looked down at me, his eyes bright with a myriad of different greens. He bent and kissed me softly on the lips and then wrapped his arms round me.

'I will keep you safe Elinor,' he said. 'At all costs—at any cost—you will be safe. I promise.'

'I believe you really mean that,' I said.

'I very rarely say things I do not mean. It would be a waste of time.'

7 March

I am perturbed by Elinor's nightmare. It means Khiara has already forged some kind of connection to her, and this is not a good thing. Initially I felt tempted to leave the city – perhaps the country – altogether for a few months. However, I do not think we can solve the problem that way. I fear we must sit this out, and try to beat Khiara at her own game.

I am sure some vampire lives will undoubtedly be lost in the coming weeks, but I am equally sure it will be neither mine, nor Elinor's. Khiara's worst trait is her naïve belief that she is more powerful than any other vampire. How the mighty will fall – and the more painfully, the better.

Chapter Fifteen

Dusk

I felt so relieved to be out of the house and away from my nightmares. Although it might have been possible we were actually going toward them, if those women were in Will's club. From what Luke had said, some of Khiara's cronies had visited the club over the last few nights. The thought of meeting any one of those women in the flesh filled me with abject terror. Our cab drove nearer to—to who knew what? At that moment in time, I felt truly thankful to be devoid of any psychic abilities.

I had been too busy to go clubbing much in recent years, because my evenings were always taken up with performances, but I knew a lot of clubs and trendy bars had sprung up in the Hoxton area during that time. It used to be a fairly deprived and somewhat forgotten part of London. Now it was considered one of *the* places to go clubbing, even more popular than the West End. No doubt Will had started his club at just the right time. I was looking forward to an evening out, even though I was filled with trepidation at what it might entail.

The cab pulled up outside the old railway arches in Rivington Street, and the nearest arch had a discreet blue sign over its door that said, simply, *Dusk*.

'Here we are mate,' said the driver unnecessarily.

'Thank you,' replied Will, and thrust a £20 note through the open window for him. The driver scrabbled around to get him change, but Will waved him away, and sprang lithely out of the cab. He leaned back in to offer me a hand out. I could get very used to his effortless charm and manners. Most modern men would have been in the club ordering a drink by now, leaving me to scramble out of the cab – and probably pay for it too.

'You've made him very happy,' I said. 'You must have given him a hundred per cent tip.'

He shrugged. 'He probably needs it.'

We walked toward the door, where a tall West Indian man stood. He was immaculately dressed in a tux, and looked pretty impressive, although more than a little intimidating.

'Good evening to you, Zachary,' Will nodded a greeting.

'Good evening Sir, it's nice to see you again,' he replied, as he opened the main door for us.

There was a small reception area just inside the door, where an attractive dark-haired girl sat behind a gleaming mahogany desk. She brightened up immediately when she caught sight of Will, but her enthusiasm dimmed noticeably when she saw me. She recovered well, and smiled brightly at Will as she angled her body forward to rest her arms on the desk, showing off her ample cleavage to maximum advantage.

'Good evening Will, how wonderful to see you again,' she said huskily, batting long, dark eyelashes.

'Hallo Tanya,' he said, and smiled back at her. 'How are you this evening?'

She dimpled and batted her eyelashes again. How much more *obvious* could she be?

'I'm very well, thank you Will,' she breathed, and gazed up at him in adoration. 'Is this your wife?'

Was it my imagination or did her voice grow colder with the question? Some women are so transparent.

Will glanced at me, and his look was one of pure mischief.

I raised my eyebrows, but said nothing.

Will turned back to Tanya, who was clearly dying for the answer. *Oh I wish …*

'Yes,' he replied. 'This is Elinor.'

'We haven't seen her here before, have we?'

Before I could think of a suitable response, Will answered for me, 'She has been away.' He raised my hand to his lips and kissed it, his amused eyes never leaving mine. Pulling my arm through his, he escorted me through the doorway that led to the dark, welcoming interior of the club.

'Did I miss something?'

'Miss something?' Will still looked amused.

'Like a church ceremony, reception, honeymoon—all that stuff.'

He laughed. 'Trust me, you would not have forgotten the honeymoon.'

Incorrigible.

We walked in to the main area of the club. The interior shrieked elegance as I had known it would. The walls had been kept as plain brick, although they'd obviously been treated with some kind of varnish. The floors were carpeted in the seating areas, but left as solid flagstones elsewhere. The low ceiling was dotted with hundreds of tiny bulbs, which kept the lighting soft and discreet.

The club stretched the length of three railway arches. The first was a lounge and reception area filled with soft leather sofas and low tables, with a bar running the full length of the room. The second room had a stage and an under-floor lit dance area, with tables and chairs around the outside. The last room contained another bar and an elegant restaurant. It was all beautifully designed, and no expense had been spared.

'Impressive,' I said.

Will led the way to the bar in the lounge where the sole barman was arranging clean glasses. He glanced up and grinned as we approached, showing incredibly white teeth.

I nearly did a double take. Surely I should be able to spot a fellow vampire? Whatever he was or wasn't, he clearly appeared to be yet another example of a heart-stoppingly handsome man. I had never found too many when I'd been alive, but maybe I'd just been looking in all the wrong places.

This man would be hard to miss, that's for sure. He stood well over six feet tall, lean and lithe with thick hair so dark it looked black, until the club lights picked out the chestnut and mahogany highlights. Dark eyebrows framed a pair of the bluest eyes I'd ever seen, which gave him an ancient Celtic look. Although, the fact his left eyebrow had been pierced by a gold bar put him right back in the twenty-first century. Dressed in faded jeans and a white vest t-shirt, he looked more like an advert for Diesel than a barman. Around his right bicep was a tattoo made up of Celtic knots, interwoven with a kind of Celtic dog design, which I thought a little strange.

I glanced back at Will. Amused green eyes glinted back at me and my stomach gave a little flip. It was at that moment I knew no other man would ever be able to compete with him as far as I was concerned.

'Hallo Stevie,' said Will, leaning his arms on the bar. 'How are things?'

'Hi Scary Undead,' replied Stevie with a cheeky grin, his voice deep, yet soft. 'Business is good. We're pretty busy most nights.'

'Excellent,' said Will, and as he turned to me, 'Elinor this is Stevie, a good friend, and the manager of my club.'

Stevie held a large hand out to me and I put my own in it. His clasp was strong, but he released my hand quickly as if afraid of hurting me.

'Good to meet you at last,' he said with a smile.

At last? That's what Luke had said when he met me. Weird.

Stevie regarded me seriously for a moment, then said, 'So Ellie, how are things?'

I was taken aback by the question, but Will answered

it for me. 'She is getting there,' he said, his emerald eyes holding mine captive. 'It has been a tough call though, has it not?'

I nodded, and he traced a finger down my cheek, which made me shiver.

'Good for you,' said Stevie. 'You're in good hands anyway.'

'So I believe.'

Will's eyes held mine. He smiled his slow, sexy smile, the one that melted me inside from head to toe.

Stevie gave a quiet laugh, and wandered off to serve a gaggle of admiring females who'd gathered at the other end of the bar. He soon became engaged in flirtatious banter, and I watched the professional way he dealt with them. He kept his distance whilst flirting and giving the impression he desired them all. Clever.

'I'm surprised all your clientele aren't female with Stevie behind the bar,' I said.

'Do not tell me he has you captivated as well?' asked Will with raised eyebrows.

'There's no contest and you know it,' I said with a smile, feeling absurdly pleased he appeared jealous.

'That is the safe answer,' he said half seriously. ' So, ask me your question.'

'Do all the staff here know about you—us?' I didn't even bother asking how he knew I had a question this time.

Will leaned back against the bar. 'Stevie knows, obviously,' he said. 'He is a lycanthrope, and we share each other's secret. Zachary is a vampire, which you should have picked up on.' He gave me a stern glance, but I was too busy digesting the earlier part of his answer. It was just as well the music from the dance area was so loud, because I almost shrieked the next question, much to Will's evident amusement.

'A lycanthrope? What the hell is a lycanthrope?'

'Stevie is a werewolf,' said Will, with a half-smile.

I stared at Will. He didn't appear to be joking. Three months ago I hadn't even believed in vampires, and now the normal world as I knew it lay in tatters. Werewolf?

'Does he work when there's a full moon?' I remembered the full moon as being very important to werewolves in all the films I'd seen.

'It is safer for our guests if he does not.'

I turned to watch Stevie mix and dispense drinks with speed and efficiency. Another barman had joined him now. The newcomer was at least a head shorter than Stevie, and conventionally nice looking as opposed to drop dead gorgeous. That really was a novelty in Will's world. The man must be human.

'Henry is human.' Will pre-empted my next question.

'I guessed,' I said. 'So how come the lovely Tanya hasn't got herself eaten?'

Will laughed with genuine amusement, and a couple of girls passing by looked at him with longing in their eyes. I shot them a venomous glare, and they looked away hastily. I may not have completely made my mind up about Will quite yet, but I had still begun to regard him as mine. However illogical that was.

'You sound as though you wish she would get eaten,' he said, still laughing.

'She's just annoying,' I said. 'I hate eyelash-batterers, they always turn out to be professional man-eaters.'

'Overt and obvious flirting cuts no ice with me, my love,' said Will. 'I have seen it all before, many, many times.'

I'll just bet he had. I felt momentarily surprised at the way the endearment slipped out so smoothly, and more than a little flustered, so I made no further comment. He stood away from the bar and held a hand out to me. 'Come and have a look around.'

I took his hand and followed him to the lounge – almost full, mainly couples in huddles on the sofas, chatting and drinking. The atmosphere was one of relaxed friendliness, I felt at ease in there at once. That could, of course, have been due to Will's calm presence at my side. We went into the dance area where the music was absolutely deafening – at least it sounded deafening to a new vampire like me. Will didn't seem too bothered. The dance floor was crowded, and I felt the familiar adrenaline rush that dancing always induced in me. I'd missed music so much over the last few weeks. I had never gone without it for so long before, certainly not in recent years.

'Would you like to dance?' Will looked at me with a smile.

I shook my head. 'I'm not sure I can at the moment,' I felt strange at the thought of dancing. My usual confidence seemed to have deserted me.

'Give it time,' was all he said.

'Do you have bands play here?'

'We do. Stevie arranges that side of things. He is adept at finding the good up-and-coming bands before they become too big and unaffordable.'

Will led the way back towards the main bar, to a staircase on the right-hand side of it.

'I need to say hallo to Errol.'

I wondered what Errol would turn out to be. Another vampire ... a demon? Maybe even a warlock?

We went up the stone staircase to a balconied upper floor, where there were more sofas and armchairs and several low wooden tables dotted about. A small bar took up the corner of the room, where another good-looking West Indian man served a tall Goth and his girlfriend. Will wandered over to the bar. The Goth couple walked away with their drinks as Will greeted the barman. 'Hey Errol, this is Elinor.'

'*Ellie*,' I said.

'Hi Ellie, it's good to meet you.' His voice was a deep, rumbling bass.

He held out a hand sporting several heavy gold rings. I shook his hand and smiled back at him.

'Hallo Errol, how are you?'

Errol turned back to Will, and grinned cheekily at him. 'So is she the reason you've been AWOL for so long?'

'She is,' said Will.

'Gets my vote man.'

Will acknowledged him with a slight nod, and I wondered how long he had been absent from the club.

'About six months,' said Will.

I frowned at him. 'I do wish you wouldn't keep doing that,' I muttered. 'I never know whether I'm speaking aloud or not these days.'

'Stevie says the club's been busy,' Will carried on his conversation with Errol.

'Yeah man, real good,' said Errol, nodding. 'Every night is real good, we're getting a lot of good publicity in the music press too. Zac had to turn away the youngest Geldof girl again the other night, but it means we got pictures and a mention in *Metro* the next day'

'They will all be old soon enough,' said Will. 'I wonder what the great hurry is.'

'Will.'

We both turned to see Luke coming up the stairs.

'Let us find a seat,' said Will. He waved a hand at Errol. 'See you later Errol.'

'Sure thing,' came the reply.

Will's fingers touched the small of my back as he guided me toward the only unoccupied sofa in the farthest corner. We sat down on the sofa, and Luke sat on the low table facing us.

'Any news?' asked Will without preamble.

'Katarina has just come in with a couple of others,' he replied, and Will grimaced.

'How lovely.'

'And Honyauti has arrived,' he continued.

'How is our Native American Chief?' asked Will.

'In a nutshell?' Luke smiled. 'Cold and exceptionally pissed off.'

'Why is he here then?' I asked.

Will glanced at me. 'Because I asked him to come here.'

'Are you the boss of him too?'

'Something like that,' he said.

Will and Luke suddenly turned their heads at exactly the same moment to look back toward the bar. Approaching us came a trio of beautiful young women. The girl in front was small and dark-haired, with a wicked elfin face. Her tiny frame was clothed in low-slung black trousers and a shimmering silver midriff top. Her long nails were painted blood red – and I recognised her. She came to stand at the end of our sofa, which put her between Luke and myself. The two women behind her were taller, both blonde and both beautiful. The first girl directed her dark gaze to me and gave a malicious smile.

'How have your days been lately, *fledgling*?' she said, her voice husky and heavily accented. 'Are you getting plenty of rest?'

The two blondes laughed. I'd heard that sound before too – in my nightmares.

'What do you want Katarina?' asked Will coldly. 'This is a club for paying guests, so if you do not want to buy a drink, may I suggest you crawl back under the stone from which you emerged.'

Katarina raised a perfectly shaped eyebrow. 'Khiara would be most upset to hear of your inhospitality.'

'If you have a message for me, deliver it, then get the hell out.' Will's tone sounded icy and uncompromising.

Katarina looked slightly nervous, and she stepped back from him. As Will stood up, all three women moved quickly further back. He changed his position to stand in front of the sofa where I sat, effectively preventing me from either seeing or being seen by the women. I glanced across at Luke who had remained seated, although he appeared tense and ready for anything. I sidled along the sofa so I could still see the women, but kept Will within grabbing distance just in case.

'Khiara wishes a meeting with you,' said Katarina. 'At your house.'

'Because?'

'She says you owe it to her.'

'Why are you all in London without my permission?' Will asked. 'Khiara of all people should know the rules.'

'Khiara does not need your permission,' Katarina pouted prettily. 'She was in London many decades before *you* were so important.'

'Times change,' said Will. 'And whilst Khiara may have some privileges, you three do not.'

'She wishes a meeting.'

'So you said.'

I saw Will nod his head once. Oh God, surely he wasn't going to allow them to come to the house? Would I have to meet the woman who turned him all those centuries ago? I didn't feel strong enough for that yet. For pity's sake, I couldn't even fight them off in my dreams.

'Five nights from now.' He said, confirming my worst fears. 'Now leave, if you know what is good for you, and do not come here again.'

I saw Will's hand move so quickly it seemed to be blurred. I thought he caught hold of Katarina's arm, but as he had blocked my view again, it could have been her nose. That thought cheered me slightly.

'Tell your mistress I do not allow humans to be killed

anywhere in my city, especially not in the area where I live,' he said in a low, cold voice. 'If there are any more of these *incidents*, I shall hunt you down like the murdering scum you are, and destroy every one of you. Give that message to your vicious bitch of a mistress.' He spat the last words out, and I felt a shock run through my body at the venom and hate. Emotions I had never before heard from Will, and my blood ran cold.

He stood still for a few more minutes, and then sat back down next to me. The women had gone. He looked at Luke, who nodded and went off towards the stairs.

'He will make sure they leave,' he answered my unasked question.

'Will—' I began, but he stopped me, putting a gentle hand on my cheek.

'They are the women from your nightmare, I know,' he said softly. 'They will not harm you, Elinor, they cannot.'

'Why does this ... Khiara ... ' I stumbled over the name. 'Why does she want a meeting with you?'

He gave a small smile as he carefully tucked a wayward strand of hair behind my ear. 'Because of *your* existence of course.'

9 March

Khiara. The very sound of her name brings back memories I do not care to dwell on. The woman is a cold-hearted monster, and I remember the night of my rebirth as though it were yesterday. I can still remember the initial revulsion when I first fed on human blood, and I have never forgotten the shame I felt when she callously killed the woman after we had fed from her. She knew it would tie me to her, and for a while it did.

Many years later, I had become strong enough to believe that my mind was once more my own. The time had come to leave the woman who had sired me.

The night I left Italy was the beginning of a new life for me. With great relief I returned to my beloved London, and over the decades I acquired several properties and a business. I heard nothing from Italy. Khiara left me alone, or at least she had until now. I know only too well that her appearance in London is because of Elinor.

Khiara would never understand how anyone could prefer another woman to herself. Somehow she must have discovered that Elinor is an important part of my life, and I fear she will do everything in her power to change that.

We must all be on our guard.

Chapter Sixteen

Honyauti

My mood was distinctly black. I'd showered, dressed and sat on the bed brushing my hair for what seemed like ages. I couldn't see all of my hair obviously, with the no reflection thing – there were no mirrors in the house anyway that I had ever seen. My hair was long enough for me to see its ends gleaming, so I presumed the rest of it shone too. There had been no sign of Will that night, which was the reason for my black mood. Unusually, he hadn't been sitting in the bedroom waiting for me when I awoke, and as yet he still hadn't appeared, which made my mood worse.

I muttered curses under my breath about a certain vampire, but didn't say anything too loudly in case he was closer than I thought. He really did have the ears of a bat. I tried to picture Will's handsome face with bat ears on either side and snorted at my own joke. Thinking enough was enough, I decided to go looking for my absent 'host'.

I went to the bedroom door and opened it. Running up the first few stairs, I stopped and listened intently. I could hear voices coming from the drawing room. I ran up the rest of the stairs, but hesitated when I reached the drawing room door. I could easily recognise Will's deep voice, melodious and calm as usual, but another man's voice constantly interrupted. Although deep in timbre, it didn't sound so calm.

Both voices stopped suddenly, and Will said, 'Come on in, Elinor.'

No point in asking him how he had known I was there, so I opened the door and went in.

My eyes went straight to Will, who smiled a greeting,

and then I turned to look at the other person in the room. My eyes met dead eyes that were pools of pure evil, and I stepped back. The owner of those eyes could have come straight out of an old Hollywood movie about the Wild West. There was no mistaking his origins, that's for sure. He stood a little less than average height, with long blue-black hair tied back in a ponytail. His skin was the colour of dark wood and his muscular frame was dressed simply in jeans, a white T-shirt and a long leather coat. Around his neck were many strands of turquoise beads, and as he folded his arms I heard a jangle of bracelets.

'Elinor, this is Honyauti,' said Will formally.

'Hallo.' I held out my hand, which Honyauti ignored, and he continued to regard me with his flat, black eyes. Looking at Will, he said, 'She needs to learn some respect for her elders.'

I raised my eyebrows, and opened my mouth to make some kind of scathing comment, but Will silenced me with a look. 'Her lessons are my responsibility,' he said, 'she is rather young and foolish at the moment.'

Young and foolish?

'How young?' Honyauti returned his gaze to me.

'Just a few weeks,' replied Will, as he lit his customary cigarette.

To my surprise Honyauti laughed, but it wasn't a nice sound, and I shivered as though iced water trickled down my spine.

'She will be good to share.' His dark gaze travelled insolently, and very slowly, up and down my body.

I definitely did not like the sound of that, and judging from Will's expression, neither did he.

'No.' His voice was cold, and I flinched. 'This one is mine. There will be no sharing of her.'

Honyauti looked more puzzled than angry as he regarded me again coldly. I kept quiet. I seemed to be getting pretty good at that these days. Will had moved, and now stood by my side. There seemed to be more to this conversation than I was aware of, but obviously no one wanted to enlighten me as to what the hell was going on.

'How unlike you, Elder,' said Honyauti, with just a trace of sarcasm. 'Changing the rules for one such as she.'

Will grinned devilishly, his good humour restored instantly. 'But my prerogative as Elder, I believe. I can claim the right to any fledgling I so choose, and I have chosen this one.'

Honyauti inclined his head slightly. 'As you wish.'

It had become pretty obvious that some kind of power struggle was being fought out here. My money was on Will.

The nauseous pangs of the Thirst were beginning to stir, but I didn't want to say anything aloud, in case the Chief suddenly thought I might taste good.

Did cannibalism happen amongst vampires?

Will turned to me as if I had spoken and raised one eyebrow at me. 'Hungry?'

I nodded, still choosing not to speak.

Will turned to Honyauti. 'Would you care to join us?' To my relief, he refused curtly.

'I shall return tomorrow,' he said.

He nodded his head at Will, ignored me, then left the room. Seconds later I heard the front door close. I turned to Will to question him, but he laid a finger across my lips in a sudden blur of movement.

'Not yet,' he whispered.

After a few more moments, he visibly relaxed, and turned to give me a quick smile. 'I apologise for Honyauti's lack of charm,' he said. 'We have to allow him some leeway, as he is considerably older than I, and from a completely different culture.'

'Is he an Apache?' I asked. Apache was the only Native American tribe I could remember.

'No, he is descended from the Anasazi – which means Ancient Ones in his language. He is of the Hopi Tribe who dwell in parts of Arizona and New Mexico.'

'How on earth do you know him?'

'I spent a number of years there,' he replied.

I nodded. I remembered him telling me that night in the garden. How long ago it seemed now.

So that was Honyauti, an ancient Hopi Indian Chief. He must have been summoned to England by Will, which posed two rather perturbing questions.

Firstly, just how bad was this vampire turf war going to be, if Will was drafting in help all the way from the deserts of America, and, secondly, would he ever be able to control Honyauti if he chose to run wild in London?

12 March

I have begun to wonder now about the intelligence of summoning Honyauti to England. He has always been a little unstable, and his assumption that Elinor would be available to share was something I had not expected. The assumption had to be quelled immediately. Initially, I had called him here because he is one of the most powerful warriors I know, and our numbers in London are but few. I did not know at the time of contacting Honyauti how many people Khiara would bring with her, which is something I still need to discover.

Honyauti's behaviour will have to be monitored carefully, and it is a small comfort to me that he is staying near Luke's house. Luke will be able to assess him nightly, and, should he begin to be more of a hindrance than a help, he will ensure that Honyauti returns to his homeland without delay. I hope it does not come to that, however, as his experience and support may well be needed.

I believe I have become slightly paranoid where Elinor is concerned. She is, as yet, not strong and still drinks warmed-up blood from a china mug, as opposed to from the direct source. This is not too much of a problem, as regular supplies are easy to come by in this city, although I would not wish any of the Italians to discover that fact. It could easily be used against her. I fear she could be kidnapped and starved. Constant vigil is still paramount.

Chapter Seventeen

Assault

Older vampires, or Elders, sleep less than the newly sired. Will had told me this some weeks before, explaining how he often awoke in the early afternoon. So that's another vampire myth shot to pieces. It just shows how legends and folklore get embellished over the centuries.

It is still not possible for a vampire to wander around unprotected in broad daylight, however, especially in sunlight, as it tends to make them go up in flames. That part of the myth is sadly true.

Unfortunately, I still keeled over – courtesy of the 'sleeping death' – just before dawn, and didn't stir again until almost full dark. I found this incredibly frustrating. Will assured me I would begin to wake earlier in a year or so. I suppose when you had eternity, another 'year or so' made little difference. But I hadn't yet managed to get my head around the whole eternity thing, and it sounded like a *very* long time to me.

For the second time in only a few nights, there had been no sign of Will when I finally did wake up. I told myself he had a lot to contend with at the moment and, as Elder of the City, he had to be around wherever and whenever he was needed. The fact *I* needed him was apparently not as important.

I tried to ignore my stupid self-pity and took myself down to the bathroom, intent on soaking my undead skin for as long as the water remained hot. I had overcome my initial revulsion at heating blood in the microwave, so my thirst had been duly quenched for the night.

I wandered into the bathroom, marvelling again at the beauty of the huge sunken bath and Will's impeccable taste.

Turning on the heavy brass taps, I chose a bottle of citrus bath liquid from a newly acquired row of expensive and elegant bottles, and poured a generous dollop into the gushing hot water. I watched the fragrant bubbles rise and glisten with their rainbow colours. I'd put in a request for some feminine fragrances, and Will seemed to have bought out the whole of L'Occitane and Molton Brown for me. He'd added beautiful scented candles as well, but somehow I didn't feel like lighting them. To me, candlelight meant romance, and he wasn't there, neither had he asked to join me again since my first bath all those weeks ago. Contrarily, I just might say 'yes' now. But I felt as though the arrival of the unfriendly vamps had taken his mind off trying to seduce me, and, sad to say, I actually missed the flirting. Maybe that was the idea. Who knew?

When the bath had filled up enough, I stepped in, and sank down in the fragrant foamy water with a grateful sigh. Closing my eyes, I hummed softly to myself, allowing the water to lap gently against my cold skin. It was wonderful.

I suddenly sensed I was no longer alone, and quickly opened my eyes.

Honyauti stood staring down at me, his black eyes filled with cold hatred.

I sank farther under the water.

'What the hell are you doing here? Get out,' I said, sounding a lot braver than I felt.

Honyauti said nothing, just stared arrogantly down at me.

'Will is upstairs,' I lied.

Honyauti moved closer to the edge of the bath, his eyes never leaving mine. I felt sure he would actually make the water disappear if he could, so he could see my body in all of its wet nakedness. Terror filled me. *Where the hell was Will?*

'The Elder is not upstairs,' Honyauti's deep voice rumbled in the bathroom.

'Well, he won't be happy to find you in here.'

'I shall be gone before his return.'

'I'll tell him you were here.' Sheer panic had set in now.

'If you are able,' said Honyauti with a sneer.

For the first time I realised just how much trouble I was in. Whatever Honyauti had in mind, it wouldn't be at all pleasant for me, judging by his expression.

I couldn't believe Will had ever allowed that psychopath into his house, and then introduced him to me. Surely he must realise just how dangerously unstable the man was.

I stared up at Honyauti as he slowly removed his coat, and dropped it to the floor.

His t-shirt clung to his muscular body, and his cold dark eyes bored into me as he leaned forward, putting one strong hand on the rim of the bath.

I felt the weight of his gaze as though he had physically struck me, and shivered in spite of the warm water.

Where the hell was Will?

Would rape hurt a vampire as much as it did a human? Is that what Honyauti intended? Or did he simply have my destruction in mind? Very slowly, I moved myself backwards in the bath. I felt any sudden movement could trigger the man in front of me into action, and that wouldn't be good. *Will! Where are you? WILL!*

'You must be very entertaining for Will to keep you around,' Honyauti settled on the side of the bath, his eyes still staring into mine. 'I intend to sample some of your best qualities.'

I didn't answer, just continued to inch slowly away. His grabbed my arm before I was out of his reach, and bent it enough to hurt and make me squirm, although not enough to break it. Not yet.

'Be still,' he snapped. He began to drag me closer

through the foamy water, and I bit my lip to prevent a terrified whimper from escaping.

'A fledgling's task is to keep *all* master vampires entertained,' he continued, 'and as your master is not here, you must entertain his guest.'

With a movement so swift I didn't even see it coming, Honyauti grabbed me by the hair, and hauled me effortlessly out of the water. It felt as though my hair was being torn out by its roots, and my scalp burned in protest. As Honyauti stood up, he held me in front of him like a prize catch, and the look in his eyes filled me with abject terror. I knew exactly what his intentions were now, and I screamed.

Water streamed down my naked body in rivulets, and he laughed harshly. The sound hurt, glancing off my wet skin. He shook me so hard, it made my teeth rattle, and I screamed again. He suddenly smashed a huge meaty fist into the side of my face, a blow of such violence that I crashed back into the bath, causing the water to surge out and over the sides like a small tidal wave. I couldn't see anything for a split second, except the swirl of bright colours that danced in front of my eyes. I struggled to get up from the remaining water, but Honyauti grabbed me around the throat before I could move, and hauled me out of the bath again.

'Struggle little fledgling,' he laughed. 'I love it when you wriggle.'

I screamed again, but he just continued to laugh.

'Be silent *plaything*.' He pulled me towards him and, crushing me against his body, ground his lips into mine so hard that his fangs pierced my lips and drew blood. A vile parody of a kiss holding neither affection nor warmth, and expressing nothing but the desire to dominate and control.

I tried so hard and so desperately to push him away, to be free of his revolting presence, but my efforts were futile against his immense strength. He forced his tongue deep into my mouth, causing me to gag, and it felt as if my throat would actually tear. I could feel the blood, sticky and cold, as it trickled from my bruised and battered lips, but still he continued his assault.

A muffled sob escaped from me when one of his large hands grabbed and squeezed my breast painfully, the other hand still holding my throat in a vice-like grip.

Suddenly I became aware of someone else, and knew beyond any doubt it was *Will. Oh God … Will …* Terrified that Honyauti would snap my head from my shoulders at any moment, I went limp and still in his grasp.

Will entered the room like a tornado, his face demonic with rage. I'd seen him angry before, but I had *never* seen him like this. He was truly terrifying. His eyes blazed, and his handsome face had transformed to resemble a livid creature from the very depths of hell.

He grabbed Honyauti with a feral snarl, and hauled him off me. Honyauti lost his hold on my throat, and I dropped back into the water again. Although barely conscious, I still couldn't take my eyes off Will. I cowered in the far corner of the bath, and stared at the snarling stranger whilst holding a shaky hand to my bruised, throbbing throat. A soft keening noise came from my mouth but it didn't sound like me at all. I felt too hurt to even cry properly.

Will growled at Honyauti, consumed by feral rage. 'I believe I said she was not for sharing.'

The words reverberated around the bathroom like angry snakes, and I covered my ears at the sound.

In one violent and contemptuous move, Will threw the smaller man bodily at the wall, and Honyauti smashed into it with such a force that several tiles shattered on impact. Before he had a chance to move, Will was on him. The wet sound of blood splattering on the floor made me gag again, as Honyauti clutched at his own throat. He rolled on the tiled floor, gasping for a split second, when Will dragged him to his feet by his long hair.

'You *never* try to take what is mine Honyauti,' he said, almost spitting out each word. 'Do not *ever* dare to abuse my hospitality again.'

Honyauti stared without speaking at Will, as the blood gushed from the gaping wound. It appeared to heal itself as I watched, and I couldn't be sure which horrified me more – the wound or the instant healing.

'If you ever touch her again – even come *near* her again – I will personally pull out your spine and feed it to you. Now get the hell out of my sight!' Will released Honyauti suddenly, which caused him to stagger and almost lose his balance.

He left, but not before he had turned and shot a look of pure venom at me. I stayed in my corner of the bath, not sure what to do or say to Will. Not sure if I could even speak yet. I rested my bruised face on the cool edge of the bath, and wished I could gain control over the violent tremors which shook my whole body.

Will threw me an angry, cold glance. 'Get dressed.' His icy words hit my body like stones. Without looking at me again, he strode from the bathroom and slammed the door behind him.

I flinched at his tone, but got shakily out of the bath without a word. My teeth were chattering and I shook from head to toe. The various wounds on my face and neck throbbed with a vengeance, but all I could hear were Will's furious, impersonal words.

Get dressed.

That was it?

Get dressed?

A big bad vamp tries to rape me and all I get is, '*Get dressed*'?

OK, I may have had some kind of death wish (which is pretty strange for a vampire) but I was angry and desperately traumatised, and I couldn't think straight. So I went for the door, grabbing a towel on my way out. I wrapped the towel tightly around my shivering body, and ran up the stairs towards the drawing room.

I pushed the door open so hard it smacked back against the wall, and I stalked in to stand in front of Will with hands on my hips. I was vaguely aware that I dripped water all over his expensive rug, but found it hard to give a damn.

He sat on the sofa, an unlit cigarette between his lips. He didn't look up at my violent entrance, although I knew he was completely aware of my every movement.

He struck a match and lit his cigarette, flicking the match into the fireplace with practised ease. He drew calmly on the cigarette, but still didn't look up.

'How ... how *dare* you treat me like that?' I yelled croakily at him. 'How the hell *dare* you dismiss me like some – some possession – or – or a *pet* that has stepped out of line?'

He did look up at me then, and his eyes glinted with angry, emerald sparks.

'You really need to ask?' he said in chilling tones, making new shivers run down my spine like icy fingertips.

'Yes I bloody well do,' I snapped. 'Thanks very much for saving my life from the psycho Indian that you let come here in the first place. No wait. You *took* my life in the first place didn't you? So thank you then, for saving my so-miserable *existence* – and before you say anything else – *he* attacked *me* and in case you didn't notice – he was about to pull my bloody head off!'

I stopped my almost hysterical rant when I saw Will's expression, and stepped back out of reach just in case. I still shook from head to toe and fought to regain control of my emotions.

'And you were naked in the bathroom with him. Why?'

The cold, harsh words hurt me more than I would have thought possible, but still I stood my ground. Brave me.

'I didn't even know he was in the house—I was waiting for *you*. He—just came in—' I choked back a sob. 'Where *were* you Will? Why are you never here at sunset any more?'

Will stared into my eyes for a moment before he leaned back in the sofa again. I stayed where I was, it wouldn't do to get too close just yet.

Tears of hurt and frustration trickled down my cheeks now, and I brushed them angrily away with my hand. Surely he knew me better than this?

'You are telling the truth,' he said at last.

Well, I knew that.

I didn't recognise this Will. He was cold and uncompromising. I wanted the cool, fun-loving Will back.

I watched him silently. I watched him stretch his long legs out in front of him, and I watched him lace his fingers together behind his dark hair.

With one rapid movement, he suddenly had me pinned against the wall, my arms above my head, held fast by one strong hand. He leaned into me until our lips were almost touching. I looked at him – feeling so scared, but determined not to cry again.

'What to do with you now, I wonder?' he said.

I stared. Surely he didn't really believe I had welcomed Honyauti's attentions?

I swallowed painfully. My throat really hurt. I had thought all vampires were supposed to heal quickly, but knowing my luck, it would probably just be me who didn't.

I looked into the depths of those green eyes, and said the first thing I could think of. 'Cut the possessive, macho crap and take me to bed.'

Will looked genuinely astonished for a split second,

before he laughed. He released my arms, and put his hands on the wall on either side of my face. Normal Will was back, and inwardly I breathed a huge sigh of relief.

'That is one offer I have no intention of refusing,' he promised. 'But perhaps it is not a good one for you to make tonight.'

His gaze lingered on the side of my face, and I touched it self-consciously, wincing as I felt the tenderness there. Capturing my hand in his, he took it away from my face and his eyes narrowed as he looked at the bruises. 'Bastard.' He muttered further curses in Italian to himself.

He lifted my chin with his forefinger and looked at my neck. I knew it was also badly bruised just by the feel of it. His fingers gently brushed the bruises on my face where Honyauti had hit me, and carefully traced my bruised and ravaged lips.

'I wish I had killed him,' he murmured. He pulled me carefully into his arms and I shuddered both from relief and from the closeness of his body.

'Are you hurt anywhere else?' He asked, and I knew what he meant.

'No, you came in time,' I whispered, and closed my eyes to prevent further tears from escaping.

'Then I think perhaps you had better go and put some clothes on, before I change my mind, and relieve you of this rather wet towel,' he said against my hair.

I pulled back from his embrace, and smiled up at him weakly. 'Clothes,' I said.

15 March

When I walked into the bathroom and saw Honyauti touching Elinor, the rage that filled me was swift and terrible. I knew the Indian had to be taught a lesson then and there if my authority over him could ever be acknowledged. I tried not to feel Elinor's terror as she cowered crying in the corner of the bath, but I was always aware of her.

I left after I had thrown Honyauti out. I just could not trust myself to speak to her for a while.

But I had reckoned without her indomitable spirit and sense of injustice.

Brave girl.

She rampaged into the drawing room, like a tiny, red-haired nymph, clad only in a bath towel. That alone would have been enough to appease me under normal circumstances, but I was striving to control my temper. She appeared bruised and battered, and very frightened, yet she was still very angry with me.

She berated me for not believing her, and rightly so.

I always know when she is telling the truth and she told the absolute truth then.

I could not stay angry with her. The assault had not been her fault. I knew that deep in my heart. But jealousy is an evil age-old vice and sadly I have it in spades.

She stood her ground against me – again – she even told me to stop being possessive and, I believe the term was, 'to cut the macho crap'. Colourful.

Immortality will never again be dull.

Chapter Eighteen

Lessons

The night after Honyauti's attack, Will thankfully stayed put in the house all night. The thought of being left alone at all, ever again, terrified me beyond belief. Will seemed contrite about his former absences, yet offered no reason for them, and I couldn't bring myself to question him.

Paranoia filled me, especially when I thought he might just have found a more compliant woman to seduce. I didn't feel strong enough to face that. Try as I might, I still found it difficult to sort out my true feelings for him. That I found him devastatingly attractive wasn't in any doubt, I would have to be made of stone not to feel something. His very being filled my thoughts more than I could cope with, and his charismatic presence drew me to him whenever he entered a room. I had never felt like this about any man … but would it be enough? Would it grow into love? I hadn't enough experience to tell. Will had been right when he said I had always been searching for something. But was the 'something' love? What the hell defined love anyway?

I gave myself a mental shake. Tomorrow night we were expecting the elusive Khiara and her cronies. I certainly couldn't muster up even a scrap of enthusiasm at the prospect of coming face to face with the woman who had captivated Will. Having encountered her advance party the other night, I knew instinctively she would be far worse. I tried to dismiss my dismal thoughts as Will came to sit beside me on the sofa. He took both of my hands in his, and regarded me seriously.

'Elinor, I have to apologise.'

I said nothing. He frowned.

‘I should have been here,’ he continued. ‘The attack would never have happened had I been here.’

I still remained silent. Actually I agreed with him, but couldn’t bring myself to add to his guilt. He seemed to have suffered enough.

He leaned forward and touched my lips gently with his forefinger. ‘You seem to be healing slowly for a vampire.’

‘I seem unable to do *anything* a proper vampire can,’ I said bitterly.

‘Are your lips able to be kissed I wonder?’ A mischievous glint appeared in his eyes.

‘I’ll give it a whirl,’ I said, pleased to have him flirting with me again. I’d missed the banter between us more than I cared to admit, even to myself. I shuddered as I remembered Will’s incandescent rage. Thankfully, his mood seemed calmer, although his usual flippant manner appeared somewhat subdued. He may have had centuries of seduction experience to his credit, but he seemed to be treading very softly around me. It was almost as though his confidence had taken a battering. Personally, I didn’t think it would do him any harm at all, but rather perversely I didn’t want him to stop trying to seduce me. Unless, of course, there really were other women on the scene.

Will put his hands on either side of my face, threaded his long fingers through my hair and pulled me towards him. ‘Good,’ he murmured, leaning down to press his lips against mine. His kiss was soft and gentle, yet it stirred feelings deep within my body. I found myself moving closer to him, and wound my arms around his neck. He took that as an invitation to deepen the kiss. When he drew back, he touched my lips again. ‘How are the wounds holding up?’

‘OK,’ I said half-truthfully, and he laughed.

‘Would you like to go out?’

The thought of sitting in the peace and quiet of Highgate Cemetery was suddenly overwhelmingly attractive, and I nodded.

'The cemetery,' he said. He stood up with a smile.

I frowned at him. 'You're in my head again.'

He pulled me to my feet. 'Apologies.' He sounded anything but sorry.

Twenty minutes later we sat on the grass, leaning against an old tomb. I listened to the sounds of the night, the many rustles and scuffles of night creatures as they scurried through the long grass. Badgers, hedgehogs, foxes – all, no doubt, in search of a midnight feast. Bats flitted and swooped over our heads, and I heard the soft hoot of an owl and the whir of feathered wings as it searched for an evening meal.

It was so peaceful there. The gothic beauty of mausoleums gleamed in the moonlight and stone angels stood etched against the dark sky like silhouetted immortal beings. My right hand was clasped firmly in Will's and, for once, I felt comforted with a sense of belonging to this nocturnal existence. I closed my eyes and continued to listen to the sounds of the cemetery.

'Elinor?' Will's deep voice interrupted my thoughts.

'*Ellie*,' I said without opening my eyes.

'Can you forgive me?'

I opened my eyes to look at him then. 'For?'

'For being absent when you needed me the most.'

'You can't be everywhere all the time.'

'You should be my priority at all times. I was unbelievably remiss to leave you unattended. If it had been one of Khiara's people ...' he mercifully left that sentence unfinished.

'I can forgive you, providing you never leave me alone again.'

His eyes glinted. 'That I promise,' he said, and his lips twitched into a smile. 'I shall be with you every hour, every minute and every second that you are awake.'

Why did I get the feeling I'd said something I might regret? I narrowed my eyes at him. He feigned innocence.

'Can we turn into bats?' I changed the subject.

'Bats?' He looked bemused by the change of subject. 'What *have* you been reading?'

'*Dracula*,' I replied. 'He turned into a wolf and a bat.'

He laughed. 'Sadly we cannot, but if we ever need a wolf, we have Stevie.'

'And mist?'

He shuddered. 'Thankfully no.'

'Shouldn't Stevie be in a pack or something?'

Will nodded. 'His home pack is in Hertfordshire and he has to return every full moon, but his Alpha does not object to him living in London.'

'Is that usual?'

'The Alpha is his father,' replied Will. 'Should anything happen to him, Stevie would have to return permanently, but until that time, he is permitted to stay here.'

I fell silent again.

Will released my hand and stood up. 'Let us take a walk,' he said, offering me his hand again. I put my hand in his, and he pulled me to my feet, stepping close enough to trace cool fingers down my neck. I shivered.

'You may not be able to transform into a bat or wolf, but you have the strength of several men. You are able to jump from incredible heights and land unhurt, you can mesmerise most unwitting humans with just a glance from those beautiful blue eyes, and you are, of course, immortal.' He put his arms around me, and pulled me in closer to his lean body.

I looked up into his own captivating eyes. 'Can I mesmerise you?'

'Always.'

He led the way down one of the overgrown paths, and headed towards the Circle of Lebanon. I loved this part of the cemetery best. Comprised of a semicircle of old vaults, its architecture looked Egyptian. The vaults sat silent and brooding in their pillared splendour, with moonlight glinting on their ornate lintels. We went down the steps to stand by the nearest vault, and I touched the stone door frame almost reverently. Rumour has it that a vampire was bricked up in one of the vaults, although I didn't know which one. Swain's Lane earned its dubious notoriety from reported vampire activity in the early 1970s, when the renegade vampire ran rampant in the area. The story has become an urban legend over the years known as the Highgate Vampire. Will had several books on the subject, and I'd been reading them, more out of curiosity than anything else.

There were many 'sightings' and claims of attacks, which were grossly over-exaggerated in the tabloid press. One girl claimed to have sleepwalked her way to the cemetery where she was subsequently bitten by the vampire. One of Will's books even has a photograph of the girl showing her bite marks.

Soon after these reports, a few amateur self-appointed vampire hunters scaled the cemetery walls, armed with wooden stakes and crucifixes, searching for the errant vampire. The local police were at their wits' end, harassed by the wealthy residents of Highgate Village, the situation itself, plus all the adverse publicity. Those events happened some twenty years before the emergence of the fictional Buffy and her cohorts, which seemed amazing to me. It appeared some humans really did believe in the paranormal, or at least wanted to. Not a comforting thought.

There was a considerable amount of damage inflicted on the elegant Victorian tombs and gravestones, as enthusiastic hunters attempted to dig up many of the graves in search of the vampire. Several members of the public were even arrested and charged with vandalism. The main protagonist was actually jailed. Unfortunately, vandalism was the only crime the law could charge them with. The cemetery was closed to the public for a long time after that, and even guarded for several months by the long-suffering police.

When the vampire attacks began again, it was somehow kept out of the press and the real 'experts' were called in. (*Who would you call?*) The renegade was tracked to an old tomb in the Circle of Lebanon section, and bricked up in one of the vaults. According to the reports, the people doing the sealing had the foresight to use cement mixed with garlic, and they had also sealed the cracks in the door with garlic. Apparently, the hunters sprinkled Holy Water everywhere inside the vault, as an added bonus, and left a few Holy Crosses too. I imagined the vampire wouldn't get out of there any time soon, and I almost felt sorry for him.

I wondered whether Will had been living in Highgate at the time, and knowing how he felt about renegades, whether he'd been involved in some way.

I came out of my thoughts to find Will standing very close to me. He placed two fingers gently on my forehead.

'It is very busy in there, your thoughts are like buzzing hornets,' he said.

'Will, what do you know about the Highgate Vampire?'

'I know he was a renegade who endangered us all,' he replied shortly. 'Shall we go?'

I nodded. Clearly he didn't want to say any more on the subject.

Instead of turning back toward the main gates, Will led me over to the high wall. He flashed a roguish grin at me, let go of my hand, and suddenly leapt straight upward with amazing speed. Grabbing the top of the wall with one hand, he pulled himself up to sit astride the wall, looking for all the world like a demonic jockey.

'Now this is something you can do Elinor,' he said. 'Come on up.'

Oh crap. Me, the one person who never got chosen for any sports teams at school because I ran like a ballet dancer. No one wants grace when speed is of the essence.

I looked at Will in frustration. He had stretched out flat on his back, balancing effortlessly on top of the wall. He casually lit a cigarette as though he were lying on a sofa.

'Of course I can't,' I said in exasperation. 'I was always rubbish at sports when I was alive, and I can't imagine it'll be any better now. I'm a dancer not a ... a high jump person.'

Will sat up in one fluid motion and dangled his long legs over the wall. He glanced down at me with considerable amusement. I could see the wicked glint in his eyes from where I stood.

'You are a vampire,' he said. 'You have been asking me about changing into a bat or a wolf, wanting to know what you can do, things that you could not do as a human. Believe me when I say that you could probably jump *higher* than this wall, but you do actually have to believe you can, until you get more ... accustomed to things.'

I looked up at him sulkily and pouted.

'Help me then,' I said childishly.

Will sighed theatrically, and rolled his eyes. 'Very well,' he said. 'Do exactly as I say.'

He swung his legs behind him, so they dangled down the other side of the wall, balanced on his stomach, and then stretched his arm down towards me, holding his hand out invitingly.

'Jump up to me.'

I steeled myself to jump, flexed my knees and bounced lightly on the balls of my feet.

Come on Ellie, get a grip, you're a dancer. You can do this – just jump!

I jumped upward, putting all my strength into it, and stretched my hand out to Will's at the same time. Without warning, he moved his hand, and swung himself back to a sitting position. He sprang lithely to his feet, and stood on top of the wall, watching me as my arms flailed in the effort to grab the top of the wall. To my surprise, I made it with ease, but it was no thanks to him.

'You bastard!' I yelled, after I'd pulled myself up to sit astride the wall. I tried to punch him, but he merely laughed and grabbed my hands, holding them fast. He hauled me easily to my feet so we were both balanced on top of the wall, myself somewhat precariously, because heights aren't among my favourite things either. So many phobias.

'Did I not tell you, you could do it?' Will grinned wolfishly.

'*Will* ... ' I said a little desperately, beginning to wobble.

He put an arm firmly around my waist, and suddenly launched us both off the wall. I gave an unattractive squeak as we landed easily on the other side, with Will still laughing.

'Great joke,' I said, the sarcasm heavy in my voice. 'Like I haven't been terrified enough in the last twenty-four hours.'

'I thought a little light relief would chase away the blues,' he said. 'Allow me to escort you home.'

Insufferable. I glared at him, but he simply leaned down to kiss me.

'I seem to remember you inviting me to your bed, or actually, back to my own bed,' he raised an eyebrow. '"*Cut the macho crap and take me to bed*," as I recall.'

'Is *that* what you recall?'

'I have also promised never to leave you alone whilst you are awake,' he grinned. 'That is a promise I intend to take most seriously.'

'Uh-huuh,' I said slowly. 'How did I know *that* promise would somehow come back to bite me?'

'No biting involved,' he assured me blithely as he pulled my arm through his. 'Unless you request it of course.'

I stifled a laugh, Will seemed to have regained his self-assurance.

It was still hours from dawn, and Will was happily channel surfing at a speed that made me dizzy. How he could take in programmes at that speed was beyond me. He stopped at an episode of *Homeland.*

'Very restful,' I said.

He put the remote on the pine chest in front of us, and swivelled around on the sofa to face me. For once his expression was serious as he put the back of his hand gently against my cheek. He stroked my cheek softly as his eyes searched my face for a reaction.

'How do you feel about me this night Elinor?' He asked. 'Do you hate me for allowing the attack to happen? Are you angry with me for leaving you alone? I need you to talk to me.'

'You've apologised enough,' I said slowly. 'But I would like to know why you haven't been around for the last few sunsets. Although if the reason is another woman, I probably don't want to hear about it.'

Will looked nonplussed. 'Another woman? Why the hell would I want another woman?'

'Please don't make me spell it out,' I said tartly.

He shook his head as he ran a hand through his glossy hair. 'I want to sleep with *you*, Elinor. I have said so many times. I have no interest in other women anymore. I am more than prepared to wait until you are ready to make a commitment to me, but that will not stop me from encouraging you at every opportunity.'

'Supposing I said I was ready now?'

Will moved in closer. 'I would be ecstatic.'

I could see a huge explosion on the TV in my peripheral

vision, not exactly the stuff that romance is made of, but I had probably the sexiest man on the planet sitting in front of me, and he wanted to sleep with *me*. I moved closer until I could touch his face, and he turned his head to kiss the palm of my hand.

He looked back at me, his beautiful eyes glowing. His arms went around me, and he pulled me against his body.

'Shall we retire early?'

'Definitely.'

The TV was immediately switched off, and we both stood at the same time.

'I could carry you downstairs ...?' Will's question was only partly serious.

I rolled my eyes at him. 'Don't you dare try any of that clichéd macho crap on me.'

His lips twitched into a roguish grin, and he strode across the room to open the door. He motioned me through with an elegant gesture. Clearly, he didn't intend to give me a chance to change my mind.

When we were both in the bedroom, I turned to find him closer than I'd thought, and a twinge of panic fluttered through my stomach.

Will leaned down and rested his forehead briefly against mine. As he raised his head, he cradled my face in his hands. 'Elinor, I will never hurt you, you know that.'

His soft lips brushed mine, and his arms encircled my waist as he pulled me close. I breathed in his expensive cologne and the heady masculine scent of him, and reached up to wrap my arms around his neck. His tongue flicked a path along my lips as it sought its way into my mouth and began to tease my own tongue in a slow sensuous dance. Any coherent thoughts I had scattered, as I melted under the onslaught of his hot passionate kisses. I felt positive my legs wouldn't support me for very much longer.

His hands slid down my back and, with one swift

movement, he cupped my bottom, lifted me effortlessly, and carried me over to the bed. When he'd put me down, he positioned himself close to my body and propped himself up on one elbow, watching me with feral eyes that glittered with nefarious promises. I looked at his handsome face, so close to mine, as he ran his forefinger slowly down my neck and between my breasts. 'We appear to have too many clothes between us.'

He leaned in closer, and trailed sultry kisses down my neck. The slight stubble on his jaw awakened chills of desire that shivered through my body. Gentle hands teased their way up my jeans-clad legs and my eyes closed. 'Are you partial to this shirt?'

I heard the amusement in his voice and opened my eyes to look at him. 'More macho crap?'

Big mistake. Will tore it in half as quickly and easily as though it were paper, and his hand traced a soft path to my breasts. With the consummate skill of a professional, he'd removed my bra in seconds and tossed it to the floor. His hungry gaze fixated on my breasts, and he ran his fingers gently over them. I arched my back off the bed to get closer to him when he took both breasts in his hands, and a soft moan escaped my lips as he caressed and teased them. He lowered his head, and pulled a nipple into the warm moistness of his mouth. His tongue licked its wicked way around the nipple and I cradled his head in my hands as I whispered his name. My aroused body felt sensitive to his every touch, and my breath escaped my lips in short gasps.

I felt the zip to my jeans slide down and trembled in anticipation as his hand slipped inside to fondle me. He kissed and licked his way across my breasts, up my neck and then settled upon my lips again.

'Still far too many clothes,' he murmured. He drew back to sit up in one slow sensuous movement. He watched me through half-closed eyes as he pulled his t-shirt over his head. I stared at that perfect upper body; so lean and muscled – my mouth almost watered at the sight of him. He dropped the shirt to the floor whilst I watched his every move. I couldn't believe this incredible man actually wanted me, when he could have any woman he wanted. Desire for him coursed through my body as I continued to watch him. I'd never felt desire like this for any man before. It was almost as if just the very sight of him shirtless could seduce me. I wanted him close again. I suddenly needed to feel his naked body against mine.

He slid from the bed, stood up and very, very slowly unbuckled his belt. His eyes held mine the entire time. He pushed his jeans down and stepped out of them.

The fact that he'd been completely naked under the jeans somehow came as no real surprise to me. The vision that stood before me was utter male perfection. His pale body glowed like marble in the dim overhead lights. He looked so incredibly gorgeous, perfect in every way, like one of Rodin's sculptures. His eyes glowed with their ethereal light as he edged nearer to the bed, and I lost myself in their green depths. My head spun as Will's spicy, masculine scent filled my nostrils, and he moved in closer to kneel in front of me. I wanted to touch him – *had* to touch him. I couldn't be this close and not touch him.

Without realising, I'd sat up and swung my legs around, to enable me to move nearer. I reached out with hands that trembled, and laid them gently on the smoothness of his chest. I felt the muscles flex against my fingers, and then he pulled me toward him. I sighed as I reached up to wind my arms around his neck. The moment our bare chests touched, it felt like a fusion of power, and the flicker of desire in my stomach became flames of passion. Sensations such as I'd never experienced before flooded through my body like molten lava.

Will planted soft kisses along my jaw until his lips found mine once more. He felt his way down my bare back with fingers so gentle that they were like erotic feathers brushing my sensitive flesh. His hands stopped short at the waistband of my jeans.

'Allow me,' Will's deep voice startled me as he pulled my jeans off, pushing them to one side, and his gaze never left my own enthralled one. Strong hands gripped my waist and thrust me back on the bed. He began to crawl towards me, slowly and sensuously, like the predator he was, and a slight smile played upon his lips. A tiny panicky part of me wanted to run away. This man was an expert in the art of making love after all, and I had no illusions about my lack of expertise.

Without a word, he gathered me up in his arms and held me close, and the moment he did, I felt safe – *loved* – and very, very desirable. Will made me feel all of those things at once, and no one else had ever done that.

'Trust me,' he whispered, as he placed his lips on mine – gentle at first, then passionate and possessive.

The effect of his naked body so close to mine stoked the fire in my belly again, and I moaned softly as sensuous thrills ran through my body from the top of my head to the tips of my toes. Every nerve ending tingled, eager for his touch. Will didn't disappoint, his hands teased and caressed my body as he kissed his way to my ear, then licked the inside of it with his sinful, talented tongue. I squirmed as the unfamiliar sensations continued to course through my body, but he was relentless. He suddenly turned his attention back to my lips, with hot, intense kisses. Never had I been kissed like this before.

His lips traced down to my belly button, and I sighed as his tongue swirled around inside it. He licked the place where the silver belly bar used to pierce my flesh. I ran my hand through his dark lustrous hair, and it felt like expensive, heavy silk – just like I'd known it would – as it slithered through my fingers.

Will licked his way even lower, and my stomach clenched in wary expectation. He hooked his strong fingers into the top of my lacy underwear, and pulled it down out of his way. His tongue flicked and teased its way over my small mound of curls to the centre of my body. He gently pushed my legs apart with his hands to allow him easier access. I gave a surprised gasp as his persistent tongue darted and swirled intimately inside me, and cried out as the first orgasm shook my body. Still he continued, whilst I clutched at his hair as wave after wave of orgasms erupted through me.

Just when I felt I couldn't take any more, he pushed the underwear completely off with his foot and made his way up my trembling body. He slid his hand up the inside of my thigh and slipped two fingers inside me, as I writhed and pressed against him.

With well-practised ease, those sensitive, skilful fingers teased and probed. Another orgasm built, and I screamed in ecstasy.

Will whispered endearments both in English and Italian, swiftly rolled us both over, and pulled me on top of him. His eyes, darkened with passion, captured my own almost drunken gaze, and his hands held my hips to keep me still, while he eased himself inside me. The feel of him, so strong and so sure, was almost too much.

'Will!'

His hand cupped my neck, and he pulled me toward him so his lips could claim mine again. I gasped when he penetrated me in a steady slow rhythm. His free hand guided my hips as I rode him. The tempo rose and the strong, pulsing sensation of each thrust caused wave after wave of mind-blowing orgasms to rack my body. Starbursts lit behind my eyes as I clung to him.

Will flipped us over again in a dizzy blur of speed, and took complete control. The momentum of each powerful movement made me moan with pleasure. Then I heard his own husky groan of satisfaction as he relaxed on top of me.

He held me close against his sweat-slicked chest, and then eased us both back onto our sides. He pushed a hand through my hair, and twined long strands of it through his strong fingers, as he kissed me gently on the lips.

'Elinor, Elinor, what have you done to me?' he whispered.

He remained inside me, with my legs wrapped around his hips, where I would happily have stayed forever, but he slowly pulled out, and playfully nipped at my shoulder.

He brushed the backs of his fingers down my cheek, and smiled as he followed the outline of my lips with his forefinger. 'So, how was it for you?' A redundant question, because he knew exactly how it had been for me.

I smiled back, feeling languid and satisfied. I'd never experienced anything so breathtaking and wonderful in my former, and frankly rather dull, sex life.

'Incredible.'

He leaned in to kiss me. 'For me too.'

'Even after all those other women?'

Nice one, Ellie. Go ahead and ruin the moment.

Moving closer, so our bodies touched again, he rested his hand on the curve of my hip, and brushed my sensitive flesh with the pad of his thumb. 'Most of those women were purely recreational.'

'What does that make me?'

Will's hand came to rest on my stomach, and he began to caress it softly with circular motions, making my body quiver under his possessive touch.

'You were always meant to be with me, and only me. You are my eternity.'

Will turned his attention back to my breasts then,

and fondled my nipples. He smiled with satisfaction as they pebbled. 'Apparently, there is someone for everyone somewhere,' he said, 'and I should know, because I have had plenty of time to look. *Il mio cuore é pervoi*, Elinor.'

The whispered Italian words sounded so sexy, and although I had no idea what they meant, I knew it was an endearment. He put his lips close to my ear, and whispered, 'My heart is for you.'

I couldn't answer. He was still too close, too gorgeous and too naked for me to think straight.

Dark brows raised, his lips twitched into a sexy smile. 'So, are you tired yet?'

14 March

This has been, without doubt, the most wonderful night of my entire existence. I have never felt this way with any other woman, and three hundred years is a long time to exist without real passion.

I have taken plenty of women to my bed over the centuries, both mortal and undead. Vampires are nothing if not sexually decadent, but those couplings were, as I told Elinor, simply recreational. Fun, and sometimes merely a necessity. I spent fifty years or more as Khiara's consort, but there was never any real affinity between us. Lust certainly, obsession maybe, but never love. Had I stayed longer with her, we would almost certainly have destroyed each other.

Just before dawn, I gathered Elinor into my arms, cradling her against me, as her limbs became useless. I know she is still afraid of the sensations she suffers at the dawn's invasion of her body, and I hoped that by holding her close, I could lessen that fear. I saw the grateful expression in her eyes just before her eyelids closed for the day. I kissed them gently.

Rest, my love, eternity is ours.

Chapter Nineteen

Khiara

The bed was strewn with virtually every item of clothing I owned. Nothing seemed appropriate. It was the night we were to entertain Will's ex-lover. His maker. If entertain is the right word.

I had only spent one night with him, which had been one night of incredible sex, admittedly, but *she* had slept with him countless times, and knew him considerably better than I did. The very least I could attempt to do was look absolutely amazing, but with these clothes, no reflection and no makeup, it would be impossible. I sighed. Perhaps I could feign illness, and stay downstairs all the time she was there. *Did vampires get ill?*

I sat on the bed, surrounded by the remnants of my human life; clothes that were fine to wear to rehearsals and the local pub, but would never pass muster when confronted by a sophisticated Italian vampire. *Khiara*. What kind of bloody name was that anyway? Sounded either like a car or a can of trashy drink to me.

Suppose Will took one look at her, and realised she really was the love of his life? What then? Suppose she just refused to leave?

I had successfully worked myself into a paranoid – almost hysterical – frenzy, when there was a soft knock on the bedroom door.

'Come in,' I said without thinking. *Good call Ellie, suppose it's Honyauti?* I leapt to my feet just in case I needed to run, but in the doorway stood a small dark-haired girl with a pretty, mischievous face. Her hair was short, beautifully cut in a shiny bob, and she wore black leather trousers with a tiny purple top that revealed an incredibly flat stomach. She carried several large carrier bags, and smiled shyly at me. 'Hi, I'm Roxanne – Roxy,' she said coming further into the room.

'Ellie,' I said.

'Will said you were called Elinor,' she said with another smile. 'But then it took him years to call me Roxy.'

I laughed. 'Perhaps I should start calling him William.'

She held out the carrier bags to me. 'He asked me to get some new clothes for you to try. I hope you like them.'

'How did you know my size?'

She gave me an amused look. 'They'll fit.'

I took hold of the carrier bags: Dolce and Gabbana, Armani, Vivienne Westwood. It seemed no expense had been spared here.

'Did you ransack Selfridges?' I asked as I looked at the various shoe bags. 'Prada, Alexander McQueen … *Christian Louboutin*? I could never have bought shoes like this, even if I'd saved up for five years.'

Roxy shrugged. 'Will has plenty of money,' she said nonchalantly. 'He's very generous.'

I started taking various items from their expensive bags. Whoever had actually done the buying had exquisite taste. Everything looked perfect, and any one of the items would suit me. I could tell that at a glance.

'How dressy should I be?' I asked Roxy, holding up a full-length dress in one hand, and a gorgeous pair of black velvet trousers in the other. Roxy pointed to the trousers.

'Save the dress for Trials,' she said.

'Trials?'

'If they happen,' she added quickly. 'You do have to hurry though, everyone will be here soon.'

Roxy handed me a small box. 'That's to replace the silver belly bar.' She seemed to know a lot about me already.

I opened the box, and got out a platinum belly bar,

which boasted a beautiful sparkling diamond in the centre. 'I love it.'

With a pleased nod she left the room, and I closed the door behind her.

Eventually, I settled on the black velvet trousers that hung low on my hips, and fit like a glove, teamed with a black midriff-revealing halter-neck top, adorned with tiny black sequins around the neckline that glinted whenever I moved. I brushed my hair behind my ears, securing it at each side with diamond-studded clips, also thoughtfully provided by Roxy. The diamond belly bar was the final touch. I wished I could see how I looked.

I started to look at the other clothes. The dress was amazing. I'd never owned anything so gorgeous, or so expensive. I was happily trying on different pairs of shoes when there was another knock at the door.

'May I come in?' Will's voice.

'Sure,' I replied, for once feeling confident in my appearance, even though I couldn't check it for myself in a mirror.

Will came in, shutting the door behind him. He leaned against the door, and his bright gaze travelled appreciatively down my body, but stopped at the sandal on one foot and soft leather boot on the other.

He raised an eyebrow. 'Well apart from the odd footwear, you are heart-breakingly lovely this night,' he said.

'How did you know?' I asked. I flipped off the sandal, and pulled on the other boot. 'About the clothes?'

He glanced at the bed strewn with my entire wardrobe. 'I like women,' he replied. 'I have learned many things about them over the years.'

'Everything is perfect, thank you.'

'You are most welcome.'

I looked up at him then, and took in his appearance

for the first time. I'd got so used to him wearing jeans and t-shirts that the sight of him dressed more formally very nearly floored me. He wore an emerald green shirt that almost matched his eyes, tucked into a pair of tight-fitting black leather trousers that accentuated his long legs. At his waist, he wore a heavy leather belt with an ornate brass buckle. A black velvet jacket finished off the outfit – although in style it looked more like a Victorian frock coat. His glossy hair hung almost to his shoulders and I truly had never seen anything sexier.

'You look pretty tasty yourself, Mr Spooky,' I murmured. 'Are you going to lean against the door all night?'

He raised an eyebrow again. 'Are you going to be flippant towards me all night?'

'I wouldn't dare,' I replied, standing up to test the height of the boots.

Even with Will's confident presence by my side, I really wasn't looking forward to the evening ahead. If Khiara was as powerful as I thought she must be, it didn't bode well, plus I was dreading the thought of coming face to face with Honyauti again. I hadn't even met the other vampires that were attending, apart from Luke and Roxy, but if the others were anything like the Tonto from Hell, I would far prefer to hide downstairs.

Will closed the gap between us and wrapped his arms around me.

'Honyauti will never come near you again,' he said quietly. 'If he so much as sends a glance in your direction, I will kill him.'

I looked up at him, and noticed that his eyes had a faraway look. I pushed gently at his chest. 'What is it?'

'Whatever happens tonight, promise me you will not overreact,' he said.

'What does that mean?'

He raised a hand to trace the curve of my face, his eyes concerned. 'There may be some baiting – particularly of you – and you must not rise to it. Promise me, Elinor, that you will keep that temper of yours in check. It is important.'

'*My* temper?' I felt insulted.

He tightened his arms around me. 'Yes. *Your* temper. Promise me.'

My feeling of foreboding increased at his words but I nodded anyway. He released me and moved toward the door, a split second before there was a light knock.

'Yes, Luke?'

The door opened, and Luke peered around. 'It's time,' he said.

Will nodded and turned to me. 'Shall we?'

It wasn't a question, so I followed him and Luke upstairs.

I could hear a buzz of conversation coming from the drawing room, yet I hadn't heard anyone arrive.

Strange.

Was that why Luke had come down to collect us as if he were some kind of bodyguard?

As we neared the door, Will turned to me, confirming that thought. 'Whatever happens, Luke is here to ensure your safety,' he said. 'Try to follow my lead in protocol and, if in doubt, say nothing, and I do mean *nothing* Elinor.'

With his usual courtly gesture, Will offered his arm to me, and I threaded my arm through his gratefully. If I'd had a pulse it would have been visibly jumping. I glanced back at Luke, who inclined his head to me with a smile.

I felt comforted to have two strong men with me, especially as Honyauti was in that room.

Will strode confidently into the room, with me on his arm, and Luke behind us. The buzz of conversation stopped immediately, and everyone in the room turned to look at ... well ... me, actually. Perfect. After a quick sweep of the room, I lowered my eyes, so as not to engage anyone. My initial impression had been that of a varied collection of incredibly good-looking people, and I was once again so grateful for the expensive new clothes.

A fire burned cheerfully in the large fireplace, and the warm glow from its flames flickered on the pale faces of the gathered throng. I remained clinging to Will's arm, hating myself for looking like a trophy wife. I decided to treat it like a performance, and raised my head as though I were on stage. Will placed his other hand over mine in a reassuring gesture, and let his gaze wander around the room.

'Good evening,' he said. 'I hope you are all well this evening.'

A tall, slender woman with long pale blonde hair sauntered up to Will, looking as though she'd just stepped off the catwalk. Gazing up at him in adoration, she then bowed her head deferentially.

'Greetings, Will, Elder of the City of London,' she said in a breathy voice. Her Italian accent sounded sexy and inviting.

'Good evening to you Josephine,' said Will mildly. 'Welcome to London.'

'Is this the fledgling?' She managed to make the question sound like an insult, even though there was nothing in the actual words that could be termed offensive.

'Yes,' Will replied. Then, looking round to include everyone in the room, he continued, 'Allow me to introduce Elinor.'

Josephine's glance took in my appearance with an experienced glance, no doubt assessing the value of my outfit. Once again, I felt relief at Will's intuition with the designer clothes. Having decided I was no competition, Josephine turned and gracefully walked over to where

Honyauti sat in one of the armchairs. She perched prettily on the arm of his chair. The buzz of conversation continued as Will led me over to the only vacant armchair. He settled me on the arm before seating himself. OK, this was definitely a form of vampire protocol that I didn't understand, but I'd make damn sure we got to discuss it later. Will gave me a quick wink as if he had sensed my negative feelings, when suddenly all conversation stopped, just as if someone had thrown a switch. Will tensed beside me, and I knew without looking round that Khiara had arrived.

She swept into the room, and I caught my breath. She looked completely amazing. Tall and reed-slender, with waist length black hair that shimmered and gleamed under the soft lights. Her pale olive skin glowed creamy and perfect, but her eyes immediately commanded everyone's undivided attention; they were a brilliant, deep blue with even darker blues in their depths, and they glittered with a fire to rival the green fire in Will's eyes. She wore an elegant, black, full-length evening gown, which fell to the floor in perfect folds and appeared to be an expensive couture number, if I wasn't mistaken. It skimmed her slender body perfectly as though it had been made to measure, which of course it probably had. Her creamy shoulders were bare, and she wore an elegant, but understated, diamond pendant at her throat.

She probably made every woman in the room feel either over, or under, dressed, and I wasn't quite sure yet which category I fell into. Her beautiful hair was completely unadorned and I immediately wanted to take out the diamond clips holding mine. Almost without thinking, my hand went toward one of the clips, only to be caught by Will's larger hand and held.

He turned to look at me briefly, and the look in his eyes told me that I looked beautiful to him, and I smiled. He let go of my hand, and stood up to greet the woman who had brought him over to this existence, all those centuries ago.

Khiara stepped up so close to Will that even a postcard wouldn't have fitted between them. 'William,' she purred, draping a perfect arm around his neck. 'How perfectly wonderful to see you again.' Her voice sounded husky and very sexy, with an exotic hint of an Italian accent. She kissed him lingeringly on both cheeks, but remained pressed close to his body. It was Will who stepped back. A tiny frown creased her delicate brows at the move.

'Khiara,' he said. 'You look breathtaking as always.' She accepted the compliment with a slight incline of her head, and then looked down at me. I stayed silent.

'Stand child,' she said, as she took in every detail of me with one contemptuous sweep of her amazing eyes.

I stood, resisting a ridiculous urge to curtsey. Khiara continued to look me over, and, reaching out, grabbed my arm to turn me around. I now knew how a heifer must feel at a cattle sale. I saw a flicker of annoyance cross Will's face, which disappeared swiftly, leaving his expression calm and dispassionate. She let go of my arm and looked back at him.

'William, surely after all this time, you could have chosen more wisely for a companion. Take her for your pleasure, by all means, for that is the best use for the newly turned, but do not allow her to reside in your home. By all the Ancients – a mere *fledgling* – it is hardly fitting for an Elder to be seen in public with such a creature.'

Before Will could answer, I found myself answering her.

'Can I get you anything Khiara?' I asked, as she raised one perfect dark eyebrow at me. 'Holy Cross? Wooden stake – a few cloves of garlic perhaps?'

Will laughed, as did Luke and a couple of the others.

Khiara's eyes blazed with anger, 'Are you daring to mock me child?'

'Modern women are quite different in this century, Khiara,' said Will, 'and Elinor is a very modern woman.'

'Or a very stupid one.' She turned those startling eyes on me again.

I immediately felt her gaze pierce my body like sharp knives. My legs trembled as though they could no longer support me, and Will had to put an arm around my waist to prevent me from falling. He put his body in front of mine instantly, his eyes flashing angry green sparks.

'That will be quite enough Khiara,' he said. 'This is my house and Elinor belongs to me. You have no right to insult her, and you certainly have no right to hurt her, especially not in my presence.'

Khiara stared at him then as though he'd suddenly become very interesting, and put an elegant hand up to caress his face as she smiled at him. Her smile dazzled and completely transformed her lovely face, making it irresistible and impossible not to look at her.

'You are so right *cara*,' she said softly. 'How unforgivably rude of me.'

I felt as though the whole room had suddenly breathed out collectively. Luke had moved quietly to my other side, and Khiara suddenly transferred her attention to him.

'So, Luke, the ever faithful bodyguard, you are still here, and as handsome as ever.'

Luke bowed his head to her. 'Welcome to London.'

Khiara held her hand out to him, palm upwards, and as he covered it with his own, she drew him closer to her, until their bodies were almost melded together. She reached up to Luke's face with her free hand and swiftly sliced his cheek, causing beads of blood to appear. Then, very slowly, she licked the blood from the wound with one erotic gesture. Luke remained passive and still.

Well, that was a different kind of greeting.

Will drew me back from Khiara, and we both stood

to one side to allow her to move further into the room and away from us. It was then that I saw the rest of her entourage for the first time.

Entering the room immediately behind her came an enormous, rather ugly man, who appeared to be at least seven feet tall. His large head was completely bald, and his skin the colour of seasoned oak. Dressed rather incongruously in an expensive looking tuxedo, which screamed professional bodyguard, he made an impressive and scary figure. Even the muscles in his arms appeared to be fighting to escape from his jacket. He strode up to Will, and bowed his head politely.

'Greetings Will, Elder of the City of London,' he said in a deep, heavily accented voice.

'Welcome, Grigori,' replied Will. 'May I introduce Elinor.' Grigori turned to look at me with dark eyes. Eyes that weren't pure evil, like Honyauti's, but just expressionless. I couldn't determine whether he was friendly or not, so I just looked up at him, saying nothing. He really was a very long way up. Sometimes I really hated being short.

'Greetings woman of Will,' he said. Well, that was new, not that I was complaining exactly, but I did have a name.

'Good evening, Grigori,' I replied.

Grigori wandered over to the corner where Honyauti and Josephine sat. I heard them mumbling greetings. Grigori then took his place slightly behind the chair in which Khiara sat.

I just wished I could be sure who were Will's vamps and who weren't. There were not too many happy, smiling faces in the room, that was for sure. To make my night complete, Katarina glided into the room. She exuded confidence, strutting in like a confident dancer or fashion model. I had tried to put her out of my mind since our meeting in the club, yet here she was again. Oh joy.

She gazed adoringly at Will.

'Will,' she breathed huskily. 'How perfectly lovely to see you again so soon.'

She smoothed her black sequinned top over blood-red leather trousers, and moved in closer to Will. If she sliced his cheek, we were going to have words.

Will stepped away from her, and gestured for her to join the others in the room. 'No threats tonight?'

She smiled coquettishly, and I wondered whether there had ever been any history between the two of them, although if Khiara had been on the scene, I thought not.

'I assure you no threat has ever been made seriously on *my* part,' she replied. 'But I do think your fledgling is rather ordinary to cause all this upset. Don't you agree?'

'Elinor is many things,' said Will pleasantly. 'But ordinary is certainly not one of them.'

'I meant no offence,' she said sweetly, but she made no attempt to look at me.

'Like hell you didn't,' I muttered.

She did look at me then and her face contorted to an angry, evil mask.

'Are you speaking to *me*? Will, is your creature speaking to me?' She made a gesture towards herself with a tiny hand, as though she couldn't believe my nerve. Then she came closer to me. 'Do you really think you can come along and take Will for your own? Just like that, *fledgling*?' she spat the last word venomously but very quietly. 'Oh you are *so* mistaken little girl. You really have no idea who you are dealing with.'

'Is that a threat?' My voice had been quiet, but I became suddenly aware that the room had gone still and silent. Every vampire in the room would have better than excellent hearing, and they were all extremely interested in our conversation.

Khiara rose and glided over to us. Her anger was palpable. She took the smaller woman's arm in a grip that looked really painful. 'Remember your position, Katarina,' she warned.

Katarina dropped a graceful curtsey and bowed her head to Khiara.

'My deepest apologies, mistress,' she said. 'I exist only to make you happy.'

That didn't sound like a lot of fun to me, but I found it difficult to care.

Khiara turned her deep blue gaze to me. 'You need to curb that tongue of yours, fledgling,' she said coldly, then, turning to Will, 'I really cannot be responsible for my people all of the time. You will have to control her if she is to remain safe. Keep her chained up in a cellar somewhere perhaps.'

'Are you threatening my fledgling *again* in my own house?' Will's tone was mild.

Khiara stared at him, clearly surprised. 'Of course not William,' she said. 'We are all friends here, are we not?'

'I think your people have been anything *but* friendly in their short stay in my city,' said Will. 'If they cannot behave themselves, they will have to be prepared to face the consequences.' He put a possessive arm around my waist, a movement that Khiara followed with narrowed eyes. 'I had a similar conversation with Katarina the other evening, but allow me to reiterate the rules of the city for everyone now. I simply will not tolerate any more humans being killed in my city, and I certainly have no intention of tolerating threats made against any of my people. Please be aware that I am merely issuing a friendly warning in this instance.'

Khiara's face was impassive. 'We need to instigate Trials,' she said.

Everyone in the room went still again. I had no idea what was going on but, remembering Will's advice, I kept quiet, standing there like a good little Stepford Wife.

'Let us not fool ourselves as to the reason you are really here Khiara,' said Will. 'You had no need to see me for decades – centuries – but suddenly it is important for you to be here in England. It is strange how the matter of Trials has never arisen before. I have been the Elder of London for two centuries after all.'

Khiara's face tightened with rage at that. She raised a hand and clicked her fingers imperiously. Her people instantly came to stand behind her.

'We will meet again in five days' time,' she said. 'It can be a place of your choosing, as this little city appears to be yours, and Trials will begin then.'

Will inclined his head. 'Very well, it shall be arranged. *Buona serata.*'

She swept out of the room, followed by Grigori, Katarina and Josephine along with a couple of dark-haired male vampires.

There was silence from the remaining throng.

Everyone looked at Will.

He sat down on the sofa and motioned to me to sit with him. I walked over and sat down next to him.

'Well, I think that all went rather well,' he said with a smile.

15 March

This night was indeed a baptism of fire for Elinor. She is an intelligent woman, but I fear the wiles and politics of the vampire world are confusing for her at the moment. I knew she would not be able to desist from retaliating should anyone threaten or insult her. She has looked after herself for many years after all, and is no doubt used to coping with objectionable people. It was rather unfortunate that the person in this case happened to be Khiara.

I think Trials were always going to be insisted on, knowing Khiara as well as I do.

I fear for the City of London should things not go as planned.

Chapter Twenty

Retribution

A mere two nights later I discovered how well Will kept his promises. Almost in a 'be careful what you wish for' kind of way. I had showered and dressed whilst Will was upstairs, making phone calls. I had a horrible feeling that the calls were connected to the pending Trials. What these Trials would entail, I had no idea and definitely no desire to ever find out. Unfortunately, the date had been set, and the venue, of course, was Dusk. Will told me I had to attend, because I was the reason they were being held at all. So hiding wasn't an option.

Will came into the bedroom just as my thoughts began to veer off in a scary direction. He looked unusually serious. 'Please accompany me downstairs.'

I felt a jolt of fear go through my body. Perhaps he was going to take Khiara's advice after all and keep me chained up.

'Why?' I didn't feel at all inclined to accompany him back down to that damp, dark place.

'There is someone I want you to see,' he began to lead the way down to the cellar.

I really, really didn't like the sound of that. 'What's going on?'

'You need to see for yourself.' His voice drifted back to me as he started down the stairs.

I followed him into the second cellar. An unconscious man had been chained to the wall, and his head lolled down onto his chest. *What ... ?*

Will strode over to the man and, grabbing a fistful of his grey hair, yanked his head back with one contemptuous move.

'I believe you know this person,' he ground the words out between clenched teeth.

It was a statement, not a question.

I looked at the man's face, and immediately reverted to twelve years old, feeling the familiar sick fear of my adolescence.

Memories flooded back – crowded my mind – one horrific scene after the other. Dark, terrifying nights ... long, lonely, dark nights. Nights filled with fear and pain, and the humiliation of no one ever believing me. The things he had made me do ...

I looked at the face and I did know it.

I hated it. I hated it more than I had ever hated anyone before or since.

It was the face of my nightmares.

The actual *cause* of my nightmares.

A face that had haunted me for years.

I shook my head violently. *No – no. Why ... ?*

Tears trickled unheeded down my cheeks as I looked at Will.

He came towards me straight away, and wiped my tears away with his fingers. I couldn't stop crying.

Will held me in his arms, and spoke quietly against my hair. 'I have brought him here to show you that all he is now is a dysfunctional old man. To prove once and for all that he can never harm you again. He will never come near you again, and he most certainly will never touch you again. You will now have the ability to move on and to be happy again, unencumbered by any former revolting memories.'

Years of pent-up emotion suddenly released inside of me. Years of no one believing anything I said, and of having to live with the perverted actions of the man that everyone did believe. Those childhood nights filled with pain and terror – the horror of hearing my bedroom door open late at night, and what it signified.

Will pulled me closer as sobs racked my body. He spoke quietly, his deep voice soothing, 'My love, if I could take all of your pain, you know I would do so in a heartbeat. But all I can do is provide the instigator of that pain and punish him.'

I looked up into his eyes, expecting to see judgement, but saw only concern. He kissed me gently on the forehead. Then he stepped away from me and went back over to the shackled man.

'Look at me,' his voice was cold and compelling.

The man raised his head slowly to look at Will, and fear emanated from him. I felt it wash over my skin, and I'm ashamed to admit that I liked the feeling. It excited my senses. But I felt shocked to the core, at coming face to face again with the man who had ruined my childhood. How Will had ever found him was a mystery, I had never even said his name. His timing, however, left a lot to be desired. With so many things going on at the moment – Khiara, Trials, bodies in the park, even our own blossoming relationship – and yet for some reason he thought he'd bring my former foster father here. Now.

Will's unexplained absences suddenly made perfect sense of course. I felt terrified that he actually intended to kill him and I didn't think I'd ever be able to stop him. Then his death would be my fault, and I knew I couldn't live with that.

'Who are you?' He looked Will straight in the face.

'Your worst nightmare.'

A hackneyed, much overused line from many movies, but delivered by Will under those circumstances, it sounded truly terrifying.

Will held a hand towards me, and I walked forward to put my hand in his.

'Do you recognise this lady?' He pulled me closer, so that I stood next to him.

The unfortunate wretch shook his head.

'Look again.'

Obediently he looked at me again. His face blanched and his eyes widened in sheer terror. '*Ellie Wakefield?* But you're dead! Didn't you *die*? Ellie, if it's really you – call this madman off. I won't call the police, honestly I won't.'

'Silence,' hissed Will. Edward Oldman fell silent instantly.

I clung almost desperately to Will's hand. I felt convinced he'd kill Oldman without any compunction whatsoever. I really couldn't cope with that, even though this perverted creep had ruined whatever childhood I'd had left after my parents were killed. I'd never even been allowed the chance to grieve for them properly. Oldman had robbed me of my virginity whilst I was still a child, years before I'd become a woman, and then he'd abused me night after terrible night. No wonder I'd always been so afraid of the dark.

No one had believed me. He'd always been very plausible and charming, and everyone believed him. Even his wife, apparently. I'm not sure I've ever allowed any man to get close to the real me – until Will. Perhaps my destiny had always been to die early, and be reborn as a vampire.

I glanced up at Will at exactly the same moment he turned to look at me. His eyes glowed in the dim light, and his expression looked deadly serious.

'I *am* going to kill him. But you do not have to watch. Unless, of course, you wish to watch. It is your choice.'

I looked at Oldman, feeling nothing but emptiness. Will put an arm around my waist, and drew me close to his side. I leaned shakily into the strength of his body.

He kissed my cheek. 'Would you like to torture him or shall I?'

With those terrible words hanging in the air, he released me and walked toward Oldman. He ripped the shirt violently from his back, and Oldman struggled in his chains. But Will had clearly chained people up before, and he would never escape.

'She was a dirty little girl. Always asking for it,' protested Oldman in a whining voice.

With a sudden movement that was too fast ever to be mortal, Will smashed Oldman in the face with the back of his hand. Blood spurted from his broken nose, and he sagged in his chains. I leaped back in horror at the sudden violence, and tears filled my eyes again.

Will grabbed Oldman's hair. 'She was only twelve years old, her parents had just died, and I seriously doubt she even knew what "it" was.' His cold, disdainful words were like angry blows, and I shivered, so very thankful they weren't directed at me. Oldman looked at Will, the lower part of his face almost a mask of blood, yet his eyes held the same black hatred that I remembered from more than thirteen years ago.

Will spun on his heel and strode to the far corner of the cellar. He came back with a lethal-looking dagger, so large it was almost a sword.

I watched with wide eyes. I had no idea what he had in mind, but I didn't think I'd ever be able to stop him.

Will twirled the dagger with professional ease, and then started to cut at Oldman's trousers. He managed to cut all his clothes off completely without slicing any flesh at all, leaving the overweight, flabby man naked and cowering against the damp wall.

'Just how many little girls' lives have you ruined?' Will pressed the knife against Oldman's genitals, not hard enough to draw blood, not yet. Oldman gasped and stared up at him in sheer terror.

'Don't.' Oldman's voice sounded thick with his own blood. 'We're human beings – not animals – please don't!'

Will gave a short, mirthless laugh. 'Now whatever gave

you the impression I was human?' He smiled wide enough to show gleaming fangs.

Oldman fainted.

'Let us wake him.' Will turned back to look at me again. I definitely didn't want this to go any further now. I may have detested the man, in fact I would *always* detest him, but I could not – *would* not – be an accomplice to his murder. I didn't think I would ever see Will in the same light again if he did murder him in cold blood. I had no illusions that he would be ruthless when he had to be, but Oldman was still human, and not some evil vampire who had come to destroy us.

'Will, you can't kill him.' My voice sounded strangled and scared. 'It would make us no better than him if you did.'

'Would you object if I fed off him?'

'Surely his blood would choke you.'

Will shrugged. 'Blood is blood.'

Practical as well as ruthless, obviously.

He went back to Oldman, pulled his head upwards by the ears, and dug his nails into the lobes. Oldman gasped and his eyes flew open. When he saw how close Will was, he started to babble in terror.

'Ellie – call him off! He's mad – a madman. He'll kill me.'

'He'd *like* to kill you,' I agreed.

'Are you sure you are not hungry?' Will turned to me once more. 'I am feeling more than a little peckish myself.'

Oldman looked back at Will. 'What the fuck are you?'

'What the fuck do you think we are?' replied Will conversationally.

'Lunatics on drugs.'

Oldman struggled feebly in his chains, and Will laughed pleasantly. He leaned closer to Oldman. 'I shall tell you what I am, shall I?' His voice sent shivers down *my* spine, so heaven knew what Oldman was feeling.

'I am a vampire.' Will stood back from Oldman with his hands on his hips, and his head on one side, as he watched his prey through slitted green eyes. 'Therefore I feed on human blood and tonight, my friend, it is going to be yours.'

'Stop him Ellie,' pleaded Oldman again.

Will grasped Oldman around the throat, and smashed him against the wall. 'How many times did Elinor ask *you* to stop?' Oldman gasped and wriggled futilely against Will's unrelenting hold. 'How many times did you abuse her tiny body, taking your pleasure with her, whilst she screamed in agony for *your* mercy?'

Oldman looked ill.

Without warning, Will suddenly dug the point of his blade into Oldman's neck, rupturing the jugular vein and causing arterial blood to gush out like a dark, red fountain. He laughed. The laugh had an unusually chilling sound. Then he turned his dark head to one side, which allowed the blood to enter his mouth with the minimum of effort.

'Tastes fine for a pervert,' he commented without looking back at me. 'Just blood. *Quod erat demonstrandum.*'

I averted my eyes from the blood as absolute horror overcame all other sensations. 'Will, stop. Please, please stop this ... before it's too late. *Please.*'

He stepped away from Oldman, who had fainted again, and his eyes softened when he saw my stricken expression. Closing the gap between us, he tenderly stroked my cheek with the tip of his thumb. 'Do you want me to save his life?'

I nodded. 'Yes. I ... I don't want to see you as a murderer.'

He brushed tears from my cheeks. 'Very well, Elinor. For you, but against my better judgement, I will allow this perverted maggot to live.'

He stopped the bleeding with his saliva, and began to

pull the shredded clothes back over Oldman's unconscious body. Unlocking the cuffs at his wrists, he allowed him to fall in a crumpled heap onto the stone floor. He stood looking down at him for a moment, a strange expression flitting across his otherwise stern face. 'Go upstairs Elinor.'

I glanced down at Oldman. 'You told him you were a vampire.'

'So I did. No doubt everyone will believe him too.'

I gave him a puzzled look.

Will's lips curved slightly. 'How many times did you want people to believe you as a child?'

'Too many to count.'

'Then this should be the perfect revenge for you. He will regain consciousness in a hospital somewhere, babbling about vampires and seeing his former foster daughter, whom everyone knows is dead, and I guarantee he will be put in some kind of institution. At least for a while.'

I gave him a weak smile. 'That is pretty clever.'

He inclined his head. 'It is. Now go upstairs and Luke can help me deliver this creature to a hospital out of London somewhere.'

I walked to the door, but stopped and looked back at the last moment.

'Will?'

'Whatever you are going to say, you worry too much.'

I went upstairs and wandered into the drawing room. Switching on the television, I flicked through the channels, trying in vain to find something that would hold my attention and stop me from thinking.

I heard Will's key in the lock some forty minutes later, and looked at him anxiously as he came into the room.

'Oldman will live, Elinor, thanks to you. He has been left at Watford Hospital. Luke informed them that he had found the man unconscious in the street, and assumed he had been mugged, as he carried no wallet or identification about his person. Luke then witnessed him being wheeled away for a blood transfusion. He had a very informative chat with a pretty little nurse, who assured him that he will make a full recovery.'

Part of me felt relief at his words, but the abused child within was still afraid.

I stared blankly at the television screen, 'It's just as well you didn't kill him, the police might have traced him back to you, they have all sorts of DNA equipment these days.'

Will laughed.

'It would not have helped. I have not officially existed for centuries.'

He flicked the remote control at the television and the screen went black.

'Talk to me,' he invited, sitting down next to me.

I looked at him, searching his face, but found nothing other than his usual calm expression.

'They'll discover that he really was my foster father.' My eyes widened with panic.

'Then they will also discover that you are dead. That should effectively close that line of investigation I think.'

'He'll say he saw me.'

'And they will remind him that you are dead.'

'He knows where we live—' I began, and Will gave me a long-suffering look.

'You give me no credit for any intelligence,' he sighed. 'Oldman was unconscious when he arrived here, and unconscious when he left. He is now in a Watford hospital with their report stating he was found on a Watford street, and brought into the hospital by a Good Samaritan.'

'Why didn't the Good Samaritan just phone for an ambulance?'

'He had no mobile phone with him and it was quicker to drive him. I have no doubt that the Hertfordshire police will try to find their most helpful witness at the address in Watford

Luke gave them, but of course they will not be successful. They will probably then assume that Luke was one of a gang who lost his nerve when he thought Oldman might die.'

It all sounded plausible enough, but I still shuddered. Somehow I couldn't erase the sight of Will drinking Oldman's blood with so much relish. I had never seen him feed, but even I could tell the difference between feeding simply to survive and the way he had fed from Oldman. 'You really wanted to kill him, didn't you?'

He nodded. 'Of course I did. From the moment I knew what he had done to you as a child, I wanted to tear him apart with my bare hands. I will not apologise for torturing him.'

I stared at the dark TV screen, willing it to spring to life so I could concentrate on something else.

'Do you fancy going to see a film?' He had probably picked up on that random thought.

'As long as it isn't a horror movie.'

'How do you feel about pirates?'

17 March

It has been a very long time since I have tortured a mortal, and even longer since I felt such an overwhelming necessity to do so. I have lived quietly and unobtrusively for many decades, but the anger I felt at hearing about Elinor's terrifying childhood awakened my primal need for revenge.

I am sorry to say that I felt no compassion for the bastard whatsoever. I may be a creature of the night and a predator, but I abhor rape, and the abuse and rape of a child is even more abhorrent to me. I loathe the scum who perpetrate such acts, and if I had had my way this night, there would have been one less paedophile in the world.

Elinor has lived with the horror of his actions for years, and she blamed herself, as is so often the case. He was the reason for her previous failed relationships with men and I have no intention of letting him come between us.

I am not too concerned about allowing him to live. He may well insist he has seen Elinor alive, but I think most people will dismiss the claims, and think them merely the babblings of an old man. Should he become a problem, however, I shall have no qualms about killing him, and Elinor need never find out.

I know where to find him now.

Later that night, I took her to see a light-hearted film, and she held my hand tightly throughout the performance. She was very quiet and I didn't intrude on her thoughts. It is my belief it would be for the best if she came to terms with the night's events on her own. Time is the best healer after all, and we have that in abundance.

Chapter Twenty-One

Trials

In some books, there's often a chapter that begins, 'The dreaded day dawned,' as being the dawn which opened on a dreaded moment. Obviously we, as vampires, try very hard not to see the dawn of any day. So, I'll just say that the evening of Trials 'dawned' far sooner than I wanted it to. Like a dentist appointment you've been dreading, and the days just fly by, until you suddenly find yourself sitting in the waiting room. You listen to the whine of the dentist's drill and know you're next. Although I will never need to visit a dentist again. I'm grateful for that at least.

Will's mood appeared as calm as ever. He seemed to be almost looking forward to the night's forthcoming events, which I found strange beyond belief.

Once again, I had tried on several different dresses in an attempt to forget the actual reason why I needed to get dressed up. Apparently Trials were a huge deal, and trying to imagine just *how* huge made me want to run for the hills. Dressing up. I hated dressing up.

I knew I'd have to wait for the winter months and darker evenings again before I could personally go late-night shopping in South Molton Street or Selfridges. But Will had very generously got another load of clothes sent round for me to try. His credit rating must have been really good, as most shops were more than happy to supply samples from their various collections.

I held up a gorgeously slinky Armani dress, in black of course. I had drawn the line at colours or patterns, and actually would have far preferred to wear trousers. But Will uncompromisingly remained adamant, and insisted I must wear a dress. As he rarely, if ever, made any comment as to what I should wear, I decided going along with him wouldn't kill me. Again.

It had to be the fourth dress I'd tried on. I couldn't even see what any of them looked like. What a pointless waste of time and energy. I sighed and slipped it over my head. It felt perfect, but I couldn't quite reach to zip it up at the back. I sighed again.

Will came in at that moment, immaculate and devastatingly sexy in an expensive-looking black suit and dark red shirt. He looked at me with raised eyebrows. 'Is there a problem? I can *feel* you sighing upstairs.'

I held my arms away from my body in a frustrated gesture. 'I can't see how any of these dresses look. But I can remember I always look like rubbish in anything formal, and I can't do the stupid zip up.'

Will's lips curved. 'Huge tragedy,' he agreed. 'Come here.'

I walked over to him and turned around, presenting him with the offending zip. His cool fingertips brushed my bare back, and I shivered. He bent and brushed his lips where he'd touched. I leaned back into his chest as he wrapped his arms around me to hold me close.

'Are you so sure you want to put this dress on?' He began pressing soft kisses to the back of my neck.

'I'm not even sure of my name when you're this close.'

He turned me to face him, and I looked up with a wry smile. 'However, we don't have very much time do we?'

Will didn't answer at first, just stared down at me, his expression unfathomable. He brushed his fingers down my cheek. 'I am banking on having eternity. So let us get this night over with.'

He turned me around again and zipped up the dress, rather expertly, I thought.

'How many times have you done that over the years?'

He laughed, completely aware of my thoughts as

always. 'Too many times to count, and mostly before your ancestors were even born.'

'That makes me feel *so* much better.'

He held me at arms' length, and his glowing green gaze travelled up and down my body appreciatively.

The dress certainly felt good. It clung where it should cling and swirled elegantly to the floor. The tiny straps at the shoulders crossed over at the back, leaving most of my own back bare. It was deceptively simple – a beautiful, elegant dress – and I wished again that I could see how it looked. I really missed my reflection.

'What do you think?'

'Exquisite.'

'Shall I put my hair up?' I asked, sweeping my hair back with my hands. Luckily, we dancers are adept at twisting our hair up into various styles, without looking in mirrors. Years of practice.

'No.'

Will wasn't a fan of long hair worn up. He maintained that if hair was long, it should be left loose, otherwise get it cut. He entwined his fingers in my hair and pulled me to him. No wonder he preferred long hair. It made perfect handles.

'I wish it was tomorrow.'

'Be careful what you wish for.' Will spoke against the top of my head.

I pulled back and looked up at him. 'Let's leave London.' I suddenly felt desperate.

'Some things have to be faced, my love,' he said gently. 'We can get through this. I will always look after you. Trust me.'

'I do, but who's going to look after you?'

He smiled then, and cradled my face in his hands. 'I am more powerful than Khiara realises, she may well regret her decision to instigate Trials.'

Will looked up at the ceiling with a start. 'The others are here.' He reached into his jacket pocket and pulled out an ancient-looking velvet box. I glanced at it, and then back at him. He opened the box to reveal a beautiful ring. It looked very old and intricate in design. The delicate, gold filigree shoulders supported a large emerald, which sparkled with a green fire to rival Will's eyes.

'It looks like your eyes,' I said softly, touching the stone almost reverently.

'Would you wear this for me Elinor?'

I nodded, lost for words, and Will took the ring from its box, slipping it onto the third finger of my left hand. It fitted perfectly, just like all the dresses had.

'You will be safer now,' he said. 'Apologies for the lack of a church wedding.'

I laughed. 'Any excuse for a honeymoon.'

He raised a dark eyebrow. 'I need an excuse now?'

'Well, a permission slip maybe ...'

He pulled me back into his arms. 'I shall have to think of something for later then.'

'Seriously Will, the ring is incredible. Thank you.'

He bent to kiss me. 'The pleasure is mine.'

That man could have charmed bats out of a belfry.

He kissed me again, letting his lips linger against mine, and I melted against him. All thoughts of Trials and what the hell they actually were fled from my thoughts, which was almost certainly his intention. He tightened his hold as our bodies melded together, and one hand lightly slipped down my bare back, coming to rest on the curve of my bottom.

There was a light tap at the door and Luke's voice came through. 'Everyone is here.'

'I would be grateful if you and Jake could drive people to the club, and then you returned for us a little later,' Will replied. His other hand was already pulling down the zip of my dress. I looked up, and to my surprise, he winked.

'Twenty minutes?' came Luke's voice again.

'Make it forty.'

'You've got it.' Luke sounded amused. I heard him run upstairs, and then came the sounds of people leaving. The front door slammed, then silence. My dress slipped off my shoulders, with a little help from my friend, and pooled at my ankles.

'It'll crease ...'

Will lifted me bodily out of the dress, and set me down away from it. He picked it up and draped it across the chair. Never taking his eyes from my face, he slipped his jacket off and began to deftly unbutton his shirt. Seconds later, the shirt joined his jacket on the bed. Clad only in his elegant black suit trousers, he was the epitome of everything I'd always been warned about. Drop-dead gorgeous, sexy and oh-so dangerous. I swallowed nervously.

He held a hand out towards me. 'Come here to me Elinor.'

I closed the gap between us, taking hold of his hand. He pulled me closer still, his other hand tangling in my hair.

'I think we need a little together time,' he murmured.

He began to kiss me, his lips urgent and demanding.

'We'll be late—'

'*Ssssh.*'

'Khiara—'

With an exclamation of frustration, Will grasped my upper arms and held me away.

'I am the Elder of London,' he said patiently. 'I shall arrive when I choose to arrive, and I will also make love to my lady when I choose.'

'Do I get a say?'

'Do you wish to stop?'

'No.'

'Then please stop talking.'

* * *

Another shower later and we were dressed and waiting for Luke, but with only seconds to spare. The moment we were upstairs, there was a rap at the front door as Luke let himself in.

Will draped a black cashmere wrap around my shoulders as he ushered me toward the door. I had no idea where he'd got that from, I'd never seen it before. Its luxurious warmth enveloped me, and I smiled at his thoughtfulness. OK, so vampires don't feel the cold, but wandering around London in a flimsy backless dress at this time of year might have attracted some unwanted attention.

We followed Luke out of the front door and through the open gateway to the quiet road outside, where a gleaming BMW was ready and waiting. Will pulled the gates closed and they clanged together with a sound of finality. I shivered, wondering when we'd be back or if we'd even get back at all. Will opened the rear door of the car and gestured to me to get in. I expected him to sit in front with Luke, but he went around to the other rear door and slid in next to me.

'I could never pass up the chance of sitting in the dark with you.' He gave me a roguish grin.

'Insatiable,' I muttered.

All too soon, Luke pulled up outside Dusk. The tall figure of Stevie came out to meet us.

'You do not need to stay tonight, Stevie,' said Will. 'In fact, it would be safer if you do not. Some of the other vampires are rather keen on werewolf blood.'

Stevie nodded. 'You know where I am if you want me,' he said and, with a nod to me, he left.

The club felt strange without the bustle and chatter of humans, their warmth and their beating hearts. It felt eerily quiet too, without the usual pounding music and the cheerful chink of glasses. There must have been about forty vampires inside. Some stood by the long downstairs bar, others were in the comfortable seating area, and no doubt there were a few upstairs as well. I picked out the big doorman, Zach, who nodded to Will, and I spotted Roxy with the tall, dark-haired man I'd noticed the night Khiara came to the house. He had short straight hair, carefully spiked on top, and his left ear had been pierced several times with gold and diamond studs. He was dressed in a dark blue suit with a white t-shirt instead of a more formal shirt, and looked like a member of a successful rock band. He leaned up against a wall, but managed to look as comfortable as if he had been seated. He looked across at us, nodded to Will, and stared at me. His dark eyes appraised me openly. He stood up away from the wall, and turned to speak to Roxy. She nodded and they both came over to us.

'I'm Jake,' he said simply when he was standing in front of me. His accent was pure North London. He held a hand out and I shook it. 'Hi, Jake.'

He turned to Will. 'Khiara isn't here yet.'

Will nodded. 'I am aware of that. It is not entirely unexpected.'

Another woman walked over to us. She was tiny and beautiful, and appeared to be either of Chinese or Japanese extraction. She had the glorious, glossy blue-black hair that seems to bless most Asian people. Exquisitely dressed in a black satin kimono, with tiny dragons embroidered in gold silk down one side, she appraised me with dark, almond-shaped eyes. She held a tiny hand out to me. 'I am Aimee-Li Chann.' Her voice, like her, was small and perfect. I smiled at her and shook her hand. 'It's good to meet you Aimee-Li.'

'Would anyone like a drink?' Luke asked.

Drink? Drink blood in front of all these vampires? Did blood come in cans now?

Will turned to me. 'We can drink alcohol, although you, as a fledgling, will have to keep your intake to a minimum at first.'

I sighed. Just like being a teenager again. 'Can I have a beer?'

Will shook his head and turned to Luke. 'Could you bring some champagne upstairs?'

He started to lead me over to the stairs. Aimee-Li, Jake and Roxy followed us.

'So I can drink champagne but not beer?' I was confused.

'I did not say I was allowing *you* to drink it.'

'What are you, my father?'

His deep laugh did nothing to alleviate the frustration I felt. I didn't want to ask what the problem was with alcohol, I just knew I could do with some. I had no clue what would happen later, and something 'medicinal' to chase away the pit of dread residing in my stomach would have been very welcome indeed. Will led us to the farthest nest of sofas, and a couple of vampires who'd been sitting there stood and left hurriedly at our approach.

'Scary Mr Spooky,' I muttered quietly, knowing he'd hear me.

'Some good healthy fear is a useful commodity to instil,' came the dry reply.

We all sat down, with Will on one side of me, and Aimee-Li the other. Luke soon appeared at the top of the stairs, carrying two bottles of champagne in ice buckets, followed by Honyauti carrying several glasses. *Oh joy.* Almost involuntarily, I found myself pressing closer to Will at the sight of him. Luke set the bottles on the table in front of us, and Honyauti put the glasses down at the same time. Luke expertly opened the champagne and began to pour it. Will lifted a finger, as he began to fill another glass, and, picking it up, offered it to me.

'Alcohol will affect you differently now,' he said. 'At first it will make you feel inebriated very quickly, just as it did when you were a teenager.' He smiled. 'When you are older, it will affect you less and less.'

'So at your age you can't get drunk at all?'

'That is correct, although I still enjoy the taste.'

'Boring,' I laughed. 'What do you do to celebrate then?'

Green eyes sparkled at me. 'I have ways.'

I lifted the glass to my lips, but he stopped me before I drank any. 'I mean it Elinor, sip it at first, the effects will be instantaneous.'

Well, I didn't want to be the embarrassing girl who danced on tables, so I took a small, tentative sip of the sparkling liquid. Immediately, my taste buds exploded, and my head began to spin.

'Wow,' I whispered. 'I see what you mean.'

He took the glass from my suddenly nerveless fingers, and put it back on the table. Looking up at Luke, he said, 'Any sign?'

Luke shook his head. 'Shall I call her?'

Will stood up. 'Perhaps I should do that.' He looked back at me. 'Please stay here, I shall not be too long.'

He strode toward the stairs, and left me feeling just a touch desperate. Luke sat down next to me, and I felt better with him there, but with Honyauti sitting opposite in an armchair, staring at me with his dead eyes, I felt scared and very intimidated. I really hoped Will wouldn't be long.

Aimee-Li suddenly leaned across and, taking my left hand in her tiny one, stared at my ring. After a few minutes, she looked at me with a strange smile. 'The Ring of Porphyry, it means you are Will's chosen one for all eternity,' she said. 'He is wise in some ways to give you the ring tonight, but in other ways very foolish.'

'Why?' I asked, although I could probably guess the answer.

'Khiara will be so angry. Never in all her centuries has any one of her men found a love they preferred to hers.'

'Would she know the ring?'

'Every vampire will know the ring,' replied Aimee-Li. 'It is well known among us for its magical properties.'

I looked down at the beautiful emerald, and watched it shine with the same green lights that shone in Will's eyes. It glowed on my hand as though it were truly alive, and I wondered what magical properties it contained. Will had said it would keep me safe, whatever that meant.

'Porphyry was a magician, devoted to magical practices in both the white and black arts,' she continued. 'It is many centuries old.'

'How did Will come to have it?'

'His family was aristocratic and the ring has been in his family for centuries, but I do not know how it came to be there. Although I do know that Khiara expected it to be hers, yet it is now yours.'

'Should get the evening off to a good start then,' I said. Aristocrats, eh? That explained a lot. One day Mr William Whatever-His-Full-Name-Happened-To-Be and I were going to have a really long chat about his family. He knew all about me after all, so it was only fair.

I picked up my glass in an attempt at nonchalance and sipped the champagne carefully.

My head spun again. I blinked trying to clear the dizziness, and was left with the warm fuzzy glow you normally only get after several glasses of the stuff, not just a few sips. Rather shakily, I put the glass back on the table, and was relieved to feel Will close again. I looked up as he emerged at the top of the stairs and flashed a dazzling smile at me.

Luke stood up as he approached.

'Khiara is not at the house,' Will said without preamble.

'Neither is anyone else. Most of her people are downstairs, except for Vincente.'

'What should we do?' Luke looked perturbed.

'Wait another hour or so.'

Aimee-Li was chatting with Jake and Roxy now, and didn't appear to be listening to Will. I stood up, needing to be close to him, and he held a hand out to me as if he knew. Which I'm sure he did.

'Downstairs I think,' he said half to himself. He pulled my arm through his and began striding back toward the stairs.

'Slow down,' I pleaded as we reached the top of the stairs. 'I'm wearing a dress.'

He turned to look back at me with a wicked grin. 'Oh, believe me, I noticed.'

Will and I stood at the top of the stairs like a royal couple making an entrance. I looked down at the assembled throng of vampires below. Sure enough, there was no sign of Khiara. She was exceptionally beautiful enough to stand out in any crowd, even one such as this – where absolutely everyone assembled appeared incredibly attractive. A quick sweep of the people below assured us she was, indeed, conspicuous by her absence.

'Where do you think she is?' I asked.

'Playing one of her many mind games, no doubt.'

'Does this mean we win if she's a no show?'

'Oh, she will show at some point, I have no doubt. But not necessarily this evening.'

I still didn't understand what was going on, but then I didn't think I was expected to. I refrained from asking Will interminable questions, because they tended to irritate the hell out of him. A fact I'd discovered to my cost a few times.

We descended the stairs and all vampiric eyes suddenly focused on us. Everyone gathered below fell silent.

'For those of you who have not yet met her, this is Elinor, my chosen consort,' said Will, his deep voice strong and authoritative. *Consort?* No one spoke. He continued, holding my left hand up for everyone to see. 'She wears the Ring of Porphyry and no doubt you all recognise its significance.' There were a few mutters and nods amongst the throng. I spotted the hateful Katarina who was glaring daggers at me. The sooner she went back to Italy, the better. Luke appeared behind us on the stairs.

'Do you wish to make an announcement about Trials?' He asked Will.

'Not yet. My suggestion is that we stay here for an hour or so, and if Khiara does not arrive within the time we set, we will call Trials off for tonight.'

Luke nodded, and wandered off towards the bar and a rather attractive brunette. Will turned me to face him, his arms encircling my waist.

'Do you have regrets Elinor?' he asked softly. 'Do you still miss being human perhaps?'

'It's been hard to come to terms with,' I said. 'But you know that. I miss the theatre sometimes ... even rehearsals ...'

He stared down at me, his beautiful eyes shining with the emerald fire I loved so much. 'I am so sorry for the things you miss, but there really was no other way my love,' he said softly. 'I could not let you die, not once I had found you. I could not lose you. I *would* not lose you.'

'There's one thing I am sure of, there is no way on this earth I'll ever regret meeting you.'

His eyes sparkled as he smiled, and, bending his head, he kissed me. Just the scent of him made me shiver and want him again; the mixture of expensive cologne and the underlying masculine, exotically dangerous smell that was just him.

Holding me away again, he looked at me with a mixture of emotions. '*Ti amo*, I love you Elinor,' he said. 'I love everything about you, your hair, your eyes, your spirit'—he laughed softly—'even your reluctance, to a point.'

'As touching as these little declarations are, some of us would like to find Khiara,' said a cold, spiteful voice to my right.

Will and I turned as one, and came face to face with Katarina.

'Katarina, as unwelcome as ever.' Will's voice was cold. 'You are interrupting.'

'Perhaps so,' she continued viciously. 'But it is difficult to speak to you alone these days. Is the little fledgling permanently affixed to your side now, Will?'

'If you cannot keep a civil tongue in your head, Katarina,' said Will mildly, 'perhaps it should be permanently removed?'

Katarina took a step back from Will. Very wise. I knew that tone of his, and I was sure she did too.

'I meant no offence,' she repeated her phrase of a few nights ago, her voice meaning completely the opposite.

I drew a breath to speak, but somehow Will's voice sounded instantly in my head, '*No*.'

'Luckily for you, none has been taken,' said Will, and then, in a louder voice for all to hear, 'If Khiara does not arrive within the hour, we shall call it a night.'

Katarina stalked off towards Josephine.

I frowned at him. 'How did you speak in my head?'

'Do not frown, it mars your beauty.'

'You're enjoying all this aren't you?'

Laughing, he turned to watch Katarina and Josephine talking together.

He put a hand on my bare back, which was somehow both reassuring and erotic at the same time. 'Shall we go back upstairs and find a private corner?'

'I've met people like you before in clubs.'

'I seriously doubt that.'

A loud knocking on the club's front door made us both turn back. Will signalled to Luke to answer. Obediently he went over, closely followed by Honyauti. As he pulled open the heavy doors, something crashed in, causing Luke to stagger back. I heard Honyauti curse in his own language and Will moved with lightning speed to investigate. I followed him merely because I didn't want to stay alone. I had a very bad feeling about what we'd find.

On the floor was a body, a decapitated body, half-naked and covered with burns and abrasions such as I'd never seen in my life before. The wounds were filled with yellow pus and still weeping. Bile filled my mouth as I covered it with my hand. Just as we were taking in the grisly sight, a canvas bag was thrown through the open doorway, and I didn't need to see inside to know what it held. Luke turned it upside down and a head rolled out. The eyes had been gouged out and the mouth stuffed with garlic.

'Well,' said Will dryly, 'at least we know where Vincente is now.'

20 March

I gave Elinor the ring of Porphyry tonight. I had intended to wait a little longer, at least until she was sure of her feelings towards me, but a strange premonition made me give it to her tonight. The ring should ensure that if we were ever separated for any reason, I would always be able to find her, and hopefully it should also work in reverse. The very thought of a separation fills me with an unbearable pain, but with Khiara in town, I cannot rule out the possibility of a kidnap attempt. Khiara is many things, but she is, above all else, ruthless and completely without conscience. I shudder to even imagine how she would make Elinor suffer, were she to ever get the opportunity.

The ring has protective abilities; an ancient spell was cast upon it centuries ago. The magician Porphyry had studied vampirism along with the black and white magicks of the time. According to legend, his spell was a strong and effective one. The ring enables the wearer to have a certain amount of invincibility against holy items, such as holy water, the wafer and the sign of a blessed cross. It will not, however, protect the wearer from a finely sharpened wooden stake. But what could protect one from that? A stake through the heart will kill anyone, vampire or human.

I discovered these facts when the ring first passed into my family in the seventeenth century. With the ring was an ancient parchment, which listed its attributes. This was long before I met Emily and even longer before I, myself, became a vampire.

Some coincidences are just too strange to contemplate.

The parchment told of the rebirth of a red-haired night creature, a fledgling sired by a powerful vampire, an Elder, and this would precipitate the birth of a partnership that would make both vampires exceptionally powerful.

At the time I thought it all a fairy tale, and in latter years I thought the red-haired fledgling was Emily, as I had no belief in vampires. How wrong I was.

I can only surmise that one of my ancestors had been studying vampirism and then somehow acquired the ring as part of his studies.

I often wondered whether Khiara had known of the existence of the ring all along, and it was perhaps her reason for pursuing and eventually siring me. Not that she is flame-haired, but she would not have read the parchment, so it is possible she thought the powers would be attainable to whomever held the ring. It most definitely explains why she wants to destroy Elinor.

Whatever the reasons for events, which happened

during my long existence, the fates surely led Elinor across my path on that wonderful day over a year ago. I know she sometimes wonders about Khiara, but one day soon, when the Trials are over, I will sit her down and tell her everything, just like I promised I would months ago.

She needs to know she is the only woman who holds my heart.

Truly, I never loved Khiara, nor she me, although I once believed I was in love with Emily. It would have been difficult not to care for her. She was beautiful, sweet-natured, acquiescent and she loved me with all her soul. But Elinor is different, certainly not acquiescent, even the thought makes me smile.

Gentlewomen in the sixteenth and seventeenth centuries were taught to defer to their husbands at all times. I have grown with the centuries, and as women have changed, so have I.

Men have to be stronger now, in some ways, more than ever before. It takes a strength of character and a certain amount of confidence to be acceptable to this century's women.

I have seen firsthand the emancipation of women, I have witnessed the suffragette movement and I have watched as women became ever more independent and self-sufficient.

In more recent times, I watched history being made again, with Britain's first female prime minister.

Now we are in ever changing times, some good, a lot of them bad, but time marches ever relentlessly on and we are powerless to stop it.

I am well aware that in the twenty-first century any true, loving relationship is first and foremost a partnership. When Elinor is stronger and more well-versed with our way of life, I know she will be the perfect partner. That she is strong-willed is evident, but she is also extremely intelligent, caring and, of course, heart-breakingly beautiful. It is terrifying how quickly she has become an integral part of me, and a necessity to my well-being. I cannot be without her.

It is this very fact that makes me so very vulnerable, and vulnerable is something I have not been for centuries.

Chapter Twenty-Two

Threats

Will's eyes met mine briefly. 'Get her away from here,' he snapped at Jake, who was standing behind me with Roxy. She took hold of my arm and began to pull me back further into the club. I was too shocked, too dazed, to protest, even though I desperately wanted to stay near Will. Things had happened too fast, and I didn't want to lose sight of him. Supposing the next time I saw him, he was without his head?

'Let's go upstairs.' Roxy continued to drag me away from the grisly scene by the doorway.

When we were seated upstairs, I ran a shaky hand through my hair, 'Wasn't Vincente one of Khiara's people?'

Jake nodded. 'Clearly a dispensable one.'

'Why would they do that?'

'Either to try and put the blame with us or simply to start Trials off with a bang,' replied Jake.

Roxy still had her arm through mine and I was grateful for that. As I looked around at the various assembled vampires, I realised I still had no clue who was friendly and who wasn't. I felt more relieved than I can say when Will emerged at the top of the stairs. He strode unerringly toward us. I felt sure he would always find me easily, and for once I found that comforting.

'Are you all right Elinor?' he asked when he was close to us.

'I don't know.'

Jake and Roxy were suddenly gone from my side, and halfway across the floor towards the stairs, before I'd even missed them. Will lowered his tall frame onto the sofa next to me. He placed cool fingers to my face and turned me to look at him. 'I am more sorry than you could ever know for what you have just witnessed.'

Tears filled my eyes at his quiet words, and he wrapped his arms around me, pulling me close. 'Khiara's love of the macabre does not seem to have lessened much over the years.'

'Why would she do something so terrible to one of her own people?'

'Khiara rarely cares for anyone, she is interested only in power and control.'

'But what can it achieve?'

'Proof to me that she cares not whom she destroys, and if she can do this to one of her own, she is capable of far worse to one of my people.'

'Can you keep everyone safe?'

Will released me, keeping one arm around my shoulders. 'The truth is, I fear not. My main concern now is to keep you away from her.'

I shivered.

'Would you like to go home?'

'More than anything … but—'

'The body has been removed, there is no trace.'

Will stood and helped me to my feet. 'Luke will drive us.'

We walked slowly back toward the stairs, and Will kept his arm firmly around me. At that moment I felt as though I never wanted to let him out of my sight again. I'd never felt so insecure before in my life, if it was, in fact, insecurity I felt.

Luke appeared at the foot of the stairs, almost as though he'd materialised from thin air. 'Do you need a ride home?'

Will nodded. 'Please. Perhaps, afterwards, you would be good enough to oversee the securing of the club for me?'

Luke nodded, and led the way to the front doors. I stiffened as we neared the place where Vincente's mutilated body had been, and Will's arm tightened around me.

I tried to keep my eyes straight ahead, but couldn't help a sidewise glance. There was nothing to see.

As we drove away from the club I began to relax slightly, and the closer we got to Highgate, the better I felt. I knew I'd feel even better once the gates and the doors were secured against the outside world.

Two more nights passed and there had still been no news of Khiara. I wondered whether I was the only one who desperately hoped she'd gone back to Italy.

Will was non-commital, slipping into his inscrutable 'Elder' mode.

I felt as though everything had happened too fast, and I was trapped on a rollercoaster careering madly out of control. The confrontation with Edward Oldman had been shocking enough, but with Trials following so closely, my grip on reality seemed to have slipped. The phone rang constantly, which didn't help my shredded nerves.

After four more nights of constant phone calls and no more news, Luke arrived for a meeting with Will. I fully expected to be banished to another room, but strangely I wasn't.

'Katarina and Josephine are stirring up trouble amongst the ranks.' Luke sat in one of the armchairs.

I wouldn't say I felt overly surprised by that piece of information.

'In what way?' Will's voice was mild.

'Saying one of our people must have killed Vincente and kidnapped Khiara.'

Will gave a short laugh. 'Yes, I have heard that amusing little ditty. In fact, I probably have the bloody t-shirt.'

'Don't you think Khiara could be hiding just so we can be blamed?' I joined in the conversation. It all seemed clear as crystal to me. Scheming bitch. It was a good way to ensure Will couldn't beat her at the Trial thingies.

Luke shrugged and looked at Will, who was busy blowing perfect smoke rings at the ceiling. Good to know he was taking everything so seriously.

'What do you think Will?' asked Luke.

Will leaned forward and extinguished his cigarette in the ashtray. 'It is, of course, possible. But I must admit I do not have a clue what to do at the moment. Perhaps we should nail a "missing" poster on a lamp post in the immediate vicinity?'

I began mentally to write the copy.

Missing – one Italian female vampire.

Black hair, pointy teeth and a very nasty temper.

Answers (sometimes) to the name 'Khiara'.

The phone rang, Will sighed heavily and got up to answer it. Plucking the phone from its hub, he spoke curtly into it. 'Speak to me.'

I could hear a female voice chattering away, which verged on hysterical, but I couldn't make out the actual words.

'Preferably in English.'

There was a slight pause and then the voice continued at a slower pace.

'Very well, we shall come over.' Will replaced the phone and turned to face us, his expression stern. 'It would appear Grigori has been attacked.'

'Destroyed?' Luke asked the question I hadn't wanted to.

'No, for some reason, he has been left alive. Presumably so he can tell us all a tale.'

Luke muttered a curse.

Will continued, 'He is barely conscious and has been badly beaten, burned, and bound in silver chains with crosses.'

I shivered, remembering the pain of just one small silver belly bolt. 'Do you think it could be a trap?'

'It was certainly a trap for Grigori, one way or another.'

'*If* it's true.'

He looked at me then, and raised a dark eyebrow. 'When did you get so cynical?'

I shrugged. 'Around twelve years old.'

Will's steady gaze appraised me. 'That matter has been resolved.'

I wondered if it had. I didn't want to think about Edward Oldman ever again. Part of me wished I'd let Will kill him, although deep down I knew I could never have lived with it. Just seeing him again, after all those years, had brought some of the old nightmares to the surface. But I knew now was not the time to talk about it.

I glanced at Luke who had been watching both of us with a strange look on his face. Suddenly, he smiled. 'I've known Will for more than a hundred years, yet I've never seen him look at a woman the way he looks at you.'

I thought Will may well dispute Luke's words, but he just threw me an amused glance. 'Thanks for that Luke, you have just ruined my reputation as an incorrigible flirt.'

'I never said you weren't a flirt.' Luke grinned. 'Just that none of the other women meant anything. No one has until Ellie.'

Will's eyes glinted. 'I believe she knows that.'

Did I? I'd never been very good at having any kind of personal conversations, and the fact that one had suddenly become a three-way conversation was considerably adding to my discomfort.

'It is a good job vampires do not blush.' Will smiled, touching my cheek gently. 'Otherwise I have a feeling my little fledgling's cheeks would be matching her wonderful titian hair by now.'

'Are we going or not?' I stalked over to the door with as much dignity as I could, which thanks to years of dance training was quite considerable.

Luke opened the drawing room door for me with an exaggerated flourish, and as I went through he said to Will, 'Mind you, she is lovely.'

'And I am exceedingly jealous with a very violent temper.' Will followed me out.

'Don't worry, she only has eyes for you.'

'Just stop—God—how old *are* you two? You're like a couple of adolescent schoolboys.' I stood by the front door with my hands on my hips, and looked back at them as they stood together outside the drawing room. Mouth-wateringly gorgeous, and definitely dangerous, they were the kind of men most women could only dream about – if their imagination stretched that far.

'We are merely trying to lighten a distressing situation.' Will smiled. 'Shall we go?'

After securing the house and gates, we got into Luke's car, and he drove smoothly away. When we neared Chalk Farm, Luke turned into Adelaide Road, one of the many residential roads that led to Camden High Street.

Just before the main road, he took a left turn onto Eton Road, and I looked out at the elegant Victorian terraced houses. Who knew what secrets lurked behind their doors? I shivered again. Even with Will and Luke beside me, I wasn't feeling up to whatever was in there.

Luke pulled up under a Residents' Permit Only sign and turned off the ignition. We sat in silence for a few minutes.

'Showtime,' Will announced into the darkness, and I jumped.

I glared at him, and he leaned in to kiss me gently on the forehead. 'Come on, let us get this over with.'

We got out of the car, and Will ran lightly up the steps to the front door. After unlocking the door with a key from a large bunch of keys, he motioned us to follow.

I went in, and Luke followed me, closing the door behind him.

The sound of the door closing had an ominous finality about it, and I didn't like it one bit.

The vampire coming towards us I didn't like one bit either.

Katarina, of course.

She was casually dressed for once, in tight-fitting blue jeans and a red velvet hooded sweatshirt. She looked almost human, but where she came from, that was probably an insult.

'Katarina.' Will's voice was cold.

She took his saying her name as an invitation, and ran to him flinging her arms around his neck.

I really didn't like her.

Will disengaged her arms none too gently, pushing her away from him at the same time. 'Cut the theatrics. Just tell me what has happened.'

She gave him a baleful look, which would have cowed most men I'm sure. But Will is very definitely *not* most men.

'Grigori is in there,' she pointed at a door to my left.

OK, I very nearly felt a bit sorry for her then, but she suddenly shot me a venomous look, and all sympathy evaporated.

Will nodded and went to the left-hand door with Luke and myself following. Grigori was lying on a sofa, wearing nothing but a pair of black trousers, which were torn and filthy. His face was barely recognisable, it was horribly swollen with so many cuts, bruises and bites all over it, I doubt even his own mother would have known him. Both his eyelids were bruised and inflamed, and his eyes were partially closed. His large chest had been slashed with what could only have been a sword, because the wounds were deep and long. Cross-shaped burns covered almost every part of his flesh, whilst angry, weeping welts marred his upper body, and had almost certainly been caused by silver chains.

I couldn't begin to guess how anyone had managed to overpower such a giant of a man. Even if he'd been human, he would still have been a force to be reckoned with. The wounds were so similar to those of Vincente that I found myself picturing that dreadful scene again.

Unfortunately for Grigori, he was still conscious, and whoever had done this had clearly intended him to remain so, which meant they knew exactly what they were doing.

'What happened Grigori?' Will stood close to him and stared down at his battered face.

'They have my mistress,' he rasped through his swollen, black lips.

'Is that so? And "they" were?'

'Masked.'

'Handy.'

Grigori's eyelids fluttered closed, and I glanced at Will's stern face. His expression looked uncompromising. I went to speak, but he lifted a hand without looking at me, and I swallowed the words. I stared back at Grigori's swollen, beaten and bitten face, and his scarred body; surely no one would deliberately hurt one of their own people so badly. Would they? Could it really be some kind of trap?

Will strode to the door and I looked to Luke for guidance. He nodded and gestured that I should follow Will, which for once I did reluctantly.

He went a short way down the narrow dark hall and stopped at a door on the right-hand side. Opening the door, he turned to me. 'It would be better if you waited in here, Elinor.'

I went into the room and heard him shut the door behind me, and breathed a sigh of relief. Unfortunately, I didn't feel better for long, because I found myself face to face with both Katarina and Josephine.

Josephine was seated in a large armchair, elegantly dressed in slim-fitting black trousers and a loose knitted blue jumper, perfectly flattering her pale beauty. Her blonde hair hung loose to her shoulders like a shining waterfall, and she pushed it back from her face with a languid, almost bored movement. Her cold, light blue eyes raked down my body and back up to my face, although she didn't speak.

Katarina perched on one of the arms of the chair, looking like an evil little gnome, and she glared at me with such open hatred that I took a step back.

'Hallo *fledgling*,' said Josephine in her clear, cold voice. 'How very unusual not to see you attached to your Master.'

I held my arms out to my sides and waved my fingers. 'No strings.'

Katarina's face twisted in a contemptuous sneer. 'How long do you think you can hold onto Will, *fledgling*?'

Great. Just to make my week even more perfect, I was facing a confrontation with the bitchy twins of evil from Will's chequered past. I glanced down at the beautiful emerald ring glinting on the third finger of my left hand, its fiery depths still reminded me of the green lights in his eyes. I looked back at the vampire gnome. 'I don't think that's any of your damn business.'

Josephine snorted with derision. 'If Khiara couldn't hold him, then *you* definitely have no chance at all.'

'Khiara hasn't been with him for a long time. What can I say? Except he obviously prefers a younger woman.'

Both female vampires were suddenly very close, and invading my personal space.

These women were out to hurt me for reasons I knew nothing about. I couldn't believe it was just because of Will – gorgeous though he certainly is – there had to be more to it than that.

Will is only two rooms away, I reassured myself. I didn't really believe they would dare try anything with him so close. They might be psychotic, but I didn't think they were suicidal. Thoughts flew around inside my head at manic speed, whilst I kept both women in sight.

They began to circle me in opposite directions, for all the world like hungry sharks, making it really difficult to keep them both in my sights at the same time.

Katarina ran long, red-painted fingernails down my cheek, whilst Josephine came close behind me, pulling long strands of my hair between her slim fingers. She began to pull my hair gently at first, then harder, and finally she twined it around her fingers, so she could force my head back to expose my throat. I struggled to free my hair but she only held it even tighter.

I could feel their icy breath on my face now. They were so close they hemmed me in, and I didn't think I'd be able to fight them both off, but I'd make damn sure I took one of them down.

Katarina laughed suddenly, a sound like shards of ice shattering. It was the same laugh I'd heard in my nightmare weeks ago. I recognised it. My nightmare had suddenly become real life.

'Oh poor little fledgling. So young and so *afraid*,' she mocked. 'How will you ever become a *real* vampire?'

'I have a good teacher.' I struggled against Josephine's vicious hold on my hair.

Both women laughed nastily. Katarina suddenly dug her fingernails deep into my cheek, and raked her nails down my face and exposed throat with one swift malicious strike. I screamed as loudly as I could, and shoved her away from me with all my bodily strength. She lost her balance and fell to the floor, but sprang to her feet again in seconds. She'd grabbed my arms before I had a chance to do anything to Josephine.

The door behind us crashed open.

'What the fuck is going on in here?' Will's voice.

Relief flooded through me at the sound of his voice. Katarina and Josephine let go of me instantly as if I'd burnt them.

They turned to look at him innocently, and Katarina smiled sweetly. 'Just a little female bonding,' she purred.

Will came further into the room and, grabbing an arm of each woman, hauled them roughly away from me. They hissed and spat, which had no effect on him whatsoever.

He put his body between us and looked at me properly for the first time, noticing the scratches on my cheek and throat made by Katarina's talons. I felt the cool blood as it seeped from the wounds and trickled slowly down my skin.

Will narrowed his eyes. 'Which one of them did that?'

Both women looked really afraid now. I wasn't sure I should give him the answer, I felt afraid of what he might do.

'Elinor?'

I shook my head slightly.

'I see.'

With a blur of movement, he punched suddenly backwards, hitting both women simultaneously.

Both fell to the floor.

'Now *that* is a definite improvement.' He came close and kissed the blood from my face. 'Blood-thirsty bitches. Always have been, and always will be, unless they cross me again, in which case they will cease to exist altogether.'

Katarina and Josephine chose that moment to stir, and Will released me to go back to them. He walked forward and stood on each woman's arm, to prevent them from moving.

'I shall now tell you the same thing I told Honyauti.' His voice sent chills down my spine. 'If you ever – *ever* attempt to hurt Elinor again, I shall have you both destroyed. In fact, I will personally end your miserable existences, with very great pleasure.'

Katarina tried to move, but Will ground his boot heel into her arm to prevent her. She screamed and snarled, her face bestial. 'Khiara will be so angry you've hurt us,' she spat.

'I think not. You drew first blood amongst my people. Not just any person either, but my chosen consort. I could have you both torched for this, *with* Khiara's approval, and you know it.'

The women looked terrified.

Luke came into the room at that point and surveyed the scene before him without emotion. 'All right Ellie?'

'Yes, thank you.'

Will turned to look at Luke. 'Everything sorted out in there?' Luke nodded. 'Then let us get the hell out of here.' He turned back to the women still on the floor 'Have I made myself clear, *ladies*?'

'For now,' said Katarina, her pretty face spoilt by the evil hatred that twisted her tiny features.

Will reached down and pulled her up by her hair. 'Do not presume to think I do not know who attacked Elinor,' he said. 'I ask again, have I made myself clear?'

'Yes,' she replied. Her eyes wide and scared now. 'It's just that ... I ... love you Will.'

He made an exclamation of disgust and, lifting her up by the arms, flung her across the room. She hit the far wall with a crash, but landed like a cat on all fours, hissing.

'Keep. Away. From. Elinor.' Emphasising each word heavily, Will grabbed my arm, and pulled me toward the door, which Luke opened for us. Keeping a firm grip on me, he opened the front door, and bundled me through it.

Luke closed the door behind us, and pressed the remote on his key fob to open the car doors. I clambered thankfully, but not terribly gracefully, into the back seat, and Will followed me in.

Luke got in the driver's seat, and we pulled away from that horrible house and its hateful inhabitants.

I slowly breathed a sigh of relief. Will turned my face to his. 'Poor Elinor, it is difficult being with me is it not? First Honyauti and then the bitches from hell.'

'Would it be anyone you were with, or is it just me?'

'You are a very young vampire and I am a very old one, plus I am Elder of the city. It is not protocol for the two of us to be together as partners. Fledglings are usually kept around merely as amusement for the older ones to share – especially the pretty ones.'

'Which is why Honyauti—' I began as realisation dawned on me.

'Which is why Honyauti thought he could join you in the bath.'

'Honyauti did *what*?' asked Luke.

Will laughed, putting an arm around me, 'It will never happen again. Bad mistake on his part.'

'Just a bit,' said Luke with heavy sarcasm. 'What happened?'

'I showed him the error of his ways.' Will calmly lit a cigarette.

'*That* I believe.'

We pulled up outside the house. Will opened the car door and sprang lithely out.

He leaned back in, and held his hand out to me. I put my hand in his, and slid out of the car. As I shut the door I smiled at Luke. 'Thanks.'

He flashed a grin at us as he drove off.

Once inside the house, Will went through the usual rigmarole of locking the door and setting the alarm before he turned his attention to me again. 'I think I am going to start killing.'

'What? Who?' I felt startled.

'Anyone else who tries to hurt you. Enough is enough.'

He grabbed my hand and made for the stairs going up. OK, this was different. I'd never been up those stairs. A few weeks ago, Will had nearly given me a tour of the house, but we'd got a bit distracted.

He ran up the first flight of stairs, pulling me behind him. Then we were on the first floor's spacious landing, carpeted in the same dark blue as downstairs.

A Knole sofa, upholstered in a heavy blue brocade fabric, nestled in an alcove, and a wooden settle stood underneath a large, shuttered window. There were four doors, which led off the landing.

'Bedrooms,' said Will without stopping at any of them. He carried on up a narrower staircase, which opened up onto a tiny carpeted landing. A single door faced us, which Will opened and pulled me in after him.

We were now in a small windowless room, which had a large domed skylight made entirely of glass instead of a more conventional ceiling. It looked absolutely amazing.

I could see the velvety night sky through the skylight and the stars that twinkled down at us. Almost like our own private observatory.

'How beautiful,' I said, and felt a little perturbed when Will gave a bitter laugh. I gave him a startled look.

'It is at night.' He put his hands on his hips, and looked upwards. 'But come daybreak, it is not a nice place for vampires.'

I stared at him in horror. 'You've actually *left* people in here?'

'Only anyone who overstepped the mark.'

'No ... no ... no ...' I shook my head as I backed out of the room, and Will moved swiftly forward to grab my arms.

'I did not show you this room to scare you, merely to illustrate what I intend to do to anyone who steps out of line in the future.'

'But they'd disintegrate—turn to dust—it would be cold-blooded murder.'

'Elinor, sweetheart, there are people out there who would torture you for simply existing, and some who would certainly destroy you for even speaking to me. Others would rape you in ways more horrific than you could ever imagine, just for fun.'

He cupped my face in his hands. 'I will not tolerate anyone else hurting you *ever*, so examples have to be made. It is a show of power and as such is vitally important.'

'What are you going to do?'

'One more false move from the vile Katarina, and she will be dust. I intend to put her in this room, and shall then make the decision whether to allow her to leave the next night, or whether to extend her stay, and force her to greet the dawn.'

I looked into those pitiless, green eyes and I knew at that moment in time he was in a different place, and it was nowhere I wanted to be.

25 March

I would have loved to drive the nearest fence post through that evil bitch Katarina's heart. Tonight she tried my patience beyond belief. Drawing blood from Elinor has sealed her fate as far as I am concerned, it is just a question of when ...

Something will have to be done and done swiftly, to show the rest of Khiara's foul entourage they simply cannot undermine my authority in my own city.

Chapter Twenty-Three

Punishment

The nights had at last turned warmer and lighter, so the sunset was now much later each evening. Although Will had assured me I would eventually wake earlier, it hadn't happened yet, and it meant I had less time with him, which I really hated.

I knew Will, as a Master vampire, could pretty much pick and choose his hours, almost like a human, and I desperately wanted to be with him all the time. Will, as usual, dealt with my frustration with his customary patience and sensitivity. He spent a lot of time reassuring me about his feelings for me. My own confidence as a vampire had grown, thanks to his patient teaching, and I grew stronger every night. At long last, I had begun to embrace my immortal status, although I still could not – *would* not – feed directly from a human, a fact that only Will and Luke were aware of. This was probably due to the fact that I found the very thought of it abhorrent. Drinking blood was bad enough, but drinking blood from a *person*?

Several weeks passed, and there had still been no sight or sign of Khiara. Grigori had recovered from most of his injuries now, although he would always bear the cross-shaped burns. Apparently, injuries caused by holy items do not heal on vampires.

My face and neck no longer bore any sign of Katarina's attack, although it remained all too fresh in my memory. Will hadn't mentioned the incident since, and I hoped his threat to turn her into a pile of dust had been forgotten.

I should have known better.

One night when we came back to the house, a figure

emerged from the shadows by the front gates to confront us.

Katarina herself. Joy.

Will instantly pushed me behind him, and regarded her coldly. 'Why are you here?'

She widened her dark eyes reproachfully. 'You are the Elder of this city and in Khiara's absence you are responsible for us.'

Will lit a cigarette, blew a plume of smoke directly at her and narrowed his eyes. 'There is such a thing as an invitation, and to my knowledge, you have not been issued with one.'

'We still need your help to find Khiara. Josephine and I are afraid.'

I suppressed a snort.

Afraid? Somehow I didn't see the Twins of Evil being afraid of very much at all.

'Why don't you go back to Italy?' I said, unable to keep quiet any longer.

Katarina shot me an evil look, and continued talking to Will. 'We have no protection in the house here.'

'Then I suggest you either join Grigori, Honyauti or Luke, in one of my other houses,' replied Will.

'Or go back to Italy,' I said again in my most helpful manner.

'Elinor,' chided Will softly, then turned back to Katarina. 'You will be far safer with Honyauti than with anyone else. I am not prepared to have either of you near Elinor.'

'We won't hurt your precious little *fledgling*,' said Katarina viciously.

'I wonder whether my feelings are clear enough on the matter.' Will pushed Katarina away from the gates, so she couldn't see when he entered the code into the panel to open them. As they swung open, he turned back to her.

'Why not come into the house for a while and we can discuss everything more fully?'

Katarina eyed him warily, but his face was impassive and devoid of expression.

He looked outwardly as calm as ever, and his eyes gave nothing away.

However, I knew Will well enough to know that anyone with even a modicum of sense would have declined his kind offer, and run away as fast as possible. Katarina, quite clearly, had no sense whatsoever.

Tossing her head she flounced through the gateway in front of him. Stupid woman.

She'd been around for a hundred years or more, and still had no more sense than she'd been sired with.

Will closed the gates and walked toward the front door. As he unlocked it, Katarina pushed in front of me so she could get behind him. Childish, for someone so old.

We all went into the drawing room, where Will flopped gracefully onto the sofa and pulled me down beside him.

Katarina's eyes narrowed jealously at the gesture, and she pouted as she sat sullenly in an armchair opposite us. 'We would prefer to stay here.'

Will gave a short laugh. 'Of that I have no doubt. But you would never be my first choice for a house guest.'

'You have plenty of rooms.'

'A castle would seem too small if you were in it.'

He stroked the back of my hand with his thumb while Katarina watched.

'Your upstairs rooms have wooden shutters.' She tried again. She'd clearly had a better nose around than I had.

'I really would not want my housekeeper to have a heart attack.'

Housekeeper? I'd never seen one, but I had always wondered how the house always looked so clean.

Somehow I couldn't picture Will wielding a Dyson, and I laughed suddenly.

Will turned to look at me in surprise and raised his eyebrows.

'Sorry,' I said at once, 'I was just picturing you cleaning the house.'

His lips twitched, but when he turned back to Katarina, his face became impassive once more. 'I do have one room I am prepared to allow you to stay in.'

He stood and walked over to her. She immediately gave him a provocative look with wide eyes. So transparent. He went towards the door and Katarina rose gracefully to her feet and followed him.

I followed both of them, hoping he didn't have in mind what I thought he had.

Naturally he had. He headed straight upstairs with the vampire gnome behind him, and, reluctantly, I followed.

Will opened the door to the skylight room and, grabbing Katarina's arm, pulled her inside.

'Will …' I began, but he shot me a warning look.

'Now Katarina,' he said in even, dangerous tones. 'This is a room you are most welcome to stay in. Elinor thinks the view of the night sky is beautiful.'

Katarina looked upwards at the skylight, and drew in a hissing breath. 'You cannot kill me. Khiara would destroy you – you *and* your little fledgling.'

'You drew first blood Katarina, against Khiara's express orders, *and* after she had warned you,' replied Will, his eyes glinting dangerously. 'I simply will not tolerate this kind of behaviour. An example has to be made, and you are it.'

Katarina gave a feral snarl as she lunged for the door, but she could never be faster than Will. He hit her violently with the back of his hand, sending her hurtling back into the room. She fell to the floor, where she lay like an exotic, broken doll.

'Will—' I said again, but stopped when he turned to face me with a muttered curse.

'Elinor, please do not interfere in matters you do not understand.' He sounded angry. 'Either keep quiet or go downstairs.'

I stared at him, stricken. It had been a long time since he'd been short-tempered with me, and my first thought was to get the hell out of that room. I turned to walk out, but he crossed the room swiftly, and wrapped his arms around me to prevent me from leaving.

'Forgive me,' he said. 'Being an "evil elder" is rather too much responsibility with you watching me.'

When I looked up at him, he gave a rueful smile. 'You may, however, go downstairs if you prefer.'

'Would the outcome be any different?'

'No.'

Releasing me, he crossed the room again, and opened the door of a built-in cupboard. He pulled out some heavy chains with handcuffs attached, and snapped the handcuffs onto Katarina's slender wrists. He then secured the other end to a ring on the wall I hadn't noticed before.

'She will be secure enough for a while now. Shall we go?'

He held the door open, and motioned me to go through. I went back out to the landing. My thoughts were muddled. The fact that Katarina and I had a mutual hate thing going was undeniable, but I really didn't want to be instrumental in her ultimate destruction.

I had started down the stairs blindly, when Will caught hold of me around the waist and stopped me. 'You really hate all this, don't you?'

I turned to face him and the unhappiness must have shown on my face.

He put his hand against my cheek gently. 'I do not want you to see me as a monster,' he murmured, 'but I have to be strong in this matter. Any sign of weakness will ultimately threaten our future together.'

'I don't understand.'

'Then I shall attempt to explain.'

When we were back in the drawing room, we sat on the sofa, and he took hold of both my hands as he faced me. 'I have already allowed Honyauti to survive after he attacked you, theoretically he is on our side, and made a genuine mistake, so I got away with that.'

'You just tore his throat out.'

'The fact is, I still allowed him to survive. We heal fast Ellie, you know that.'

I nodded.

'Katarina, if you like, is on "the other side". If she goes unpunished, others will hear of it, and it will be seen as a sign of weakness. Other Elder vampires will come to London. You certainly won't be safe, and eventually, neither will I.'

With his words, I realised for the first time what a dangerous game he was playing, if, indeed, it could be called a game.

'But do we really have to kill her?'

Will's eyes sparkled. 'My lovely, sweet Elinor, you are still far too nice to be a vampire.'

'You're just making fun of me now.' I was getting seriously pissed off. 'It was a reasonable question.'

'I apologise.' He didn't look remotely sorry. 'What would you have me do rather than kill her?'

I really didn't want the responsibility of choosing Katarina's fate, but I knew Will would insist on an answer. 'Perhaps do something that wouldn't heal, then everyone could see she's been punished.'

Will smiled at me, pleased. 'Exactly right and a very intelligent deduction. So what do you suggest?'

I suddenly realised he was skilfully backing me into a

metaphorical corner. I looked down unable to meet his probing gaze.

'Elinor?'

'Why do I have to say?'

His lips curved. 'Because, my sweet, it was you she attacked, and it is *you* who does not want her turned to dust.'

Oh. Lucky me.

'I think you already have an idea, but you just want me to say it,' I said miserably. 'Will, I can't do this.'

Well, if I'd thought he would relent, I was sadly mistaken. He just reached for his cigarettes and lit one, watching me steadily as he smoked. 'You have to, I am afraid, otherwise she is dust.'

I looked at him reproachfully, but he was unmoved.

'No amount of reproachful looks from those beautiful blue eyes are going to get you off the hook either.'

I stood up and crossed the room, staring unseeingly at the rows of books on his bookshelves. It was easier than sitting uncomfortably under Will's steady stare. I clasped my hands together and closed my eyes briefly.

I felt Will's hands touch my shoulders and jumped. I hadn't heard him move. He pulled me back against him, and brushed my cheek with his lips.

I turned in his arms. 'A Holy item.'

He nodded approvingly. 'Yes.'

'A cross ... holy water perhaps ...' My voice faltered.

'Somewhere visible naturally. So where do you suggest?'

I balked at the idea of disfiguring Katrina's face, much as I hated her. 'On her arms?'

To my consternation, Will laughed. 'Well maybe as an added bonus.'

'Not her face—please—not her face.'

Will moved in closer, pinning me against the bookshelves with his body.

He tunnelled his fingers in my hair, looking down at me with a serious expression. 'I am very much afraid it has to be her face. Surely it is better than being reduced to dust?'

'She'll be back for revenge.'

Will smiled grimly. 'Then she will definitely be dust. We simply cannot afford any sentimentality as far as she is concerned. We have to give a show of strength. Khiara would have no qualms about punishing her, and, indeed, if she ever deigns to come back, I have no doubt that Katarina will be on the receiving end of more wrath from her mistress.'

'Why is she so stupid?'

'Well, as with humans, not all vampires are intelligent. She has probably only lasted this long because of Khiara and Josephine, otherwise she would have been dust long ago.'

He walked away from me and over to the pine chest, where he swept the magazines on its top to the floor with one swift gesture. Opening the lid, he riffled through the contents, eventually pulling out a large black box and a phial of water.

'You keep those things here?' I was horrified.

'Never know when you might need a holy item. It is our secret though.'

That was one secret I could have done without. He put both items in his jacket pocket, and replaced the lid and the magazines.

I suddenly remembered what he'd said earlier about a housekeeper. 'Do you really have a housekeeper?'

He gave me an amused glance. 'Of course. How else do you think the house and our clothes get clean? Elves?'

I laughed.

He touched my hair gently. 'It is the first time you have laughed for hours, and pleasing to hear.'

I ignored the comment because I wanted to know more. 'Doesn't she wonder why she can't see you?'

'But she does see me. She just does not see you yet.'

'How can she see you?'

'I am often around in the afternoon as you know, I have to pay her after all. She thinks my wife is at work all day, and she knows I am a club owner. It explains my nocturnal lifestyle. She only comes in three times a week, it is really not a problem.'

'How can she clean the bedroom and the bathroom?'

He gave me a long-suffering look. 'I move you to the dressing room and keep the door locked.'

He made everything sound so easy, and I suppose for him, it was. Plenty of practice at being devious made him perfect. The thought of Will having to move my 'dead' body around did make me smile though. It was like some old Ealing Comedy farce.

An unpleasant thought suddenly struck me. 'Please tell me I don't have to torture Katarina myself.'

'No, that is something I can help with, although unfortunately you must be present. It will not be pleasant for you, I am afraid.' He walked towards the door, expecting me to follow. Reluctantly, I did. If it would make us safer, then there was no choice. I followed him back upstairs, feeling worse with every step.

When we reached the top landing, he turned to me. 'We do not have any alternative in this matter, Elinor, you have to trust me.'

'I do trust you.'

'All I ask is that you do not interrupt or interfere. Remember, this is a show of strength, and it is vitally important that this "message" gets across to others.'

I nodded and he smiled briefly. 'Good. Let us get it over with.'

He strode into the room where Katarina was sitting

sullenly on the floor, a large bruise on her cheek where Will had hit her, and angry, bleeding welts on her wrists where she had been trying to break free from the silver handcuffs.

'Khiara will destroy you both for this,' she hissed.

'I doubt it.' Will sounded unconcerned.

'She will tear your little fledgling into tiny pieces and feed on them,' Katarina continued, spitting out each word with venom.

Will raised an eyebrow. 'Well, interestingly, it is my "little fledgling", as you call her, that did not want you turned to dust. For some reason she does not want to see you destroyed. So a different punishment is to be instigated.'

Katarina glared up at him. 'It is not her place to make decisions. She should be nothing more than a plaything. She has no right to be by your side as an equal.'

'Would you rather be dust?' Will walked around her, and she moved to keep him in her sight.

'Of course not.' She twisted to give me a contemptuous glare. 'But be very careful what you do to me. It may also be done to her *tenfold*!'

'More threats Katarina?' Will reached into his jacket pocket, bringing out the black box. He took off the lid and handed it to me to hold. My hand trembled as I took it. Will took hold of a thin leather strap that lay nestled in the satin lining of the box and pulled it carefully out. A large silver cross on the end of the strap spilled out, momentarily blinding me, and I averted my eyes from its glow.

Will moved toward Katarina, dangling the cross from its strap. She stared at it, mesmerised. 'You wouldn't dare ...' She sprang lithely to her feet and backed away from him. He continued to walk towards her.

'Oh, I dare.'

She had her back against the wall now, and there was nowhere else to run. With a rapid movement, Will had her handcuffed wrists held above her head. She struggled and kicked out at him, but he was far stronger. I turned my head as the cross seared into her flesh, and she screamed in agony. Seconds later, she howled like a wounded animal as he pressed the cross to the white flesh on her forehead. She spat and cursed in Italian, and the smell of burning flesh filled the room, making me feel weak and nauseous. As Will released her hands, she slumped to the floor again, her dark eyes burning with such hatred that I stepped back.

I leaned against the farthest wall, desperately wanting to be out of this room, away from the torture, and the smells and sounds of such excruciating pain. I screwed my eyes tightly against tears that threatened to fall, and clenched my hands tightly, digging my nails into my palms.

'Stay where you are Elinor.' Will obviously felt my desire to escape. He picked up the box where it had fallen, and coiled the cross and its strap back into it. He held out his hand to me for the lid, which I'd inadvertently dropped to the floor. Obediently I picked it up and gave it to him. He glanced at me briefly before returning the box to his jacket pocket.

Katarina's beautiful face was marred forever. There were two livid, cross-shaped burns, one on her forehead and one on her right cheek. She continued to glare up at Will, her eyes burning red with blood lust and anger.

Will took the phial of holy water from his pocket and turned it around with his fingers, looking at Katarina all the time.

'You dare not do anything else to me!' she screamed. 'You would never survive Khiara's wrath.'

Will stood directly in front of her, his eyes blazing with anger as he looked down at her. 'Do not ever presume to tell me what I do, or do not, dare. You are lucky that my love for Elinor has made me listen to her voice of reason, otherwise you would have been a pile of dust by morning. I have already told you I will not tolerate attacks on Elinor, your empty threats, or your pathetic attempts at undermining me in my own city. You will damn well show me some respect from now on, or quite simply you will not survive.'

He squatted in front of her and carefully uncorked the phial. 'I take it you know what this is?'

Katarina just continued with her torrent of verbal abuse in Italian.

Will merely raised his eyebrows and, standing up, hauled her up by the neck at the same time. Leaning over her, he slowly and very deliberately dribbled some of the Holy Water onto Katarina's neck, where it trickled its tortuous way down her body. Her flesh bubbled and burned instantly as each drop touched her, and she howled like a wild animal. Blood-flecked spittle flew from her lips as she cried in agony. Her screams were in turn pitiful and then vengeful.

Will remained completely unmoved. 'You are extremely fortunate I am not forcing you to drink it.'

Tears trickled down my cheeks, as I once more dug my fingernails into the palms of my hands. I squeezed my eyes tightly shut again to stop more tears from falling. When I opened them, Katarina was unconscious once more.

'That should do.' Will calmly corked the phial and returned it to his pocket. Unlocking the handcuffs from Katarina's wrists, he picked up her lifeless body as though it weighed no more than a feather. How ironic that the only way she could be in his arms was when she was unconscious.

Tears flowed unheeded down my face, and I drew in a shaky breath as I tried to control them. Will looked at me then, his eyes sympathetic. 'Well done Elinor,' he said. 'I know how hard it was for you.'

Carrying Katarina, he walked to the door, and I followed silently. He went downstairs and I stumbled behind like an unhappy wraith. Outside the door to the drawing room he gestured with his head that I should go in. 'I shall be back in a moment.' He carried on downstairs.

I went in and sat on the sofa, burying my head in my hands.

Weren't vampires meant to be strong, cold and unfeeling? Why was I so different? I didn't think I would ever make a very good vampire. Perhaps Katarina was right after all, and I was the worst partner that Will could ever have chosen.

What if he changed his mind and thought me more of a liability?

What would happen to me without his protection?

He came back in at that moment, and I raised a tear-streaked face to him. He dropped to his knees in front of me, and put his arms around me. '*Sssh*—Elinor, it is over.' He gently wiped the tears from my face. 'She is safe in the cellar, and Luke will take her and Josephine to his house tomorrow. It had to be this way, you know that.'

I nodded miserably. He put his forefinger under my chin, and raised my face to his.

'So what else is worrying you?'

I might have known nothing would ever escape his notice.

It never did.

I was betting no previous girlfriends had ever got away with anything either.

He was one very scary man.

'Suppose you decide I'm too much of a liability and you don't want me around anymore?' I asked, as more tears threatened to fall.

He sat next to me on the sofa, and pulled me close against him. 'I do not know what else I can do to convince you of my feelings for you. I do not give my love lightly, I never have. There have, of course, been many women. I may be hundreds of years old, but I am still a man with a man's appetite.'

I stayed quiet for once.

'I want you here with me—not just for a few months, Elinor and not merely for a bit of entertainment, I want you with me for eternity. We have been through all this before.'

I looked into his lovely green eyes and felt better – calmer.

'You were right before when you said I'd never been truly in love.'

'I know that.'

'I couldn't survive without you now.'

'I think you would,' he smiled but when I went to speak, he put a finger against my lips. 'But you will never have to find out because it is not going to happen.'

'I love you.'

He leaned forward to kiss me. 'And I love you, my beautiful fledgling.'

It had been a very long, painful night, and I became aware of the dawn's hungry approach. I closed my eyes and leaned back in the sofa.

Will immediately looked concerned, 'What am I thinking?' He helped me to stand, and then scooped me up in his arms. I relaxed against him immediately, and his arms tightened around me.

'Dawn's very close, it is time for all good fledglings to be in my bed.'

'All of them?'

He laughed his low, sexy laugh. 'Only the one in my arms.'

His voice seemed to come from a great distance and almost immediately the darkness swallowed me.

2 May

In almost three hundred years, I have not found administering punishment exactly difficult, at least, not until tonight. The sight of Elinor suffering along with Katarina very nearly broke my resolve. In my opinion, the little witch deserved to die for what she did to Elinor, and die very painfully. But Elinor did not want her destroyed, and the choice had to be hers to make.

I am relieved, however, that she is as she is, it is what makes her so very different from the rest of our kind.

I feel no guilt whatsoever at defacing the odious Katarina. It is beyond my comprehension how, or even why, Khiara has continued to tolerate and shelter her. Khiara generally does not suffer fools gladly, if at all, so Katarina must have had her uses, although I cannot imagine what they could possibly be.

Elinor was completely exhausted, and I felt concerned and appalled for not noticing her discomfort earlier.

The newly-fledged vampire has similar traits to those of a human child or young animal in many ways. Its strength seeps away quite dramatically with the approach of dawn and it tends to collapse wherever it may be at the time.

Most nights I am well aware of the time and am able to make sure Elinor is safely in bed long before dawn, but tonight I was preoccupied, and I have to reproach myself for the omission.

To the untrained eye, the fledgling would appear dead, as indeed we all do when we are at rest, which is another reason to be safely at home well before the dawn.

I am hoping Khiara's return is imminent, and she will take her revolting followers back to Italy. I cannot believe she has stayed away so long, but I am convinced it is all part of Trials.

I long for my city to be back to normal. I have a relationship to nurture and, for that, I need the enemies within to be gone.

Chapter Twenty-Four

Recreation

Exactly an hour after sunset the next night, Luke arrived to collect the poisonous gnome. Will went downstairs to let him in the cellar door, and said I should go with him. It wasn't a request.

The livid, red scars on Katarina's face stood out violently against the pale beauty of her face. I still felt wholly responsible for her ordeal and, judging by her curses and threats, so did she. From what little I did understand of her ravings, both my human parentage and my siring were extremely questionable. Many of her screamed threats were in Italian of course, but I still had the feeling most of them were directed at me. Will, I knew, spoke fluent Italian, but he didn't seem inclined to translate the threats for me.

'Well if she meant only half of the threats I vaguely understood, I'm in big trouble,' I said wryly as Will closed the cellar door behind them.

He smiled. 'I think you would be more than a match for her now.'

'You think so?'

'I know so. You are, after all, descended from an exceedingly superior line.'

'Wasn't she sired by Khiara?'

'No. A renegade attacked her and I believe Grigori dusted him some eighty years ago. Josephine took her in as a servant for Khiara.'

Once again I almost felt sympathy for her. 'That's revolting. No wonder she hated me from the word go.'

Will rested his hand on my back as he guided me upstairs. 'You are indeed most privileged.'

'To be hated?'

'To be so adored by me.'

'No less arrogant tonight then.'

'Mind your manners, young lady.'

Once upstairs, I automatically headed for the drawing room and sat on the sofa. Will came and sat next to me. 'How are you feeling tonight Elinor? Would you like to go out?'

I thought about leaving the safety of the house for a moment. Part of me felt safer inside with everything that had happened over the previous few weeks, but another part of me wanted to simply escape its four walls and do something completely different.

'I'm not sure. What do you have in mind? What did you do before I came here? Have a few beers with the boys, watch a football match and chat up some girls?'

That did make Will laugh. 'Sounds too indescribably dull for words.'

'So what *did* you do?'

He regarded me thoughtfully for a moment. 'Hunted, fed, slept. Come to think of it, that sounds too indescribably dull for words too.'

I smiled. 'Somehow, I can't imagine you suffering anything dull.'

'I happen to know there is a large rock concert at Wembley tonight. Do you fancy that?'

'Who's playing?'

'I believe the collective age of the band almost totals my own.'

I laughed. 'You have to be talking about the Stones. But their tickets get sold out months before a gig, unless you pay the exorbitant prices the ticket touts charge of course.'

Will merely put a hand in his inside jacket pocket and produced two concert tickets with a flourish.

'How?'

His lips quirked upwards. 'Oh, I know a man, who knows a man, who ate a ticket tout.'

I shook my head at him. He was completely incorrigible. 'I'd love it.'

'Good. I have a cab coming in half an hour.'

I raised my eyebrows. 'Pretty sure of my answer, huh?'

'I know you are a dedicated rock chick.'

I wondered how he had ever discovered the Stones were playing at Wembley. Perhaps Stevie had told him. Although I supposed he kept his eye on the music press because of the nightclub. Will struck me as far too sharp a businessman not to take his own business seriously.

About an hour later, the taxi dropped us as close to the main entrance of the Arena as it could. After we'd got out, Will leant back in to pay and have a short conversation with the driver. I watched the throng of music fans making their way to the various entrances. The familiar thrill of a prospective live rock concert ran through me, and it was as much as I could do not to grab Will's hand and run for the nearest entrance. There were so many people. More humans in one place than I'd seen since being turned.

I looked around to drink in the atmosphere, loving every moment already. One of my favourite things had always been to go to as many concerts as I could afford, when I wasn't working of course. As Will had been stalking – sorry – *observing* me for a year, he would have been very aware of that.

Taking hold of my hand, he strode confidently toward the nearest entrance. As usual, a great many women turned to look at him, and, as usual, he didn't appear to notice. He had dressed in blue jeans, t-shirt and his favourite black leather jacket, but he still stood out from the masses. The old vampire charisma again perhaps. He showed the tickets to a security person at one of the turnstiles who scanned them and waved us through.

Once in the outer ring of the arena, I became instantly aware of the noise, both of the crowd, and of the support band who were already on stage. The place seethed with a mass of people, all ages, shapes and creeds, buying t-shirts, programmes, badges, alcohol and the rather dubious greasy fast food on offer.

An overwhelming smell of hot dogs and hamburgers hung on the air, so heavy it was almost visible. I saw everything through different eyes now, with sight I now knew had become enhanced since my rebirth as a vampire. I felt as if I'd been somehow starved of life before, missing the many scents, sights and sounds which were so very clear to me now.

I'd always loved people watching, and I stood still to soak in the excitement and the electric atmosphere that pulsated through the stadium. Will stood very close to me and took hold of my arm, so as to speak quietly in my ear. 'How is your control?'

I looked up at him, and smiled at his concern. 'I'm fine. Really.'

He nodded, satisfied, and led the way to the Arena's inner sanctum, turning back to me just before going in. 'Do I have to buy you a T-shirt?'

'I only ever buy Bowie t-shirts.'

He raised a dark brow. 'Should I be worried?'

'You can hold your own. Anyway, the man may be a legend, but he's almost retired these days.'

'And still only in his sixties,' murmured Will. 'So young.'

And he thought I always had an answer.

When we were in our seats, I continued to watch everyone around me. The age range at a Stones' concert is always incredible. The youngest fan I saw looked about six years old, but the oldest could easily have been seventy, or maybe even more. Obviously, Will remained senior to everyone in the audience, by quite a few centuries, but without looking it, of course. He leaned back in his seat, perfectly at ease, his arm resting across the back of my seat. I could feel his eyes on me and turned to face him. 'OK—what?'

He smiled, and raised his hand lazily to touch my hair. 'You are just like a child in a sweet shop. I really should have thought of this before.'

'You thought of it tonight, and that's good enough for me.'

A huge roar suddenly erupted from the crowd as vibrant lights flooded the stage, and Ronnie and Keith stormed into the opening riff of their usual opening number.

The audience rose to its feet as one and the cheers were deafening. The familiar music pulsed louder than anything at any concert I could ever remember. I found myself on my feet swaying in time to it along with everyone else.

Will remained sitting, looking cool and often watching me more than the band.

I could feel his amused gaze like a weight, and turned to glance at him several times. His eyes glowed in the dark as he watched me, a half-smile playing on his lips. Too sexy for his own good.

When the Stones had played most of their back catalogue, Mick had strutted his last strut and the final throbbing notes had died away, Will rose slowly to his feet.

I tilted my head up at him. 'So *now* you stand up?'

'I needed to conserve my energy.'

I had a fairly good idea why. Even vampire elders can be predictable sometimes.

We made our way to one of the exits along with hundreds of other people. I looked at Will as he slipped a proprietary arm around my waist. 'Thank you for this.'

'The pleasure is mine.' Seventeenth-century manners were certainly endearing. A smile lit his face briefly. 'Do you have any idea how many concerts you have attended over the last twelve months?'

I thought for a moment. I'd been dancing in the chorus of *Chicago* for three months, and I frowned as I mentally counted the gigs I could remember. 'Not the exact amount, no.'

'Well it has been quite a few. Including Glastonbury.'

'You aren't telling me you were at all of them too?'

'Not all of them, no.'

I stopped walking and turned to face him. 'I remember now. I talked to you at Glastonbury.' I couldn't believe I'd forgotten.

He traced his fingers down my cheek. 'Memories cannot always be recalled for some time after rebirth, Elinor.'

I nodded slowly. 'But Glastonbury's on for three days. What did you do during the day?'

He gave me a wicked look. 'Kept out of the sodding sun.'

'How?'

'Camper van.'

Oh. Simple then.

We emerged from the Arena, and I started to follow the masses towards the tube station, when Will grabbed my arm and pulled me in the opposite direction. 'We need to find our cab.'

I snorted with derision. 'Fat chance around Wembley after a concert.'

He made no reply, just continued walking away from the station. He turned suddenly into one of the small side roads. Sure enough, a black cab idled there, with the yellow 'for hire' sign turned off. I really shouldn't have been surprised to see the same man who'd driven us here earlier, but I gave Will a questioning look anyway.

He shrugged. 'Everyone has a price.'

We got into the back of the cab, and it pulled away almost immediately.

'Good night mate?'

'Very good, thank you.'

'Can't believe they're still goin' at their age.' The driver shook his head. 'Bleedin' mad if you ask me.'

Will draped an arm around my shoulders, a roguish smile lighting his face. He relaxed back into the seat, crossing his long legs. It seemed just as I'd begun to enjoy the dark intimacy of the cab, we drew up at the back gate of the house. Will leaned forward to pay the driver with, I noticed, several twenty pound notes.

'Cheers mate, you're a gent.' The driver stuffed the notes into his pocket, and the cab shot off the minute we'd got out, presumably in case Will changed his mind.

'Generous.' I commented.

'I had no desire to travel home by tube, so I bribed him to come back for us.'

'Have you ever wondered what a taxi driver sees – or rather *doesn't* see, when he looks in his mirror at us?' The thought had been bothering me more than a bit on the journey home.

Will threw his head back and laughed. 'You are fantastic! Just fantastic.'

I tried not to laugh. 'Stop laughing at me. You're always *laughing* at me.'

He held me around the waist, still laughing. 'I apologise, Elinor. I have spent so long covering my tracks around humans, and now everything is second nature. I sometimes forget that you do not know some of our more fundamental parlour tricks.'

'Parlour tricks?'

'How do you think I persuaded the driver to come back for us?'

I shrugged. 'Money?'

'Money certainly assisted, yes. We have hypnotic qualities to our gaze, Elinor, it is extremely helpful.'

Of course. Silly me.

Will stopped laughing suddenly, and raising his head, sniffed the air. His eyes flashed dangerously, as he motioned me to be quiet. His voice whispered through my head. *We have visitors.*

He walked to the entry panel on the wall and quickly punched in the code. Opening the gate, he pulled me through and shut the gate behind us. Two shadowy figures loomed into sight immediately.

'Waiting for me, girls?' Will's quiet voice sounded amused.

The nearest man snarled, but it was the last thing he ever did, as Will plunged a hand through his ribcage and relieved him of his heart. The second man launched himself at Will only to have his head wrenched violently around and I heard a sickening crunch as bones splintered.

My legs suddenly gave way, and I crumpled to the ground. I pressed a trembling hand to my mouth to prevent the scream in my throat from escaping. I stared dumbfounded at the results of Will's mini massacre. Everything had happened incredibly fast and so silently, I wasn't even sure I'd seen it happen at all. I crouched against the wall, not trusting my legs to support me yet.

Will drew an evil-looking silver dagger from an inside pocket and plunged it through the disembodied heart. Without any hesitation he suddenly thrust it into the other vampire's body. Both bodies disintegrated immediately. A small sound escaped my mouth, and Will turned to me. Leaning down, he grabbed my arm and brought me to my feet. I pressed my hands against his chest, and just stared at him. He hoisted me up into his arms and made for the cellar door. 'We need to get inside.' His voice sounded quiet but urgent.

He got us both to the cellar door and inside in seconds. Once inside, I turned to him in panic. 'Who else is here?'

'The lovely Khiara is by the front gates, and she is not alone.'

Chapter Twenty-Five

Confrontation

Will's words sliced through me equally as deadly as his silver dagger. Khiara *here*? After all this time? Just when I thought she'd left the country. Maybe that was the point, the old lulling into a false sense of security trick.

'Why is she outside the gates? The other two managed to get into the garden.' Will didn't answer.

I watched him as he went to a far corner of the cellar to pick something up. Retrieving the object, he twirled it around his head, as though he were leading a Royal Marine Band or something. It was a wooden stake, whittled to a deadly point at one end. He threw it from hand to hand deftly, coming to stand in front of me. 'This piece of wood could ultimately mean destruction for any one of us.'

'I thought that was pure Hollywood, you know, *Buffy* stuff.'

Will looked stern. 'You really do need to do your homework.'

I didn't answer.

Will tossed the stake carelessly back to its dark corner. 'Never forget the things that can maim or destroy us. Other vampires will not hesitate to use them against you should they ever get the chance.' He looked down at me. 'So, can you tell me the items we should avoid at all costs?'

I thought for a moment. 'The sign of the cross, holy water, holy wafer, silver, the direct rays of the sun, a wooden stake, or a silver dagger through the heart …' I faltered at the last item, remembering how Will had dispatched the vampires outside.

Will pulled me against his body. 'Very good, most excellent student of mine,' he said against the top of my head.

'Do I get a gold star?'

'Something like that.' He was smiling now, and his eyes were shining with the fanatical gleam they got when he was looking forward to a challenge.

'What shall we do about Khiara?'

Will laughed softly. 'The fun is only just beginning.'

'If I didn't know better, I'd think you were actually enjoying all this.'

'You do not know any better, and I am.'

'*William.*' A voice sounded, loud yet strangely soft, reverberating around the stone walls of the cellar.

Will just smiled and looked upwards. 'Khiara, how nice. We missed you.'

'*Let us end this.*'

Will's laugh echoed around the cellar walls, and it sounded as though the room had suddenly become filled with different people all laughing at once.

I stared at him wide-eyed. *What the hell?*

He stood in the middle of the cellar, hands on narrow hips, with his dark head thrown back as he stared up at the ceiling. I felt really glad he was on my side. I'd seen many of Will's mood swings, but tonight the power seemed to emanate from him, and he was more terrifying than I'd ever seen him before. More terrifying even than the night he'd beaten up Honyauti, and definitely more scary than when he'd dispatched the two vampires in the garden.

He looked at me and held out his hand. 'Come. We need to greet our guests.'

I took hold of his hand. 'What the hell is happening?'

'A show of strength. Can you not feel it?'

I could feel a new kind of power surging through my body just by holding Will's hand. That had certainly never happened before.

I turned to face him, putting my free hand on his chest.

He glanced down at me, his eyes still glowing like green embers from a demon's hellfire. 'Embrace the power Elinor. Breathe it in.'

He moved toward the stairs pulling me reluctantly behind him.

Oh dear God, and I'd thought performing on stage had been scary.

When we reached the hall, Will opened the front door with a flourish. Khiara stood outside the front gates, dressed elegantly in a black jacket with matching trousers and a dazzling white shirt. Her amazing hair had been swept back from her face like a shining, dark cloud. All very dramatic and monochromatic. At her side was Grigori – an almost healed Grigori – his face impassive as usual. I knew they could have got over the gates or the walls with ease, but I supposed they were pretending to be human in case they were noticed.

Will pressed a button near the entry phone and the gates swung open. Khiara swept through the opening, followed by Grigori, and Will pressed another button to close the gates behind them. Khiara came up the steps to the front door, and after a disdainful look in my direction, she turned her cold blue gaze to Will, her face unsmiling. 'Get rid of the fledgling.'

Will leaned against the door frame insolently, folded his arms and regarded her with a cold stare that easily matched her own. 'Define "get rid of". What *can* you mean?'

Khiara narrowed her eyes. 'Chain it up somewhere. The sight of it is unpleasant to me.'

Oh very nice, I didn't feel too enthralled with her either. I kept quiet, I was getting quite good at that. I'd learned there was often someone around who could hurt me if I said the wrong thing.

Will's soft, sexy laugh made me look at him. Trust him

to find something funny in any situation. 'I have no need for chains.'

Khiara turned to Grigori. 'Remove the creature from my sight. Put it downstairs somewhere and tie it up.'

It?

Grigori moved forward to do her bidding, but at exactly the same moment Will stood up straight, and put a firm hand against the other man's broad chest. 'Touch her and you die,' he said.

Grigori stopped immediately, and Will turned back to me. 'Elinor, be so good as to wait for me in the drawing room.'

'I want to stay with you.'

'Go. Please.'

Reluctantly, I left him in the hall with Khiara and Grigori and made my way to the drawing room. Once inside, I made myself close the door quietly behind me.

I leaned against the door, straining to hear their conversation. I could hear Will's patient, deep voice and Khiara's cold, angry answers.

Then silence.

I waited to hear the conversation start up again, but it didn't.

I waited for what seemed an eternity. I waited until the silence itself was deafening.

And I knew something was wrong – very, very wrong. I simply couldn't feel Will's presence any more. As always, when we were separated, cold fear filled me, followed by absolute panic.

I flung open the drawing room door and spilled out into the hall. The front door was wide open, mocking me with the emptiness beyond. No Will, no Khiara and no Grigori. I ran to the doorway and looked out. Still no one. The front drive was empty, the gates closed. Terror gripped every fibre of my being – a terror such as I had never felt before. I ran to the gates and peered through. The entire street was empty and quiet. There was neither a car parked outside in the road nor a car driving away. The only sound was the balmy night's breeze gently ruffling leaves on the trees.

Fearing an attack without Will to protect me, I bolted for the front door and virtually leapt through the doorway, slamming the heavy door behind me. I put the various chains in place and leaned trembling against the door. What now? I struggled to regain some semblance of composure as I tried to think what to do.

Luke.

He'd help me.

I had run back to the drawing room before I realised I had absolutely no idea of Luke's phone number. Will always dialled it from memory. But I had to believe he'd written it down somewhere accessible at some point. But where?

The cabinet on which the phone was kept seemed a sensible place to start. I pulled open the top drawer. I found it to be stuffed with various papers, including the black leather-covered notebook I'd noticed Will writing in so often.

I took out the notebook and opened it.

The first page was neatly written in Will's beautiful writing. I guess one had to be a few hundred years old to be able to write like that. My name leapt out at me, and so, of course, I read on:

Tonight I have discovered her name is Elinor Jane Wakefield. She is truly the most enchanting creature I have ever seen. She moves with the grace and confidence of all dancers, and I find I cannot take my eyes off her. I have to meet her, speak to her. She fills my every waking thought.

Dated over a year ago, it had obviously been written after Will had first seen me. I flicked quickly through the pages of what appeared to be some kind of journal – all about me. Will's sightings of me had all been carefully dated and noted.

I found it more than a bit creepy, but decided I needed to get back to the job in hand. I closed the book, putting it back carefully. I sifted through the papers, which were mainly paid bills and old statements. *They should be kept somewhere safer than a drawer*, I thought. Eventually, I discovered a small book underneath the papers, and almost cried for joy when it revealed phone numbers. I found Luke's number and dialled it with trembling fingers.

Please, please be home.

I heard the phone ring once … twice … *please, please be home* … three times … and then on the fourth ring it was picked up. Luke's deep voice came on the line.

'Hallo?'

Relief flooded me. 'It's Ellie.'

'What's wrong?'

'Will's gone. Khiara came—'

'I'm on my way.'

The line went dead, and I listened to the buzzing of the dialling tone for a few more seconds before replacing the phone. Luke was coming. He'd know what to do.

There were only a few hours left before dawn, but I knew they were going to be the longest hours I'd ever experienced in my short vampire existence.

I also knew we wouldn't find Will tonight. Dawn was too close. My only hope was that we'd find him alive. Supposing Khiara's plan had always been to destroy him?

I'd never see him again, never gaze into those wonderful eyes, never again be held in his strong arms.

I couldn't bear it.

Tears began to trickle down my cheeks.

I've got to be strong. Will would want me to be strong.

I knew I wouldn't rest until I found him, whatever it took. I started to pace the room. No prizes for guessing where I'd picked up that habit. After what seemed an eternity – another one – there was a sharp rap on the front door. I ran into the hall, but stopped myself just in time from undoing all the chains and flinging open the door. Best to be safe.

'Yes?'

'It's Luke.'

Recognising his voice, I undid the many chains with trembling fingers and pulled the heavy door open. Luke stepped over the threshold swiftly, and closed the door immediately behind him. 'Are you all right?'

I nodded, not trusting myself to speak, not yet.

'What happened?' Luke took my arm and led me into the drawing room.

He pushed me gently until I sat on the sofa, and then sat opposite me in the armchair. 'What happened?' he asked again. I told him as briefly as possible the events of the last few hours.

He smiled at the thought of Will at a Stones' concert. Then his eyes grew serious.

'What does it mean? Will was so sure he was more powerful than Khiara, but he's gone. Luke, will she kill him?' I dreaded the answer. 'He spent so much time making sure I'd be safe.'

Luke didn't reply at first, but he looked up as I finished speaking. 'Ellie, it was never about you, you were merely the catalyst. It has always been about Will and his power.'

'But will she kill him?'

'No. At least not yet. Although, we do need to find him, and fast.'

'It's nearly dawn.'

'I'm sure nothing will happen to him tonight. Will is very strong Ellie.'

'So how could she take him?'

'He almost certainly went of his own accord.'

I stared at him aghast. '*What*?'

'Khiara would have threatened you in some way or another. Will must have gone with her in order to keep you safe.'

Luke leaned forward and took hold of my hands. 'He loves you more than he values his own existence, Ellie.'

'But I can't exist without him.' I took a shuddering breath to keep control. 'And I don't want to.'

'We'll find him.' Luke stood up. 'Would you like me to stay around until tomorrow night?'

'Yes please.'

I was terrified of being left alone, and even more terrified at being without Will. For all my bravado, I was still a very new vampire. I'd only just learned that wooden stakes through the heart really did turn us to dust, for heaven's sake.

Luke went toward the phone. 'I must let the others know.'

He made several calls, but I wasn't really listening. I sat miserably on the sofa, my senses reeling. I felt empty, desolate, every fibre of my being longing for Will. Since my rebirth, Will had always been there for me, a little late on several occasions, angry and demanding on others, but there nonetheless. My love for him had suddenly grown too, in spite of everything.

There was a dull ache in my body, which wasn't just the approaching dawn. My eyes ached from unshed tears. My throat felt constricted with grief.

I had to find him. *I had to*.

'Have you fed tonight?' Luke's voice broke into my miserable thoughts.

I nodded.

'Then may I suggest bed?'

I must have looked as startled as I felt, because he

smiled, and held his hands up, laughing. 'Don't worry. As attractive as I find you, you are completely safe with me.'

'I know that.' I gave him a small smile.

'Anyway, I have no doubt Will would kill me in a particularly nasty way if I attempted anything untoward with you.'

'Where will you sleep?'

'The cellar's fine. It won't be the first time I've slept there.'

I stood up and went toward the door. Luke reached it first and opened it for me. 'Be sure to lock your door.'

'You think they'll come back tonight?'

'No. But we'll lock all the doors anyway.'

'I didn't think locks could keep vampires out.'

'They can't, not once we have been invited over a threshold anyway, but any intruders would make a noise breaking in, and then I can kill them.'

I followed him round the house as he locked the front door and replaced the chains once more. He activated the burglar alarm – Will had taught him well. We went downstairs together.

Luke opened the bedroom door for me, and I went in, turning to face him as he walked over to the far door. 'Thank you Luke, I don't know what I would have done without you tonight.'

'We will find him Ellie, I promise. Rest well.'

He went out and closed the door behind him. I locked it.

The bed looked large and lonely, and I could feel tears threatening again. With a huge effort, I pulled myself together and got slowly undressed. It was so much more boring, undressing alone, especially as I'd grown used to Will's roguish, lascivious comments as each item of clothing came off. In fact I usually had his help taking them off anyway, whether I needed it or not. His absence affected me far more than I could ever have imagined. I felt incomplete. Every slight creak or sound in the house made me feel more insecure than ever. As Will himself once said, I had become a part of him now. I even felt that I couldn't be a 'whole' person again until he was back with me. Not exactly how a twenty-first-century woman should feel, I know. I'd spent most of my adult life avoiding being dependent on a man too. *Good job Ellie.*

I climbed into the large bed, and pulled the duvet up over my naked body. Not that vampires feel the cold, or the heat for that matter, it was just force of habit. Lying in bed waiting for the dawn, I found myself thinking of the girl's murder in Waterlow Park, Grigori's torture and Vincente's murder. There was no doubt in my mind now – Khiara had been behind everything from the very beginning. Cold, scheming bitch. What kind of creature would torture her own people? She must have known both of them for decades, perhaps even centuries, and yet she'd done unspeakable things to both of them, or at least instructed someone else to. I somehow doubted she would stain her own fair hands with their blood.

I could feel dawn's approach at last, and for once relief filled me. At least the pain and fear would be blotted out for a while.

Will my love, where are you?

I pictured his handsome face as my eyes closed for the day.

My last thoughts were of him.

I had always known that Khiara would return, and, sure enough, she was there, waiting for us, when we returned from the concert.

The two thugs in my garden were merely cannon fodder, young and inexperienced, and destroying them was hardly taxing. I opened the gates and my front door to Khiara, and then had to persuade Elinor to leave us to talk alone. I wanted to keep Khiara's attention on myself, and not allow it to wander toward Elinor. I leant against the door frame, looking down at the woman I had once followed across continents. The fact she still looked breathtakingly beautiful was beyond any doubt, but her cold beauty had no effect on me. I understood her better than most. I knew her heart was as cold as her flesh, without a shred of compassion or the ability to love. She wanted merely to possess, manipulate and ultimately to kill.

I asked her what she wanted to happen now.

'You must come back to Italy with me.'

I raised an eyebrow at her – that was not the answer I had been expecting. 'Why the hell would I do that?'

'I shall see your fledgling destroyed if you refuse. It is the only way you can keep your creature safe.'

'I feel sure our Council will think differently.' I reined in my temper with some difficulty. *Threaten Elinor and die, it really is quite simple.*

'The Council will believe she has turned rogue. Come with me now or she will suffer far worse tortures than those you inflicted on Katarina.'

'Katarina drew first blood, as you are no doubt well aware. She is fortunate I allowed her to continue with her miserable existence at all.'

'Your fledgling will never see another sunset, if you do not come with me now.'

At that moment Grigori came closer to me and I narrowed my eyes at him. 'If your flunky comes any closer, I will destroy him. You know me, Khiara, so you know I mean what I say.'

Khiara made a gesture with her head and Grigori walked to the open gates and out to the Mercedes that waited in the road, its engine purring, nice and ready to drive us to hell.

Khiara no longer had the power over me she thought she had, but I realised in order to keep Elinor safe the best solution, at that moment, would be to accompany her. I needed to keep the stronger vampires away from Elinor – she was young, and not yet strong enough to be able to defend herself against the likes of Grigori. I knew she would be intelligent enough to alert Luke, and I also knew that Luke would protect her with his life if he had to.

The ring of Porphyry will keep Elinor safe from torture with holy items, but I remembered only too well what Khiara's men did to Vincente. No vampire could survive decapitation.

I followed Khiara outside, leaving the front door wide open, hoping Elinor would realise something was wrong. The soft May breeze caused blossoms on the trees to swirl around us in a bitter parody of confetti. I almost laughed at the thought. Khiara slid gracefully into the back seat of the Mercedes, and God help me, I followed her. Again.

Chapter Twenty-Six

Torture

I can still remember, so many centuries later, my first night as a vampire. The hideous night I followed Khiara from the cemetery like a good little puppy. We left in a horse-drawn carriage then of course. Myself to experience, for the first time, many decades of bloodshed and horror. Grim encounters I have since tried to erase from my memory. Unfortunately, I felt sure the end to Trials would also be steeped in bloodshed, and very many bodies, if Khiara had anything to do with it.

The car drove smoothly away, taking me to whatever joys she had in store for me. We continued the journey in silence, neither of us being great fans of small talk.

We stopped outside one of my own houses in Hampstead – what a delicious irony. It was the house I had, in fact, allotted to Grigori initially, and presumably the same one that had also housed Katarina and Josephine. Interesting. Somehow, I had not expected Khiara to stay anywhere connected to me. Surely she must have realised that Luke would easily find me there. But perhaps that was the point? Perhaps she intended to take out the top people in London, leaving only the weaker and more malleable vampires.

I got out of the car and stood with my thumbs hooked in the belt of my jeans, as Khiara extricated herself elegantly from the back seat. She swept past me and, without a word, I followed her into the house. The moment I stepped over the threshold something smashed into the back of my head, and the world went away.

When I regained consciousness, I found I had been taken to the damp basement and chained to a wall. Without opening my eyes, I tried to reach Elinor with my mind, but the blow to my head prevented any clear thoughts for the moment. I remained still, instinctively feeling both Katarina and Khiara in the room. I kept my eyes firmly closed.

'Is he dead?' Katarina's voice.

I heard Khiara make a disapproving noise. 'Ridiculous child. A blow to the head will not kill an ordinary vampire, far less an Elder such as he.'

'Then I want to make him pay for what he did to my face.'

'I have no interest in your wishes.' Khiara's cold voice chilled the very atmosphere. 'You will not touch any part of him, and you will certainly never touch his face.'

They were conversing in Italian, which I followed with some difficulty through the mists of pain permeating my skull. Mercifully, we vampires heal rapidly, unless we are attacked with anything holy or silver, and I doubted they had used either. The throbbing had already begun to lessen, although I remained motionless on the floor.

I heard light footsteps approaching, and knew it was Khiara. I felt her grab a handful of my hair, and she suddenly wrenched my head back viciously. 'I know you are conscious William, do not play games with me.'

I opened my eyes and stared insolently at that perfect face so close to mine. 'I thought you liked games.'

'You would do well to respect me as your maker.'

'What is it you actually want Khiara?'

'Your humility will do for a start. Then your compliance and your allegiance.'

I gave a short, bitter laugh. 'Like that is going to happen.'

'It is the only way you get to survive.'

She stood with a swift, graceful move and, turning towards the door, snapped her fingers.

Two large men came in whom I did not recognise, although I did recognise the implements of torture they held, and I somehow knew we were not all going to be friends. They walked to stand behind Khiara, putting their hands behind their backs like good guard vamps. She looked down at me, her blue eyes cold, yet they gleamed with a manic light. I realised then that she had become deranged over the centuries, or should I say, *more* deranged.

'Stand.' She waved an imperious hand at me. Seeing no point in aggravating her at that point, I complied. 'My men will torture you until you beg for mercy, and then they will continue simply because I allow it. It pleases me to make you suffer.'

I did not bother to reply. *Twisted bitch. Torture and I were no strangers to each other. Let them do their worst.*

I knew Luke would find me eventually, and if that was what it took to keep Elinor safe, then so be it.

Khiara made an imperious gesture, and the taller of the two men turned me to face the wall and shortened the chains to hold me still. I felt him rip my t-shirt almost in half. *Bugger. One hundred and eighty pounds down the drain.* 'That was a Paul Smith, and is most certainly going to cost you.'

There was a sharp cracking sound and a searing pain exploded across my back, making me stagger. I knew the tips of the cat o' nine tails were made from solid silver, in order to cause the maximum amount of excruciating pain to a vampire. I barely had time to regain my balance when a second crack heralded another bout of pain, then another and another. The pain accelerated with each stroke, the nine thongs with their deadly silver tips burrowing their insidious way through my flesh. I could feel the blood trickling down my back as the bastards opened the wounds more with each lashing. I wound the chains around my wrists and hung on, determined not to fall to the floor, as they continued to shred the flesh from my back. I had seen these particular toys used on vampires before. Somehow I never thought they would be used on me.

In my city.

In one of my own houses.

I forced my mind to go blank, and took the beating without a murmur. There was no way I would give the Wicked Witch of the West the satisfaction of knowing she had caused me insurmountable pain.

'Enough,' came Khiara's voice after a while.

I never thought I would be glad to hear her voice again.

I allowed myself to slide to the floor then, my arms still held above my head because of the shortened chains. I turned to look up at Khiara. 'Well, if this is what you call love, remind me never to piss you off.'

Khiara stared impassively back at me. 'Always the funny man, William.'

She left the room followed by her cohorts. I could see it was definitely going to be a fun-filled night.

After the door closed behind them, I rotated my shoulders carefully, feeling the cool blood trickling down between my shoulder blades as the many lacerations throbbed. I knew the actual wounds would heal, but I also knew they would heal slowly because of the silver tips on the whips' tails. I was in for a painful time.

Knowing Khiara, I felt sure she would also resort to using holy items fairly soon.

We all know they leave scars.

I opened my mind to Elinor again. I needed to open the channel between us, which I knew would be there. It was early in our relationship for such a connection, but I hoped the ring she wore would assist us both. I called to her, mind to mind, hoping the prophecy had been right about the ring … and about her. *Elinor …*

Chapter Twenty-Seven

Decisions

'*Elinor.*'

It was Will's voice.

I couldn't see him, but I could hear him. I knew this was a dream, of course I did, but his voice sounded so real – so very close.

'*Elinor.*'

The voice sounded louder, in my head.

'Will? Where are you?'

'*Listen to me*,' his voice came again. '*Tell Luke I am in the third house. You must not come with him Elinor. I want you safe.*'

'What good is *safe* if it's not with you?' I shouted. 'I don't care about me.'

I was crying again., Huge, heartfelt sobs. 'Will—'

'*Luke will keep you safe. Trust no one else, Elinor. No one.*'

The voice was fainter and I could hear someone else calling me now.

The other voice was nearer. I opened my eyes with a start and felt my body shudder awake.

I sat up in bed. So it had been real. I was alone.

There was a soft tap at the door and Luke's voice called, 'Ellie, are you awake?'

'Yes. I'll open the door,' I said, getting out of bed.

I struggled into my robe, a beautiful, green robe that Will had bought for me. I pulled it around my body fiercely, and went to unlock the door.

Luke stood there, a plastic bag of blood in his hand. He handed it to me. 'Breakfast.'

'What about you?'

'I've fed. Have you heard from Will yet?'

'How did you know?'

Luke shrugged. 'I would have been surprised if he had not been able to communicate with you telepathically.'

'Luke, he told me to trust no one but you.'

He frowned. 'That's odd, I wonder why. Did he say where they are holding him?'

'The third house. He said you'd know.'

'Hampstead, that's also odd. I'd have thought Khiara would have taken him out of London.'

'We can't take the others with us.'

'We may have no choice, those who know of this will insist on coming with us.'

I shook my head violently. 'He was adamant, Luke. He—he doesn't even want me to go with you.'

I pushed my hair out of my eyes with hands that trembled, and looked up at the tall blond vampire standing before me.

'But you're going to come anyway,' he said with a slight smile.

'Of course,' I agreed. 'Nothing would ever stop me coming, not even Will.'

'Good for you. The phone's ringing.'

His hearing had to be even more acute than mine. I hadn't heard the phone at all. Clutching the bag of blood, I hurried up the stairs and into the drawing room. I plucked the phone from its hub. 'Yes?'

'Fledgling,' came a cold, bitchy voice I hadn't wanted to hear again this side of Hell.

Katarina.

Wonderful. My night was already perfect.

'Yes.'

'You really should have destroyed me when you had the chance. Silly little girl.'

'Not a mistake I'm likely to make again.'

'We're torturing your master, although he has yet to call your name as he suffers.'

'Why should he?' I tried to stay calm and not allow the despair I felt sound in my voice.

Luke moved nearer, in order to listen to Katarina's side of the conversation.

'It is customary on these occasions for the tortured one to call for their most beloved when the pain is at its greatest. Maybe you are *not* his most beloved.' Katarina's smug tones continued to grate down the line, and I resisted the urge to scream at her.

I dug my nails into the palms of my hands to enable me to gain some control over my emotions, but looked up when Luke touched my arm gently. His blue eyes were warning me about something. But what? I waited a heartbeat before I replied in a relatively calm voice.

'Should I be concerned?'

Luke nodded, and then I understood. I shouldn't rise to any bait the poisonous gnome might throw down the phone at me.

'Are you not *concerned* that your master is so hurt and badly disfigured, you will never want to look upon him again?' Katarina had warmed up to her subject now. 'No one will be able to look at him again without feeling disgust.'

'What possible gratification could you gain from that?' My thoughts thrashed around my head in turmoil. Just how badly hurt was he?

There was a short silence, possibly while Katarina looked up 'gratification' in an English dictionary.

'I shall be *gratified* when your happiness is in shreds.' she spat at last.

I didn't reply, just looked at Luke who shrugged and stayed silent.

I heard an exchange of voices in the background, and then Khiara's cold, clear voice came on the line. 'You have until dawn to find and claim your master, fledgling. Should you fail, you will lose him forever.'

'You yourself said these Trials were not about me, so why are you involving me?'

'Breaking you is the surest way to break him. I am adept at breaking fledglings, and he will soon be on his knees, begging my forgiveness.'

The line went dead.

I looked at Luke. 'Breaking me? What the hell does that mean?'

Luke took the phone from me and put it back. 'Khiara believes your failure is a certainty and you cannot survive without Will.'

'But she must know you'll help me?'

I was having a few problems following the Machiavellian thoughts of a master vampire's complex mind.

'She thinks Honyauti will work against you and try to turn others against you,' said Luke. 'She is very well aware of the jealousies and anger your arrival has caused.'

'That's more than I am,' I admitted. 'Poor Will, he tried so hard to keep me from finding any of this out and now it's working against him.' My voice broke and I pressed my hand to my mouth to stop from breaking down again.

'Hey, Ellie,' said Luke, gripping my arms. 'You're stronger than this.'

I stared up into his blue eyes, and felt a steely determination flow through me.

'I can't bear being without him, but there is nothing and no one on this earth that will ever stop me from finding him. If Khiara thinks otherwise then she really has no idea who she's dealing with.'

Luke smiled then, and his eyes filled with admiration. 'Will's right, you are brave for one so young. His judgement, as always, is impeccable.'

Flustered by the praise, I went and sat on the sofa. Luke

sat opposite me in the armchair, as he had the previous night. I knew that I needed to tell him more about Will's voice in my dreams.

When I'd gone through everything, he looked astounded. 'It's so early for all this to be possible, telepathy is one thing, but you are actually conversing. Tell me, Ellie, do you wear the Ring of Porphyry even as you rest?'

I looked at the ring sparkling on my finger and touched the glittering emerald reverently. 'I have never taken it off from the moment Will gave it to me.'

'Then it is true.'

'Aimee-Li said the ring has magical properties, but she didn't say what they were.'

'If the wearer of the ring is truly loved by the donor of the ring, and it is a reciprocal love, then the magical properties know no bounds. Or at least so it has always been believed amongst us,' said Luke as he continued to stare at the ring. 'If the love is true for you both, then the ring makes it possible for communication such as you have already experienced. It also enables you to find Will, or he, in turn, to find you, should you ever be separated.'

'That explains the communication through dreams.'

'It is a combination of Will's own powers and the powers of the ring. Also there is the fact that he's your sire, which, of course, means you already have a bond.'

'Which Khiara wants to destroy?'

'More than anything.'

'But she's Will's sire, don't they have a bond too?' This was all very confusing.

'Will was able to break free, he has been apart from her now for two centuries,' said Luke. 'I suspect she wants to try and re-establish her power over him by terminating you.'

Great. Now I feel a hundred percent better about this whole mess. Not.

'How can any of this work if Will doesn't love her?'

Luke gave a bitter laugh. 'Khiara cares nothing for love. She likes to own – to *possess*.'

I remembered Khiara greeting Luke. 'Did she ever possess you?'

'She possessed most of us who are now with Will,' said Luke. 'We who are now free stay with Will through choice.'

I took that information on board, and it certainly explained many things.

'So, what *aren't* you telling me?'

Luke didn't answer that. 'We need to go to the third house.'

'Surely Khiara will be expecting us? Can't she read his mind?'

'Not anymore,' replied Luke. 'He has no love for her and they have been apart for a very long time. He is able to block her from entering his mind.'

'Bet she loves that.'

Bizarre thoughts flitted manically around inside my head again, as I absent-mindedly opened the container of blood and sucked at it. A first for me, not drinking from a cup.

'Luke, do you think she'll kill him?'

Luke shook his head. 'She wants him too much.'

'But they are torturing him aren't they?'

'Possibly. Ellie we will be in time, please don't worry.' Luke gave me a sympathetic smile. 'Jake is bringing the others and when they arrive we'll leave.'

'Can't we go now?' I insisted. 'They can catch us up. We might be too late—please Luke, please let's go now.'

I stood up suddenly and realised I was wearing nothing but a satin robe. 'But I probably should get dressed first.'

'Not on Will's account I'm sure.'

'I'm not wandering around London like this, even for him,' I said. 'Give me a few minutes.'

Luke inclined his head and I hurried downstairs to the bedroom.

I pulled on jeans and a sweatshirt, then hurriedly tugged on my trainers. Not exactly the epitome of elegance, but very practical.

When I went back upstairs, I found the drawing room full of vampires. Honyauti, Jake and Aimee-Li had joined Luke. They had been fast.

Luke stood up as I entered the room. 'Ready?'

I nodded. 'As ready as I can be. Do we need weapons?'

Honyauti snorted. 'You may well need weapons.'

For once I was in complete agreement with him. I merely nodded. It tends to take the wind out of people's sails when you agree with them, and I did so enjoy deflating Honyauti. Everyone needs a hobby.

They all filed out into the hall, and once they were out of sight I opened the chest and took out the phial of holy water. It looked slightly depleted since the Katarina incident, but it might just have made the difference between undead life and absolute death.

I came across the box with the silver cross in it, and pocketed that along with the holy water. I hoped the stopper on the holy water stayed stopped, otherwise my legs were going to sizzle.

'Ellie?' Luke called from the front door.

I went out into the hall. 'I haven't got any keys.' I wondered how we would make the house secure and, more importantly, how I would get back in later. If I needed to.

'I have keys.'

Of course. I remembered Will telling me that Luke had copies of all of his keys.

Two gleaming cars waited in the road on the other side of the gates. Luke's I recognised, and I presumed the other belonged to Jake. Honyauti and Aimee-Li got into Jake's car, whilst Luke motioned me to get into his. So there I was, ready for battle, backed up by four very powerful vampires, two of them extremely ancient and scary. I just hoped it would be enough. I wondered why Will had insisted I shouldn't trust any of the others. It worried me. Luke and I fell silent in the car, each lost in our own thoughts. Jake drove off in the direction of Hampstead and we followed.

'What's the plan?' I asked eventually. '*Is* there a plan?'

'I told Jake to park in the road parallel to the street where the house is, and once we've parked, I suggest you see whether you can contact Will.' Luke deftly negotiated his car down the narrow road. Some parked cars on both sides of the street had already lost their wing mirrors, but he managed to avoid hitting any of them.

I had never wanted to drive in London, although I'd passed my driving test at eighteen. I certainly could never have afforded to run a car anyway. It felt really ironic I'd been almost killed by one.

All too soon, Jake turned into a leafy, residential road in Hampstead and parked his car. Luke pulled in smoothly behind him, and we sat in silence for a while.

I remembered Will's warning again. *Trust no one but Luke.*

Surely he must have meant at least one of the others was not on our side.

I touched Luke's arm. 'I need to talk to you alone.'

He turned to face me. 'What is it?'

'Remember Will said to trust no one but you,' I said. 'There has to be someone with us he doesn't trust.'

Luke looked grave. 'I fear that is so. Try to contact Will now. Clear your mind and think only of him. I will watch over you.'

I nodded. Getting out of the car, I went to sit on a low garden wall.

I cleared my mind, closed my eyes and thought of Will. I pictured his face and tried to call him with my mind.

Will. I felt rather ridiculous sitting on a wall with my eyes closed. *Will!* At first nothing happened at all, and a cold dread filled me.

Supposing they'd killed him anyway? Vampires aren't exactly renowned for fair play after all, that much I had learnt.

Will ... can you hear me? Where are you? Please answer me.

After what seemed like an eternity, I felt Will's presence inside my head like a touch of soft velvet, and relief flooded through me.

'*I am in the basement.*'

Are you hurt?

'*Hungry.*'

I had to smile. Even in such a predicament, he still made feeble jokes.

How many are guarding the house?

'*Who is with you?*'

I told him who was with me, and there was no answer for so long that I felt sure something terrible had happened. At last, his warm voice spoke again.

'*Send the others to kill the guards. Only Luke must come to the basement.*'

But—

'*Safer.*'

I miss you.

I felt his warm laughter fill my head.

'*So you should.*'

Are you sure you're not hurt?

'*I am ... fine.*'

His voice faded slightly and I didn't want him to leave me.

'*Elinor?*'

Yes?

'*I want you to stay in Luke's car. Lock the doors and remember your homework. I have ... to ... go ...*'

I felt the void immediately as his presence left, followed by such anguish I didn't think I could bear it. I slid from the wall, and sat on the pavement. Tears ran down my cheeks as Luke came over and lifted me to my feet.

'What is it?'

'They're torturing him. I can feel it.'

'He's strong, Ellie, more powerful than you could ever imagine.'

'He's hurt ...'

'Did he say where he is?'

'In the basement. He said only you should go to him. The others should go in first to deal with the guards.'

Luke nodded. 'Makes sense.'

'I have to remember my homework too.' I deliberately didn't tell Luke that Will had told me to stay out of the house. As if I would hide while everyone else went in like the cavalry.

'What?'

'We need some wooden stakes.'

Khiara's torturers had been having a fine old time, alternately beating me and slashing silver swords dipped in holy water across my back. I did not add to their enjoyment by making any kind of sound.

I had endured much torture when I was with Khiara. It was almost a daily routine with her. Some vampires have a strange way of procuring loyalty. I kept a picture of Elinor in my head all the time: it helped to alleviate the pain when I concentrated on her lovely face. I knew Luke would arrive with help, and felt sure my rescue was imminent. But I had to believe Khiara would not actually destroy me. I did not think she would, but she has become ever more warped since last I saw her, and she seemed to be sinking into the madness that some ancient beings succumb to.

I hoped with every fibre of my being that Elinor would stay out of harm's way, but somehow I doubted it.

Khiara called for a halt, at long last, and they left me hanging from the wall, supported only by the chains.

I drifted in and out of consciousness, but eventually, mercifully, some of my strength began to return.

Then I felt Elinor trying to contact me. She has had no practice at telepathy between us, yet I could still feel her attempting it. Clever, clever girl.

I answered her at once.

I managed, I think, to allay some of her fears until Khiara's flunkeys returned with more of their torture implements. My newly returned strength ebbed almost instantly, and I lost contact with her.

Khiara erupted into the cellar like a raven-haired maelstrom and ordered the two men to go upstairs. She looked at me, her face twisted in fury. 'Your Indian friend is here. Along with the English boy and Aimee-Li.'

I said nothing.

She knelt in front of me and took hold of my chin to force my head up to look at her. Her eyes were wondrous, yet empty and cold. How wasteful that someone so beautiful could be that cruel and corrupt.

'Where is the oh-so-handsome and faithful Luke I wonder?' She raked her long nails through my hair and I suppressed a shudder at her touch. 'I feel sure I can persuade him to join us. It would be a shame to leave such male beauty behind in this pitiful city.'

Again, I said nothing.

She stood in one lithe move and walked away. Halfway up the stairs she paused to look back at me. 'I look forward to your return to my bed. You were always so … adventurous.'

She laughed then. The same cold, pitiless laugh that I remembered from the night of my initiation. Some memories, unfortunately, stay fresh for eternity. As she opened the door at the top of the stairs I could hear sounds of a skirmish. I knew Khiara would keep out of the way until the fighting had finished. She had plenty of minions prepared to die on her behalf, after all – more's the pity.

I closed my eyes trying to sense Elinor's location. She felt close. Far too close.

I hoped Luke was keeping her safe. I would have his head if anything happened to her.

Chapter Twenty-Eight

Nemesis

Luke took hold of my arm and led me back to the others. They stood in an uncomfortable, ill-assorted group by Jake's car. Talk about drawing attention to themselves. The only one who looked anywhere near normal was Jake, who had dressed casually in faded jeans and a black t-shirt.

Aimee-Li wore some kind of black martial arts suit, which I felt sure would be sporting an embroidered dragon on the back of it somewhere.

Honyauti didn't have a hope in hell of blending in anywhere in Europe, let alone in London. He was too striking and actually just too Native American. He could have stepped straight out of a Hollywood B-movie. At least tonight he wore an ordinary t-shirt and jeans, but he had ropes of turquoise beads strung around his broad neck, and the bangles, which he always wore, jangled as he moved. His long, black hair hung loose, almost to his waist. He looked completely amazing, but European – never.

Not exactly an everyday sight, even for colourful North London. In fact, they looked as though they could be members of a really embarrassing Seventies' pop group, whose name I forget, save to say one of them always dressed like a Native American.

'Elinor has consulted with Will,' Luke announced without preamble.

Three pairs of eyes stared at me in disbelief.

'She is too young for that.' Honyauti folded his arms with a jangle of bracelets and stared coldly at me.

Ageism amongst vampires. Interesting.

'She's done it just the same.'

'Very advanced for a fledgling,' said Aimee-Li, a thoughtful gleam in her almond-shaped eyes.

'Perhaps I can graduate now then,' I said.

Aimee-Li smiled. 'Patience,' she said, touching my arm. 'Graduation comes at a price.'

'Price?'

Now what?

'Responsibilities, duties,' said Luke. 'Take my advice and stay as you are for as long as you can. Leave the hard work to us.'

'So, what's the deal?' Jake joined in the conversation for the first time.

'Deal?' Honyauti frowned.

Clearly he wasn't too well-versed in modern idioms.

I looked at Luke, hoping he would do the talking, and luckily he took the hint.

'Will thinks you three should take care of the guards,' he said. 'There are six apparently.'

'Where will you be?' asked Jake suspiciously. 'If there are six guards we need all the help we can get.'

'I'm thinking diversion tactics,' said Luke. 'All six guards won't be together, and Honyauti could probably take them out two at a time on his own if he had to.'

Honyauti looked slightly mollified at that.

'So where is Will?' asked Jake.

'We're not sure,' lied Luke. 'He was kind of *interrupted* before he could tell Ellie.'

I felt desperate to get into the house, but knew I had to let Luke do the organising. He was Will's 'second in command' after all, and the others would listen to him. I already knew they didn't take any notice of me.

'Let's get going then,' said Jake.

At least someone wanted to get going.

I felt more and more anxious as time ticked by.

'Ellie and I will go around the back of the house,' said Luke. 'I suggest you three go to the front.' He took out his bunch of keys and, slipping one key from the ring, handed it to Honyauti. 'Front door.'

Honyauti nodded.

At that moment, a burning sensation in my back caused me to cry out, and I crumpled to my knees in agony. Luke tried to help me stand, but my legs wouldn't support me. Pain ripped through my body again and again. It felt like many red-hot pokers searing my flesh, all at the same time, over and over again. A red mist coloured my vision and I cried out again. I curled into a ball on the pavement and sobbed in agony. I heard Luke speaking to me from a great distance, but I couldn't hear the words and my tongue felt so thick and swollen it made speech impossible.

The pain gradually subsided, and I opened tear-filled eyes. Slowly I uncurled my body and lay shivering on the pavement, too weak to move anymore. Jake and Luke stood on either side of me. Neither spoke a word.

'Torture.' My own voice sounded strained and hoarse.

'She's chattin' breeze.' Jake looked to Luke for his opinion. 'She's much too young.'

Luke crouched down at my side, and I clutched his arm. 'He's still alive, but very badly hurt. We need to hurry'

'How do you know this?' For once Honyauti spoke directly to me.

'I can feel him, and I can feel everything they're doing to him.'

'This should not be happening yet,' said Aimee-Li.

I was beginning to get very tired of what should or should not be happening.

'The fact is,' I said through gritted teeth, 'that it damn well *is* happening and if it's hurting *me*, then it must be bloody well *killing* him.'

To my surprise, Honyauti lifted me to my feet. 'We waste time we do not have,' he said abruptly.

For the second time that night, I agreed with him wholeheartedly. Worrying. 'Thank you,' I muttered.

'Right, let's do it,' said Luke. 'Are you well enough, Ellie?'

'Well you're not leaving me here.'

'Fair enough,' he said. 'Honyauti, Jake and Aimee-Li, go and sort out anyone you find in the front of the house. Ellie, you come with me.'

He strode off, but not before he and Honyauti had exchanged glances.

What had that meant, I wondered.

I had to run on legs that were still shaky in order to catch him up. 'Is there a plan?'

'The others will create a diversion by attacking the guards in the front of the house,' replied Luke, 'which should allow us time to get to Will.'

He went over to a small, wooden picket fence, and pulled at one of the stakes. He snapped it off from its neighbours, and pulled it from the ground.

'Homework,' I said.

Luke nodded, and broke it in half, handing me one half. 'Tuck it in your belt, it's safer.'

The thought of falling on a wooden stake and disappearing in a cloud of dust had me tucking it into my belt with all haste, and I followed Luke into the next street.

The expensive, suburban street looked beautiful with its elegant houses. The pristine pavements lined with leafy trees and not a scrap of litter to be seen anywhere. It looked peaceful and very upmarket, just like the previous street.

Such a nice, classy area for a spot of torture and murder.

The terraced houses had probably been built in the early Victorian era; they were tall, graceful houses with a hugely expensive price tag – and one of them sheltered monsters.

Every second house had a passageway running alongside it, each with a tall wooden gate that joined onto the house itself and presumably gave access to the gardens. Luke retrieved the keys from his pocket again, chose one and held the rest in his hand to prevent them from making a noise.

The others were still behind us, and Luke silently motioned them across the front garden, toward the front door. Honyauti went up the steps to the front door, as quiet and graceful as a cat, and unlocked it. I watched the three of them enter the dark house without a sound, and then turned to follow Luke. He walked down the short passageway at the side of the house without making a sound, and just as quietly unlocked the high wooden gate.

We walked into the small back garden, and came face to face with a tall male vampire. I barely had time to notice that he had short blond hair, and a body Arnold Schwarzenegger could have been proud of, when Luke smashed a fist in his face and rammed the stake in his heart. It was all over so quickly and I'd barely even followed the moves.

In seconds, the vampire had been turned to dust. How frightening was that? A being who had lived for centuries, reduced to something resembling the contents of an ashtray in the blink of an eye. A being just the same as myself and Luke.

'Inside quickly,' Luke said abruptly, breaking into my manic thoughts. He headed across the small paved garden toward the back door.

I could hear shouts coming now from the front of the house, but when I turned back to Luke, he was already inside. More terrified than I'd ever been in my life, I followed him quickly into the house.

'Stay close,' he said softly. 'If anything happens to you, *I'm* dust.'

We found ourselves in a small utility room, and Luke went straight for the far door.

The sounds of fighting seemed even louder now, and I wondered how long it would take before one of the worthy neighbours called the police. We ran through a deserted kitchen, and I thanked any gods who might be listening. Luke opened another door onto stairs, which led down. I felt more than a little relieved that he seemed to know his way around.

He ran quickly and silently down the stairs, and I ran after him, pulling the phial of holy water from my jeans pocket as I ran. I just knew we'd meet some kind of opposition soon and I wanted to be ready.

Almost as soon as the thought flitted through my head something large and incredibly heavy smacked forcefully into me from behind, making me lose my balance, and tumble head first down the remaining few steps. The holy water flew from my hands, and the bottle skidded unbroken across the stone floor and disappeared into the far shadows.

I was momentarily stunned when my head hit the floor, and blinked several times in an effort to clear my vision. Whoever, or whatever, had landed on my back was still there, so without any further hesitation I rammed my elbow back as hard as I could. The blow connected with a solid wall of flesh, and I heard a grunt of pain.

The weight on my back disappeared as quickly as it had arrived, and I looked up with eyes still blurred to see Luke holding a male vampire by the neck.

'Would you like to dispatch this one?' He shook the unfortunate vampire like a dog would shake a rat, whilst his captive hissed and spat at him. 'It is your turn I believe.'

He noticed my hesitation, and waited a split second, before he staked the man himself. 'Hesitation costs lives,' he said. 'This is no time to be squeamish.'

I rubbed my head again. 'Sorry.'

He nodded, and turned back to the gloomy room beyond. Lucky for me the phial of holy water had been in my hand when I fell, or I would have been sizzling like bacon in a frying pan.

For the first time, I wondered at the wisdom of going blindly down into the basement.

Who knew what horrors lay in wait down there?

Almost on cue, another vampire stepped out of the gloom, and Luke kicked him in the groin. As he doubled over, he dealt him a bone-crunching blow on the back of the neck with clasped hands. Before he'd even fallen to the floor Luke had staked him, and he too was history.

'Good job you thought of stakes Ellie,' he said. 'Very useful.'

I knew Luke wanted to make me feel better about my loss of nerve, and I smiled my appreciation.

'But I think you should go back upstairs now.' He made it sound like an order.

I gave him a questioning look.

'We've killed three of the six,' he said, and I felt thankful for the 'we' in a weird way. 'I'm confident Honyauti will have despatched the others by now.'

'Khiara?'

'She won't do any fighting herself,' he said. 'Once we get to Will, everything stops. Trials are over, one way or another.'

'You don't want me there when you find him do you?' Stark realisation washed over me.

Luke grimaced. 'My job is to ensure his safety at all times, and now also yours. But I need to make sure I can move him.'

I looked away so he wouldn't see the tears that had sprung to my eyes. But I was too late. I felt his hand touch my shoulder lightly.

'Let me do this my way, for Will's sake, and for yours.'

I nodded without turning round, and retraced my steps quietly to the kitchen.

There were no sounds coming from any of the other rooms upstairs, so either everyone was dead or ...

I quietly opened the kitchen door. It led out onto a high-ceilinged hall. A horrific tableau met my eyes. Honyauti lay comatose on the floor, and the tiny figure of Aimee-Li stood over him holding a sword high with both hands.

Honyauti's head bled profusely from a vicious looking wound, his blood pooled around him, staining the black and white tiles. A machete coated with blood lay discarded on the floor beside his body.

Chapter Twenty-Nine

Finale

Aimee-Li pressed the large silver sword against Honyauti's heart. There wasn't a second to lose, she'd already pierced his skin, and one wrong move on my part could have provoked her to turn him to dust.

How Aimee-Li had overpowered the strong Indian was beyond me, although obviously a machete to the head would render most people unconscious.

'Do you still intend to follow the *usurper*, or do you wish to join me and my glorious mistress?' she hissed.

'Traitorous bitch!' Honyauti spat some blood from his mouth as he struggled to raise his head.

I didn't hesitate; this was no time to be squeamish again. I ran towards Aimee-Li and pulled the wooden stake from my belt as I neared her. She turned a split second too late, and I rammed the stake straight into her treacherous, black heart. She literally exploded into dust, and I jumped back, aghast with horror and shock at what I'd done. The silver sword clattered to the floor with a hollow, metallic ring.

Honyauti sat up, and tentatively I held a hand down to help him stand. After a moment's hesitation, he took it and stood easily. We both knew he hadn't needed my help. Jake appeared in another doorway.

'What's going on?' he asked. 'Where's Aimee-Li?'

Honyauti and I exchanged swift glances. 'Will's woman has just saved me,' he said, and Jake raised his eyebrows at me.

'Well, that's not a sight you see every day,' he said dryly.

It took several attempts to put the stake back through my belt because my fingers trembled uncontrollably. I glanced up briefly when I finally managed it.

'I have to find Will.' I muttered, and retraced my steps towards the cellar, leaving the two men together.

Honyauti could tell Jake whatever he wanted.

I ran lightly through the kitchen and the utility room, and started down the cellar steps.

Halfway down, I stopped to listen for sounds of movement.

Big mistake.

A spiteful voice spoke behind me, sending icy marbles of fear rolling down my spine.

'You really should have let Will kill me,' said Katarina coldly, as I turned to face her. 'That will now be your epitaph. Pathetic little fledgling.'

She launched herself at me, and we both tumbled down the rest of the steps. My second time that night. My head bounced from step to step, as her weight bore me down.

Katarina's cold hands reached for me, and when I tried to stand her hands tightened around my throat like a cold, steel vice.

Blindly, I tried for her eyes, but missed, grabbing instead a handful of her thick hair. I pulled as hard as I could, and tore a huge clump out by the roots. She screamed like a banshee, and I pushed her away from me.

Her fury and hatred of me made her stronger than ever, and she leaped on me again. We both went down, and she went for my throat. I brought both my hands up in the martial art defence move Will had taught me weeks beforehand. She was knocked off balance, but jumped to her feet in a second. A blur of vicious vampire, intent only on revenge. I kicked out at her with every bit of strength I had.

I heard the splintering of a knee joint and she writhed on the ground whilst screaming obscenities at me, but this time I didn't intend to show any mercy.

I fumbled for the bottle of holy water in my pocket,

but remembered it was still on the floor somewhere, and scrabbled instead at the stake tucked in the belt of my jeans.

I pinned her to the ground with my body, and plunged the stake into her chest as hard as I could, and hoped desperately I would get the heart. I felt past caring about my guilty conscience, this was survival, pure and simple, exactly what Will had been teaching me for so many months. I would *not* let him down.

Katarina gave a loud, piercing shriek and as her head slammed back against the floor, I caught a brief glimpse of her surprised expression before she exploded into dust.

So I definitely got the heart then?

I stood and looked at what little remained of my handiwork, but couldn't find a shred of pity for her.

I became suddenly aware of Will's presence, and turned as he softly said my name.

With a cry of joy, I ran to him and literally jumped up into his arms, wrapping my legs around his waist and my arms around his neck.

He winced slightly, and I remembered he must be badly hurt. He lowered me to the floor until I stood within the safety of his arms. I looked up into familiar green eyes, and felt my own fill with tears.

He looked at me with his familiar mocking expression. 'I thought I told you to stay in the car?'

Chapter Thirty

Graduation

I looked at Will, and many emotions flooded through me at once. His handsome face was unmarked, as gorgeous as ever. I felt relieved beyond belief to discover Katarina had lied. I moved closer so I could touch him, and put my hand gently against his bare chest. 'How badly are you hurt?'

He ignored the question. 'My brave, resourceful Elinor.' He leant down to kiss away the tears on my cheeks.

Well, that didn't work, it just made the tears fall harder, and he laughed, pulling me close. 'It is over. We won.'

'I killed people. *Two* people.'

'Well, good. I am positive they deserved it.'

'You said I mustn't kill.'

He stroked my hair back from my face, 'I said you must not kill humans, and I do not believe you have.' He raised a dark brow in question.

I shook my head.

'Then we have no problems.' He turned to look behind him. 'Hey Luke? Any sign of my damn shirt?'

The wounds on his back became visible for the first time as he turned, and I gasped in horror. An angry criss-crossed pattern of welts and livid burn marks marred his pale skin. With trembling fingers, I touched them gently, and he drew in a sharp breath.

'Will, what did they do to you?'

'The wounds will be gone in a few days,' he said. 'Although the burns caused by holy water will take longer to heal, and they will scar.'

'We should have got here sooner.'

He looked serious. 'That would have been impossible

my love.' Then he flashed me a wicked grin. 'However, I think we may need to find a creative position tonight.'

'Holy Water—that must have been what I felt,' I said, half to myself.

He gripped my arms suddenly. 'You felt the pain?' When I nodded, he swore. 'Elinor, I am so sorry. I had no idea this would happen so soon.'

'So everyone keeps saying,' I said. 'Too early for this—too early for that. Blah, blah, bloody blah.'

He shot me a humorous look from under raised eyebrows. 'How I have missed you.'

Luke came back at that moment, carrying what was left of Will's shirt. He handed it to Will, who looked at it ruefully.

'Have to do, I suppose,' he said, struggling to put it on.

I helped him get the torn t-shirt over his shoulders, and his arms into the tattered sleeves.

I gave him an appraising look. Let's face it, he could look good in anything, and he looked exceptionally good in nothing. 'Very out there,' I said. 'Perhaps you could sell the idea to Vivienne Westwood.'

He burrowed a hand through my hair in order to pull me close again, and looked over at Luke.

'A lift home would be good round about now?'

Luke smiled. 'You got it.'

Home. Home with Will. I couldn't think of anything better.

We all trooped upstairs, and I clung to Will as though I hadn't seen him for weeks.

Jake and Honyauti still stood in the hall, practically where I'd left them. Jake gave me a quick smile, which could have meant anything – or nothing.

I smiled back tentatively.

Will raised an eyebrow, and looked back at me. 'Anything I should know?'

I shook my head, not exactly sure what he meant.

He continued to look at me for a moment longer, then turned back to the others.

'Where's Aimee-Li?' asked Luke, and I stiffened at Will's side.

Will glanced at me again, and then answered. 'She was a traitor.'

'How did you know?' I asked. 'Why didn't you tell us?'

'It did not become apparent until I was brought here,' he replied. 'I heard Khiara and Josephine talking about her.'

Luke and Jake looked astonished.

'She attacked me with a machete, and was about to pierce my heart with a silver sword,' said Honyauti. 'But your ... Elinor saved me. She is brave for a new one. She will make a fine warrior.'

A compliment, indeed, and also the first time he'd ever said my name. I really felt as though I'd graduated.

'Well done,' said a cold voice to my left.

We all turned to look at Khiara, and Will slipped an arm protectively around my waist.

'Your fledgling must have surprised you,' she said, giving me an appraising glance.

'Always.'

'I leave for Italy tonight,' she continued.

'*Chi mangia solo crepa solo*.' Will's deep voice made the Italian words sound so beautiful, but as usual I had no idea what they actually meant. He turned back to me. 'He who eats alone, dies alone.'

It clearly had a deeper meaning for Khiara, as a shadow of pain flickered across her beautiful face. 'This is only over momentarily.'

'Get a fat lady to sing,' I suggested, and everyone stared at me.

Will gave a short laugh. 'What?'

'"*It's not over until the fat lady sings*,"' I quoted.

Will shook his head in amusement, and then turned back to Khiara, his smile disappearing instantly. 'If you ever feel the urge to visit London again, ask permission first.' His voice was cold and uncompromising.

Khiara's beautiful eyes flashed dangerously, but she knew she was beaten.

She inclined her head slightly. 'So it is to be war between us?'

'Not at all,' replied Will. 'But I will not tolerate you just turning up, and hurting my people. Ever again.'

'It is only I who have lost people.'

'One of which you killed yourself, and another you had tortured. Another two appear to have been dispensed by Elinor.' He smiled slightly as he met my eyes.

As Khiara looked at him again, there was a sense of loss about her, and her eyes held more than a hint of sadness.

'Be happy *cara*,' she said softly, and she turned and disappeared through one of the doorways.

We sat together in the drawing room – alone at last.

Will had bathed and dressed in different un-torn clothes, and I couldn't take my eyes off him.

'I think she really does love you.' I still couldn't forget the last look in Khiara's eyes.

'Love is about making someone happy, not about being more powerful, or more important.' Will turned his glinting, green gaze to me.

He took hold of my hands. 'Love is not being complete unless that person is with you. It is the happiness that fills you each time they enter a room.'

He kissed the backs of my hands with his soft lips – his eyes never leaving mine.

'Charmer,' I laughed. Did all vampires possess the ability to charm anything that breathed, or didn't breathe? I felt sure it was just him. Wonderfully, gloriously him.

He smiled, and let go of my hands to push a strand of hair out of my eyes. 'Every word is the truth. You make me complete.'

'One night without you felt like eternity.' I moved closer to revel in the sight and feel of him again.

He cupped my face in his hands. 'So, you are now best friends with Honyauti, I understand.'

'Jealous?' I teased with a wicked grin.

His eyes took on a dangerous glint. 'Do I need to be?' His voice held just a hint of displeasure.

'Of course not,' I said. 'How can you even ask me that?'

'He is a good-looking man,' he replied. 'Very macho. Then, of course there is Jake, who has definitely developed an interest in you since you dispatched Aimee-Li.'

'Will—'

He laughed, and twined his fingers in my hair. 'Elinor, I can always tell if you are lying, you know that.'

'Well maybe I'd forgotten just how bloody clever you are.'

'Fancy turning in early?' he suggested, his voice now deep and seductive.

'What about your injuries?'

'Trust me, I can manage,' he said, as his hand traced down my body to cup my breast. He leaned in to kiss me whilst his thumb gently aroused my nipple. 'I will always manage.'

11 July

It is now several weeks since Khiara and her followers returned to Italy.

Elinor has suffered many traumatic nightmares, many of which were courtesy of Khiara herself. Happily, she now seems to be over the worst.

I have found it more difficult than words can say, to come to terms with the fact that Elinor felt much of the torture inflicted on me. But I am certain Khiara would have known this might happen.

Even if I had not loathed Khiara before, her little parlour trick would definitely have ensured my hatred for eternity.

My own injuries have all but healed, leaving, of course, the scars caused by holy water.

All my vampires, without exception, now see Elinor in a completely different light. She certainly seems to have gained strength exceedingly quickly for a fledgling, and I assume the Prophecy is not only true, but has been fulfilled.

I have spent much time during the last few weeks being part counsellor and part teacher. My favourite role, however, is that of full-time lover.

I can barely remember now when Elinor was not in my life. Her presence is a constant joy to me and she is definitely helping me to be a better man.

Even after three hundred years as a re-birthed demon, it seems it is never too late for improvement.

Epilogue

Late October has given us back the long, dark nights. I never thought there would be a time when I'd look forward to the long winter nights. But times change.

Longer nights mean more time with Will, more time awake and more time for ... well, just more time.

It had been a difficult learning curve for me, dying, being reborn, the various changes, my new nocturnal existence and especially the realisation of my deep love for Will.

Very difficult.

Will has been a constant source of strength, a kind of guiding light, in a way. Even I couldn't call him a guardian angel, but he feels close to one, all the same.

I know now I would never have found a love such as his, even if I had lived for many human years. Some things really are worth dying for.

Khiara and what was left of her entourage returned to Italy, and I was ecstatic to see the back of them.

Honyauti went back to his desert home. I don't think we'll ever become email friends exactly, but I knew he wouldn't pose a threat to me anymore.

Any lingering feelings of guilt I may have harboured about killing Aimee-Li and Katarina have been firmly dispelled by Will.

It seemed I'd won my vampiric spurs, so to speak, and earned the respect of the other vampires. The fact that I, a mere fledgling, killed a master vampire in Aimee-Li, thus saving Honyauti, another master vampire, had elevated my status beyond belief. The London vampires have completely accepted me as Will's consort, and sometime soon I am to be officially presented to them as such. No pressure there, then.

To say I have impressed Will is an understatement, and I shall always be grateful to Luke for not telling him about my extremely squeamish moment in the cellar.

I still cannot feed directly from humans, and the idea of actually biting humans remains abhorrent to me. The thought of accidentally killing someone through feeding fills me with terror, too. Will knows all this, and it's one of the reasons he keeps a watchful eye on me – well, that, and the fact he's a three-hundred-year-old control freak.

Everything will become easier in time, and time is something I have a lot of.

I still miss the sun – lying on a beach and soaking up its warm rays. Most of all, I miss the daylight. Sadly, no one is able to do anything about any of these things, not even Will.

Being without a reflection is just plain annoying, but Will always says I look beautiful, and, for the moment, that's good enough for me.

About the Author

Berni Stevens lives in a four-hundred-year-old cottage in Hertfordshire, England, with her husband, son and black cat. She trained in graphic design and has worked as a book cover designer for more than twenty years.

Books and art remain her passion, and her love of the paranormal began when she first read Bram Stoker's *Dracula*, aged fourteen. She is now on both the committee and the book panel of the Dracula Society, a society for fans of gothic literature and film.

Berni has had several short stories published. *Dance until Dawn* is her debut novel with Choc Lit and the first in a series of three.

Follow Berni –
www.twitter.com/circleoflebanon
www.bernistevens.blogspot.co.uk
www.facebook.com/berni.stevens.5
www.goodreads.com/author/show/4587596.Berni_Stevens

More from Choc Lit

If you loved Berni's story, you'll enjoy the rest of our selection:

Visit www.choc-lit.com for more details
including the first two chapters and reviews

CLAIM YOUR FREE EBOOK

of

You may wish to have a choice of how you read *Dance until Dawn*. Perhaps you'd like a digital version for when you're out and about, so that you can read it on your ereader, iPad or even a Smartphone. For a limited period, we're including a **FREE** ebook version along with this paperback.

To claim, simply visit ebooks.choc-lit.com or scan the QR Code.

You'll need to enter the following code:

Q281401

This offer will expire April 2015. Supported ebook formats listed at www.choc-lit.com. Only one copy per paperback/customer is permitted and must be claimed on the purchase of this paperback. This promotional code is not for resale and has no cash value; it will not be replaced if lost or stolen. We withhold the right to withdraw or amend this offer at any time. Further terms listed at www.choc-lit.com.

Introducing Choc Lit

We're an independent publisher creating
a delicious selection of fiction.
Where heroes are like chocolate – irresistible!
Quality stories with a romance at the heart.

Choc Lit novels are selected by genuine readers like yourself. We only publish stories our Choc Lit Tasting Panel want to see in print. Our reviews and awards speak for themselves.

We'd love to hear how you enjoyed *Dance until Dawn*. Just visit www.choc-lit.com and give your feedback.
Describe Will in terms of chocolate
and you could win a Choc Lit novel in our
Flavour of the Month competition.

Available in paperback and as ebooks from most stores.

Visit: www.choc-lit.com for more details.

Keep in touch:
Sign up for our monthly newsletter Choc Lit Spread for all the latest news and offers: www.spread.choc-lit.com.
Follow us on Twitter: @ChocLituk and Facebook: Choc Lit.

Or simply scan barcode using your mobile phone QR reader:

Choc Lit Spread

Twitter

Facebook